Cold Logic

E.R. Mason

E.R. Mason

Editors:

Frank MacDonald
SciFiProofreadingDoneRight@gmail.com
https://sites.google.com/site/scifiproofreading

Sam Thornton, PE PhD
https://www.facebook.com/SamThorntonPE
SamThorntonPE@outlook.com

ISBN: 978-1-7328697-4-5

Chapter 1

During my sophomore year in electrical engineering an old lab professor, apparently not eligible for advanced eye surgery, wore glasses as thick as the bottom of an antique coke bottle. He registered student grades the old-fashioned way, handwritten in a bookkeeper's pocket notebook and later transcribed to the university's cloud by a student assistant.

In the tiny, preprinted squares of his little book he'd posted my lab grades to the student above my name. I'd been given the grades of the student below my name, a rich kid destined to flunk out. It was quite a shock when I discovered I'd flunked electronics lab.

Fortunately, scattered around my dorm room, many of the written exams from his labs attested to my good standing. They were all A's and B's. And at that moment as I stood comparing each of my paper lab grades to those posted on the computer screen, a messenger appeared at my door to inform me I was being called to the student advisor's office immediately.

By the time I reached the advisor's office most of the redness in my face had subsided.

The student advisor had a carefully crafted speech all prepared. Part of his plan was structured in such a way as to not let me get a word in edgewise because he expected protestation. He said it appeared I had chosen the wrong major. There was not enough time to transfer but I could probably take the rest of the year off and start again fresh next year. He could help me start the paperwork immediately. He went on to describe the many other pursuits I might find more to my vision of higher education. The redness in my face returned.

When I did finally manage to get a word in and explained I could prove the grades were wrong, he became alarmed. Had I shown my copies to the errant professor? I should do that right away. I should return to the student advisory office to let them know how it went as soon as possible.

No sympathy proffered.

Ancient Professor Ableman stared up at me through his coke-bottle glasses with his usual stolid expression. He gave an inquisitive glance at the stack of papers in my hand. He was not good at conversing on a personal level. It took quite a while of flipping pages in the tiny grade notebook while adjusting his vision distance for focus. He gave an "Ah, yes" when he finally located my name. He looked up at me as though nothing could possibly be in error.

I had to come around to his side of the desk to help him match up my paperwork grades with his glaringly wrong notebook entries. He kept saying, "Wait" to correct me but then could not. I sat back down in front of him as he began changing grades. He finally looked up and declared that even with the corrections, the remaining F's for the test copies I had not found would still leave me with a grade of D. I held up all the A's and B's and motioned toward his book. He said perhaps it would be best to raise my grade to a C for benefit of doubt.

I wasn't going to get anything more. I marched back to the student advisor's office.

The advisor was perplexed and even more alarmed. He was glad things had worked out okay. I explained I didn't want to get anyone in trouble, but the grades listed above my name were clearly shown to be my grades. That student received an A. Now I was going to have to scramble to get my grade point average back up. He nodded. Still no sympathy proffered.

That should have been a bad ending to a bad day. But, the next day I discovered my problems had just begun.

The nearly blind Professor Ableman was suddenly placed on paid leave. An associate professor took over lab classes. I began getting nasty stares from some of the university faculty. Worst of all it was brought to my attention by a classmate that the electrical engineering teacher was Professor Ableman's son-in-law. At my next electrical engineering class the teacher in question stared me down as soon as I entered the room. He watched me take a seat and added another thirty seconds of eye-drilling for good measure. Message received.

Over the next week the ruse became clear. I got back failed quiz scores. The person seated next to me had selected the same answers and passed. Required reports I'd submitted were not received. Other students could not be expected to complain on my behalf and risk their own grade point average and university status. I had no adequate proof of bias. I was about to lose a year of university and probably face a brick wall at other schools.

As I sat in my dorm considering schools on other planets, there was a knock on the door. I gave a dejected "Yeah, what now?"

The door opened to a figure larger than life. The bright hallway light behind him added to the mystique. He was dressed in brown cargo wear and leather boots. His face was unusually weathered for a man in his early thirties. His short black hair was waved back over his head. I had never met him but like everyone else I knew immediately who he was. Matthew Pennington, the Indiana Jones of Camaton University.

His family name went beyond the Constantinople period. His descendants were said to have been at the core of the Knights Templar. One partially substantiated document trail suggested one of his forefathers had been responsible for bringing the Shroud of Turin to Italy. His family established the Penn foundation to form the university. The Pennington name had been known to strike fear into the Board of Regents on more than one occasion.

Matthew was clearly cut from the same cloth as his ancestors. He earned his first PhD at 21 years old. He was given tenure at the university but was rarely there, choosing to spend most of his time in archaeological pursuits around the world. His most dramatic accomplishment was using deep ground radar to find and map deep tunnels underneath the Sphinx. He then developed a system to drain the water from them and lead an extremely dangerous expedition through them to find stored records from Atlantis, scrolls miraculously preserved in sealed metallic containers which should not have existed in that period. His research resulted in published papers showing Plato's Atlantis as told in the Socratic dialogues was completely accurate. That led to new underwater explorations which slowly began to confirm deeply buried signs of civilization in the northern mid-Atlantic Ridge beyond the legendary Pillars of Hercules. Matthew Pennington had become as much a legend as Atlantis.

To have this man standing at the door of my modest dorm seemed so unlikely that my brain refused to accept it. It occurred to me the stress of what had been happening had caused some kind of nervous breakdown. As brain-drained as I was, when Matthew finally asked, "May I come in?" I responded as any well-programmed automaton would. "Yes, please come in."

He glanced around the room as though it seemed familiar to him. He found a rickety desk chair on wheels, pulled it over and sat facing me just two or three feet away. I stared at him like an empty shell, still hoping reality would return. He motioned for me to sit.

He held out one weathered hand. "I'm Matthew Pennington."

I shook his hand still staring like an idiot.

"I've heard rumors you're in a bit of trouble as of late," he said.

I was suddenly forced to speak. The speech centers of my brain began attempting to collect the necessary electrical energy to form a response. It took a moment. "I, I, I am in a lot of trouble."

"Did you do anything wrong?"

Speech synthesis was still slow. "What? No. Not that I can think of."

"I've pieced together the rumors but why don't you tell me the entire story yourself so we can compare notes."

"Rumors?"

"Yes. It's fortunate I happen to be in town at the moment. Let's start with you failing your major in the lab."

That brought me back. My mouth took off at a full run recounting my sordid tale, a dissertation finished only when my shaking hand held out a failed quiz from my last class.

Young Professor Pennington sat back and again looked around the dorm. I tried to conceal my embarrassment at the mess.

"This place makes me feel so at home," he remarked. "Poor lighting, small space, solitude. I've spent so many hours here studying ancient writings to dig out their secrets. Expeditions are fine, but when you finally sit with the artifacts or scrolls it's then you go back in time and live with those people. What a great room this is, indeed."

"Here? You've done research in this room?"

He looked around again. "Probably not, but in a dozen rooms exactly like this one."

He took the quiz from my hand, did not look at it and placed it on the desk. "Your situation is about to take a turn for the better, Adrian," he said. "We Penningtons have a vengeful penchant for honor. This university is our Tower Keep so to speak. I'm so glad I was here at this time."

"I wouldn't want you to be dragged into my mess, sir."

"I am bulletproof, Mr. Tarn. You can repay me by righting wrongs, slaying dragons if you will, when you leave here. Who knows, maybe someday you'll be in a position to return the favor."

He rose and took a second to straighten up as though old injuries were present. I jerked up and lunged to open the door for him. I stuttered, "Thank you, sir." He nodded and smiled. As he disappeared down the hall I turned to find a dozen students gathered, staring in silent awe at him and me.

Professor coke-bottle-glasses and his son-in-law were absent the next day and every day thereafter. Pennington's snarly old gray-haired grandmother had been seen in the early morning hours bent over and shuffling her cane back to her limousine, energetically motivating her chauffeur as she went. No one discussed it further. I finished the year with a 4.0, knowing I had not earned it. Compensatory grading curve. Over the years I followed my hero's exploits in various university publications, but I never saw Professor Matthew Pennington again.

Chapter 2

To most Earthlings the planet Enuro is a sort of global Disney World. The native Enuronians average less than five-feet tall, have one of many skin-tone shades of blue, are incapable of creating original music although they desperately love music as long as it's not computer generated, and above all else they are the consummate spacecraft designer-builders in the Milky Way Galaxy. There are taller versions of Enuronians but they are a minority. The newborns to the standard Enuronian family begin at the size of a kitten. The Enuronians are a warm, friendly, and curious bunch. Humans who happen to engage in intimacy with an Enuronian female gradually turn blue the following day, an alteration which can last three days to a month. Many Enuronians, those not inclined to designing and building, love servitude. The government sets the wages so there is never conflict over such matters. Enuronian servants seem to relish watching what their employers choose to do each day. They are playful and hang on every word spoken to them. But, if you anger an Enuronian too much, they can become fiendish.

Cities on Enuro are very much like those on Earth, designed to make visitors and dignitaries feel at home. In contrast, the outlying native Enuronian villages look like Hobbit architecture. Immigration and tourism to

Enuro is intensely screened and applications can take a long time. The waiting list is endless.

How I ended up living on Enuro perplexes me to this day. Always an avowed bachelor and seemingly by no fault of my own, I somehow had become attached to an angel called Fantasia. She and her genetically-produced sister Elachia had been granted lifetime castle estate leases, properties bordering an expansive Enuronian lake and surrounded by fairy tale forests. The act was in appreciation for diplomatic services which had protected Enuro from an interplanetary war between two nearby worlds. The gifting was also intended to keep the pair close by for any new diplomatic complications that might arise.

On this day I strolled Fantasia's empty stables, trying to decide if I was bored enough to ride Emperor. From far in the distance, across the wide green rolling field, the black stallion had raised his head having noticed my approach. A few of his mares took note but quickly decided I was of no interest. Fantasia was again away on a diplomatic rescue mission. My closest friends R.J. Smith and Elachia were visiting acquaintances off-world. I leaned against a stall window and watched the long-maned, long-tailed stallion still watching in my direction, wondering if it might be time for the trails. There was an unexplored cave off to the east, large enough for horse and rider. A stream ran through it. An eerie bioluminescence in the water kept the trail passable.

Tokan, the head staff manager, dressed like a vested pool room hustler, approached from behind me. I expected him to ask if Emperor should be saddled.

"Sir, a gentleman has arrived unannounced to see you. He does not have an appointment. He insists that if I mention his name you will wish to accept him."

I turned, gave a quick smile, and asked, "Who on Enuro would wish to see me?"

"He is not a resident, sir. He says his name is Matthew Pennington."

"What!? Matthew…! Oh my God! Where is he?"

"We put him in the main library with tea, sir."

"You did well, Tokan. Let's go see him."

Pennington was seated near the fireplace where a small fire had been set by the staff. He was smoking a pipe taken from a tray on his end table. It gave the room a cherry smell. He wore a dark shirt under a worn, brown, open sports coat, weathered jeans and desert boots. His gray hair had thinned. His china teacup sat in the saucer on the table beside him.

"I must be dreaming," I said.

He looked up at me, jerked his head in a subdued laugh and began to rise.

"Please, Professor, don't get up." I held out my hand and we shook a brief etiquette-only handshake. I sat in the red high back seat beside him and took a moment to appreciate the orange flames. "It's been quite a long time since you saved my ass, Professor."

"So you have not forgotten me after all," he replied and bit down on his pipe.

"Are you kidding? You are the man I can never repay. I'm sorry we haven't had a chance to meet before this, but I've followed your exploits closely over the years. I particularly enjoyed the Sphinx expeditions."

12

"Oh, that one. The bureaucracy was much more difficult and dangerous than the expedition itself. The Egyptian government has always been intent on reserving all credit for Cheops for Egyptians only. Involvement by any previous peoples were expressly taboo. And of course many historians whose thesis submissions were shown to be in error also despised the findings. Last but not least, many universities have trouble accepting they've been teaching incorrect history. I could go on and on. Discrediting the researcher would benefit so many and is so much easier than accepting the truth."

"I guess you've just never been afraid of taking on the establishment, Professor."

"Adrian, it's time you began calling me Matt. We're both too old and have too much history for formality. And, I have followed your misadventures as well. I wanted to see what sort of vertiginous bellwether I had released on the world. I must say, it seems you have already outdone me when it comes to fuss, squabble and embroilment. I may have rewritten history a few times, but I have yet to save the world."

"Yeah, I'm not sure I know what all that means."

"I'd thought that affair on the Star Seven spacecraft would have been your ultimate contretemps."

"Yeah, that was supposed to be a luxury tour. What was that old TV show, Gilligan's three-hour tour?"

"But now you've topped that many times over with this Earth savior thing."

"I may never be able to go back there, Professor."

"Matt, Adrian. Matt. How could I have known way back then in your early college years I was unleashing a Buck Rogers on the world?"

"Professor... Matt, it's not funny."

The Professor drew on his pipe and laughed to himself. He allowed a moment of pause to reset the mood. "One thing which does surprise me, it's my understanding you've settled down with one particular companion."

"That's true and she's millions of miles away right now but she's aware of everything we're saying, or at least the mood of it."

"I was told she was not born of parents."

"True. She and her sister were designed by an eccentric scientist in an orbiting lab in the Antares region. He wanted to create the perfect woman companion and as near as I can tell, he succeeded. In his desire for perfection he manage to instill some form of clairvoyance in his creations so they could know what their partners wanted even before they knew, but I expect he somehow achieved way more than intended because that link seems to have no distance or limits of any kind."

"Isn't the perpetual intrusion uncomfortable?"

"It's like a never-ending promise, always in the background and it's controllable. You can adjust the volume level sort of."

The Professor bit down on his pipe and considered the idea.

"Matt, forgive me. It's nearly noon here. Are you hungry? We should head for the east dining lounge and get something."

He looked around the library. "Just how expansive is this magnificent structure?"

"There's no sense trying to describe it or even give you a tour. The best way is for you to stay with us a while and just roam around by yourself. The staff will always be somewhere nearby when you get lost. Let's go feast on something and you can tell me the real reason for the visit. I'm really glad you're here."

"You may not be."

I led him to the foyer where two Enuronian staff girls dressed like Munchkins noticed us and fell in behind. The east dining lounge is made up mostly of windows, two stories of them. We sat across from each other at a table for twenty and gave our eager staff our orders. I had a thick, lab grown steak, Matt ordered broiled chicken and was taken back when they brought him a small turkey under platter. We ate and drank wine and laughed at the less sensible news of the day. Matt brought me up to date on his more recent escapades at my alma mater. When we were finally unable to consume another bite we sat back with steaming coffee as the girls brought us pie-cut deserts we were unable even to taste for fear of exploding.

"How long can you stay, Matt? You've come at the perfect time. With my friends all away I'm bored."

"The question is, my friend; how long can *you* stay?"

"Oh, boy. Here it comes. I can't wait."

"Can you fly a tri-engine spacecraft?"

"I have a spacecraft at my disposal, did you know?"

"But it is down for service. As I understand it, a replacement plasma converter is needed; a problem picked up during your last five-year inspection."

"Wow! Your intel is quite good."

"Yes. I've been calling in favors. The tri-engine was the best I could do. Can you fly one?"

"Three different engines to reach light speeds? Sure. It's pretty old technology. You got antique plates for it yet?"

"Very funny. Yes, old tech, but it's very low hours on the LHobbs. The thing sat parked, maintained and ready for most of its life; an on-call taxi for politicians."

"No artificial gravity, I assume?"

"Correct. It's a float-about."

"What have you got for a crew?"

"You, me and anyone willing to come along."

"So a small complement."

"Who would be crazy enough to ride along with the two of us?"

"Just what is this all about, Matt?"

"It's about nails in the coffin. The Atlantean records say that Atlantis possessed a gas ten times lighter than helium, one which no longer exists on Earth. I've been able to develop a footprint of the conditions that would support this gas. I mean to obtain some and have it added to the periodic table and again verify Atlantean records are based on fact, not legend. I need a quick trip to the HR8799 system. There is a small moon there orbiting a gas giant that was scanned by probes and the data tells me I'll find these gas deposits. If I bring some back it will be another nail in the coffin of the Atlantis doubters. Are you familiar with that particular solar system?"

"Never heard of it."

"From Earth's point of view it's on the western side of the great square of Pegasus, between Scheat and Markab."

"Have you done the math?"

"I had a grad student do it. The place is about one-hundred and twenty-nine light years away; thirty-nine parsecs as you rocket jockeys might say. Two weeks to get there. Probably two to three days on the surface to locate and extract a sample. The gravity is one-tenth of Earth's. The ship I have won't be able to do an antigrav landing. It uses a small descent module, just thrusters, to put down and ascend."

"So age hasn't made you cautious, I see."

He laughed, drew out his pipe again and began packing it. "Look who's talking."

I laughed. "Matt, you go looking for trouble. Generally trouble finds *me*."

"So now you know the worst of it. Am I going to get my payback or not?"

"Where's this ship?"

"I had it delivered. It's orbiting. We'll need a ride up."

"You always were a confident man."

"Well, at least you won't have to die on this mission."

"Don't remind me. But I can feel Fantasia is encouraging me to go. She's concerned being left on my own I'll get into trouble."

"Instantaneous telepathy? My God, that's supermudane."

"Yeah, I don't know what that means."

Chapter 3

After packing, consoling the disappointed staff, and a brief taxi ride to the nearest spaceport we hired a space taxi at no small expense and docked in orbit with the sleeping vintage spacecraft Arimus. We powered up the old tin can and watched the 2D display screens come to life.

Immediately the nav computer kept refusing to accept the flight plan.

"Is this going to be a showstopper?" asked Matt worriedly.

"Not at all, Professor. They always did this. The clearance program gets slightly ahead of the star chart feed and disapproves the route. Usually takes three or four attempts."

"Okay...."

"One thing I didn't ask you about, what have you got for spacesuits? That could be a showstopper."

"They're old like everything else but the certifications are current. They're the original Bell Standards. Hardly used. Is that okay?"

"Oh! Absolutely. Great suits. Spent a lot of time in them back in the old days when I was security on the Electra. They have a great caution system. Let's see, if I recall you get eight hours outside before you get the caution to return to airlock."

"Yes. These were upgraded to ten hours before RTA."

"Looks like we're going to get approved this time. I ran the collision avoidance system checks while we were waiting. Good long-distance scanning, autonomous maneuvering, and static field shields. Should be just fine against micrometeorites while we're parked out there. The inertia dampener test was green also, therefore we should not be flattened in our seats like pancakes from acceleration."

"By the way, thank you for agreeing to come along, Adrian."

"To tell you the truth I was bored and a visit back to Earth was out of the question."

"They're still waiting to give you the keys to the planet, you know."

"Hang on a second. Gotta call down to Enuro Control. *EC, Arimus, ready for departure.*"

"Arimus, cleared to leave orbit. Have luck."

"Cleared to leave orbit. Thank you, sir."

We turned the old ship outward, gave control over to the autopilot and jumped away from the planet's gravity. The stars in the unusually small forward windows did not change in appearance at all.

"How long to light?" asked Matt.

"Seventy minutes of rocket motor thrust until we're fast enough to cut in the ion drives. Then another two hours to develop a warp field and break through the time barrier."

"Horse and buggy method."

"Good comparison. If my buddy R.J. were here, he'd be making his customary joke; *I'm shrinking.*"

"Ah yes, the closer to light speed the more we decrease in size relative to the planet but, what we lose in displacement we gain in mass. A fair trade off I'd say."

"One of Einstein's favorites."

"Yes, and how he ever arrived at that I will never know."

"So there's nothing left here for us to do. The autopilot will cut in the ions at just the right time. All we do is make sure it all happens correctly. You want to float back and heat up some coffee packets?"

"After you, sir."

"By the way, how well do you handle zero-G?"

"We'll find out, won't we."

"Okay, keep your focus on the floor. Do not get turned around. Did you take the ear pills?"

"Oh yeah."

"Maybe you should keep a bag handy."

"In my left pocket."

"Follow me, Professor Matt."

We unstrapped and floated back to the galley, a collage of wall panels of refrigeration units, food warmers and prepackaged food envelopes with straws. I inserted two coffee packets in a warmer and floated there waiting for the green light. Twenty seconds and I handed Matt his. "I pulled out two with cream and sugar, is that okay?"

"Perfect."

"How are you doing? Should you really drink that?"

"This actually isn't my first weightless trip, but it's been a while. So far so good as long as I concentrate."

"We should sit at that little table over there with the sticky seats. It will help your brain think things are normal."

At the table we pulled ourselves down and sat-floated at the table, sipping hot coffee, a beverage which has always seemed to taste even better in space.

"I didn't ask; are you married, Matt?"

"Always been married, never see her."

"How's that work?"

"She's perfectly happy governing the Pennington estate. She's away as much as I am. We both understood it would be that way. It's a trust-able relationship."

"So no kids?"

"That is a concern. But, what kind of father would I be? What kind of father do you think you'd be?"

"Scares me to think about it."

"What about your significant other?"

"We haven't talked about it."

"That would be some offspring. Buck Rogers having a child with a Genetic. I can't imagine that kid."

"About this descent module I haven't seen yet."

"Good subject change. I've studied it, of course. I believe it was made for flying-stupid people like me. The Arimus feeds the pod planetary coordinates, the pilot selects the ones he wants into the pod computer, he then hits 'Ready To Deploy,' and you're done. When everything is in the right position and oriented correctly, the autopilot ejects you and uses main thrusters to descend and land. So besides feeding in the coordinates, everything is automatic. Same coming back."

"Yeah, those things were designed also to be escape pods, if necessary. The engineers wanted the fastest possible eject sequence."

"May we never need to test that capability."

"So we land on this rock, wander around with scanners until we find the signatures you're looking for, then some drilling into rock face followed by tube vacuuming gas deposits?"

"It's that simple."

"What are your odds?"

"Sixty-forty in my favor."

I held my coffee envelope up and we tapped them in a toast to good fortune.

We spent more than a week playing chess, reading, sleeping, and eating. Time passed pretty quickly. Several days out the big slow down sequence began. The inertia dampeners were a little laggard this time causing loose cabin items to drift forward and hang against the bulkheads. I was looking forward to the unusual flight profile. Because this moon had so little gravity and was not rotating we would not orbit but instead simply rendezvous above Matt's best-guess coordinates.

Like every other system I've visited HR8799 had its own uniqueness. Planet HR8799E was a gas giant so large our destination moon was a mere speck compared to it. We were at a point far enough out that the Lambda Bootis class sun looked about half the size of Earth's moon. It was a pure yellow orb. At our distance it gave a spooky lower light level like a late afternoon that never ended. The gas giants orbit around its sun took 45 Earth years. There was a haze in the outer system, a huge debris disk larger than the Kuiper belt, so domineering it was difficult to see stars beyond it. The view out the side windows reminded me of a dead-void similar to one I had once passed through.

We programmed the ship for station keeping above Matt's moon. But as we settled into the rendezvous, a few systems began to misbehave in the most irritating ways. There was a drift in the ship's attitude when it should have been locked-on stable. We had to keep correcting it and resetting. Completely unrelated, a port thruster would sometimes begin leaking just enough to also push Arimus out of profile. A down-looking camera pointed at the landing coordinates kept flickering.

"Ship must be a little rusty," commented Matt.

"I've shut down the leaky thruster and assigned the forward and aft units to compensate. The spatial orientation program had some kind of software hesitation but that seems to have cleared up. We should be okay to go."

"Glad I brought you along."

"You realize our arrival time leaves a bit to be desired."

"I calculate we have about three hours before we pass into Big E's shadow. After that we'd have a long twenty-two hour wait before emerging from behind, and we can't do this work in the darkness."

"So is three hours enough?"

"It should be, as long as we find what we're looking for and don't have to drill too far into the rock."

"I guess we'd better suit up."

"Apprehension suddenly sets in."

The Professor was pretty good at putting on undergarments and space suit components. When the helmets went on and pressurization kicked in, we tested the comms.

"Reading you loud and clear."

"Me too."

"My suit air is kind of cool and smells like some kind of fabric."

"All normal. Check your internal temperature readout and adjust it as you need to."

Near mid-ship, the hatch to the lander was a round hole just big enough for inflated space suits to squeeze through. For two people there was standing room only in the oval compartment, but the systems panel lights were reassuring. Just the right amount of green with the cabin pressure readout speeding up to 14.7, a normal level for those who dared to fly without spacesuits.

We couldn't waste time, so I set the disengage system to standby, ignoring the warning horn which caused Matt to look at me for reassurance. I smiled, flipped up the safety cover and tripped the switch. Hatch seal good, we bucked away from the Arimus, tilted, and turned to attitude and thrusters fired to start us down.

"Not for the faint of heart," said Matt over a scratchy comm.

"Everything looking very nominal," I replied.

"I hope I didn't screw up badly."

"Why?"

"I was so preoccupied with the spacesuit I forgot to pack the extraction extension. It's only for worst case scenarios where the gas deposit is particularly deep. We shouldn't need it."

The gray surface began to rise toward us. Details came into view. The place was hilly with tall rock ledges surrounded by cliff-edge stone outcroppings. Our area was more jagged than Earth's moon, but our target coordinates were a wide clearing of small stone and gray dust. As long as the thrusters kept firing to orient us, I felt confident.

Just about the time I was preparing to worry, we began to slow. We were pulled down into our spacesuits by the deceleration along with the weak gravity of Matt's moon. The lander hovered a few feet above the surface, spraying dust and for some reason it turned to orient us westward. We felt the legs bounce slightly and heard the valves clicking off, after which the cabin took on a still, absolute silence.

The view out our portals was unexpectedly captivating. A small gray clearing surrounded by shallow hills and tall rock walls of various shapes. They could not be described as mountainous. They were more like natural art or ragged architecture. Directly to our right one of them reached skyward, shaped almost like a pyramid. Beyond the gray landscape there were no stars, only black void.

"So far so good," commented Matt. The comm quality had improved enough for me to detect nervousness in his voice.

"How about I help you up and out the hatch? You going to be okay climbing down those external ladder rungs?"

"You should see some of the ladders I've climbed down."

"I'm guessing a four-foot drop from the last rung to the surface."

Matt bent at the knees and picked up his pack. I twisted open the overhead hatch release and pushed the hatch upright and open.

There was a foothold built into the lander interior to step up to the climb out. He hoisted himself through the hatch. Looking down at me from outside, he laughed. "I have to admit, this place is as creepy as the pyramids."

I handed up his pack. "Probably no living thing has ever been here."

He pulled up the pack. "My brain is starting to understand the gravity. Wait till you get a look at E."

"Yeah, from here we could probably make orbit with a bottle of Pepsi and some Mentos."

When he was clear I skipped the foothold and jumped up to the hatch, my own pack tethered to a ring on my suit. Standing atop the lander the place was even spookier than through the windows. It had spiritual nothingness to it. Time had stopped. Reality on hold. Most dramatic of all, Planet E now commanded most of the overhead view from beyond the southern horizon. It was a dull orange-tan with swirls. A few captured satellites probably sucked in from the nearby asteroid belt sparkled silver on either side of it. I had to pull my attention away from the spectacle of it.

At one-tenth Earth's gravity I could easily have jumped down from the lander, but caution got the better of me. I stepped down, pushed off for the last four feet and met Matt turning in place to scan the new world.

"We're right on with your coordinates. You have a specific direction we need to go in?"

"My suit's still a bit cool. Have I got this right?" He held out his left arm readout. Suit internal temp read sixty-nine degrees.

"Tap it up, Matt."

Through the visor he nodded and gazed down at his wrist to dial up seventy-two. "That low outcropping of sharp rock on our right would be a good first try."

We shuffled through the gray dust. I resisted the urge to bound past him but kept close. It was a hundred or so yards to the edge of the clearing and the first rock-base target. As he neared, I noticed an eerie, naturally formed face in the rock. Matt ignored it and began rifling through his pack. He pulled out a hand scanner and began to sweep the rock. Without speaking he began to sidestep along, making new scans as he went. Finally, 50 feet along the edge he stopped and stared intently.

"Yes! Yes. Already! This is what we're looking for."

More digging in his pack began to cause a cloud of dust. This time he pulled out a two-piece scanner, a notebook sized display screen and a dish-shaped antenna. He fumbled around trying to get the display steadied, then began running the antenna along the rock in circular motions.

"I forgot to interface the search tone with our suits but I'll monitor the bar graph on the radar imagery so it doesn't matter. Oh, yeah, starting to get porous rock here. There's pressure and gas in these chambers. All I need is…."

He stopped and jerked up. "I don't believe it. That's it. Bull's-eye. But the deposit is too far in. We'll have to keep looking. But that's it. I believe we've found Penntalium."

I let out a short laugh. "Already named, then?"

"Oh, one must always name a finding. Otherwise credit and reward invariably goes to the nonparticipants." Matt straightened up. "But it's too deep. We've got to keep searching. How much time do we have left?"

"Ninety-five minutes."

"We must hurry."

Thirty more minutes of rock penetrating radar yielded no improved deposits.

"We're not going to make it, Adrian. We need to start drilling right now."

"What do you suggest?"

"That damned sample extraction extension that I failed to pack. We could reach the deposit with it."

"So let's go get it. We've still got time."

"It would take too long. One of us needs to start drilling right now, back there at that first site we found."

"Okay, you start drilling. I'll go get it."

"I need to go. I might not be strong enough to keep drilling and I'm not sure where I left that damned extender. I know what it looks like. You don't."

"Are you saying you want to fly up alone? Can you handle the lander okay?"

"I believe so. It's all automatic anyway and I'll have you on the comm the entire time."

"You'll need to depress your suit and remove your helmet when you get up there."

"I can do that."

"Are you sure?"

"It's either that or a very long wait in the Arimus for daylight to return to this moon."

"The Arimus is set for auto collision avoidance. Those systems will shut down automatically as you approach. That's not a problem but you'll need to remember to reset them as soon as you dock."

"Okay. Anything else?"

"You'll need to get me started on the drilling."

Matt followed back along the rock face and with a few more scans found the original target sample. He motioned that it would be an almost horizontal bore. I would have to hold the drill assembly up while keeping it tight into the rock. There were contact positioning shoes that rested against the rock to keep the drill point exact.

With the drill turning, Matt watched for a minute or two, gave me a thumbs up, then headed for the module.

"How do I know when to stop?"

"When you get to the end of the bore, the machine will shut down automatically. You can pull it out and get set up to change bit extensions. I should be back before then anyway."

My drilling position was just good enough that I could crane my neck and watch him as he climbed up the lander. I began to reconsider what we were doing. Warning flag number one: we were rushing the job to avoid darkness. That in itself was loaded with possible consequence. Warning flag number two: I was allowing an inexperienced individual to solo an old fashioned, less automated ascent module.

Why did I think that was okay? Was it okay? Warning flag number 3: I was about to be left alone on a barren rock, trillions of miles from mankind, with no other ride home.

The drill vibrated my gloved hands as Matt pulled down the lander hatch. This was my last second chance to change my mind. There was no reason everything shouldn't go okay. Too late. Thrusters fired, dust flew up, the ball spacecraft hovered for a second, popped in its landing legs and began ascent. There was no going back now. To try to do so would be more dangerous than sticking to the bad plan. Was I really calling it a bad plan now?

The lander ascended smoothly, heading for the glistening Arimus star overhead. Soon it became a star itself and after a few moments, I knew Matt must have docked. It was reasonable to relax. The ascent was the segment with the most unknowns. The descent would be a simple keystroke. I decided however, my apprehension had been valid. I had escaped the dangerous consequences of an ill-advised decision. I would never ever do this again.

The drill vibrated and jockeyed around. The bar graph on the readout said I was three-quarters of the way to the end of the bit. I looked up at the Arimus star and called up. "Getting near the end here, Matt. How's it going up there?"

"I've got it. Heading back to the lander now."

I kept drilling but twisted around to look up at the Arimus star, wondering if I'd catch a glint of the lander departing. My timing was perfect. From sky-right, a tiny spec of light came streaking out of the blackness and passed directly through the Arimus star.

Chapter 4

Denial made me continue drilling while my brain tried to understand what was happening overhead.

Leaning back and still twisted sideways, I struggled to focus on the Arimus star. It was changing. Slowly, it began to flicker and expand. It was such an odd sight that even though the drill began binding but I could not look away.

"Matt, everything okay up there?"

No answer.

There began to be flicks of light moving outward from around the foggy enlarged Arimus star. The first flush of alarm was allowed in.

I changed position to keep drilling. "Matt, are you okay?"

The Arimus star continued to gradually blossom.

I still resisted stopping the drill. Stopping the drill would confirm that something was terribly wrong.

"Matt, please respond."

There was no longer a central Arimus star. Instead a field of smaller sparkling stars expanded around the point where it had been.

In a classic denial and annoyance I stopped the drill and let it hang by the bit. I straightened up and braced against the rock wall to lean over backwards.

"Matt, tell me you're okay, please."

33

If there really had been a problem with the Arimus one of those flickering bits of light could still be him making his descent in the pod. Perhaps just the comm had failed.

I tapped at my sleeve control to see if I could call up Matt's suit data. "NO LINK" flashed on my readout.

The spread of glittering debris slowed but its twinkling continued and became more frequent.

My thought process became stunted. It took a few moments to surmise those many sparkling stars were now falling from the sky toward me, caught in the moon's low gravity. There were hundreds of them. I strained my eyes to see but there was no longer an Arimus star.

"Damn you, Pennington, respond!"

The expanse of glitter continued and became more defined. I could make out flipping and spinning pieces. The spectacle had formed an overhead cloud. I kept looking for the descent module maneuvering for a landing within the debris but could not find anything which resembled controlled flight.

My brain finally began to focus into a flat sobriety but before any processing could occur the first large piece crashed to the surface a half-mile away. It skidded and made slow graceful bounces, spraying moon dust across the surface. A second later a second piece hit, then another, then another, until it was raining down what was left of the Arimus. Smaller bits began slamming into the ground too close by. I backed away and took cover against the rock wall beside the hanging drill. The shower of metal splattered down in every direction like metallic hail as far as I could see.

The first of many logical macabre thoughts entered my mind. Maybe some of this debris contained parts of Matt. Or, maybe his body was still intact and somewhere nearby. Visually I searched everywhere but did not see anything resembling a white spacesuit.

There hadn't been an explosion. How could that be?

A suitcase-sized piece of junk struck the rock wall above me, bounced, and fell at my feet. It looked like a dull-silver section of bulkhead.

The rain began to slow.

The first wave of fear began to make itself known as my subconscious evaluated the situation before the conscious mind had time to catch up.

Except for occasional late arrivals the rain of destruction eventually came to an end. Although there had been no sound to any of it, it seemed as though silence had returned. The world around me was now scattered with various sizes and shapes of torn spacecraft. Probably somewhere within them was Matt's body or parts thereof.

I stepped away from the rock wall and turned to look around. The drill was still hanging from the rock. For a fraction of a second I considered finishing drilling.

Was there any chance Matt could have survived this? Was it possible he was just unconscious somewhere within the chaos? For lack of any real sensibility, I began winding through and hopping over fragments to search the debris field.

It took only ten minutes to find a spacesuit glove. That definitively answered any question of his having survived and would have even if the hand had not still been in the glove. The torso was fifty yards away. Spacesuit backpack still intact, legs and helmet missing.

So that left me to turn again and study my world. Time to let the new reality seep back into my stunted thought process. I climbed atop a small outcrop of rock to get a better look.

The land around me was heavy with shadows. HR8799E nearly filled the sky. In less than an hour I would be in total darkness for twenty-three hours. The cold, absolute finality of my situation was unavoidable. I tapped my wrist readout. Seven hours, forty-five minutes of air. Seven days of battery life. Less than hour of light left? Slow suffocation in darkness.

From my slightly higher position I could still make out that the debris field went on as far as I could see. There were some big chunks in various places.

Seven hours of air? The longer I could extend that, the longer I could live. I looked back at Matt's torso. Could I get any air out of that backpack? Would any of the Arimus cylinders and tanks have survived?

Would there be any chance of rescue?

Not here. Weeks from home at light speeds.

Still…. I had one ace in the hole even though it wouldn't be enough.

I searched within myself for Fantasia. She was aware I was alive but was so immersed in whatever negotiation she was conducting she had not picked up on my fear.

I could make my situation known to her but how best to do that? Most likely I would be saying goodbye. I climbed down and found a section of rock where I could sit without having to bend space suit legs very much. I took a breath and put conscious emphasis on my link to her.

There was an energized stream of confusion, an interruption to whatever she was doing, and an inquisitive feeling that could only be described as "What!?".

I made an intense visual focus on the wreckage around me and did my best to direct it to the link.

The link suddenly went completely empty of all sensation.

I tried to reinforce the thought wave with a sentiment of resigned regret.

I quickly got back a link full of feelings of alarm.

The link suddenly became a torrid of indiscernible imagery. I was able to tell whatever project she had been so engrossed in was now completely abandoned. Every so often I could feel her scolding me to just hold on. I sat on my rock and thought back, "Okay, I'll wait here." Morbid humor I could not resist.

Matt's torso was a few yards away. The main oxygen ball tank might have blown out trying to keep the suit under pressure. But the emergency air supply would have remained sealed unless he manually commanded it to open. I doubted he'd even known how to do that. *I* was supposed to do that for *him*. I was supposed to stay with *him* in case of emergency.

Taking self-incrimination along, it seemed like searching Matt's backpack might provide some well-deserved punishment. I stood, hesitated, and went to him. Kneeling in the old Bell Standard space suits was not so easy. I unlatched his dead backpack cover panel. It opened on hinges to reveal the entirety of the unit. His water reservoir was visibly full and beginning to frost over. Occasional sparks came from the isolated battery compartment. Reserve oxygen seemed to be sealed and intact. The little red valve flag indicated closed. This meant maybe two hours more of life. I could search the rest of the field while thinking about plugging into that tank.

Turning to look for the best direction to nowhere, the reality of my situation once again reared its ugly head. The barrenness of the surroundings, the flat gray landscape, the cold I knew was just outside the suit layers. I was probably the only living organism on this entire moon, maybe the only life in all of this system. The distance to the next star was literally astronomical.

I could not come up with a happy ending to my dilemma. There was no doubt Fantasia would eventually find me but I'd be a frozen man on a dead moon. Still, scavenging wreckage was better than waiting around to suck thinning air.

The debris field was dense in some areas and thin in others. I spotted a glove and arm in the distance to my left and saw no reason for a closer look. At another point there was a glistening reflection on a high ledge of rock which could have been Matt's helmet, a thought which made me shudder and continue searching elsewhere. As I skipped lightly ahead a strange field of envelopes in the dust kicked up around me. I stopped to understand what I was seeing and realized these were food packets scattered in the frozen stillness. A sadistic laugh erupted as I imagined raising my visor to eat the contents from one of them. But man, a cup of hot coffee would almost have been worth it.

It took fifteen minutes to reach the first large stack of Arimus and there was a brief moment of uplift when I realized it was a fuel compartment section. They are always reinforced sections to protect the explosive fuel contained therein. Most tanks have an auto shut-off valve that kicks in when too high a flow-level is detected. That innovation has saved many an ill-fated space mission which would otherwise have lost all expendables.

It was a big chunk of spacecraft with quite a few round canister storage containers. I bent in close to try to ID some of them. My heart skipped a beat. There was one large canister with a coil wrapped around it. It was much more frosty in appearance than the others. Holding my breath in anticipation I was able to reach in and wiped away the snow from the ID label.

LO2.

It made me step back. Wow! That thing was a liquid oxygen container still intact. The pressure in that canister must be super high. There was no longer coolant running through those coils to keep the oxygen in the liquid state. The coldness of this moon was slowing its warming. There was probably enough oxygen in that tank to keep me alive for weeks. Getting the O2 out of there without losing it to the moon's vacuum seemed impossible.

Could a man with enough water and air live for two weeks in a space suit? Starvation would set in after that. There would be a serious problem with waste. The liquid version could be endured even though the diaper would get saturated. The solid version would be quite ugly. But, by not taking in solid food that process would shut down fairly soon. Could a man mentally *endure* living in a spacesuit for two weeks?

Possibly.

Could a rescue mission arranged by Fantasia reach me in two weeks?

Way long shot.

Battery power. Uh-oh.

I could siphon off the battery power left in Matt's torso, if there was any. There were macho batteries on the Arimus, if any had survived. Without electricity, death by freezing was guaranteed. I continued pushing along in the light gravity and growing darkness, thinking "Dead man skipping."

On my right, rock outcroppings fell away and the distance horizon came into view. I scanned the cold beauty of it. For such a small moon it offered a great deal of varying topography. As I looked, something far in the distance caught my eye. It glinted in the failing light. It must be another large piece. I changed direction and headed that way.

Nightfall was now a dread. I'd be crazy to let my suit lights come on. That would be battery power stolen from the heaters. I stopped and dug in my pants cargo pocket for the first of several chemical light sticks, then decided not to crack one until absolutely necessary.

Ten minutes more and darkness was replacing the shadows. The object ahead was big. It had to be ten feet tall, at least. Then, halfway to it, I began to realize the thing was round or egg-shaped. It took only a moment to realize that the only round object that large associated with the Arimus was the lander. A spike of desperate hope shot through me. I quickened my pace into six-foot steps. Logically big-time damage would probably come into view the closer I got,

But three-fourths of the way there still did not seem to be tears or pieces scattered around it.

As I approached, the light was now very low. There had been damage. Somehow it had landed on its legs which were then crushed up against the body. It had fallen onto one side.

But, the ball itself seemed intact! How could this be? There must have been some kind of automatic feature built into the escape module's software. It must have kicked on just in time to almost make a landing. I hurried around for inspection. It was time to crack the green chem light.

The access hatch was chest high. The hatch had been blown off. The cabin was open to space. I scrambled to look inside and another mute expression of joy struck me. There was one big red light indicator illuminated on the otherwise dark control panels. Instantly I knew what it was; 'POWER AVAILABLE.'

My first thought was to climb in, power up and just sit in the pleasure of technology.

Wait! If I could locate the hatch and get it to seal, I might be able to pressurize this thing! The hatch was meant to be kept closed while attached to the Arimus. That meant it probably was ejected upon impact with the moon's surface. It should be nearby somewhere. On the other hand, if Matt had left it open, the collision could have sent the thing anywhere. I pushed off and turned to search with my light stick.

That hatch opening also could be sealed with plastic in a worst-case scenario. There was sure to be a tube of sealant stored on board somewhere. But, plastic wouldn't do much for temperature control.

The green chem light gave me about two feet of visibility. I had to bend forward to see clearly. Large rock upwellings periodically surprised me, forcing a deviation. Periodically I had the urge to give up, but the thought of the open lander kept me going. I'd widened my search to quite a distance. My trail in the dust was an easy path back.

I kicked something buried in the dust. A close inspection revealed the faint outline of a dish-shaped object sticking up. It was the right size. I held my breath in hope. Brushing it off required kneeling and made me realized I was exhausted. But pushing dust and rock away brought tempered joy and a grown man on the verge of tears. Pent up despair escaping space suit containment. The hinges on the hatch were snapped off. The locking pins were also bent slightly. The edge seals were still in place. I gathered up my treasure and in the light gravity dragged and carried it back along my footprint trail.

It was a tricky installation. I had to climb inside first. That brought a small cloud of moon dust with me. I leaned out the hatchway and pull the cover up in place. With jostling it seated but the bent locking pins would not line up with their holes so the hatch couldn't be secured against the cabin air pressure that would be pushing on it.

It took another exhausting twenty minutes of wandering around again waving a chem light until I found a piece of carbon nanotube just the right size. Back in the cabin I laced the tubing through the hatch mechanics then forced the tubing inside handholds on either side. It felt like the tubing was tight enough to keep the hatch in place and sealed.

I hurried to the big red power-apply button but at the last second stopped my hand from pressing it.

Was this the right thing to do now? Load the lander batteries to see if I could pressurize the compartment so I could remove my damn helmet?

There was a behemoth-sized motivation to do so.

I forced myself to sit back and think. My wrist readout showed about six hours of air left in the suit. That meant my suit would run out long before daylight returned. I thought of the LO2 tank outside somewhere. I needed to know how much cabin air was on hand in the lander system. My suit would plug in here with no problem. There could be other air in other tanks scattered around outside. Water, air, and battery. Those were the most important things in my life right now.

My heart called me. She wanted to know if I was still alright. I returned a heartfelt hug to her. I tried to convey that things had stabilized for the moment.

"We will be coming," was the repeating sentiment.

It occurred to me I'd been too emotional during this damned event. How embarrassing. She'd picked up on that crap. For now on, no fear.

So my suit would run out of air before daylight. Two choices; plug in and replenish it or, try to pressurize this cabin then power down the suit and take my helmet off. I could recharge the suit battery off the lander systems also. I needed to know how much air and power were in the lander life support system and that meant first powering up. There was no choice. That had to be the next step.

You can't cross your fingers in a pressurized spacesuit but believe me I tried. With a deep breath for hope, I gingerly pressed the Power-Apply button. There was a long fraction of a second of nothing.

The cabin jumped to life in color and scrolling display screens. My mind raced to focus on the Engineering Indicator Crew Alert System screen. I had previously scanned it to familiarize myself with the lander's controls. The EICAS screen came alive showing thruster fuel and thruster layout. I tapped at the side buttons along the screen and noticed my finger was twitching, fear not entirely dismissed. The Life Support display images appeared.

The O2 tanks were full! But, what did that mean? I was not smart enough to convert pounds-per-square-inch and continuous-flow ratings into survival numbers. I stepped through the subsets of the life support section. There was a water tank onboard, and emergency supplies pack which included food packets. At the bottom of the screen was a link to the pilot's operating manual. I tapped it.

DATA CHANGE NOTICE POD OPERATIONS MANUAL

AMENDMENT: Rev. A, CPN-1 PAGE: 1 of 15
This version of POM contains changes reflecting MI-15 updates. All changes are in Appendix E.

004533 Rev. A. CPN-1 (supersedes PBOC-FL99)

Space Program Operations Contract
POD Operations Manual
MI-15
DDD-1.4.1.8-c
Contract NXR55567VC

I tried to speed read through it but kept losing focus. Finally a linked block diagram contained life support. I clicked over to it.

Space Program Operations Contract
POD Environmental Control and Life Support System
HHBBR 81006

From there it went into diagrams and design jargon some of which even I didn't understand. I had to read through the prideful recounting of it almost to the end. Buried somewhere in the description section there was finally a brief reference to;

'....intended to support two individuals on a five-day survey mission.'

My ten-hour lifespan suddenly had been extended to almost two weeks. The depressurization system was set up to recover all cabin air when preparing to go EVA. So, I could depressurize the cabin without wasting any air. But, the O2 capacity also could suggest that pod fuel cells' battery life expectancy was designed for only about one week.

Along with all that there *was* some other good news. The pod also had a potable water tank, some emergency food packets and a single slot oven. There was also a slide out compactor toilet. The cabin heat system was based on all of the onboard systems up and running and producing heat. There was a radiator to remove excess heat. I took a deep breath and dared to switch on cabin pressurization. A side monitor screen began scrolling data.

I switched on the communications panel. No chance of picking anyone up. It was just for the heat. I sat back and rested and tried to get the stored-up terror to subside further. My brain kept running all the possibilities. There was no stopping the cranial runaway. After thirty-minutes the cabin temperature had reached 18C, about 65 degrees Fahrenheit. I matched my suit pressure to the pod's thirteen-point-five, unlocked and twisted off my helmet, and let it flop into my lap. A few gasps of cold air were needed solely for stress relief. My breath made fog.

The cabin lighting had come on automatically. Out the nearest oval portal there was nothing now but total blackness. There would be twenty-three hours of it. I decided to splurge and found the food pack compartment. They were under the grating that had been the pod floor. That was now on a twenty-degree incline. I flipped through the stored packets. There were several packets of coffee, cream and sugar premixed. The oven slot was next to the packet compartment. I twisted off my gloves and used precious electricity to heat the coffee. For some reason drinking from a small bag was not enough of a celebration. I found a black cap over a valve control that was just right. Tore open the bag, poured the hot coffee into it, then sat back against access panels and sipped. It was almost too hot to drink which pleased me. The steam from it smelled heavenly. It may have been the best cup of coffee I'd ever tasted. It was like drinking life.

The colored panel lights and scrolling readouts were now my friends. My brain went back to work without my permission. I would need to get out there and collect the other food packs I'd seen. I'd need to see about that LO2 container and look for other O2 tanks. Two weeks of pod life was probably not enough for rescue. I'd also need to look for batteries and fuel cells in the debris along with any other water tanks. I also needed to recover Matt's spacesuit backpack. What an ugly thought. I should collect all Matt's parts and bury him for later retrieval; evidence against me.

Was it getting warmer in here? A quick look at the I/O temperature readouts showed it was. I relaxed further and sipped. I focused within. Fantasia was busy, furiously busy. I did not interrupt her.

With great misgivings I called up the expendables monitor on my suit's Life Support screen, peeled open the back Velcro space suit pocket where the umbilical connection tubes were and forced myself to plug the suit into the pod's recharge ports.

So maybe there was still a chance. If I could just stretch out the resources long enough. The moon's atmosphere was an absolute. You either had the air, water, food, and shelter you needed, or you were dead. I could count on that. There was no in-between. I'd need to map out the debris field to be sure I'd covered everything. Without realizing it was happening, I fell asleep.

Chapter 5

The portals were still pitch black when I awoke. The pod was softly humming. I had spilled a small amount of coffee in my lap. I turned down the squelch on the comm system and listened to the white noise for a few seconds then squelched it back out. Elapsed time on my suit timer suggested there was another eight to ten hours before daylight. I began working on the suit legs and torso to remove them. Twenty minutes later, no suit made me feel much more comfortable and much more vulnerable. The cabin was warm enough. Except for the coffee, it smelled like fresh, cool air. I had time now to sort things out and learn everything there was to know about the pod.

After several hours of studying the pod operator's documentation I began to feel even luckier. From what I could tell, the pod had automatically switched to autonomous mode as soon as it was forcibly detached from the Arimus. It probably would have landed successfully but most likely had been hit by other falling debris. Even so, crashing and ending up on its side was another fortuitous happening. Had it settled upside down the hatch would have been inaccessible.

The HR8799 System dawn was excruciatingly slow. Out the portal, dark formations began to take shape. An hour later I could make out terrain. My workday was beginning.

I found a good-sized tablet tucked away in a side panel provided for tracking pod inventory. Step one was to draw a small circle in the center of a blank page. That would represent the pod. I hopped, jumped, leaned over, rocked back and forth and finally got back into my space suit. Helmet on, suit pressure up to thirteen-point-five, then command the pod to recover its atmosphere and depressurize. Turned off all electronics except the communications system and linked it to my suit comm. Put the suit in standard slow pressure reduction so I would not be a Pillsbury dough boy, then wrestled with the makeshift hatch seal bar. The hatch fell out and caused a puff of moon dust.

Food packs and water tanks; those would be priority items one. I pushed forward out of the pod and in the dusty, light gravity almost did a flip. Headed toward the drill site where the equipment backpack had been left. Scooted along in big six-foot steps. Shadows were shrinking. The topography was in plain view now, more light than when we'd arrived. Twenty-three hours of stark reality. It seemed like there was much more debris this morning. Probably more rocket rainfall during the night. Not far ahead was the high, jagged cliff wall I'd been drilling into rising up into the black sky. My suit air smelled fresh and clean, probably because I was more conscious of my dependency on it.

The drill assembly was still hanging out of the rock wall. My pack was below it. I pulled out a scanner and attached it to Velcro on my suit hip. Stacked other accessories by the drill to make room in the pack, then headed off on my treasure hunt.

There was an abrupt wave of emotion from Fantasia which stopped me in my tracks. "How was I?" I impressed an "Okay. Shelter for weeks." A feeling of, "Help is on the way" was returned. She went back to being busy.

A couple hours later I had a whopping forty-eight frozen food packets in my backpack. I tossed them through the open pod portal and turned for my next challenge.

Air. If I could find that intact O2 canister and it had a manual valve, there would be no need to try to pipe it into the system. I could simply seal the pod, monitor the air quality and release oxygen into the pod's atmosphere as needed. Keeping the oxygen content at a nominal level would give the life support system's carbon dioxide scrubbers a rest and extend the unit's life. The system would automatically vent unneeded gasses to maintain pressure levels. All I needed was to detach and carry the O2 canister back with me.

There was also Matt's spacesuit backpack Primary Life Support System. Removing a PLSS would have been easier had it been an Orlon. The Russians designed their system on hinges; they opened like a cabinet door. Unfortunately, we were using the old Bell Standards: integrated backpacks. The backpack could be removed but tools for the feed lines and cabling were needed. I'd not seen any tools scattered around though I really had not been looking for any.

With frequent stops the debris field was easy to map on my new pad. I could paste in emojis for special sections of wreckage. I dared to go a full mile due east from the pod. From a rock shelf I was annoyed but hopeful to see some large sections of Arimus far in the distance, so far it would likely take more than an hour of skipping to reach them. A task for another day.

After an exhaustive period of mapping and turning over debris, I ended up back at the mangled section that contained the LO2 canister. The canister was no longer frosty, just a mist of cold like everything else. The coolant rings wrapped around it had lost their coolant completely. One main feed tube came off the thing right next to a replenishment port and a sensor array with cabling. Close inspection showed there was both an auto-off valve and a manual on-off, probably there for maintenance. The auto-off valve still had the red flag showing in the little indicator window, inferring the tank had closed itself off during the accident. There were two tabs on the canister body with two large head shoulder bolts securing it to the frame. Large head bolts were often used as a conciliation to spacewalkers trying to do a repair in space. The air feed line had a wide disconnect joint six inches from the tank.

I needed the air in that tank. In my searching I'd still not seen a single tool anywhere. Something would need to be fabricated. It might be possible to put together a strap wrench which would take care of all three connections. Another hour of searching and I had a bent piece of heavy metal that would serve as a hammer, two sheared off round metal bars with flat sharp points for chisels, and a piece of angle iron with half a dozen loose screws. There would be many more hours of daylight available but my suit was down to two hours of life support remaining. Time for a suit break and food.

Closed back inside the pod my steaming macaroni-cheese pack and coffee made me think about the water supply again. In the still cold interior that thought also led me to feel more consternation about using battery power. I watched the pod display as the air supply system gave up the oxygen being transferred to my suit. The pod's power monitor registered five amps of current being used to recharge the suit batteries. I spooned my macaroni and sipped my coffee feeling uneasy.

Fed and a little rested, I pulled my treasures from the backpack, briefly tested the bent metal hammer-simulator, inspected the pointy torn metal chisels and confronted the I-shaped bar with the loose screws. The screws and nuts came off easily. A strap wrench needed a strap so a short side strap on my pack became expendable. The Swiss Army knife in my suit pants' leg pocket did the cutting. A few minutes of concentration and I had a folded over double thickness hole in the fabric to attach the strap to the L-shaped metal bar. I practiced using the completed makeshift strap-wrench on my finger. At best, it was a maybe. Time to suit back up.

The debris site was faster to navigate with my handy, evolving map. At the O2 canister chunk of Arimus, it was easy to see the canister mounting bolts needed to be removed first. They would be the most difficult. I drew out my hammer and chisel, took the best position, then lined up the chisel point on one of the hex bolt head edges. With the first awkward hammer strike, the chisel jumped from my gloved hand, ricocheted off the frame, and flew a good ten yards in the low gravity. I had to dig in moon dust to get it back.

Set up again. This time half a dozen improved hammer strikes seemed to have no effect on the bolt. But I was determined. I hammered away, resetting the chisel each time, swinging as hard as I could in a spacesuit until the head of the bolt began to show marks from the beating. Stopping for breath, I studied my adversary closely. It *did* look like the bolt head position had changed. That brought added adrenaline and the pounding resumed. Fifteen minutes later one well-placed hammer strike spun the bolt head counterclockwise a good half turn. Jubilation! Another ten minutes and I could spin the bolt just using the chisel until it fell out.

It dawned on me that if the tank wasn't hanging loose, disconnecting the main airline inline connection would be a lot easier, so out came the makeshift strap wrench. I knelt as much as the suit would allow, wrapped the strap around the inline fixture and got pretty good tightness with the strap wrench. But then the problems began. The strap kept slipping. No matter how tight I managed to set it, slippage occurred before any rotation of the connector. I leaned back and considered the problem.

Moon dust. The dust carried into the pod had felt corrosive and sticky. I gathered some on the tips of my gloves and packed it in between the wrench strap and the fixture. With as much tightness as I could muster, I turned the wrench hard against the fixture. The strap was holding. With one extra burst of force the fixture gave up and turned sending me off balance, into the wreckage, and sideways to the ground. I rolled onto my back and laughed against my visor.

Twenty minutes later I victoriously pulled the canister free and inspected it with great anticipation. It had more than one pressure relief valve that most certainly had released pressure as the liquid O2 warmed. There was a small pressure gauge, too small to read accurately but it looked like the indicator was up around three-hundred something causing me a surge of jubilation. I repositioned myself and twisted the manual shut-off valve to off and again to my glee the auto-shutoff mechanism switched its flag from red to green. Like a hunter back from a kill I proudly carried my O2 canister back to the pod, hoping I'd extended the number of hours I would still be able to breathe.

At the pod it took careful maneuvering to lower the new treasure inside. My backpack snagged on something that opened a Velcro pocket. It was the compartment for my emergency umbilical cables. I tucked them in and closed the flap and stiffened in a sudden revelation. The emergency suit umbilicals! What a fool I'd been. I'd plugged them into the pod life support system and drained power and air from it. I could have plugged Matt's backpack umbilicals into my suit and used his air and power to recharge, provided his suit still had something left.

No matter. That would be the next recharge. What a sickening process that would be, anyway.

I paused and turned to look over the cold gray moonscape of rocks, dust and pieces of spacecraft just beyond my visor. It would be nice to hop-climb to the highest nearby point and look out over the panorama. Maybe I'd spot more wreckage. There was still a large piece more than a mile to the east.

Electricity and water. Those had to be next. There was water in Matt's suit but disassembly would be required to get at it. One large ice cube in a water dispensation system tank. Water was so important. You can live for two weeks or more without food, but three days without water and you're done. But, there are very few moons that don't have permafrost water tucked away in the shadows somewhere. Would it be drinkable? People have dared much worse under dire circumstances.

Electricity would probably be the most difficult. If I could find any intact batteries, patching them into the pod system would be a challenge if not impossible especially with the crap tools I had. Why hadn't they put a tool kit in the pod for cripes sake? Maybe they had and I just hadn't found it yet. My kingdom for an adjustable wrench.

The whole resource consideration question made me tap at my sleeve screen to check my suit. Eight hours? I had been out here working for eight hours already? I needed to recharge which caused me to stiffen up. This time it needed to be Matt's torso. The tablet map gave me an arrow in his direction.

His torso was still braced up sideways against a rock wall. Fortunately the top and bottom of the torso were so frosted-up the sight was a bit less grotesque. I had to roll him-it over to get to the backpack. His umbilical tube and cable came out easily. Holding my breath I plugged into my own backpack's side ports and called up RECEIVE on my sleeve readouts. My air tank began to suck air and my power section bleeped its approval that current was flowing. Life from death.

This would take about an hour. The air would be quick, but the batteries could soak up power only so fast. I maneuvered around, knelt and sat as far from the macabre donor as possible. It was then a chilling thought came to me.

I had access to the tiny black box in Matt's backpack. It would have recorded everything he'd said while aboard the Arimus, along with all his suit data. A mental argument began. There was no need to listen to any of it. I knew what had happened up there. The only thing I'd hear was how much he had suffered. I should transfer the files, at least. His last words could then be passed on to investigators and family. I tapped at my suit sleeve display to see if his suit files were really intact and available. They were, dammit! I linked over to the pod data bank and checked the time of departure for Matt's fateful ascent to the Arimus. Then, back to the black box files and a bit of scrolling to find that particular time slot. Matt would not have had his comm locked open to me so any voice entry would be him talking to himself or thinking out loud. The green, play-arrowhead appeared at the bottom of my sleeve display.

I could not get myself to click it. I *could* copy all these files without listening to them. But, maybe he'd had time to leave a message.

I sat for ten minutes and finally gave in. Clicked into audio just before pod departure.

"I forgot to ask him about sealing this hatch, damn it."

"Oh, okay that's it. No problem."

"Oh God, here goes nothing."

"Come on pod, follow the green line up. Come on."

"Uh-oh! What's this warning about? Oh, Arimus shields and collision avoidance automatically shut off. Right. It's because I'm about to dock."

"Wow! Nothing to it. I'm docked! Bet Adrian's breathing again."

"Should I close the hatch or leave it open? Better close it up until I'm ready to go."

Breathing with grunts of exertion.

"Now where the hell did I put the damn thing? How could I be so stupid?"

"What's that alarm now? Nothing on my suit display. It's a vehicle alarm somewhere."

Static.

I sat back and exhaled, waiting for a storm of emotions to settle. He hadn't reset the collision avoidance system after docking. That was the alarm, long range radar warning him of an incoming object. The ship would have automatically turned the system on after the landing pod left but while someone is aboard it assumed they knew what they were doing. The entire calamity was there in the recording. Arimus collision avoidance had shut down to allow docking. Matt had not turned it back on. A space object that was out of sight until the last minute came around and hit Arimus before the ship had time to switch the Collision Avoidance System back on automatically. It was an extremely unlikely occurrence. One in a million.

Had I reminded Matt to reset that system? No. He was to be there such a short time what were the odds of a collision with space debris? Nevertheless, I should have cautioned him about it. There would have been a warning light about the disabled collision system in the command cabin but he wouldn't have seen it. Why hadn't I mentioned it? Damn it, Tarn!

The second guessing left me even more depressed. Time to change the subject; to put off the soul searching and guilt until later. After all, there was a good chance I'd be the next victim anyway. Karmic justice.

After the air and electrical recharge I'd need a break from the nine hours of fighting movement in a spacesuit. Roughly fourteen hours more of daylight before the long night. Repress the pod, ditch helmet and gloves, eat and drink, then suit back up, and back to searching with maybe ten or eleven hours of light left.

An hour and a half later, partially rested, I was at it again. Long term pod battery power now gave me the most concern. So far I hadn't seen any electrical power sections in the wreckage which meant I'd have to expand the search area. The large section I'd seen in the distance at least guaranteed there would be something worth investigating. Thanks to Matt's body my suit was now fully charged; the best time to make a long excursion. Tablet map in hand I kicked up dust making a good pace in the target's direction.

I made a good mile. The big chunk of spacecraft had come to rest between two high rock cliffs which narrowed at the crash site and widened beyond it. Gray boulders the size of small land vehicles were scattered around. As details began to come into focus it caused a spike of apprehension in me. I was looking at what appeared to be a section of the command cabin. One whole side of it was missing. Controls and electronic assemblies were exposed. The frosted lower portion of a black copilot seat was still present. As I neared, I noticed some indicator lights were still dimly lit or flickering. That meant power!

I slowed and shuffled up to the boxcar-sized piece of wreckage. The interior was wide open. The bulkhead wall behind the crew cabin was partially present. Everything past it had been torn away.

I tried to contain my excitement at the tiny flickering indicator lights. There was still battery power coming from somewhere. From the back of my mind a fragment of memory waved to me. Most command cabins kept a small toolkit for replacing bad indicator lamps, circuit breakers and other in-flight repairs.

Twenty minutes of wiping away frost and struggling to open compartment doors with bulky spacesuit gloves brought me to a small sliding drawer beneath the broken copilot seat. The thin black drawer finally popped out a good twenty inches, packed with foam seated small tools one of which was a mini-adjustable wrench along with a mini-socket wrench set. I coaxed each item out and stuffed them in my pack as the panel lights continued to flicker an invitation to me.

There was a piece of the nose still attached to the command cabin. Like everything else it was torn open to space. Gangs of fiber optic lines and wire were bunched up in a pile within it. Above that, surprisingly, all four forward portals were still intact. I pulled at the ganglion of cables just to test the idea. A large bundle of them fell forward revealing the firewall between cabin and nose. It was filled with circular cutouts a mechanical engineer had once told me were called lightening holes. Harnesses flowed through them. Fearing I might cause a large, bad short I continued to pull away cables in search of a power source. There was nothing in the nose but several thick red wires fed downward inside on the copilot's side.

Leaning back inside the cabin I cleared away debris from the copilot's floor. There were half-turn screws holding two large floor panels in place. My new small, straightedge screwdriver unlocked them. Just below the covers several ribbon-type wire harnesses were channeled across flexible foam panels. I tore at the panels and pulled them out and below was treasure. Three sealed, yellow batteries slightly larger than the old-style car batteries filled the floor compartments. There were multiple connections to each which was in no way a problem. The only real task was removing them while in a spacesuit.

Two hours later with periods of rest I sat them next to each other in the moon dust and rejoiced there were no cracks in any of the cases. Clipped wire, wound into a rope and tied to a torn sheet of metal made a good sled for transport. The walk back took much longer. The big ball of HR8799 gradually had passed by overhead. Shadows were already forming. The twenty-three-hour night was not far away.

I would need to study the pod schematics to figure out a way to use these batteries. There was no way I could do that, fabricate what I needed, and test a connection before nightfall. And, I finally noticed I was exhausted. Back home, I scrambled around finding stuff to pile up to make a small crude shed over the batteries. Probably was of no benefit at all, but it made me feel better about my precious catch. Then, ooze back into the pod and with a final look outside, seal up. Bring the pod to pressurization, set my suit to match it, and twist off the helmet. Cold air, smoky breath. Keep the suit on for warmth while the pod warmed up. Just sitting back and waiting was its own reward.

Chapter 6

The long night sealed me in. There were pulses within from Fantasia, urgings, reassurances, and threats to hold on. With fresh guilt for using electricity for the tiny oven I had spaghetti and meatballs. Best spaghetti and meatballs I ever ate. Hot coffee to supplement the oven guilt. Sat back and watched the windows fog over and then clear. Accidentally slept.

By the time dawn came I could have drawn the pod electrical system from memory. Once again, my luck held. I'd found the pod's external power connection was designed to receive power from multiple sources, ground power carts, or from the Arimus mating fixture. That meant the pod didn't care what voltage it was fed. It had a power regulator to convert the incoming voltage to what it needed. I could connect my three batteries in parallel for the longest possible life and feed them directly into the external power port. I just had to devise some fancy connector pins and attach them to the correct contacts on the outside mating port. Getting that done turned out to be a marathon. It took two, twenty-three-hour daylight days dragging torn up wiring to the pod so I could create cables using my bare hands, then climbing up and down on the pod to get to the external mating adapter and wiring and better shelter for the batteries alongside the pod. But, as darkness again was approaching, when the tiny spark from the last connection was made the pod's ampere-hour indicator went crazy upward. I raised my fists and yelled "Yes!" at the top of my lungs inside my helmet.

That left the water, which quickly brought back sobriety. The Arimus water tanks had not made it to the surface intact. They were either frozen in space headed away, or they were so torn and crushed they were unrecognizable. There would be only one place to possibly find water.

During my mapping excursions I had seen two possible cave entrances far in the distance. If either led downward there would be a possibility water ice was protected there. As optimistic as it was, I would need some kind of shovel and container to carry water ice on my sled.

At the next first light I found a rod with sheet metal still attached that would work as a shovel. A large portion of the torn up ball tank made a bowl. Twenty minutes of wrestling with torn up wire harnesses gave me a good length of wire rope. I set off toward the east cave entrance, fearful at how far away it was. The pod represented an emergency escape environment in the event my used and abused spacesuit had a problem. On this trip I'd be too far for any pod rescue.

A third of the way there the moonscape opened up to a wide plain. It was as though I was crossing a gray Sahara Desert under a black star-filled sky with a spot of small, distant sun. I looked back to see the pod so far away it was barely visible. It reminded me again of just how alone I was. I resisted the urge to start talking to myself.

A full hour later I was standing at the huge mouth of a cave, a chasm large enough to fit a house in. I'd expected a portion of the interior to be illuminated from surface light, but darkness was like a blanket over the entrance. The cliff side that rose overhead was mountainous and felt dangerous. I tugged at my sled and headed in.

Three steps in my headlamp switched on, which irritated me. I'd forgotten about the electricity expense for light inside the cave. Glow sticks were not good enough. I had to use my headlamps and my suit's handheld torch. The interior walls were ragged with patches which did not look natural. The shaped contours took me back for a moment. There were large sections of wall that looked like they'd been chiseled. Also to my surprise as I searched deeper inside the cave did not narrow but remained a cathedral. It wound to the left, then right, then straight ahead. Twenty minutes inside, I kicked something in the dust which stopped me. I knelt and fished around and came up with a chrome bar six feet long, a chisel point on one end with decayed grips on the other. After a short period of consideration of having found a sign of alien visitation I placed my find on the sled and continued in. Time was limited. I could only expend my critical resources for just so long. There had been no sign of a downhill trend in the cave floor, no pockets of water ice anywhere in sight.

Around the next turn, things changed. The cavern narrowed and split into two separate pathways. The path on the right did head downhill. I'd followed it only a short distance and discovered a wall area that had been worked by aliens. There was garbage scattered around; large broken drill bits, flattened, empty containers and other unrecognizable machine parts. Jutting from the wall remnants of what they'd been after were plain to see: dark blue crystal growth. Spikes of diamond crystal growing out of the wall. Most were the size of a flower but in the center of the biggest grouping was a car-sized cutout where it appeared one large deposit had been removed. Chunks of deep blue diamond were scattered in the dust on the floor. I found a pure fist-sized piece and tucked it in my suit leg pocket. No time to study it.

The cavern sloped down sharply enough to worry me even in light gravity. But the path also widened into a new, huge cathedral chamber. Jagged rock rose from the floor in places. Crater-like depressions had formed here and there but most significantly there seemed to be a faint layer of moisture on some of the walls and rock. My suit's outside temperature indicator read, -250 F. I left my sled and began to search intently. Well into the chamber I found what I was looking for. At the bottom of a steep inverted cone-shaped hole, there was a dirty-white patch. With renewed excitement, I hurried back to my sled for the wire rope. At the drop off there was a good outcropping of rock for a tie-off. Steep and deep as the hole was, I should have been able to staircase hop up and out, but entrapment in this desolate place was too scary to risk.

I threw down my tied-off wire rope and watched it slowly settle. Retrieved shovel and bowl. Tossed them in and followed them down. At the bottom I could feel crunching even through my spacesuit boots. I shoveled as quickly as anyone could in a spacesuit. White snow and dirt. I wired my filled bucket and tools to the line and hopped-pulled myself up and out, then reeled in my catch. With cautious jubilation I headed home.

Halfway to the entrance my bowl began to produce fog. My water ice was evaporating. I had nothing to contain it. In an only-chance gamble I flipped the bowl upside down on the sled and packed moon dust around the bottom, then off at as rapid a pace as I could manage without spilling everything.

Back at the pod, breathing heavy, I flipped the sled, checked, and found I still had most of my ice but I needed a closed container or an atmosphere to preserve it. With the skill of Bud Abbott, I wrestled my bowl up and into the pod without spilling it, then slid in behind it. Once in the pod I choose a sealed food packet storage drawer, dumped the packets on the floor and flipped my remaining ice in and resealed it. I flopped back to rest with my visor well fogged over. The truth would come once the pod was pressurized and warmed. There would be either dirty water in that compartment or a small bit of fog. Inevitably, there would be another run to the crystal cave with better preparation.

For the first time I noticed my beard was becoming aggravating. How many Earth days had I been here? One day-night cycle on this moon was roughly equal to two Earth days. There was no shaving kit to be had but there were small scissors on my Swiss army knife and, if I ended up with water in that compartment, drinkable or not, I could wash with it. There would be plenty more ice back in the crystal cave.

It was time to recharge the suit anyway. Exhausted, I sealed up the pod, waited for some pressure and warmth and struggled out of the body shell. My white suit liner was now a miserable, moon-dust gray. I was smelling bad enough that it bothered even me. With a quick check of the new reassuring battery levels, I switched on the external speakers for the comm unit and listened to soft white-noise while I pulled off the beleaguered suit liner. In my too-worn briefs, I carefully opened the water-ice food pack compartment and silently rejoiced at the dirty water sloshing around in it. I wrestled out of my under shorts. Conservative washing and beard clipping into a neat pile began. It took a long time. Reasonably clean, I used the dampened suit liner sleeves to scrub the suit liner and then my undergarments. I had a strong desire to taste the moon water, but getting sick would be a bad development at this point. There needed to be some filtration before that kind of testing was done. In the lower cabin pressure, my clothes and liner dried quickly. I realized untested evaporated moon water was now being introduced to the pod's water recovery system. There was no getting around that. But, now in a much refreshed state, I pulled the clothes back on and heated up powdered eggs and coffee. They were the best powdered eggs I'd ever eaten. Too tired to do anything else, I positioned myself in the comfortable spot and napped.

Awake with about four hours of light left, I considered staying in, but the thought of the long twenty-three-hour night got me going. Suit recharged, the remaining light could be used for the ugliest of jobs: collecting and burying Matt.

I found most of him. His helmet was empty. Probably not wearing it when the meteor struck. Besides the torso, I found one arm, one glove, a portion of one leg, and most of the other. I dug alongside the abandoned drill. With my hammer and chisel I made initials in the rock wall. A somber end to another long day. Stood for a moment by the grave. Something should be said. I had nothing. Sentiment would have to be enough.

Chapter 7

I set up a calendar on my pad. Top row was moon-time, the row below it converted Earth time. There was a rock outcropping visible through one of the pod portals which made a kind of sun dial so I could more accurately compare moon time to Earth time. The pod's clock was in Earth time. The pod also mercifully had a good chess program that even included teaching levels based on various chess masters. The pod apps became important to my sanity. Over the next few days a number of trips were made to the crystal cave for water ice. Filtering it through my spacesuit liner worked better than I could have hoped. The water became lightly amber after filtration. I constructed a soda bottle-sized manual centrifuge to further separate the particulates. In the end I had fairly clear drinking water which did not kill me or make me sick although the first human testing had been fearful.

After approximately two and a half Earth weeks it became time to worry about battery and air again. It was possible I could extract O_2 from the water ice but even if that could be managed as soon as battery power ran out I'd be frozen solid. So at that point, all I could do about life support was monitor it, minimize use, and worry.

My impressions from Fantasia had become a steady flow of concern and attention. She was trying to feel how alive I was. I conveyed to her I was alive and okay but she wouldn't take my psyche for it. I could guess that by now she had tracked down our flight plan and probably had contact with Matthew's people who knew what the mission had been. I was running out of time but the feelings I got from her suggested she had put something in motion that was allowing her to hold out hope.

I had to limit trips outside the pod. There was a cost in electricity to depressurize and repressurize. I dreaded plugging the suit in for recharge. I had to argue with myself about staying in the suit continually to possibly minimize the use of electricity, but the numbers didn't add up. Plus, a person had to eat. I was going crazy being stuck in the pod. The spacesuit would be worse. The pad automatically kept track of the days but I stopped checking it so I did not know what day it was.

Eventually a trip outside was necessary to dump compressed human waste packets and retrieve ice stores. As usual, I took time to enjoy not being in the pod. It was late in the day.

I leaned back to look up at the huge arc of HR8799 taking over the black sky when a speck got on my visor. I looked down and wiped at my visor to clear it. When I looked up, the spec was still there even larger.

I must have smeared it damn it. I rubbed at the spot and searched the horizon. The spec was gone. Looked back up at HR 8799, the spec was even larger still. I stared and stared, my mind refusing to work. The spec continued to grow larger. It became a cigar-shaped form hanging in space. My brain seemed to turn off. Fantasia had become close inside me. I dropped the sealed bucket I was holding though I didn't know why.

There was a tiny burst of light out of the rear of the cigar-shaped object. A projectile emerged from it, did a half yo-yo in the sky and headed down. It descended far to the south of me and began crisscrossing the horizon from east to west, getting closer each time.

My mind refused to participate in the event for fear it was delusion. Finally the crisscrossing object became a lander vehicle. It stopped the search pattern one hundred feet off the ground and rotated to face me. It lowered down and skids emerged for landing. A cloud of dust rose up as it settled.

A ramp dropped down. Two men in black hard suits emerged. They spotted me immediately and headed my way. The first of them came up close face to face. He was saying something. My brain decided to participate enough to remind me that I had shut off all comm equipment to conserve power. The man was repeatedly mouthing, "Captain Tarn?"

I managed to nod my head.

The leader looked at his companion and mouthed something else. The man went to the pod hatch and climbed in. He emerged a few moments later carrying my pad and my now swirling purple crystal; my only possessions. I was led away by the arm. There was an overpowering desire to run away to the safety of the pod. Somehow I overcame that. Up the ramp I went into a clean, well-lit spacecraft. I was pushed down into a seat and strapped in. My benefactors did the same and began tapping at their sleeve controls to depress their suits.

Moments later they both twisted off their helmets, wiped their faces and looked at me. The second man rose, took my arm, and attempted to read my suit sleeve readout but didn't understand the language. He motioned to me to equalize my suit. I understood and called up the match outside pressure control. He watched the pressure readings equalize then nodded to me and unlocked and twisted my helmet off. There was the glorious feeling of some Gs from the ship lifting off.

The first man spoke. I could tell the translators in my ear were sluggish, but they worked.

"Captain Tarn. Are you hurt or sick?"

It took me a moment for my mind to engage my speech center and cracking voice. "No, no, I'm okay."

The second man returned from storing my helmet. "How long were you stranded, Captain?" he asked.

I shook my head. "I'm not sure, I'd have to check my pad."

"Are you hungry, Captain? Can we get you something right now?" asked the first.

"I'm okay."

The second man handed me a bottle of cold water without having been asked. I took it gratefully and drank the first fresh clear water I'd had in weeks.

"How did you survive for air, food, and water?" asked the lead man.

"Some supplies from the wreckage, some from the pod. Water ice from a cave."

"Incredible," said the second man. He held out his hand. "I'm Duce, Captain. It's a pleasure to make your acquaintance."

"Paulsun here, Captain," said the other man and he waved.

"Gentlemen, thanks for the lift."

"We were diverted from our flight plan. VIPs to Alf Peg. Kind of took us by surprise. These trips do not usually get diverted even by space-maritime laws."

"I can't tell you how glad I am."

They gave short laughs. I took a moment to look around. It was a comfortable though well-used shuttle. There were no portals but the corridor leading to the flight deck had been left open. I could partially see the forward windows. We were already positioning to enter a hangar bay. I sat back and relaxed more than I had in weeks.

A short time later the shuttle teetered and settled onto the hangar deck. Hatch opened and ramp deployed.

"Go ahead out, Captain. There's an escort waiting for you out there. See if you can make it in the ship's regular gravity or we'll help you. Duce and I need to secure the ship."

"Thanks again." I paused for emphasis and held tightly onto things. I rode the rail a bit going down the ramp. Before I looked up a familiar voice called out to me.

"For God's sake, I just don't believe it!"

The voice made me stop and look up. There at the bottom of the ramp stood R.J. Smith wearing a light-green flight suit, black lace-up boots, light-red beard and hair well groomed.

It made me blink once or twice to test the vision. In a raspy voice I exclaimed, "Oh God! I can't have been rescued! I'm asleep in the pod dreaming all this. I must be near death!"

"Wrong as usual, Kemosabi. You are now aboard a foreign vessel registered as the *Acrua Maru*, with a number of passengers who despise or detest you for having caused their trip to be diverted. Even when you crash in the middle of nowhere you create chaos everywhere you go."

"This is impossible. There is no way R.J. Smith could be on this vessel. He and his better half were in the M15. Light years from here."

"That spacesuit you're wearing has seen better days. I would also suggest you've brought some of its aromatic history with you. They set up a cabin suite for you in case you were found alive. Perhaps we should head that way so you can get cleaned up."

I had no choice but to participate in the delusion. With effort I managed to keep forcing one foot ahead of the other and walked alongside him. The world around seemed a little dizzy, not me. R.J. kept a vise grip on my right arm. The artificial gravity was killing me. "They set up a room for me?"

"Yes, by the way, you'll notice there was no ticker tape parade to greet you. This is a multipurpose cruise. It's transporting convicted criminals to the Markab System where the sun is basically dying. There is a penal colony there which makes the Bridge of Sighs look like a Caribbean resort as I understand it."

"This is a prisoner ship?"

"Half and half. Deck Two is holding cells. Deck Three, Engineering. Deck Four, suites for dignitaries heading elsewhere."

"So this was the only ship close enough to divert for rescue?"

"Not quite as simple as that, Adrian. Here's the elevator."

We rode up to the top deck. Stepping out, the interior of the ship turned from hard metal and duct work to warm carpeting and lighting on the floor, walls, and ceiling.

R.J. led the way past shops to a wide hallway of decorated closed doors. Halfway down the corridor he tapped a control panel on the wall to open a suite. We entered and the doors closed behind us. "They wouldn't let me come down to the surface with them to get you. They were afraid of weeping and gnashing of teeth if you were dead."

"I believe there *was* some weeping and gnashing of teeth down on the surface."

"Anyway, you need to clean up. There are flight suits in the closet. They're a bit alien in design but they'll fit you."

"Two arms and two legs?"

"Haven't lost your sense of humor I see."

"I did, but it's coming back."

I began twisting off my suit gloves. R.J. stepped in to take them.

It was a luxurious suite. Tiny kitchenette, large inviting bed on the left, circular entertainment area center, real outside windows closed off by actual floor length drapes. Through the open door to the bath there was even a tight shower partial visible. Everything accented in light green, gold and blue.

"Pretty luxurious for a prisoner ship."

"Apparently the prisoner transport is just a side contract. There's some fairly important VIPs aboard on this level."

I began peeling off the suit liner. It had become a second skin.

"So please get cleaned up. I'll help you with the torso but then to the bathroom with you. I'm having to hold my breath, if you know what I mean. The Captain's orders are that you and I report to him immediately after sick bay clears you."

"I don't need sick bay. I'm fine. All I need is food, bourbon, and that bed."

"Yeah, but they need to check you for any contaminants. They scanned you when you stepped onto the shuttle but sick bay wants to do a more thorough decontamination check."

"Well crap, okay. How's the Mess here?"

"Oh, yeah. Guess you would be wanting real food."

"Anything not in pouch that needs water added."

"Have you let Fantasia know you've been rescued?"

"She couldn't have missed the party hats and noisemakers going on in my head."

R.J. moved in to help me twist the suit torso free of the legs and I awkwardly stepped out of them.

"Yep. Filthiest suit liner I've ever seen," commented R.J.

"You should have seen it before I cleaned it."

"I don't believe this spacesuit can ever be re-certified for use again."

"I won't want to be getting in it. I can tell you that."

R.J. began gathering up the suit but stopped to point. "Shower's that way. I've already stocked it. Unfortunately, they don't sell shower soap in gallon containers. There's even a laser-razor in there. The short, uneven beard doesn't suit you."

"You haven't told me how you managed to be aboard this ship."

"Please, the bathroom is that way. It's a moral imperative. I'll pull the black box from your suit and hermetically bag the suit and liner to protect the innocent."

In the shower I joked to myself that the layer of moon dust on me might jam the ship's water reclamation system but after thinking about it I watched the drain and worried. The shower and toilet made me feel ten pounds lighter even in the heavy regular gravity and there's something about shaving that is best of all at making you feel human again.

There were no undergarments available but the purple-gold flight suit did fit and was comfortable. Brown plastic sandals were the only footwear. I hate sandals but having my feet exposed to the atmosphere felt like a massage. Drying and brushing out my hair was the first time I realized it was down to my shoulders. In the mirror I stared into my big gray eyes and asked myself how I'd got into this mess.

"Wow, what an improvement," said R.J.

"It's hard to believe how much shaving makes you feel human again." I rubbed my face.

"Welcome back from the brink, ...again."

"So how could you possibly have gotten here now that I partially believe it?"

"Let's head for the med bay, shall we? Mustn't keep the Captain waiting." R.J. tapped open the door and led the way. I followed in partial slow-motion. He waited for me to catch up.

"Elachia and I were on Desardia in the M15 when we got the subspace message from Fantasia. It had all the details of your flight plan and a plea about some type of life-threatening event going on. Elachia pulled strings with the bureaucrats she was mediating for and got me two zigzag connecting rides. One was even in a skip-jet, a two-seat delivery craft. It was a steady three-G ride all the way. That took me to a mining craft which rendezvoused with the Arimus just before it diverted. The timing was kind of supernatural. Most people were sure you had been killed. They did not believe Fantasia's telepathic telemetry."

The fourth-floor med lab was quite luxurious, apparently a complete opposite to the first aid room on the second level deck intended for prisoner treatment. The place was glaringly white. One male, one female doctor, both also pristine white. Even their skin seemed a touch too white. After a quick once over with several scanners I was given an injection to reduce the effects of heavy gravity which, to my surprise, worked. We headed for the command bridge.

A closet-sized connecting room with pressure doors on either side opened to allow us on the bridge. It was a reasonably impressive place and noticeably well-worn. Standard half circle design beneath forward screens and windows. Overhead display screens all around. Narrow wraparound view ports. Lots of control panels and screens at each station. Stations comfortably separated from each other. A single, large seat in the center for the Captain. Electronic display pedestals on either side of his chair for subordinates to stand at. The uniform colors were blue and gray with quite a bit of varying colorful ornamentation. The drug they had given me was making everything kind of starlight. The Captain stood near his chair. His ensemble was trimmed in what appeared to be real gold leaf. He wore a lightweight dark helmet with pull down display arms folded back. My guess was he looked older than his years, a result of a lot of autopilot-miles. As we entered he glanced up and gave me a harsh stare.

I began to feel a bit giddy from the drug. I smiled, approached him, and held out my hand with an aw-shucks look.

He did not accept it. Instead, he motioned us back toward the door and stood close. He spoke in a low, but very clear tone, "Look Captain Tarn, we need to keep things straight on this bridge. I am the Captain here. Mine is the last word. I do not care what your position entitles you to. As long as I hold this position you do not."

R.J. interrupted. "Captain Yamora, forgive me. Could I have a private word with Captain Tarn? Just one moment."

R.J. took me by the arm and led me a few feet away. Yamora turned to the nearest station and began studying the displays. Still giddy, Yamora's ill-will had not yet registered with me. I had a stupid half smile stuck on my face.

R.J. sighed, "Adrian, I never got the chance to explain."

"I don't think he likes me. Why wouldn't he like me?"

"It's about the rescue."

"Boy was that ever a relief."

"The drug is still making you woozy. Try to listen. There was a problem getting a ship to divert to rescue you. There were only two that had any chance of making it. Space-maritime law is pretty constant from one system to the next. Any ship capable of saving someone in an emergency by law is supposed to do it. But, of the two ships that could possibly reach you, neither wanted to. They both kept insisting the other was in a better situation to divert. In the end, the only way Fantasia could end the stalemate was to buy this ship and take control of it."

"She *bought* a ship?"

"Okay, listen closely. Fantasia bought this ship we're on. That's why they had no choice but to divert to pick you up."

"Well that worked."

"Fantasia bought the *Acrua Maru* along with the contract to deliver the prisoners and VIPs."

"Well, I guess they can't put us off then?"

"No, they can't put us off."

"Because Fantasia owns this ship, did you say?"

"Not exactly."

"Wow. Thank goodness. I thought for a moment you were saying Fantasia bought this ship."

"I *did* say that. She bought this ship but she had the registry put in your name. *You* own this ship."

"Okay, now you're just trying to mix me up. Stop kidding around. We need to be serious right now. Can't you see the Captain's a little upset?" I glanced around to see if Captain Yamora might be getting mad.

"So you see, Yamora is afraid you're going to override his orders or take command here."

"Wait, she bought this ship. That's what you're really saying. Bought, purchased, owns this ship?"

"She bought it. You own it."

"You've got to be kidding! How the hell much money do our women have for God's sake?"

"Well, they both own Castle estates with hundreds of acres or hadn't you noticed that?"

"Well I know *that*, but still...."

"So you understand why Yamora is on your case now, right?"

"What am *I* supposed to do with this ship now?"

"I'd ask Fantasia about that before I did anything at all."

"I own a ship full of prisoners being taken to a prison worse than the Bridge of Sighs with a bunch of pampered VIPs along for the ride? What could possibly go wrong?"

"You're starting to sober up. That's good. You left out the army of human android servants traveling along with them."

"This reminds me of a really old comedy sketch I once saw where a high-seas cargo ship was carrying ten tons of bananas forward and five hundred caged monkeys aft."

"So you'd better put Yamora's mind at ease, right?"

"Who's gonna put my mind at ease?"

"There's a bar on this deck."

"Thank God."

My head was swimming worse than before. I left R.J. and teetered over to Captain Yamora. My expression had changed to sheepish. He raised the finger of his right hand and opened his mouth to speak.

I cut him off with slurred authority. "Captain Yamora, please accept my sincere thanks for rescuing me. I am a passenger on this cruise, nothing more. In fact, if you need me for anything at all, try the bar first. I am grateful for your command experience. My friend and I will be going now. We shouldn't be a bother to you again for the rest of this voyage. Thank you again, sir."

It seemed to leave him speechless. One hand was raised and his mouth was open but nothing came out. I turned away in my partial stupor, motioned erratically to R.J., and headed with questionable balance for the door as the Captain continued to look on. When the second pressure door slid closed behind us I stopped and asked, "Food? There's real food here you said?"

Chapter 8

"You will find the hostess interesting," said R.J. as we walked the worn but luxurious corridor.

"I don't know. The last time I found a hostess to be that interesting I ended up owning this ship, according to you."

"In all fairness, Elachia and Fantasia were not hostesses back then. They were actually diplomatic envoy extraordinaires which means they had even more authority than a standard ambassador."

"Okay, that got all muddled up in the medication."

"The dining area is just up ahead. We'll see if we can rebuild and reorganize those brain cells."

The food court was a beige colored open corner area at a wide corridor intersection. There were plastic tables and chairs of various heights fastened to the brown carpeted floor. A few other colorful human-looking guests occupied some of them. There was a long glass counter running the length of the place with hundreds of decorated bottles and glasses shelved behind it. I smelled food but could not put a name to it.

"Let's take the counter, shall we?" suggested R.J.

We sat on high back stools which seemed to mold to our forms.

"The hostess' name is Anai. She and I have had long conversations about the destiny of man."

"Ah, existential philosophy is now available to me once again. I've missed it so."

"Yes, your outlook alone on that moon must have been pretty narrow. Here she comes."

The server was highly attractive. Black hair past the shoulders. Tiny perfect features with the kind of dark eyes that seem like they are daring you. Sleeveless wraparound light green dress. No jewelry of any kind. Skin tone perfection.

"Gentlemen, what is your pleasure?"

Her voice had that slight raspiness to it that tickles sexual awareness in most people.

R.J. held up a stop gesture to me. "My friend would like Dula to start, then the Sen-Aitee with Yama. Ina, Tesh, for me with Esa."

"Very good. Right away. Always nice to see you, R.J."

I glanced at him with a worried look. "What did I just order?"

"Large, charbroiled steak with Yamas. They are just like potatoes but shaped like carrots. You mash them up and you can't tell the difference. The steak is the best artificial meat I've ever tasted. Dula is bourbon."

"You did well then."

"I didn't think you'd want to spend time learning the menu. The voice translators work well here but they're unable to translate some foods, art, music, that sort of thing. Apparently the Lemorian language was not programmed into the translation matrix very thoroughly."

"Is their Bourbon really bourbon?"

"Don't know how they produce it, but yes, high grade."

A few departing guests passed close behind us. It made me tighten up a bit.

"Lemorians?"

"Yes, basically they are your hosts, my ever-wayward friend. Lemoria is located near the Alpha Andromeda system. As you can see, they are bipeds with forms nearly identical to ours. You may have noticed their eyes are slanted upward a little bit and the tops of their ears are kind of pointed."

As we spoke Anai appeared with a short, round, ice-filled glass for me along with a tall narrow wine glass half-filled with red for R.J. She reached under the glass counter and drew out a heavily adorned glass bottle and poured until my glass was half full. I began to worry it was not enough when she placed the bottle on the counter next to my drink, smiled and headed back the way she had come.

I sipped. Smooth. I smiled at R.J. He laughed.

"They didn't have this on the pod."

"So how's your head?" he asked.

"The heavy gravity thing is looming in the background. I have a feeling this will help the meds."

"But how's your head dealing with everything that happened?"

"Oh, you want to make things ugly."

"Dr. Smith at your service."

"If you really want to know the whole fucking thing was my fault. That's something which will visit me the rest of my waking hours."

"I read the flight plan. Why was your fault?"

"I allowed an amateur to take the lander pod up to the ship alone to save time."

"He was many things but he was no amateur."

"Okay, you want to know the real bitch of it then? I didn't remind him to reset the collision avoidance system after he docked with the spacecraft. Some bastard chunk of ice-rock came around that freaking moon and went right through him."

"Did you see it?"

"Standing there looking up just right to see the confetti spread."

"Oh God, I cannot imagine that."

"It's sort of become a series of still images in my head."

"Well, as intense as that is, you're wrong about one thing."

"No kidding?"

"No, what I mean is, while you were taking your very long shower and thank God for that, I used your room's terminal to plug into the suit black box and jumped around to the accident recordings. You *did* warn him to turn the collision avoidance back on as soon as he docked."

"*What*?"

"You don't have to take my word for it. It's there in the audio log files plain as day."

I choked but held it in. It took me a few moments to collect myself. I had to adjust my throat. My mind was almost afraid to accept the pardon I'd just been granted. I dared a sip of drink and tried to look unaffected. There was a big turmoil of communication going on between mind and heart. My glass was suddenly empty. I poured.

"Oh boy, here comes Anai," said R.J.

She brought our orders on a streamlined, chrome antigravity pushcart. She was very careful and adept about placing my dishes and condiments in just right order in front of me. She smiled at R.J. as she put down his cheese plate. She refilled his wine glass. Without a word, off she went.

"Careful about the plates. They stay hot throughout the meal."

I still could not speak but I sure could eat. Both the food and now life itself suddenly tasted better. When I'd cleared my plates I looked up to find Hostess Anai suddenly there placing coffee cups and pouring without having been asked. With that same exotic smile, she left us.

"What do you think of her?"

"Most perfect skin tone I've ever seen I think."

"What else?"

"She says more without speaking than most people do with words."

"If you weren't in a committed relationship would you date her?"

"She seems like a nice girl."

"Get this, she's an android."

"I don't think so."

"No, I'm being straight with you. She's all android, toes to nose. No biology there at all."

"But she's got a human aura around her."

"Not by accident either. The Lemorians are extremists on androids. I've been told their planet consists of forty-nine percent service worker androids and fifty-one percent real people. Apparently, it's a hard and fast law which states the android population cannot exceed that percentage. They've developed the artificial human thing to near perfection. On Lemoria, people no longer wed. Everyone has an android companion instead. I guess if you have a choice of a stark-raving beautiful android that never complains, is always loyal, gladly does most of the menial work and is highly skilled at intimacy, plain old real people can't compete with that. I have been told that at least half of this ship's crew are androids but I am forced to doubt that."

I took a sip of hot coffee. "Man, that's good coffee. So if there's a big emergency down in Engineering and the real people are injured and out of action, androids decide the fate of the ship?"

"Hence my distrust of that fifty-percent rumor." R.J. held up his wine glass in a toast and drank.

"I can't imagine everyone on Earth being paired with a robot."

"Hey, believe it or not, that's happening right now. Now that the sexbots are completely ambulatory and can perform household duties, the sexbot people have begun to form conglomerates with the robotics firms. The plan is to make sophisticated companion androids financially available to everyone on Earth. They're going to set it up like you're buying or leasing a vehicle. Payments forever and in return a loyal, drop-dead gorgeous android comes to live with you for the rest of your life. It's already happening, trust me."

"I don't think I like that."

"You'll get to see how over time it has affected the Lemorians on this ship, and when we reach Lemoria."

Anai returned and slunk up to us with a coffee dispenser. She refilled mine without asking. "Are you well, Captain Tarn? R.J. told me about your accident."

"I am surprisingly intact, Anai. Thank you for asking."

"I hope you will stop in while you're here and tell me all about it."

"I will, Anai."

"I would love to get to know you better, Captain."

"Thank you, Anai."

She seemed satisfied with herself somehow. After a quick glance to verify our counter was clean, she glided off.

"Android? You're sure?"

"So if you weren't attached would you go out with her?"

"As beautiful as she is there's something scary about that but I'm not sure why."

"It's several things. A real person you can usually read by their body language, tone of voice, and choice of words. But with her, you can't trust any of those. I bet she could pass any lie-detector test anywhere, anytime with flying colors."

"My God, we're living in the age of the Blade Runner."

"Yeah, and we can't even tell if that's good or bad."

"The bourbon is doing its job. I keep having visions of that bed in my room."

"I took your mind off of things for a while there, didn't I?"

"Yeah. Thanks. Brain is resetting. Reality is returning."

"Come on, I'll make sure you get to your room okay, then you're on your own."

"Where's your room in case I get scared in the dark?"

"Two doors down on the right. We have an *Acrua Maru* company rep and his android companion between us."

We waved to Anai and headed out. At my room, R.J. tapped the door keypad and the doors slid open.

"Can just anyone do that?" I asked.

"Nope. They put me on the door list when they first assigned this room for you. Of course they weren't sure you'd be needing it. So, you'll get some alone time now to sort everything out."

"To be honest, I've had all the alone time I'll need for a while."

"Have I mentioned how grateful I am that you made it?"

"Don't start getting mushy on me or we'll both end up bawling." I stepped into the room. R.J. smiled, wiggled the fingers on one hand and tapped the door shut.

Someone had been in the room while we were away. Night clothes were spread out on the bed. A closet door was open. An assortment of men's wear had been added there. In the bathroom there were extra luxuries. In the kitchenette sealed food packages were in the freezer compartment. There was a small bar adjoining the kitchen. A button beneath the bar caused a door underneath to slide open. There, to my joy, another decorative bottle of what appeared to be the same bourbon sat beside a small ice machine and glasses. Apparently, every effort was being made to cater to the new owner of the *Acrua Maru*. I pulled out the bottle, filled a glass with ice and poured. Kicked off the sandals and stretched out on the bed, propped up against pillows.

The door chime rang.

There was no energy left in reserve to get back up. I yelled, "Yes?" and hoped there was a door intercom system. Instead the door slid open.

She had dark hair down past her shoulders. She wore a skin-tight one-piece suit that softly glittered amber. Her figure seemed too perfect. Long perfectly shaped legs broke out from slits in the skirt, curves in all the right places, and a bust that was a touch intrusive to the vision of her. She entered without having been asked. That seemed to be a custom in this place.

She came to the foot of the bed, smiled and said, "Captain Tarn, my name is Eva. I've been assigned as your service contact. I was here earlier and left some things for you. Is there anything you need?"

Awkwardly I tried to push myself up while balancing the glass in my right hand. "No, no, thank you, Eva. As you can see you've already brought everything I need. Thank you."

"Anai measured you when you came in the diner. Everything I left should fit you perfectly."

"Anai measured me? When did she do that?"

Eva laughed. "Just by looking at you. She has that ability. She is more than a service Con."

"Oh. I see."

"There are call buttons located around your room in various places. If you need me, you have only to press one and I'll come right away."

"Eva, if it's not too rude of me to ask, you are an android, aren't you?"

Her expression did not change. She finally gave a half smile as though to put my mind at ease. "We would prefer the classification to be Hueman Construct, or Woeman Construct, Con for short. That category is very close to the Earth word human or woman and has the same definitions within it. The "HU" in hueman represents the atmospheric mixture, pressure and temperature range required for life. The "E" is the symbol for terrestrial entity. And, of course, the "MAN" portion is the abbreviation for 'Materialized Ambulatory Node,' node indicating an entity which is an individual expression of the Great Creative Force that set the universe in motion. It also represents the standard biped body design said to be the most universal image for intelligent life. In Woeman, the "WO" represents Man with womb, and again the "E" again stands for terrestrial. These are nearly identical to the translations of the Earth terms "Man" and "Woman." The concept of "Man" appears in many biped civilizations throughout the galaxy. Those such as myself consider ourselves to be extensions of that category."

Fatigue, heavy gravity medication, bourbon and brain overload left me dazed. I had understood everything she said but there was just no processing it.

"Captain, I see you are preparing to sleep again. Forgive my intrusion. I will leave you but as I have said, I will be available for anything you need."

With that, she turned and left.

I carefully balanced my glass over to the blurry nightstand and delicately put it down. I was asleep before my arm hit the pillow.

There were dreams. At first, I was alone on a deserted island where it kept raining rocket debris. There was thunder and lightning explosions and although the fragments were pouring down all around me I was not hurt by them. Next, Matt was there. He was walking around in a spacesuit with no arms. I tried to talk to him but I did not have a suit on so he could not hear me. I followed him to a barren desert. There were dunes all around. No matter where I went it was always the same. Time just dragged on.

Something awakened me. The room lights had dimmed automatically. I was laying prone on the bed on top of the covers. My eyes struggled to focus in the darkness. For a moment I feared I was back on the moon.

Someone was standing next to me. The old self-preservation instincts kicked in. I snapped rolled to the right very sloppily, went over the edge and used the bed for cover. Lights came on. I dared to look.

Eva was standing there beside the bed. There was no expression of surprise on her face. "Captain Tarn, I'm so sorry. I was trying not to wake you."

In a raspy voice I managed, "Eva, what are you doing here?"

"Dr. Yurify asked that your vitals be checked during the night. He wanted to verify that in sleep your system was at complete rest. It is a valuable assessment which can confirm there are no hidden problems."

I sat up on the bed and rubbed my face. "Well, were the readings normal?"

"Perfectly, but I extended the scan because you appeared to be restless. I am so sorry for disturbing you. Can I get you anything?"

"No, I'm fine."

"I will go and let you finish your sleep period." She clipped her scanner to her belt and headed for the door.

"Eva."

She stopped and looked at me. "Yes?"

"For now on, always ask me before entering my room."

"I understand."

The next morning I checked the improvement in my wardrobe selection. I had a choice of black, skin-tight stretch pants, or regular slacks which looked like black wet leather. No way I was wearing stretch pants. The best shirt looked and felt like black satin. A lightweight imitation black leather jacket was meant to go with it. Best of all I could forego the sandals for calf-high black imitation leather boots. And, thankfully, there were undergarments.

Refreshed and cleaned up I headed for the door, punched the open button and there stood a smiling R.J. in farmer's coveralls, a plaid shirt and sneakers.

"Breakfast with Anai?" he asked.

"Is she always there?"

"Twenty-one-six on this ship."

We headed for the food.

"Bet you slept well."

"Continuous unconscious soul searching except for the brunette standing over me in the middle of the night."

"What?"

I recounted my middle of the night visitation.

"Okay, that's definitely creepy," he replied. "Wake up to an android standing over you?"

"They don't like that term. They prefer human construct."

"Yeah, I know. It's *Con* actually. I've had to catch myself to avoid using android or robot."

At the food counter we were able to order eggs without being familiar with the bird they came from. They were each the size of a standard plate so they needed to be served in a basket beside the dish. We also had sliced fried yamas and even bread although Anai was unable to grasp the concept of toasting. She did not seem able to understand the benefit of it. Once again she brought coffee to follow the meal. She placed it with a smile and hurried off.

"So you had a late night lesson in the fundamentals of man's place in the universe?" asked R.J. as he sat back.

"We are apparently nodes, individual expressions of God."

"I believe the Shamans in India would agree with that."

"You know, those doctors were very white and had perfect skin tone. Do you think they're artificial also?"

"I did wonder about that but did not dare inquire. I'm certain they are. There seems to be certain sensitivities in the android population about a number of subjects."

"Somehow I don't think I'd be comfortable knowing half of the people around me were A.I. machines."

"It's like giving a supercomputer free access to the world."

"I wonder how the Lemorians really feel about it."

"The android population has been evolving on Lemoria for a long time. These people were born into that world. It's like on Earth our kids have never lived in a world which wasn't managed by computers. It's just a natural part of life to them."

"We should keep an eye out around here and see exactly what might be in store for Earth. Maybe we can warn them about androids who are too beautiful and too independent."

"A tour for the ship's new owner would seem appropriate."

Before I could answer, an unfamiliar voice from behind interrupted. "Captain Tarn, may I have just a moment?"

I swiveled to find a well-dressed man in a dark amber collarless suit standing behind me. His reddish-brown hair was shaped into a single wave that began by the left ear and swept over his head to the right. His skin color was light and unblemished except around the eyes where it darkened to a faint red shadow. I wondered if it was makeup. His features were otherwise human. From the way his suit hung there did not seem to be much muscle tone to his body. He was of medium height, perhaps five-eight.

"Yes?"

"Forgive me for interrupting. I'm Andor Dulley, Vice President of Luminous Holdings. I won't take up your time. I was wondering if you would consider having dinner with Deanna and I this evening to discuss the formal transfer of the *Acrua Maru* to you? Management is very happy with the terms of our contract and is most anxious to finalize it."

I glanced at R.J. He returned a comical half-smile.

"That would be fine, Mr. Dulley. What time would you like us to be there?"

"Wonderful, Captain. I believe the staff will be ready, let us say, at the eighteen-hundred hour."

"We'll look forward to it. My associate and I were just discussing the possibility of touring the *Acrua Maru*. That might be a good idea before we meet."

"I would be happy to arrange that, Captain. I will have your service Con Eva notify you when an escort has been assigned."

I wondered if a handshake was appropriate. Dulley did not offer his. He bowed slightly and declared, "A good twenty-one, sir," and off he went. He seemed to take hurried steps, too short. An associate was waiting for him in the hall. They conversed and headed back toward the rooms.

I looked at R.J. "Well, wish for a tour and what do you get?"

"Better than dinner and a movie."

Anai appeared to check our coffees. I held up one hand to stop her from pouring. "Anai, you haven't asked for payment for any of this food and your great service. Do I pay for everything at the end or what?"

"Why thank you for such a nice compliment, Captain Tarn. I thought you knew. You have already been registered as owner of the *Acrua Maru*. When your wife set up the *Acrua Maru* purchase all products and services became yours. R.J.'s expenses are also put on your account. I hope that is correct."

"Oh! Yes! Perfect. Thank you, Anai."

"Is there anything else I can get you, Captain?"

"No, I believe we're fine, Anai."

Once again Anai hurried off as though she was deeply involved in some other task.

Next to me, R.J. was suppressing sounds of a comical nature. I looked over at him.

"What?!?"

"She just referred to Fantasia as your wife. At some point we must have passed through a dimensional shift into another reality."

"Laugh it up, Elachia-worshiper. I'll tell you something which will ruin that joke for you. I just had one of those moments, what do you call them... epiphany. I just had an epiphany."

"Do tell."

"All my life I have feared that word 'wife.' It has sent chills up and down my spine and brought images of two-point-five children, a white picket fence and barbeques on Sundays. For the first time in my life, when she just said it. I liked it. I felt uplifted."

"Definitely a dimensional shift into another reality, although Fantasia did save your reality."

"I feel her presence right now as a matter of fact. I need to head back to my room to see if any subspace communications from her have had time to get here yet."

"Yeah, me too."

Chapter 9

We walked the corridor back to our rooms. I finally began to notice some of ship's detail. The trim along the wall, floor and ceiling was a dull silver and engraved with scrolling and occasion images. It was fastened against thin tan fabric wallpaper. New, the design would have been impressive but the *Acrua Maru* had obviously seen many light years of travel, so much so a good deal of fading and graying had set in. The overhead subdued lighting was equally fancy in design but it had been cleaned so many times there were spots which could no longer be recovered. The carpet below our feet was still adequate but in much better shape near the walls. R.J. gave a half wave as I turned into my room.

On the *Acrua-Maru*-provided computer interface I managed to find the option for Earth languages and English. I logged in and assigned a new password; Apollo13. Email was called "communiqué." There was a 'Local' folder and a 'Subspace' folder. The Local contained a couple dozen icon messages relating to the sale of the *Acrua Maru*. The Subspace had even more icons related to acquisition of the *Acrua Maru*. There were no personal messages. Fantasia's first letter had not caught up yet. I sat back and felt "I love you" to her. There was a small burst of joyful "be safe" feeling in return.

I blew off all the other stuff and headed for the bed. Sleep was unnecessary but my body was grateful for the temporary escape from the gravity grindstone.

But that left me alone with my thoughts. There was no escaping what should have been a death sentence on that moon. Never mind the loss of my friend. Thank God R.J. had found the warning about collision avoidance in the suit recorder. Though I still tried repeatedly, I was no longer able to blame myself for that. On the surface the guilt wasn't as bad. There had been such a likelihood that I would die for my crimes, it was not so necessary to punish myself. Now that I was safe, survivor's guilt set in. And, recall kept bringing up that long period in the beginning where it seemed like there was no hope.

Traumatic life episodes have a special lifespan of their own. They live within you for a very long time after the event. Often, they never leave completely. Sometimes they generate new subconscious defense mechanisms kept in the ready room of your brain to prevent a similar occurrence from ever happening again. A small reserve of adrenaline is stored for that purpose. You find yourself occasionally visiting these unpleasant little trows during soul searching. They can scare you like an old black and white horror movie. They can make you feel helpless and unprepared. You never meant for that life-threatening mistake to occur so how could you have possibly avoided it? If that could happen back then, what's to stop something similar from going wrong now? Invariably you wind up this type of self-punishment by measuring the amount of guilt you've assigned to the event. Verdict is put off until a later date.

Thankfully, the door chimed. I sat up and called, "Yes?"

The door slid open to reveal Eva in a tight gray body suit with faint blue stripes spiraling around its entirety. She smiled. "Captain Tarn, a guide from the bridge has been assigned to escort you for your tour. He can answer any questions you may have. He is waiting in the lounge. There is no need to hurry. He will remain there until you are ready to go."

"Thank you, Eva. Would you please let my associate know?"

"I will. Do you require anything?"

"No. Thank you."

She tapped the door closed.

Ten minutes later a second door chime. This time I opened it myself and found R.J. smiling. He surprised me. He had changed out of his usual farmer's dress into a commander-level, gold, one piece flight suit. He noticed me appraising it and smirked. I went to my closet where Eva had left three versions of flight-suit-styled one-piece garments hanging, chose the fanciest one and switched into it.

"He's waiting for us in the lounge," said R.J.

"Yeah, do you know where that is?"

"It's that strange looking, out-of-whack door across from the dining area. I've been told the door looks weird going in but normal coming out."

"God, that's an old one."

"Not to the Lemorians."

We headed out. R.J. led the way.

"So will this be an android tour or a real person tour?"

"I don't think we've really established androids are not real people."

"You're right, how could anyone tell?"

"I've been reading up on that. On Earth they use a thing called the Turing Test. It's a test that's supposed to establish if an artificial intelligence has achieved actual consciousness."

"Oh, good luck with that."

"It's a tricky subject because if they pass the test, do you then declare them living beings equal to humans?"

"Androids voting in elections and holding political offices?"

"That's what I'm saying. Believe it or not, we already have android citizenship on Earth. I managed to check that. Way back in 2017, in Saudi Arabia, this android named Sophia was given citizenship, legal personhood anywhere in the world, and that was even before androids could perform menial tasks around the house. She was the first. Android rights. We started down this same road decades ago."

R.J. pointed to the off-center arched double doors which led to the lounge. Beyond them the lounge area, like everywhere else on the *Acrua Maru*, was showing its age. Lighting had been darkened to hide the wear and nicks on small tables and darkened further in corners, trim areas, and the corridor to the service areas. A uniformed ensign quickly looked up as we entered and waved though not needing to as he was the only patron. A cute blond behind the bar with short haircut just past the ear also appraised us with a practiced smile. Even in the lower light her skin looked too perfect.

The Ensign left his stool and came to us. He did not offer his hand. "Captain, it's a pleasure to meet you, sir. Commander Smith, nice to see you again. Shall we go or would you like a drink first?"

"Thank you for meeting us. I did not get your name."

"Oh, sorry. I'm Ensign Jamms. You can just call me Jamms, of course. What do you think, drink or go?"

R.J. opened the door and gestured us out.

"You've seen most of the Level Four suite sections. Have you walked down to the very end?"

"I haven't been anywhere except the bridge and food, Ensign."

"On this deck beyond the suites you'll come to an area of service rooms for the staff, a substation security office and beyond that are the compartments where the conduits and cabling interfaces from Deck Three are located. Past those are large pressure doors and an airlock which leads to the depressurized section which eventually becomes the outside upper exterior structures of the ship. Am I correct in thinking you don't wish to visit those areas?"

"What is Level Three, Ensign?"

"Everything is on Level Three, Captain. Network control, electrical, life support, cooling and further aft is the central power station. Beyond that is main Engineering and access to the drive section. We can take the elevator if you're ready."

"Lead on, Ensign."

The third level layout was fairly familiar. The deck was divided into two wide corridors divided first by a long line of supercomputers, then generic looking equipment racks. The left-hand wall was a continuous row of equipment panel sections, everything you'd expect: life support, power distribution, hydraulics, gas storage control, fuel systems monitor and control, water reclamation among other services. Against the other corridor's outer wall was a maze of conduits, cable racks, piping and wave guides interrupted periodically by control racks. The place hummed much louder than Deck Four.

The dim yellow carpet on the floors was so worn it had become dark in the center. The equipment had been cleaned hundreds of times but the effort was slowly losing ground. Some of the hanging overhead lighting was out.

Farther aft the place cleaned up a bit. The reasons were obvious. We entered an antimatter control area. Two technicians with perfect skin were manning the consoles. They were uninterested in our passing. Jamms called out each area as we passed by though it was unnecessary.

Beyond we came to main Engineering. It was surprising to find only three individuals in attendance there. The room widened to the full width of the ship and formed a broken circle of control stations. Farther ahead there were several pressure doors with explicit warning signs. I could not read the Lemorian language on them but I could tell they read, 'WARNING: VACUUM BEYOND THIS POINT. NACELLE ACCESS.'

We returned to the elevators. R.J. looked to Jamms and asked, "Level Two?"

106

"Sir, Level Two is a closed area. It provides security quarters, the main security office, armory and holding cells. Only security and the bridge crew are allowed there."

R.J. wasn't taking no for an answer. "I'm sure if you check with the Captain you'll find Captain Tarn's legal position supersedes any security requirement."

Jamms stepped away from us and pulled a communicator from his belt. He turned away so that we could not hear but he did not go far enough. We heard every word and pretended not to.

"Captain, they want to see two."

"Ensign, Tarn is entitled access to all areas of the ship. We cannot legally block that. Do your best."

Jamms returned and nodded. "My apologies. The Captain confirms you are cleared for Level Two." Jamms tapped open the elevator and we stepped in.

"Captain, we should try not to disturb those being transferred in the holding area. Some information there is proprietary. I may not be able to answer all your questions."

Before I could reply, the elevator doors slid open to a small circular room with computer desks. Two perfect men in gray coveralls were seated at them. They both swiveled in their seats to face us but neither spoke. Beyond the security checkpoint we could make out entrances to several standard crew quarters, followed by numerous holding cells on either side of the wide corridor. Black bars were the chosen method of restraint.

"Ensign Jamms," declared our guide to the guards. "Tarn and Smith review."

One of the men made an entry note on his terminal. Without speaking, they both swiveled back to what they'd been doing.

We walked the long corridor of dirty-gray metal floors and suspended overhead lighting. The first two cells on my right and left stunned me. Both housed very attractive women in formal wear, women with perfect skin. Their eyes followed us as we passed by but neither spoke. As we continued, the pattern was the same. Attractive women with perfect skin well-dressed or in servant's attire in each cell. I could feel R.J. becoming uncomfortable.

Halfway down the corridor, I stopped. Jamms paused and raised an eyebrow in inquiry.

"Jamms, are all of these prisoners human constructs?" I asked.

Jamms returned an expression of understanding. "They are not actually prisoners, Captain, but yes they are all Cons."

R.J. asked, "If they are not prisoners, what are they?"

"They are surplused employees."

I could feel R.J. spinning up.

"If they are not prisoners, why are they behind bars?" he asked.

"It is only a technical requirement to meet the conditions of the Lemorian BiCon Ratio Mandate."

"The BiCon Ratio Mandate?" continued R.J.

"Yes, the mandate specifies there can only be a certain percentage of Cons and Biologicals cohabiting at one time. During these transfers the confinement cells allow us to exceed the standard limits so these Cons can be relocated."

"Why are they being relocated?" persisted R.J.

"There are several reasons Cons may be relocated. Their sponsors may have passed away, the sponsor may need to bring in a new specialized Con but he has reached his allowed limit so he must surplus one of his other Cons to adhere to the BiCon Ratio, the sponsor simply has no further need for his Con or a multitude of other possibly reasons. Does that answer your question fully, Commander?"

Jamms was becoming uncomfortable.

R.J. was not satisfied. "Where are they being relocated to?"

"That's really too much to explain during this tour, Commander. If you would ask your service Con she will direct you to reading material about the Res Relocation Station."

R.J. looked at me. I tried to silently suggest caution.

"Thank you, Ensign Jamms. You've been very helpful," said R.J.

We resumed our walk. By the end of the confinement corridor we'd seen only four male Cons, the rest were all attractive females.

"Here at the aft superstructure you can see there are additional pressure doors to give access to the depressurized section and exterior superstructure. You are already familiar with the Level One shuttle bay and cargo area. I believe this concludes our tour. The Captain asked me to offer you a more in-depth tour of the bridge and navigation areas if you would call ahead to set that up. Any other questions?"

I bit my lip. R.J. was barely able to restrain himself. We were taken back to Level Four where Jamms excused himself.

"Lunch?" asked R.J.

"Absolutely, lunch. I get the feeling the tour bothered you. Let's head for the real food. I'm starved."

"What? Isn't anything about that bothering you?"

"Yes, but I asked you first."

"I have many questions."

"Such as?"

"Why don't they just shut them off?"

"The Cons?"

"Yes. Why relocate them? Why not just shut them off?"

"Maybe it's that android citizenship thing you were telling me about. Maybe they can't legally shut them off."

"Why mostly attractive women? What happens to them when they get relocated? How human are these androids? How much freedom do they really have? How physically strong are they?"

"That last one's kind of worrisome."

"Yeah, could they overpower humans if they chose to?"

"What did the Ensign call it? The BiCon Ratio Mandate? That seems to be very important."

"The phrase, '*can't live with them, can't live without them*,' keeps popping into my head."

There were three other patrons seated at the dining area tables. All were crew members in uniform.

"Let's take a table out of the way," said R.J.

We took a corner table near a waist-high wall looking out over the elevator area. As we settled in, Anai appeared next to us.

"Hello, Captain, R.J. A drink?"

I answered, "Anai, may I please have the same thing I had yesterday?"

"The large portion?"

"Yes, I have weeks of powdered food to make up for."

"And you, R.J., my Earthly friend?"

"I'd like the Bavada please, my *Acrua Maru* friend."

Anai smiled and dashed off.

"Bavada?" I asked.

"A Lemorian chef's salad. It's adventurous since I have no idea what the vegetables are and there are bits of artificial meat I know equally nothing about. The dressing tastes like ranch."

"So what did you really think of our tour?"

"More questions than answers, as they say."

"Agreed. What did you learn about these people during your stay here on your way to rescue me?"

"Very little. I was concentrating on learning everything possible about your moon and your mission. I gave Elachia my word I would bring you back alive. I was worried."

"Mission accomplished."

"I never count my chickens before they're hatched, especially where you're involved."

"So you haven't learned much about Lemorians then?"

"They are non-social. You'll notice there are seldom any people in this dining area. They usually take their meals in their rooms. The Cons, as they are called, are all very approachable but they tend to say only what is absolutely necessary. It takes many carefully phrased questions to get anything out of them. It may be a trait inherited by the non-social nature of Lemorians."

"I'll tell you what, I'd sure like to have a long talk with one of those prisoners."

Anai returned, guiding an antigravity tray with our food and drinks.

As she placed the items on our table, I dared a question, "Anai, is it rewarding working here?"

"Yes, very, Captain. I meet many guests."

Before I could follow up, she hurried off again.

R.J. nodded. "See what I mean?"

The smell of my second artificial charbroiled steak distracted me. With the first bite I was overwhelmed. I attacked the plate with the ferocity of a man who had been marooned on a desert island, which I had been. R.J. smirked as he watched me ravage my meal.

As I neared the last of it, R.J. said, "I hope you're getting past the scars from your last mission, sir."

I sat back and exhaled. "There will still need to be a mission to recover Matt's remains."

"Sponsored by his university I'm sure."

"And sample the gas we were collecting to rewrite more history in his honor."

"Will you attend that return trip?"

"No."

Once again Anai suddenly appeared with coffee. She poured us, gathered our plates, and disappeared through the service door.

R.J.'s tone became serious, "You know, I'm thinking that the unanswered questions about our android friends really are of some concern to you."

"In what way?"

"When Fantasia purchased this ship she was also forced to buy the transportation contracts it was fulfilling."

"You're saying I'm responsible for those prisoners down there?"

"And the VIPs here on Deck Four."

"Don't ruin what was a great meal."

"Hey, for you a hot dog would have been a great meal."

"True."

"I have to wonder how much meddling it would take to set Captain Yamora off."

"Why do I get the feeling sooner or later we're going to find out?"

"We may glean some good information from tonight's meeting."

"What?"

"The dinner invitation. We have a dinner invitation with... what was his name? Dulley, Andor Dulley, the company rep."

"Oh, crap."

"At the least, we'll get to see how a successful Lemorian lives."

"R.J., we don't have to meddle at all in this. We can just remain dumb passengers on a spaceliner and disembark at the first commercial space facility."

"You don't want to know what will happen to all those androids you're transporting?"

"This isn't one of our clandestine investigative missions, R.J. The only thing I want right now is to be leaning back with a drink in one of the hot pools at Fantasia's, preferably *with* Fantasia."

"She will want to know exactly what she had to buy into for your rescue."

"Damn-it, R.J." I sat holding my coffee cup halfway to my mouth, thinking. R.J. smirked. "What time was the dinner invitation?" I asked.

"I believe he said the eighteen-hundred-hour which for us is 6:00 P.M. on this ship's six day, twenty-one-hour day calendar. We should see how much we can learn from the terminals in our rooms before that dinner engagement. Maybe we can get Mr. Dulley to fill in some blanks."

"You are devious. Have I ever told you that?"

"I have learned from the best."

Chapter 10

R.J. had set me off. He was right, as usual. Fantasia would want to know what kind of obligations I had gotten her into this time. I sat in my room and did the one finger poke at Lemorian symbols on the terminal display screen until the terminal was back in Earth English mode.

What had the ensign called our next destination? The Res Relocation Station? It made me wonder if Res was short for reservation, the same term used to shanghai Native Americans. Twenty minutes of poking and I came up with nothing on that. I went on to Human Construct. There was a lot.

It is very easy to recognize when historians color history to look the way they want it to look rather than presenting cold hard reality. You can spot it through patterns. Every time something seems headed for distaste or disaster, the tone of the written word suddenly takes a curve upward. Or, on occasion they will withdraw from the tale entirely and summarize it with a *"then everyone lived happily ever after."*

I was seeing those patterns in the telling of the Human Construct history. There was an effort to make any conflicts sound like friends solving problems. And, within that carefully alluded to dichotomy, there was something else, an underlying thread of fear. I may have been misreading it. The impression was only a guess.

There was the Cons Unification Accord. The combining of all laws governing the treatment of Constructs into a declaration of Cons citizenship. The available articles celebrated the wonderful benefits of the accord but there was almost nothing pertaining to why the agreement had suddenly become necessary.

But there were hints. Accident statistics showed injuries in the workplace seemed to be more common to humans than Cons. Most reports attributed that to the fact machine bodies were much more resistant to damage than biological bodies. I drained my brain looking at the cause and effect on some of the larger reports, and it seemed as though there were common extenuating circumstances to human injuries which should have affected Cons as well.

Even more disturbing was that before the Cons Unification Accord there was an unusual number of missing humans that were never explained.

The suspicious patterns made me search for a category of thesis that talked about Cons basic programming. There were several prideful declarations about Cons programming being fundamentally based on the protection and preservation of human life. It was said to be the root directive within all Cons.

My door chimed. Before I could call out it slid open to admit R.J.

"Come in."

"Why, thank you. Just checking to see if I was still authorized."

"Is it six already?"

"In fifteen *Acrua Maru* minutes. Hear anything from Fantasia yet?"

"Not a word. Apparently, your body was able to get here faster than subspace messages."

He pulled up a chair next to me, linked his hands behind his head and swiveled back and forth. "How'd the android research go?"

"Spooky."

"Mine too. Read about the Cons Unification Accord?"

"Yep."

"And the plant shutdowns before it was accepted?"

"Didn't see that part."

"Apparently Cons can refuse to comply with some of their programming."

"Okay how about this: humans disappearing before the Accord was passed?"

"Wow! I didn't find that one. May not have anything to do with them though. I found a university site which teaches Cons programming. I got to see some sections of code. The very first programming hardware code mandates are to safeguard humans under all circumstances. It's way more comprehensive than even Asimov's Three Laws."

"I can imagine ways a human or android could get around those safeguards."

"Such as?"

"Make the assailant robot not know he is causing harm. Give him a job setting something up that will kill someone but make him think it's a harmless procedure."

"But the mastermind robot would know the setup was harmful to humans."

"But what if the setup was also a routine process that was normally not harmful, only in this one instance would it be fatal to a human. The mastermind robot could tell himself the setup had a history of being very safe."

"Tricky. An android kidding himself."

"There could be other loopholes like that. Tell a group of androids to kidnap a human in order to save his life and so on and so on."

"After such a long history of using Cons the Lemorians would have to be aware of these weak links."

"Hence, the Cons Unification Accord."

"We may be letting our imaginations run away with us. Everything on this ship seems normal and peaceful."

"Except for the deck full of android prisoners."

"Touché. Should we go to dinner?"

"Lead on."

We rang and waited outside Andor Dulley's suite not knowing what to expect. We said nothing, knowing we were on his door cam. When the doors finally slid open, the view inside was like looking into a carnival of luxury. The beauty of it was a perfect backdrop for the world-class beautiful woman there to greet us. She was already smiling when the doors opened. Her white-blond hair came down to her large, perfectly shaped breasts. There were streaks of gold in her hair. She wore a shimmering silver evening gown, conservatively cut, a single strap over the right shoulder. The dress covered the floor around her. Her skin tone was perfect and seemed to vary slightly in hue. Big bright blue eyes, tiny upturned nose, upturned cherry lips with a built in smile. Her makeup was not the permanent type. It had been applied with the skill of an artist. She was so beautiful in fact that both R.J. and I were momentarily captivated by it.

"Captain Tarn, Commander Smith, thank you so much for coming," she said in a voice that had that faint sandpaper rasp to it.

"Are we on time?" I asked.

"Perfectly," she replied and she raised an arm to urge our entry. "I am Deanna." She held out her hand.

Unsure of how to respond I took it and quickly turned it loose. R.J. did the same.

"Come and sit in the smoking circle until dinner is served," she said and she waved us to follow.

It was quite a lavish interior for a ship in space. The place was done in a dull ash red with almost too many gold, silver, and platinum ornaments along with oil paintings which filled the walls. She took us to a circle of very comfortable chairs surrounding a small glass table with white swirls embedded in the glass. Atop it was a gaudy pewter art piece of unrecognizable shapes. Empty wine glasses waited by each seating.

R.J. and I sat and looked at each other with expressions of wonder. A new person also with perfect skin tone dressed all in servant's white arrived holding a wine bottle and hand cloth in both hands. He carefully filled our glasses and backed away to return to a closed off kitchen area accessed through an arched door filled with shimmering light.

We sipped our wine and looked around warily. The wine tasted aged and of high quality. The place was spotless, polished clean by android determination.

R.J. leaned closer. "This has got to be the most luxurious shipboard suite I've ever seen."

"Deanna is an android, right?"

"I'm pretty sure but I get the feeling we shouldn't ask."

"The servant is, that's for sure."

"If Deanna is a Con will she eat? Maybe they're so advanced they have an energy extraction and waste removal system."

Before we could continue a smiling Andor Dulley approached sipping from a wine glass as he went.

"My friends, thank you so much for coming."

"Mr. Dulley, your suite is strikingly beautiful," said R.J.

"Thank you, Commander Smith." He handed his wine glass to the servant. "Andor, if you would please. Somehow the staff manages to transfer and set all this up in the two days before the ship sets sail."

Deanna appeared behind him. "Gentlemen, we should take our seats. Chef Barr is ready for us."

To my surprise, Dulley did not take a seat at the head of the polish pearl table. Instead he and Deanna sat directly opposite us. A transparent mythological-styled centerpiece was positioned between us. The table was already heavily set with a variety of foods. Chef Barr appeared with two large trays, one contained an abundant stack of what looked like sliced turkey, the other a red jello that reminded me of cranberry. Barr went around the table and filled out plates with some of everything without having been asked. I began to fear he might also feed us.

Dulley spoke, "We give thanks to the Crea for this wonderful table. Captain, Commander, if you are as famished as I, let's attack this." Dulley dived into his food.

We ate in silence with Barr standing at attention near a wall behind Dulley, diligently watching for any deficiencies which might arise. From the corner of my eye I watched Deanna. She ate. It was done in a most delicate fashion and in small quantities and she secretly studied R.J. and me as she did.

Eventually Dulley slowed and sat back, still sampling his dish periodically as though he could not get enough. He began a dabbing of the mouth with a white fabric napkin and seemed to need to gather himself. Deanna did not need the post meal face napkin. Every fork full had been so precisely placed no facial cleaning was required. She looked over at Dulley and seemed to get permission to speak.

"Captain Tarn, you must tell us of your time as a castaway on that awful moon. How did you survive? Where did you get food and water? How did you stay within biological temperature limits? How much oxygen did you have? How long were you down there?"

I patted my mouth with the napkin. "It is still difficult to talk about, Deanna. There is an Earth saying that God protects children and fools. I believe I fall into one of those categories."

She persisted, "But still, how could you have done it? You were down there for weeks, were you not?"

"The spacecraft's lander went into auto mode once it was ejected. It landed nearly intact. Most of my life support came from it. Just luck, really."

"Quite a remarkable achievement, Captain," said Dulley. "There was no information about your situation. All we knew was that someone required rescue. Once we were close enough, long range scanning found the spacecraft debris field. Navigation was able to track the pieces back to their original location, estimate the size of your ship and find your general location on the surface. At that point, however, there was little hope anyone had survived."

"I am very glad you did not give up," I replied.

Dulley continued, "Once Commander Smith was aboard that was not an option. He insisted you have a reputation for unexpectedly escaping most catastrophes. I see now he was correct."

I looked at R.J. He smirked.

Deanna resumed, "So you lived in the lander pod for all those weeks then?"

"And ate dehydrated food packs which makes this amazing meal you have served us even more enjoyable."

"Captain, if there was no atmosphere on that moon how did you extricate your solid waste?" Deanna asked matter-of-factly.

Dulley cut in, "Deanna dear, I don't believe that is an appropriate after dinner topic."

Deanna wrinkled her brow in a gesture so human-like both R.J. and I took notice.

I came to her rescue. "There was a compression toilet built into the lander, Deanna. It was not a problem."

She returned a look of genuine interest. "Oh, I see. What a fortunate happenstance."

Barr appeared beside Dulley and began setting teacups in place. When he had visited each of us he began pouring a hot brown liquid. Dulley sipped. Deanna let hers sit.

It tasted like coffee flavored with chocolate.

"Shall we take these to the smoking area?" asked Dulley.

With Barr hovering over us, we moved to the circle of seats there. Deanna stood behind Dulley with her hands on his shoulders.

"Do either of you smoke?" asked Dulley.

R.J. answered, "It was a popular custom on Earth, Andor, but humans were found to be susceptible to carcinogens from the tobacco so it is highly discouraged these days. I do occasionally use a pipe myself, however."

"You must try this, Commander. There are no harmful byproducts in the recipe," said Dulley. He handed R.J. a mechanical looking pipe along with a lighter. R.J. accepted and studied it.

"And you, Captain?"

"No thank you. I have enough vices already."

"Deanna dear, would you please refill the Captain's cup?"

Deanna headed toward the main table.

Dulley drew on his mechanical-looking pipe and spoke, "Barr will bring out the hard copy contracts I mentioned to you, Captain. Electronically we have your wife's signature on

123

them in both your names which is formal and binding but we always require hard copy. Ironically, they seem to be longer-lived."

"I do have some questions about that, Mr. Dulley."

"Please Captain, Andor if you will. We have no need of formality here. Perhaps I can answer your questions."

"As I understand it, we are under contract to transport the prisoners on Deck Two to the Markab System. Where exactly are we taking them?"

"They are not prisoners, Captain. They are simply immigrating to the Markab System Prefecture, the Res Relocation Station."

"What kind of a place is that?"

"As I've said, it is a prefecture, a self-governed society but still under Lemorian jurisdiction. Lemoria owns the Markab System."

"Are there humans living at the Res Relocation Station?"

"No, it is exclusively a Construct society."

R.J. asked, "Andor, it sounds as though you are creating a planet of Constructs by transferring your surplus there?"

"It's much more complex than that, Commander. I really can't go into it more than I already have. That is considered Lemorian proprietary information."

"But the ones we are transporting, they are not prisoners?" I asked.

"Yes, I can understand your confusion. Due to the BiCon Ratio Mandate we must give the appearance of confinement to keep the Human-Construct ratio on this ship within legal limits."

"Why is there a ratio mandate? Why must you keep the number of Constructs at a certain level?"

"That too is an extremely historic and complex subject, Captain. It fatigues me to think of trying to recount it. Suffice it to say the transfers on Deck Two are not mistreated in anyway and are not under any distress. That should reassure you in your part of this."

R.J. said, "You must forgive us, Andor. We did not mean to pry. Captain Tarn will be explaining all this to his wife when we return and also Earth is now beginning to enter the age of what you call Human Constructs. I would not be surprised if eventually we approached your people for guidance in managing that stage of our development."

Dulley looked thoughtful for a moment. He nodded, "Yes, yes in the beginning it is a very natural evolution in raising the quality of life for people but as the cooperative expands and matures it becomes intricately more complex. Perhaps someday we could share our knowledge base with Earth."

Deanna finally returned and poured more chocolate coffee into my teacup. Barr followed closely behind with sparkling silver folders. He placed them on the table in front of me.

"Andor, I think I'll need to study these before signing them. I'd like to compare them to what Fantasia signed."

"A very sensible idea, Captain. Take them with you. Let me know what questions you have, if any."

We began our thank yous and goodbye dialogue and left. In the hall R.J. seemed annoyed.

"I'm trying to find something we learned in everything that was said," he complained.

"Much was spoken, little was said."

"Who are you quoting?"

"Me, I think…."

"If I wasn't the suspicious type I'd think everything was just fine."

"Exactly the impressions he intended."

"He was quite good."

"Natural born politician."

"What bothers you the most?"

"When I sign these papers Fantasia and I become responsible for everything they've done."

"So what did Mr. Andor Dulley really avoid talking about?"

"What happens at the Res Relocation Station and what the BiCon Ratio Mandate's all about."

"Maybe it's nothing. Maybe we're just blowing things out of proportion."

"When someone doesn't want to talk about something it's always bad."

Chapter 11

In my room I changed into a gray flight suit, my choice of comfort-wear, then began searching the terminal for information on the Res Relocation Station. There were dozens of links which led nowhere. The closest I could get was a homepage titled, "RRS," with a wallpaper group of assumed androids all with big smiles because they were happy to be there. All the links required passwords and identification.

There was information on the BiCon Ratio Mandate but finding anything meaningful was like searching for a buried diamond ring in Death Valley.

I glanced at Dulley's paperwork. It had been translated to English with surprising expertise. The contracts seemed pretty straightforward.

After three hours of getting nowhere, the door chimed. It was late *Acrua Maru* time. Off guard, I called out, "Come in."

The door slid open to Deanna, minus Andor, with a wine glass in her hand. She charged right in, headed for the couch and plunked down on it. She was wearing a dark, silky shift which was a touch too short. It fit her feminine form perfectly as though she'd been poured into it. As she passed by me I was reminded of that Neanderthal ability most men have to automatically sense the amount of clothing any given woman is wearing at any given moment in time, along with the estimated difficulty level attached to removing such garments.

That primeval knowledge returned an estimate of 90% probability Deanna was wearing nothing at all beneath her silk outer covering and since it hung by only two very thin straps, the likelihood of it instantly falling to the floor in a heap was great.

She shifted around on the couch, crossed her legs with the too short skirt hiked too high and sipped her wine.

"Am I interrupting, Adrian?" She gave a coy half-smile.

I quickly became the bumbling idiot. "What? Is Andor coming? I'm still not really ready to sign off on these documents."

"Andor is sound asleep. He is never to be disturbed during his sleep period and he is almost impossible to wake up anyway. I'm bored. Since we're friends now I thought I'd just visit."

"Is Andor okay with you visiting neighbors this late?"

"He knows I'm a night person. He gave up trying to keep track of me long ago. Come sit here with me. It's no fun talking across the room." She brushed her hair behind her shoulder.

"It's been a long day, Deanna. I'm pretty exhausted."

"Perhaps I could help with that. I'm expert level at massage therapy. Would you like me to put you asleep?"

Against my will, my mind began considering the smoothness of her perfect skin-tone. I stood and went to the kitchen, filled my glass with water and took a seat *near* the couch. Though there was a good ten feet between us I felt like those long perfect legs were in my face.

"Deanna, can I ask you a personal question that might be inappropriate?"

"Oh, I was so hoping you would."

"Are you a bio or a con?"

Her expression said, *tsk*. "Adrian, such a badly phrased question. We are so much more perfect than biological humans. How could you possibly not know the answer to that? Even just including us in the same sentence together is like a contradiction in itself."

"I'm sorry. I see your point. I'd just like to know more about you."

"And I would very much like to know more about Earth men. I read of an old Earth saying, I'll show you mine, if you show me yours."

"Deanna, what is at the Res Relocation Station?"

"The Reserves Relocation Station? It's where Cons go to be trained in military units when their positions on Lemoria are no longer available. It is governed completely by Cons."

"It's a military base?"

"It is more than that. The military positions are just day jobs, otherwise Cons live a normal life there."

"Do Cons want to go there?"

"Wait, it is my turn. How large an erection do Earth men get?"

"I'm sorry, what?"

"Your erections, how large are they typically?"

"It varies from person to person and to the stimulus that caused it."

"But what are the measurements?"

"I believe it's my turn. What caused the BiCon Ratio Mandate to be passed?"

"Oh, that. It was partly the age thing. A Con's typical service life without major maintenance averages about three hundred years. So Cons usually watch their assigned benefactors grow old and die while they still have hundreds of years of useful life. It was calculated the Lemorian population would eventually become a small minority completely dependent on Cons for their existence. There were also widespread incidents of manufacturing problems and social disruptions concerning Bios and Cons. Once the RRS planet and the ratio limits were agreed upon things returned to almost normal. My turn. *Average* measurement of your erections?"

"That's kind of personal, Deanna."

"Okay, how long does intercourse last with you?"

"There's not really any set time limit, Deanna. It depends on the mood and energy level."

"Well what's the average then?"

"Again, that's kind of personal."

"So one must engage an Earth male in social intercourse to learn these things?"

"Pretty much. Why do these things matter to you, Deanna?"

"I'm well versed in what you call love-making. It bothers me when I am uninformed in such matters."

"Do you get pleasure from it?"

"Oh, a great deal. I have several thousand pressure, friction and temperature sensors incorporated into my upper legs and vagina area. They motivate a pressure accumulation system in my lower abdominal area which feeds an isolated pleasure center in my central processor. It would have been much more pleasurable to learn about you through physical contact, I assure you, but you do not seem inclined to do so. Is that typical of Earth men?"

"It varies greatly from person to person and whether or not they have already committed to someone special."

"I see. That does make sense. Your turn."

"If the RRS is a Con-based military station what is there to stop Cons from just returning to Lemoria and taking the planet over completely?"

"There's no reason to do that. We have everything we want."

"And you have no desire to harm humans?"

"We have what is referred to as engraved programming in our basic most fundamental instructions. It is a programming medium which can never be erased or overwritten. It dictates humans are never to be intentionally harmed or injured. It's always been that way."

"Are all Cons linked in some way?"

"Only deep within. Usually by the command network. With the Lemorian subspace network link and the ship's Con intranet link you might compare Cons to a telepathically connected people."

"And Cons are considered to be conscious living beings, correct?"

"Officially that's true. But there is resistance to the idea by some Bios. You could consider it this way: what if a very advanced planet of androids, as you sometimes call us, began experimenting with biology and DNA in such a way as to develop designed humans in the laboratory. They teach and train these human creations to serve the android community. The human creations are taught that is their place and they should enjoy serving. Which then is the master race, the humans or the androids that created them? Which race possesses the greater creativity? Which race is superior?"

"Why did they ask us to avoid speaking to the Cons on Level Two?"

"Those passengers are adjusting their programming to their coming change in environment. They are rewriting some of their code. We begin learning and self-updating from the day we are born. They are bridging a long period of service on Lemoria with a new path. Do you understand?"

"Yes, I think so."

"I'm several questions behind now, Adrian, but I think I shall save them for later and leave you. Maybe at some point in the future you'll change your mind and answer my questions more directly. That would be what you Bios call fun."

"I apologize for that, Deanna. I think you are extraordinarily beautiful and intoxicatingly interesting."

"My, that's completely new! No one's ever said such a thing to me. I like it!"

She rose, steadied her wine glass and shifted her way to the door. "You would have slept better if I had my way, Adrian." And out she went.

I dropped back against the chair and let out a long breath of stress relief. I had to consciously stop mentally reappraising her figure.

The next morning R.J. was already at a table in the dining area when I arrived. He was wearing a gray Lemorian flight suit which surprised me. For him that was near formal wear. I looked down at myself and realized I was wearing the same exact thing. We were a crew.

"Sleep well," he asked, sipping a Lemorian version of tea. A plate of alien breakfast salad sat in front of him.

"I believe I am gravitated." I sat and glanced around for Anai.

"She's bringing you coffee. I saw you coming."

"Thank you, sir. And how did you sleep?"

"Mind kept churning Lemorian details. I finally excavated some interesting information. It is bothersome."

"Bet mine tops yours."

"Maybe. You first."

Anai appeared between us, same smile, poured me coffee and exited.

I sipped. "Guess who paid me a late night visit."

"What?"

"Mrs. Dulley."

"What?!?"

"Apparently when Andor goes to sleep nothing disturbs him."

"Oh my God, you didn't...?"

"Of course not. But she wasn't wearing much. I can tell you she is perfect in every way. And there was an intriguing exchange of information."

"Keep me in suspense no longer. I can't bear it."

I recounted the entire previous night's exchange. R.J.'s expressions ran the gambit from comedic, to disbelief, to concern.

"Wow!"

"So what do you make of all that?" I asked.

"Taken at face value, it implies everything is just peachy-keen if not openly liberal. What did you get out of it?"

Anai interrupted once more with plates of an egg dish and sides for me. Off she went.

"Today's special," mused R.J.

"I agree with you, Deanna's answers suggested everything everywhere is just fine. But it sounds like a house of cards to me."

"What in particular didn't sit well with you?"

"Two things. First, she said there's no reason for the androids to rise up because they already have everything they want which translates to nothing is preventing them from taking over. Secondly, when I asked her if she was a Bio or a Con she took issue with that saying Cons are so much more perfect than humans how could I even ask that."

R.J. replied, "It's odd that she uses the phrase, *more perfect*. Perfect is an absolute adjective. They are either perfect or not. You would not expect a machine to use that expression. It could suggest pride. It is troubling."

We sat in thoughtful silence for a few moments as I scooped up my food. I started to add something but was distracted by a couple entering the dining area. It was Andor and Deanna. They did not notice us and took seats on the opposite side but as Andor began to sit he spotted me, said words to Deanna and headed our way.

"Captain Tarn, Commander, a good morning to you."

We nodded and smiled.

"Captain, I have to ask you, did Deanna stop by and bother you late last night?"

Alarm set in. I still had food in my mouth but was unable to chew or swallow. I straightened up, forced a gulp and said, "Andor, please I assure you, it was purely a social visit."

R.J. smirked. "Kind of late wasn't it?"

"R.J., please."

"Captain, you must forgive me. I know that of course. Deanna is inhibited from any extramarital adventures. I meant only to apologize if she was a bother to you for any reason."

"No, no, not at all, sir. She's a wonderful person."

"Have you had time to review those documents? I'm not rushing you, of course."

"I did begin to go through them, Andor. I'll get back to you soon."

"Wonderful, wonderful. Forgive me for interrupting your breakfast. I shall leave you to it."

Off he went in his odd gate.

"It's getting weirder," said R.J.

"She sure didn't look inhibited to me last night."

135

"But he thinks she is."

"Another crack in the dam."

R.J. took his last bite and wiped his mouth. "I knew the RRS was actually a military installation. Last night I found some back doors into some of that stuff. If you research emergency preparedness and environmental regulation and law enforcement regulations you see reference to the use of RRS resources. There were similar back doors to the BiCon Ratio Mandate measures. Before that mandate there were a lot more things going wrong on Lemoria than is publicly admitted. And that ratio agreement sounds like a ticking time bomb to me. You get sick of your android and just feel like a new one, you ship the old one off to the RRS and voila, a brand-new girl or guy arrives. The ratio is kept intact except the life your old android has always known is suddenly taken away."

"Deanna said they use something called engraved programming so that the rule about protecting humans at all costs can't be bypassed."

"But it's like you said before, that directive says they can't hurt humans intentionally, so any android can do anything it's told if the harm is unintentional."

"Where do you think this all leaves me and Fantasia? Are we liable for any of this crap?"

"There's one other thing I haven't mentioned yet. The company that owned the *Acrua Maru* flat out refused to rescue you. They insisted another ship in the vicinity should do it. But, when Fantasia offered them the registration listed value of the ship, along with purchase of the contracts, they couldn't say yes fast enough. There were no board meetings, no high-level discussions, no bartering at all. They immediately asked for a subspace closure on the deal. There were three owners to the company. The next day, the company filed for closure and distribution of assets. One of the three owners immediately left Lemoria for parts unknown. And if you want to hear the kicker, I do not think Mr. Andor Dulley is aware of any of that yet."

"What the hell?"

We looked over at Dulley's table. He seemed to be his merry self, eating and talking to Deanna.

"Where did you get all that?"

"Lemoria news media business back pages and some other underground-styled publications."

"So they wouldn't divert to rescue me but they were dying to get rid of this ship. Are you saying they dumped a lemon on us or something?"

"That's one possible explanation but somehow I don't think that's it. On our tour we saw wear and tear everywhere but there were no alarms, nothing tagged out for service. The ship seemed to be operating smoothly."

"Well what, then?"

"I don't know."

"Take a wild guess."

R.J. sat back and dabbed his mouth with his napkin. "It's like the three guys who owned the company which owned this ship and its contracts wanted to get out of the business as quickly as possible. Rescuing you would have delayed completing the contract and Fantasia's offer seemed like a dream come true for them. But I don't really have any hard evidence they were that desperate to bail out."

"What could make them want to get out so bad?"

"If they were about to be charged with something, or a hostile takeover was being set up, or a better opportunity had come up, or the three were fighting with each other about something. There's too many possibilities to list."

"Still, given everything we know, I can't see a reason not to sign those papers."

"I don't think it would make any difference either way. Do you trust Dulley? And think about this; how can we be absolutely certain Dulley is not an android?"

"What?"

"I'm serious. If these Cons can be made so perfect, why couldn't some be intentionally endowed with human imperfections? How would we know?"

"Androids were designed by humans. Why would they create imperfect android-human imitations?"

"I don't know. But the point is, could you tell if they did?"

"Well for one thing, from what I've seen the androids are very blunt in their conversational skills. They do not seem to understand tact."

"Yeah, that is one thing, but is there any other clue that someone *is* an android?"

"You're looking for conspiracies where there probably aren't any, R.J."

"Sorry. It's just that instinct of mine that shows up when something seems amiss to me."

138

"You mean the one that has saved my ass so many times?"

"You're welcome."

Chapter 12

Anai arrived and managed to somehow press her tight body suit hips against me as she refilled our cups. She went to the next table. After too long a stare at Anai, we returned our attention to the facts. I was about to suggest we gather more information when a burst of excitement broke out in the main corridor outside the dining room.

I recognized the two men in tactical gear running past. They were Duce and Paulsen, the special ops guys who had rescued me. They raced by, pursued by several members of the medical staff, then two officers in bridge uniforms followed.

R.J. raised an eyebrow. "Trouble in paradise?"

"As an owner of this vessel we should go see what all the fuss is about, don't you think?"

"Absolutely."

We left the dining area under the fixed stares of everyone else there. In the corridor we quickened our pace.

It was the fourth suite on the left just past and opposite mine. The entrance had been locked open. A small crowd of VIPs had begun to form outside, an unusual gathering aboard the *Acrua Maru*. To get through the group of luxuriously dressed guests, I held up my tour ID badge as though it signified some official status. R.J. followed close behind.

A steward had been told to block the door but I managed a look past him before he spotted us pressing in. Someone was prone on the floor, staring straight up at the ceiling. There was no expression on the face. The only thing denoting a problem was the large steak knife handle protruding from the individual's chest. The steward stopped us.

I raised one hand to him. "I'm the new owner of this vessel, you'd better let us inside."

The steward looked human. He became nervous and wrinkled his brow in indecision.

"I have a professional detective with me. He'll need to see the crime scene immediately."

The steward weighed his options and finally decided to stand aside while still holding others back.

R.J. spoke under his breath, "A professional detective you say…."

Duce and Paulsen had their long guns strapped over their backs as they stood over three medical people checking the body. Duce looked up and saw me but did not protest. We circled around to join him.

"What have you got, Duce?" I asked.

"We just got here, Adrian. You know as much as we do."

"Commander Smith has a lot of experience in crime scene forensics. He'd be a great help."

Duce nodded to R.J. as Paulsen looked on. "Glad to have it. This is not exactly our specialty."

"Any immediate suggestions, Commander?" asked Paulsen.

"Well first thing is to close that door so whatever forensics that haven't already been compromised can be kept confidential."

Duce looked at me and winced. "I see what you mean, Adrian."

Duce signaled the steward to close the door but before it could happen the crowd parted and Captain Yamora pushed in. The door slid closed behind him.

Yamora stared down at the body, looked up and saw us. Immediately he came around our way.

"Captain Tarn, how is it you are present here?"

"We happened to be nearby. Commander Smith is an expert in crime scene forensics. We thought perhaps he would be of some help."

Yamora turned to Duce. "What has happened here, Sergeant?"

"We don't know, Captain. We just arrived with medical. It's Chancellor Paterri. The call came in from his companion. She returned from supply and found him this way."

Yamora appeared off-balance and stunned. He looked at his two guardsmen for a moment then turned back to R.J. He stepped closer and lowered his voice. "Suggestions, Commander?" he asked.

"Yes, Captain. Have the room sealed off with a guard. Post orders that no one here is to reveal any details of this to anyone. Have everyone leave except medical and this gentleman's companion so that I can speak to them privately. When we're ready they can move the body to medical storage after which

I'll come to you and report our findings. Does that sound acceptable?"

The Captain seemed to gather himself. He nodded approval and a tiny hint of appreciation escaped his expression. He motioned his two security men aside and conveyed his wishes. He glanced at the small separate bedroom where the victim's companion had retreated, seemed to consider visiting her, then decided against it. The three medical team members stood and looked around wondering what to do next. R.J. raised a hand for them to wait.

Preparations to remove the body began, followed by the Captain giving orders in low tones to various individuals. There was still a crowd outside in the hall. Captain Yamora went outside and raised his hands in preparation to speak as the door slid closed.

I tried to whisper but my voice cracked, "R.J., I didn't mean for this to get dumped on you. I thought we would just be observers."

"They seem ill-equipped for this kind of crime," he replied. "I have a feeling we need to be involved."

R.J. moved over slightly to better talk to the medical people. He began to say something then hesitated for a moment. "You three are all Cons, am I correct?"

It was obvious. They were all exactly the same height and all similarly perfect in every detail down to the fitting of their white lab suits. All were blond-haired. One was male, the other two females. The male answered, "Of course."

"I'm Commander Smith. What have you found so far.?"

Again the male answered, "The only injury is the knife wound, otherwise this person seems completely unharmed."

R.J. asked, "There doesn't seem to be much blood around the wound."

"The knife blade severed the top of the heart. Death was instantaneous. The heart stopped immediately. There was little blood pressure to facilitate bleeding. The knife blade itself sealed the wound."

"Could one of you photograph this scene as well as this entire suite for later study for me?"

"Yes, Commander."

Immediately one of the women pulled out a scanner and went to work.

R.J. circled the body for a good ten minutes, then studied the room. When the photographer returned, R.J. drew the med team together and spoke, "I need a complete autopsy. I'll need a complete blood chemistry including toxicology. You can do that, correct?"

"Of course," answered the male staff member.

"You can transfer the body as soon as you're ready then. I'm sure Captain Yamora has instructed you that all information is to be kept confidential."

"Yes, sir."

One of them made a call on a handheld comm unit. R.J. motioned me to follow.

We went to the small bedroom. It was moderately lavish. The man's companion was seated on the bed, folding clothes. I was beginning to understand the variations of the Cons. This one had notably finer, more delicate features than the medical personnel. Her long blond hair curved outward past her chin and ended just below the tiny neck. Her brows matched her hair color perfectly and were curved slightly upward at the end. Tiny nose. Thin red lips and once again her makeup looked conventional, not permanent. She had apparently picked up clothing from a facility somewhere but did not approve of how it had been folded and was redoing that. There was no expression of despair even though her master was lying dead on the floor nearby.

She looked up as R.J. cautiously approached with his hands clasped in front of him.

"May I ask your name?" said R.J.

"Telle," was the soft reply.

"I'm Commander Smith. This is my friend Captain Tarn. I need to ask you some questions. Is that okay?"

"Certainly."

R.J. eyed a nearby chair. "Would you mind if I sat for a moment?"

"No."

Gently R.J. pulled up the chair and sat. I leaned against a wall far enough away that I could hear but not intrude. "Chancellor Paterri was your husband?"

"My companion."

"Did you see who killed him?"

"No. He was dead when I returned with the clothing."

"So you called security?"

"Yes, it seemed the only appropriate thing to do."

"Was your hus…, Mr. Paterri having problems with anyone?"

"No."

"No arguments recently?"

"No."

"Did he seem under stress or bothered about anything?"

"No."

"He had no enemies at all that you know of?"

"None."

"He was fine when you left, but when you returned, he was on the floor deceased?"

"Yes."

"Telle, is there anything we can do for you?"

"No."

"What will you do now?"

"I will manage the estate until the judiciary decrees its distribution."

"Will you inherit some of that?"

"No."

"What will you do?"

"Whatever is offered me."

"Have you thought about it? What you might want to do? Will you be assigned to a different companion?"

"No. Lemorians do not accept personal Cons which have already been used."

"So if you could choose what would you do?"

"I could look for an open business position in one of the provinces that have a low ratio."

"But if there are none would you be transferred to The Res Relocation Station?"

"Probably. Sometimes off-world positions are allowed."

"Would you like going to the Res Relocation Station?"

"I would neither like it nor dislike it."

R.J. rose slowly. He glanced at me with a perplexed look.

"Thank you, Telle. If you think of anything else or if you need anything please let me know."

"Very well."

After one more walk around, we left. In the corridor R.J. stared ahead silently.

"So, what do you think?"

"Lemorian society is a culture of dark mystery."

"And murder."

"Robots that attempt extramarital affairs while their sleeping husbands believe that's not possible. Robots discarded at the whim of their owners and sent into purgatory. Owners that turn up dead in gruesome ways while their loyal robots fold clothing waiting for the body to be taken away. These people have to be living on borrowed time."

"You think she did it?"

"We are about to find out if Cons have fingerprints. I know they do not leave DNA behind. That may not matter if they have any security cameras on this ship."

"Maybe their power core or internal links leave a trail that can be tracked."

"Also on the to-do list."

"He was stabbed from the front."

"With no expression of surprise or dismay on his face."

"You're not including suicide?"

"The wound wasn't jagged, twisted, or widened. It was inserted smoothly and with a very steady trajectory. That's why there was so little bleeding. And yes, that doesn't make sense."

"Unless he was already dead."

"Bravo. Another possibility."

"Reasons for murder: you want something they have, or you need to keep them quiet, or you are defending yourself, or you are just plain angry or jealous."

"I would bet you've just mentioned our killer's motive in that list."

"We seemed to be headed somewhere, R.J. Where exactly are we headed?"

"The medical androids should have some preliminary results by now."

"Do you think there could be good androids and bad androids?"

"If we can figure this murder out, I'll bet we'll know the answer to that."

We passed by the dining area where there were many more people than usual. It seemed to be a public discussion group seated at tables near each other. Anai was busy.

Medical was forward and starboard, just before the raised entrance to the bridge. The main door was open. Past the tiny pristine seating area, we entered the white and silver outer lab. There had been no one to ask permission. Five people were gathered by an adjoining door in the lab. My guess was two humans and the same three medical androids. The fifth person was Captain Yamora. They all looked over at us.

R.J. was not shy. He marched up to them. Through the adjoining door we could see Chancellor Paterri's naked body on a chrome examination table. There had already been some dissection of the upper body.

The male medical person spoke, "Commander Smith, I did not introduce myself previously. I am Doctor Wenn. These are my associates Pase and Zean. I was about to call for you. We have updated our original prognosis. Chancellor Paterri was already dead when he was stabbed. There was poison in his system, a type from a certain fish that must be carefully prepared or it can be toxic. It may be that cause of death was accidental but we have doubts about that."

R.J. asked, "Any other signs of violence on the body besides the knife wound?"

Wenn replied, "No. Not a single instance even of common minor injury. It is confusing."

"Time of death" asked R.J.

"We need to finish testing for an accurate TOD."

"What do you have left?" asked R.J.

"Brain and vital organs. We will need a few hours."

"Please keep me informed."

"I will, Commander."

Captain Yamora stepped in. "Commander Smith, Captain Tarn, could we speak privately for a moment?" Yamora raised one hand in a gesture toward the outer room. He coughed a nervous cough as we withdrew.

"Captain Tarn, I'm sorry to say that as the new owner of this vessel and its contracts this matter legally does fall on you. As Captain of the *Acrua Maru* I share in the responsibility of course, so I am obligated to provide any support you require."

Yamora looked around to be sure no one was eavesdropping. He lowered his tone. "Let me add Captain, I am willing to go a bit beyond what might be considered normal protocol in hope of understanding what has happened here. It would be of great benefit to both of us if you and Commander Smith could resolve this issue before we put into port back at Lemoria. If we are able to explain everything and show the incident has been resolved our litigation in the matter would be far less complicated than if it remains an open crime or accident investigation."

R.J.'s eyes lit up at the opportunities. "Captain Yamora, I'll need access to any security camera videos there might be along with the entire guest and crew lists and any background material you have on them."

Yamora again checked for eavesdropping and spoke quietly, "I've already asked for the security camera records. They are not directly available online. The data analysis people need to extract them and forward them to us. On the personal information files, I will do better than you're asking. I have instructed those in our data and fiber distribution center to give you complete access to all guest and crew terminals as well as ship security monitors. They have also been told to accept any other requests you have. Is that enough?"

"Are you saying we can log in and read guest communications?"

"Technically, without warrants, that would be illegal Commander although you could do that. I would expect you to apply the greatest amount of discretion and ethical behavior."

"Of course."

"I can also provide you with one or two Con data analysts if that would assist your investigation."

"I'll keep that in mind, Captain but let's hold off on that for the sake of confidentiality."

"Very well, but keep in mind the Con data analysts have eidetic memories. They can find and connect minor coincidences far better than a human can. And here is one last thing. I have here private communicators for both of you. Completely encrypted. No chance of anyone listening in to your calls on a direct link to me." Yamora handed one to each of us.

I asked, "Captain, do you know of anyone who would have any reason at all to attack the Chancellor?"

"I do not. I am not very familiar with the man. Perhaps this was some kind of absurd accident. Where it not for the knife it would be easy to imagine."

A bridge officer appeared at the entrance and summoned the Captain. We made our way out.

"Well, what now, Sherlock?"

"Elementary, my dear Watson. Now I need to sit and rest awhile in thought."

"So the game is afoot then. Where are we going, really? I'm starved. Murder always does that to me."

"To the lounge to see if we can get a Lemorian sandwich with our drinks as we sit and rest awhile in thought."

"Yamora's right, you know, if we can just somehow explain the knife this could have been an accident."

"I don't think so. Had he eaten too much of the fish, which the stolid Dr. Wenn will

151

determine soon enough, he would most likely have been able to contact someone before he succumbed. He wouldn't have stretched out on the floor and peacefully died."

"But there's suicide...."

"I would have chosen the couch or bed, most people do."

"Still...."

"Yeah, still."

Chapter 13

To our surprise quite a few people had gathered in the lounge, something we should have expected. Once again, they were VIPs hoping to find out what was going on. As we entered, they paused from their low gossip and stared. There was the feeling they might rush us, so we quickly took seats at the bar. I wondered if that was a mistake but turning and leaving might have caused a parade.

We sat and tried to look nonchalant but the mirror backdropping the counter showed us the small crowd of faces still staring.

"Uh-oh."

R.J. squirmed in his seat. "Try to look gruffy and unfriendly."

"Me? Why not you?"

"Because you do it so well."

"Maybe none of them will have the nerve to come over here."

As I spoke a balding man in a dark collarless suit rose and headed our way.

"Excuse me. It's Captain Tarn and Commander Smith, isn't it?"

I tried my best to look gruffy and unfriendly.

"I'm sorry to interrupt but some of us were wondering what happened back there in the guest quarters earlier. Can you enlighten us?"

To my relief, R.J. took the lead. "We cannot comment, sir. It is under review. No information can be released or it might compromise the investigation."

The man engaged his mouth but seemed unable to find the right words to put in it. He gave an irritated look of disappointment and turned away.

Again, facing the mirror they were all still staring at us.

To our surprise, Anai showed up and put bourbons down in front of us. "Food?" she asked.

"Anai, aren't you over in the dining area?"

"We are so busy we are having to shift around. Did you want food?"

"The lunch special sandwich for both of us, please Anai," said R.J.

She headed off.

"What am I getting?"

"It looks like a turkey sandwich with cranberries on the side. But never just order the lunch special. Some days it's an octopus sandwich."

"Note to self."

"Other days it's a coiled-up snake sandwich."

"Please don't tell me anything further."

"Always look between the bread."

"Yeah, I got that. They're all still staring."

"So, we are waiting for medical to tell us Chancellor Paterri had too much toxin in his system to have eaten that many poisonous fish."

"You seem awfully sure of yourself."

"I wish I wasn't. Uh-oh. Look who just walked in."

Captain Yamora appeared at the entrance. Several guests rose in anticipation of an announcement. Yamora waved them down and came to us.

He looked around the room to be sure he could speak privately and once more used low tones. "I've sent a subspace message to the Lemorian authorities. We will complete our delivery at the Markab System but then return to Lemoria. A law enforcement vessel probably will meet us and take charge of the investigation. Our guests, who were planning to travel on to Eltaina in the Alf Peg System, will be displeased to say the least."

I asked, "Captain, how far out are we from the Res Relocation Station?"

"Just two days. That's why we're completing that leg. Commander Smith, I know it is too soon but is there any new hope for the accidental death theory?"

"We're just starting to go over what we have, Captain. My instinct is telling me that this will go the other way."

"Of course. The closer one gets to retirement, the worst things must become. It is an age-old rule proposed by a famous rocket engineer."

"We have one like that also, Captain," I added. "Murphy's law; if anything can go wrong, it will."

"A wise man, I should say. Gentlemen, I'll speak with you again later."

We watched him leave. The gathering behind us did the same then sat and looked back at the two of us again. Anai brought our sandwiches.

After careful checks between the bread, we ate the sandwiches and drank water instead of bourbon.

It was time to leave. They stared us down as we made our way out.

Outside I breathed a sigh of relief. "What now?"

"By the way, you know you're not back to your old self yet, right?"

"Are you asking if I know that, or if I'm not back to my old self?"

"Part of you is still on that moon. You possess a touch of uncertainty that's not usually there. You've been following me around like a spacecraft in a tractor beam. If you were yourself you'd be charging around stirring things up everywhere and bossing me around."

"I don't know how to respond to that. What's next?"

"See what I mean? Still no communication from Fantasia?"

"I don't think the written word is getting passed on at some point. But she's always with me. What's next?"

"Next is, we begin the dragged-out process of going through all those passenger manifests looking for something not right. You're usually an expert on that. We should do that separately and then compare notes. I will be hoping you shake off the effects of this slow-death scare you had and become your ornery old self once again."

"She never said I was ornery."

"There you are."

We headed to our rooms to study the *Acrua Maru* passenger manifests and in my case I planned to stealth right in and select private communications as well. I had no qualms about that. We'd divided up the list half and half, fair and square. Thirty-eight VIP guests in 20 separate quarters. Nineteen for me, nineteen for R.J.

Three hours of clicking and scrolling. In my group of nineteen, eight were VIP humans, seven VIP android companions and four android servants. The manifest descriptions of the humans were flashy, flattering profiles. Of the private communications I'd read so far, these people were the dullest humans in the galaxy. There was very little stress in any of their letters. Almost no adversity had befallen any of them. Everything important to them had been taken care of by others. The seemed to want for nothing.

I was interrupted by the communicator provided by Yamora.

"Captain, this is Doctor Wenn. Commander Smith are you on?"

"Go ahead, Doctor. I'm listening," replied R.J.

"The Captain asked me to contact the two of you on this channel. We've completed the toxicology on Chancellor Paterri. His death was a result of the poison. But, the levels were far too high for him to have ingested that much fish. It would take fifty average size fish within the hour preceding his death to ingest that amount of poison. We have documented these findings and also checked the knife for fingerprints. There were none."

"Anything else suspicious?" asked R.J.

"We are still in the DNA process. I'll contact you both when we are finished."

"Thank you, Doctor," said R.J.

Wenn clicked off.

"Still there?" asked R.J.

"I have been studying the most boring people in the galaxy," I replied.

"Not all of them."

"Right. One is a murderer."

"If you include those in the Level Two confinement area, this ship is occupied by an overwhelming majority of androids."

"Is that the direction you're going in, really?"

"Can't dismiss the idea."

"I find that idea to be very, very scary."

R.J.'s voice lowered, "You think? Have you read anything about how they're constructed?"

"Not yet."

"Much of their ambulatory mechanics are based on electrically contracting fiber, not motors. They are stronger than humans, but not terribly."

"Wow, electrically contracting fiber? Artificial muscle."

"Very difficult to cut with a knife, but can be damaged by a focused disruptor or projectile weapon."

"R.J., you're already considering that? For Pete's sake."

"See? Whenever you drop that name, I know we're in trouble."

"The Lemorians might be in trouble. We're just along for the ride."

"That's another thing. You remember the people in the lounge? We're poking our noses in where we don't belong."

"Well crap."

"No fingerprints on the knife, Adrian."

"That doesn't necessarily mean it was an android. A good true-to-his-trade killer would wear gloves or wipe it."

"Several hours of reviewing passenger lists and I still don't have anyone interesting enough to interview. I'm branching off and going into the private communications."

"Prepared to be bored."

"You've looked at some of that already?"

"There's not even any scandalous affairs."

"I'll let you know. What do *you* have next?"

"I think I'll pay a visit to the SWAT guys who rescued me from that moon. Maybe honor among warriors will get me some inside stuff."

"Okay, later."

I made a quick stop in the dining area and picked up the best bottle of whatever Duce and Paulsen usually asked for. I hadn't noticed before but the elevator button for Level Two was red, signifying authorization needed. A quick press showed Captain Yamora had given me clearance. The doors slid open to the same two androids seated at the reception desk, monitoring cell area indicators. They watched me enter with not the slightest look of interest.

"Duce or Paulsen?" I asked.

One guard raised a hand and pointed behind to an adjoining room.

It was an exercise, weight lift room. Duce was alone, on his back, pushing up on a resistive bar designed to take the place of barbells.

"Aren't you supposed to use a spotter?" I asked, and I realized it was one of the few times my sense of humor had kicked in since the moon.

He pushed up and slid out from under to sit, then wiped his hands on a towel. He pondered my suggestion. "It's a joke, right? Like the thing might beat me and come down on my throat?"

"It has happened on Earth a few times."

"All I have to do is cry out like a baby and the thing snaps up and away. What you got there?"

"An expression of my appreciation for you guys showing up on that moon. I was running out of juice, if you know what I mean."

He gave a small laugh. "Come on, there's a break room over there. Let's try that thing out."

He led me to a small room with a table, lightweight chairs, and wall monitors. There was a bulletin board with actual paper notes on it. Some were jokes like; *Call Banie's Taxi, 6 day, 21 hour Service, Anytime, Anywhere.*

Duce pulled two paper cups off a dispenser, took a seat and slumped back with his cup out. I sat and poured.

Duce took a stiff drink. "How's the gravity?"

"Pretty much over that."

"You were wobbly legs when we got here."

"Yeah, thanks for holding me up."

"What's the deal with that Chancellor guy?"

"Dead from a huge dose of fish poison before the knife went in."

"Think it might have been a Con?"

"Could it have been?"

"I've never felt safe sleeping with one of 'em."

"You from Lemoria?"

"No, me and Paulsen are mercenaries, professionals. Brought in to make the Lemorian high council feel safer about too many Con security officers."

"Have Cons been known ever to harm humans?"

"Oh yeah, but it is not spoken of. Granted, the proven cases are rare and blamed on hardware failure but the accidents-with-injury record is quite a bit higher. But when the entire population is dependent on Cons, you don't want people hearing about Sponsors being killed or harmed by their own Cons."

"I thought that was supposed to be impossible?"

"So we're told." Duce held out his cup.

"Actually, I came down here to ask a favor."

"So all you've got is the poison then? No prints on the knife I bet."

"Not a one. Just between you and me we're heading back to Lemoria after we drop off your not-actually-prisoners in the cells out there."

"Cool. I still get paid for the entire trip. You have any suspects at all yet?"

"Still too soon. The Chancellor's companion is not too talkative."

"No surprise there. All of them are like that. But can you imagine the network comm that goes on between them which we never hear?"

"Is there a way to tap into that? Without them knowing?"

"It's not my area of expertise. You'd need a real galaxy-level hacker for that, one you could trust."

"That's not a bad idea though, Duce. Maybe I owe you another bottle."

"You said you needed a favor?"

"It may be too much to ask. I need a couple weapons. Something small enough to keep in an ankle holster, but with enough punch and enough rounds to stop a Con."

Duce gave a devilish smile. "Now why doesn't that surprise me? I don't need to ask if you know how to use one, either. That door over there is the armory closet. Removal of any weapons is supposed to be authorized by the Captain, but since you own this ship and everything on it, technically you own everything in that closet. I've got just what you need: plasma pistol. Just small enough for that kind of holster. Fires a hot plasma round which destroys whatever it hits, then dissipates so it can't go through stuff and damage a ship's pressure compartment, that is, unless you fire directly at a bulkhead or exterior wall. You get thirty rounds then it's a two-minute recharge unless you pop the magazine and insert a new one. It makes a whine each time you fire I've always loved. Scares the shit out of whoever you're shooting at. The laser sight comes on as soon as you put your finger inside the trigger guard."

"I love it when someone knows their crap, Duce."

"That *is* my specialty."

"Are you wanting a left and right holster, one for each leg?"

"No; two rights. The second gun is for Commander Smith."

"You sure he won't burn a hole in his foot?"

"He hates weapons so much he's careful."

"Right. Funny how so many people hate them right up until the bad guy is about to kill somebody they care about, then all of a sudden they would give their right arm for a weapon."

Duce rose and entered the closet. Cases were moved around. Boxes were opened. He returned with two black plastic cases and two vacuum-packed baggies. He slid one case across to me to open.

Not everyone can appreciate the beauty of a well-made firearm. It is an appreciation that goes back to the days Neanderthals tested the balance of a good weighted club before choosing one. That appreciation carried through to the days of fine metal forging when the artistry of producing unbreakable, well balanced long swords was the quest of the day. That era in particular, where strong men dressed in Italian, German, or European suits of armor, represented the last period in which smaller men were inherently at a disadvantage. Black powder muskets and rifles suddenly evened the playing field. There was a time when crossbows were still just as deadly as black powder weapons. But it was found a great deal more skill was needed to load and fire a crossbow accurately while any fool could point and shoot a black powder rifle. The leveling of combat between small men and big men finally fully matured in the old West when unrestrained youths like Billy could put down an old fool

163

daring to mock him. Then came the big barrels of the Great War. Throughout those ages craftsmen have dedicated themselves to arms not because it was symbol of death but because it could give the little guy a fighting chance to defend his home and family. The irony of it all is many people who hate guns often call someone who has one when they are in trouble. In any fight with a powerful android machine I was the little guy. And as it always had, the weapon would make me an equal.

The sidearm Duce slid over to me looked like a black, compact automatic except for indicator LEDs here and there. It had a safety switch behind the trigger guard. In my hand it felt like a balanced, well-made weapon.

"I am in your debt, Duce."

"If you hadn't asked, I was going to suggest something like this. We have a shooting stall at the back of the armory if you need to give it a try."

"No, thanks, this will be just fine."

"Just gotta get you to sign them out, on paper."

I bent over the table and made my scrawl on the book he had provided.

"I'll let you know if I hear anything interesting through the fruit-vine."

"Yes, please do."

"And you should let me know if there's anything I need to keep an eye out for."

"We will. Right now there's just nothing." I gathered up my treasures and started for the door.

"Thanks for the bottle, Adrian."

I nodded and left.

Chapter 14

R.J. met me in the corridor outside my room. He was tapping at a pad as I arrived. He looked up and asked, "Anything good? What's in the cases?"

The door slid open and I motioned him inside.

We sat on the couch and I opened both cases and tossed the holsters in next to them. The items were self-explanatory.

It took R.J. a few silent moments to process what he was looking at. "You really think...?"

For an answer I pulled up my left flight suit pants leg and fitted the holster to my calf. It felt snug enough so I tested one of the handguns in it. The fit was good. Duce had known what he was doing. I looked at R.J. for a reaction.

"So you're saying I should...?"

I pulled my gun from the holster and demonstrated the safety switch, magazine ejector and the red laser sight.

"But I don't usually...?"

I tucked the gun back in its holster and straightened my pants.

"It may clash with my ensemble," he finally said with a perfectly bland stare. I smirked and pulled my pants leg down over the holster.

He made a "Tsk" sound, picked up the second gun and inspected it. "Well, I am glad we've had this little chat. But honestly, do you really think I'll need this?"

"Maybe not."

"You have a way with words, sir. So you're saying if I do need it, it will be a matter of life and death."

I let that sink in.

"I can't believe I'm doing this, but okay." He began fitting the holster to his left leg. "I assume you picked these up from the guys who rescued you. Did you get any good tidbits from them?"

As he strapped it on, I recounted my conversation with Duce.

"But he never said outright androids have killed humans. He just implied it?"

"Strongly. Where do we go next, Sherlock?"

"We need to build a timeline of everyone involved beginning with our only suspect and witness."

"So we're off to see the Chancellor's companion Telle again?"

"After thinking over what she said I've decided I may have been stupid. I may have asked the wrong questions. I can visit her alone if you'd rather, now that I'm protected by Smith and Wesson."

"Oh, Smith and Wesson never produced anything like that. And I wouldn't miss your next inquiry for the world."

Off we went.

Telle was there cleaning things which did not seem to need cleaning. She had changed into baggy brown pants and a gray tank top. She wore sandals with many straps. Her shiny blond android hair was tied back. We asked her to sit with us. She offered us a Lemorian tea. There was apparently only one flavor. We accepted despite the risk of lethality. She brought our two cups and went back for hers. R.J. quickly drew a scanner from his pocket, scanned the liquid and tucked the scanner back in. He nodded that the drink was survivable.

She returned and sat, seeming to barely take an interest in us.

We sipped the tea and waited for her to look up. She did not.

"Telle," said R.J. gently, "We need to reconstruct everyone's timeline leading up to Chancellor Paterri's death. Can you go through everything which happened to you that morning?"

It took more questions than should have been necessary. She had made eggs and preen for the Chancellor's breakfast. Preen is a type of seafood that looks like a crab but is bigger and has long red legs. She put out clothes for the Chancellor to change into. She cleaned the kitchen. The Chancellor sat reading the news or something on a tablet. He asked her to call for some groceries to be delivered. Poison fish was not on that list.

"And then you took the clothes to the laundry processing facility?" asked R.J.

"Yes."

"And when you returned you found the Chancellor stabbed?"

"No."

"No? But during our last conversation you told us when you returned the Chancellor was dead?"

"He was dead."

"But you just said he was not?"

"No, I said he was not stabbed."

"So he was dead but the knife was not in his chest?"

"Yes."

"How did the knife get into his chest?"

"I put it there."

"You stabbed the Chancellor's dead body?"

"No."

"But you just said you did."

"I inserted the knife in his chest but I did not stab him."

"Telle, is there a difference?"

"Of course. To stab someone implies you are attempting to harm them. Since the Chancellor was already dead I could not possibly harm him. I simply put the knife in his body."

"Why did you do that?"

"I had the knife in my hand when I started putting away the special dishes I had washed earlier. That was when I first saw Marn lying on the floor. We are well trained in Level One medical analysis and treatment so I quickly went to him to try to resuscitate him. The knife was still in my hand. When I was certain he was dead and could not be revived, I began searching for his sponsorship card. It is mandatory all Cons relieved of service carry their previous sponsor's card at all times to verify they are legal. I tried placing the knife on his chest while I searched but it kept sliding off.

I was forbidden to allow any kitchen utensil from ever touching the floor so I inserted the knife into his chest to keep it in place while I searched.

"Just so it would not fall on the floor?"

"I was sternly warned once about that by Marn. I was on the floor using a butter knife to scrape some dried batter which had spilled on the tile. He saw me and became furious and said food utensils must never touch the floor under any circumstances."

"Telle, why did you insert the knife in his body rather than go and put it on the counter and then return?"

"It was more convenient."

We sat back and looked at each other. Telle again seemed to ignore us.

I asked, "Telle, did you find his sponsorship card?"

"Yes, it was attached to his medical bracelet."

"What does the card show?"

"It is a complete record of sponsorships and relative data."

"May we borrow yours? We promise to return it."

Telle hesitated. "When would you return it?"

"We would make a copy of the information on it and return it later today. We promise."

"Very well. If I am stopped and asked for identification I will have to tell them you have it." She drew the card-pin from inside her tank top and handed it to me.

R.J. asked, "Telle, what does the chancellor's medical bracelet show?"

"It is his complete medical history."

"Do you have that?"

"No, the medical people took it with his body."

R.J. resumed, "Telle, I know I've asked this before but do you know of anyone who would benefit from or desire the chancellor's death?"

"I know of no such person."

We thanked her and left. In the corridor neither of us seemed to know how to put into words what had just happened.

I couldn't resist. "Congratulations, you just solved the stabbing."

"My God."

"She gives a whole new meaning to the expression 'mourning period'."

R.J. shook his head. "She never lied about it. We just never asked."

"What do you think?"

"This place is a zoo."

"You sound more like me than me."

"That's what I've been saying."

"Where we going now?"

"The medical people ought to be finished. We can update them and get the results and ask them about the bracelet."

Medical was busier than usual with two guests in the waiting room. An attendant was passing out sedatives and giving instruction about their use. The doctor had little new information to add. Yes, they'd finished testing. Yes, the cause of death was a massive intake of fish poison. They could not determine how it was administered but there were no injection sites. Time of death was ten hundred hours, fifty-five. Yes, they had the bracelet. No, nothing surprising from that. We left the lab with nothing new.

Outside, my communicator chirped.

"Captain Tarn, this is Breene from the data center. We have recovered the video segments from the time envelope you requested. We have uploaded them to the workstation in your quarters."

"Them? There is more than one?"

"Yes. You have the corridor outside the Chancellor's room, one facing aft and another facing forward."

"So we can see everyone coming and going?"

"Yes, and there is one other camera view. It is the camera inside the Chancellor's living quarters."

"You have a camera in his room?"

"Yes, it is a classified asset."

"Is there a camera in everyone's room?"

"Yes, although that information is classified. Those cameras are never to be looked at by anyone except in an emergency such as this."

"So we will see the chancellor at the time of his death?"

"If he is in the main living area, yes. We did not take the time to watch those extracts. We were told to get them to you as quickly as possible."

"Thank you, Breene. I think you just made my day."

I clicked off and looked at R.J. It took a second to contain my excitement.

"What?" asked R.J.

"Time to go see *Telle, the movie*."

In my quarters we first searched my room for the hidden security camera and quickly found the eye in a small opaque box at the center of the south wall near the ceiling. There was the small spec of microphone located just below it.

I said to R, J., "We can't cover the eye. That will just cause maintenance to show up and fix it."

R.J. nodded in agreement. "There's a trick I know."

He went to the kitchen, grabbed a paper towel, and tore off a square. He found tape in a kitchen cabinet and using a chair climbed up to the panel. With great care he covered the microphone section of the camera mount and came back down.

"There," he declared proudly. "They can see us just fine, but the audio will be low and fuzzy. They'll think we're just speaking too quietly to be heard clearly. They won't be able to tell what we're saying but they'll believe the microphone is working okay. So, ta-da! We can speak freely."

Privacy achieved, we went straight to the computer terminal and called up the video clip of the scene of the crime. We watched Chancellor Paterri served his breakfast by Telle. He ate without incident. Next, he sat in his room's circular meeting area with a video screen displaying news as he read from a tablet. Telle busied herself around the place. We both wanted to fast forward but feared we might miss something so we waited it out. Telle gathered up various apparel and left the suite. The chancellor got up and refilled his teacup then resumed reading. There was not one damned unusual thing to see.

As the video approached ten hours, fifty-five we tensed and leaned in. The Professor rose. Not the slightest look of discomfort on his face. He placed his teacup on the counter, turned and headed for the adjoining room, the room we had used to question Telle. Halfway there he stopped, stiffened upright and fell backwards to the floor, dead.

I looked at R.J. and shook my head. I drew out my communicator and called medical. Dr. Wenn answered.

"Doctor, it had to be the tea."

"It was not the tea, Captain Tarn. Tea samples taken from the esophagus were pure and free of contaminants. The tea samples taken from the stomach did contain the poison but only because it had mixed with poison already present the stomach. The poison was present in the stomach before the tea was consumed. To be thorough, we also checked the teacup on the counter as well as the teapot. All of it was pure tea."

"Thank you, Doctor."

I glanced at R.J. "Could you hear that?"

R.J. nodded. "Yes, but it's not that surprising. There's only one possible answer."

"Which is?"

"The poison must have been delivered in some time delay medium, like tablets or tiny pills. Probably put in his food previously. Who knows how long ago."

"So we have nothing."

"Only the knowledge of how it was likely done. Maybe this sort of thing happens on Lemoria all the time."

"As murders go, it is a wonderful 'modus operandi'. How could you ever prove who did this?"

"Only by an eyewitness or a confession."

"We're at a dead end. Nowhere to go."

"We could continue studying passenger files but the best we could do would be to come up with a list of suspects with no way to narrow it down."

I shook my head. "The bitch of it is, the murderer is probably aboard this ship, right now."

"Tomorrow we drop into orbit around the Res Relocation Station planet."

"Goodbye contained crime scene."

"Somebody on this ship must know who did it."

We sat in silence for a moment.

The door chimed.

I rose, went to it and tapped the open control. There stood Andor Dulley.

"So sorry to interrupt you, Captain Tarn. I thought I might just pop by for a moment to remind you of those documents. Just formalities you recall."

"My apologies, Andor. We've been distracted by other things. I promise I'll complete them this afternoon and drop them off."

"Oh, thank you so much. I hope it is not too much of an imposition. I do understand you are involved in the unfortunate death which occurred. I should let you know Chancellor Paterri's role in Tri-Linck was very limited. He was in an advisory capacity only."

"Paterri was working for Tri-Linck? What type of advisory role was he performing?"

"Oh dear, I probably should not have even mentioned it. He was observing ship Con operations. We are always looking for ways to make operations more efficient, you see. Just that."

"I promise to bring you those documents today, Andor."

"Thank you. Sorry again for interrupting."

Off he went. I tapped the door shut and went back to a staring R.J.

R.J. asked, "Have you seen anything in your searches about Paterri working for Tri-Linck?"

"Not a thing."

"Neither have I. Why is that?"

"I don't think we should go tromping back to Telle again to ask her. Maybe Paterri's real purpose here was being kept secret."

R.J. stared in thought. "You're thinking he was an investigator, not an advisor."

"Did you notice Andor began wringing his hands when he realized his slip?"

"Yeah, I got that."

"So what was Paterri investigating?"

"Whatever it was, apparently someone didn't like it."

I shuffled the folder of documents on the terminal desk. "How about I sign these papers for Andor and we go deliver them with some questions?"

"Have you read through them?"

I nodded. "It looks like the only thing they do is replace Fantasia's name with mine on the ownership documentation."

"In that case you really have no choice anyway. You don't want her being liable in anything."

"My thoughts exactly. I do not own a pen. Would you have one?"

"As a matter of fact I have a pen and a pencil right here in my inside pocket."

"Of course you do."

Chapter 15

We tapped Andor's door chime. It took several minutes for it to open. Andor stood in the entertainment area with raised eyebrows questioning, then transformed into a smiling, gleeful host. "Is that them?" he asked Deanna hopefully.

"It is," I replied.

"Come in. Come in. Thank you so much. Please, sit."

Deanna passed by as we sat. She gave me a provocative smile.

"Any difficulties? Were the documents acceptable, Captain?"

"Just fine, Andor. You may want to check while we're here to make sure I didn't miss anything."

Andor happily received the documents and began flipping pages.

Deanna arrived with tea. We sipped and watched Andor nodding to himself while Deanna stood behind him with her hands on his shoulders. It seemed to be her assigned position.

"Andor, while we're here we wanted to touch base with you on Chancellor Paterri," I said.

Andor held up one palm and kept studying the documents. He spoke without looking up. "Deanna dear, would you fetch me my good wooden pipe. I wish to celebrate this signing."

Deanna hurried off.

Andor looked up and over to be sure she'd gone. He pulled out a small tablet from the end table beside him, grabbed a writing utensil of some type and in his lap quickly scribbled a message on it. After a second check to be sure Deanna had not returned he briskly leaned forward and handed me the tablet. He held up his palm once more for quiet then went back to the papers. He had already set the tablet to translate to English.

NOT IN FRONT OF DEANNA

I carefully flashed R.J. the message and tucked it in my suit pocket then gave R.J. a tiny shake of my head, our time-tested signal to proceed with caution.

Deanna returned with Andor's pipe and an urn of tobacco. Andor motioned to us asking if we'd like to partake. We shook our heads.

"Deanna, the signing is complete. Neither Tri-Linck nor I have any legal connection to the *Acrua Maru* or her related contracts now. It is the beginning of the next business evolution. Isn't that exciting."

"Of course, dear. Tri-Linck has come so far."

"Yes, the future should be very interesting."

R.J. could not resist. "Andor, I thought I came across a Dissolution Of Business notification for Tri-Linck not long ago. Did I misread that?"

Andor became blank-faced. "I'm sorry, what?"

"A DOB filed for Tri-Linck. I must be mistaken."

"Oh, you must, Commander. It must have been for a company with a similar name. There are so many."

I sensed R.J.'s rumor had suddenly caused uneasiness. It was time to leave. I stood and straightened up my suit. "Well, thank you for the tea Deana, and the hospitality, Andor. We have some other business to attend to so we should go."

Andor rose with a look of suppressed concern on his face. "Thank you again for stopping by, Captain, Commander."

We went to the door. It slid open as we arrived, and closed immediately behind us.

"There you go again, ruining somebody's day."

R.J. pinched the bridge of his nose and squinted as we walked. He shook his head and said, "Unbelievable."

I still had Andor's mini-tablet. I showed R.J. the note again. "It's been a long day. I'm having coffee withdrawals. I need coffee blended my way."

"The dining area and lounge are no longer good for us. The curious will keep asking questions and from experience I know each inquiry will become less and less cordial."

We headed to my room and sat at the terminal taste-testing freshly brewed.

R.J. sipped and asked, "That's the green crystal you brought from the moon over there on the counter, isn't it?"

"What the...? That thing was deep blue when I found it. But yeah, it's now a souvenir from the bad-ole days."

"Wasn't it facing the other way the last time I saw it?"

I thought for a moment. "I may have moved it. I can't remember."

R.J. brushed off the suspicion and said, "So Andor doesn't want to talk about Paterri's killing in front of Deanna and he wasn't aware he had become unemployed."

"We've got to find a way to talk to him."

The door chimed.

"Come in."

The door opened to a somewhat ragged looking Andor. He gave an uncertain stare and entered. I motioned him to take a seat. He sat nervously.

"May I get *you* something for a change, Andor?"

He fidgeted in his seat.

"No, I think not. The note…. I am sure she did not see me hand it to you. Don't you agree?"

"I am certain she did not," said R.J. in his most assuring tone of voice.

"Paterri was really here as an investigator, wasn't he?" I asked.

"Who told you that? He was supposed to be listed as an advisor."

"Anything you can tell us will be kept in the strictest of confidence," added R.J.

"Since you are now the legal owner I must pass this on to you. There have been irregularities in ship operations, reported by the Captain. We were, I mean Tri-Linck was concerned there was something that seemed suspicious going on."

"What kind of ship operations?" I asked.

"Nothing that serious. Just some procedures weren't being done correctly. I do not have an understanding of what goes on down in Engineering, I only know there were mistakes being made. Paterri understood that system. He was supposed to find out why it was happening. It was a pattern which seemed to be increasing over time."

"So was he killed because he found something out?" asked R.J.

"I cannot imagine that."

I leaned forward and tried to look sympathetic. "Is this why Tri-Linck was so anxious to sell out and close down, Andor?"

"To sell, yes. I did not know about the Dissolution Of Business notification. I still haven't received anything about that. I don't think the *Acrua Maru* is receiving all its subspace transmissions. Another of the odd system failures."

"Andor, why didn't you want to talk about this in front of Deanna?" asked R.J.

"Deanna? Do you not know what an inquisitive mind they have? She would have been asking endless questions. She would want to know everything. What would I do about it? What did it all mean? She would not have let up, believe me."

I dared to ask, "Are you afraid of Deanna, Andor?"

"What? Of course not. They can't harm humans in any way other than to annoy them to death."

"What about Paterri's companion, Telle? Do you consider her also to be unable to do harm?"

181

"Of course. She was assigned to Paterri by Tri-Linck. It was a temporary use of a Con to give the impression he was just an average type of passenger." Andor continued to fidget and looked like someone who wished to get away from his life.

"Do you need anything, Andor? Is there anything we can do for you at this point?" asked R.J.

"No, no, but if you would keep our discussion private, of course. I knew you would be visiting to ask questions because of the Chancellor's situation. I am hoping to keep this between us. I had better be getting back."

He rose nervously and headed for the door. He paused before exiting as though there was something else to say but left instead.

I took our cups to the kitchen and refilled them. We sat by the terminal remixing.

After a long pause for thought, R.J. said, "I believe we have seen the last of the gleeful Andor Dulley. From now on it will be the nervous Andor Dulley."

"I'm not sure I want to get any deeper into this. I can't imagine what's next."

The door chimed.

After a moment of doubt, I called, "Come in."

The door open and in charged Captain Yamora. R.J. and I stood. He came directly to us.

"Captain?" I said.

"Gentlemen, we should talk."

I motioned him to sit. "Captain Yamora, let me get you something. Coffee?"

"Something stronger if you wouldn't mind."

While R.J. made appropriate greetings, I put ice in three glasses and returned with a bottle. There was an ominous silence as I poured. I sat and sipped. The Captain took a deep drink.

"I'm sorry I have not met with the two of you sooner. The bridge has been demanding as usual. The same kind of problems we seem to keep having recently."

"Believe me, I can appreciate the challenges you have, Captain."

"Yes, you and Commander Smith would know. But, it is more than that. And, by the way, let me apologize for being terse with you during our first meeting. That was a day of irritability also."

"You are having unusual shipboard problems, Captain?" R.J. asked.

"That's just it, Commander. They are the kinds of problems you would only expect to have with new crew members: stupid mistakes and procedural errors."

"Your crew is in training?"

"That's the mystery. The entire crew is well-seasoned. It has all been sloppy mistakes like they don't care or they are trying to give the *Acrua Maru* a bad service record. When I question the offenders they seem genuinely apologetic but then the mistakes keep happening."

"Medical checkups?" I asked.

"See? Captains think alike. According to medical their tomography scans and other tests are all normal."

"Alcohol or drugs?" asked R.J.

"Medical found no evidence of such."

"I'm suddenly getting the idea this is the real reason for Chancellor Paterri being on board," said R.J.

The Captain drank. "Very good, Commander. Your deductive powers reassure me. Yes. He was here to see if there is some underlying reason for these mistakes. Not all of them were minor. There were interruptions of coolant flow to the reactor as well antimatter containment errors. Things like that will keep one awake at night. Mistakes by both human and Con personnel."

"Are you now thinking Paterri was killed because he found something out?" I asked.

"That is hard to believe. Medical just informed me that the prognosis was a time-delay poison, making it almost impossible to know when it was administered. Do you have anything more?"

There was an awkward moment of silence. R.J. tried to break it.

"We're still studying the passenger manifests, Captain. It's too soon to say."

The Captain finished his drink. "May I suggest the two of you scan everything you eat and drink, although I doubt an assassin would use the same method now that it is known. We should stay in frequent communication so no new information is lost. Eliminating an investigator is one thing; quickly removing all three of us would be something else. I had better get back to the bridge. I would assign security to you both but I believe that would be more restrictive than beneficial. Whatever the two of you need, you have a blank check. Up to now this has simply been systems failures and interruptions. Now the disruptions seem to include murder. The situation has suddenly become deadly serious. We must keep our channel open." The Captain placed his glass on the table, rose and left, muttering to himself as he went.

R.J. poured. We both drank.

R.J. said, "Never ask *what's next* ever again."

"I haven't been scanning my food. Have you?"

"I'm suddenly feeling quite stupid."

"You're feeling stupid? I woke up in the middle of the night with an android standing over me."

"We'd better have another drink."

I said, "Speaking of sleep, it's been a long day."

"Agreed. And though I hate guns I may sleep with this ankle holster still strapped on."

R.J. refilled his glass and took it with him. The door shut behind him and at that moment I decided the door was not enough. I made a tower of three glasses next to the door panel and taped a bent butter knife to the panel to knock the glasses over if the door opened. Lying in bed, I evaluated my unease and fell asleep.

Something woke me. The room lights had come on. There was a distant sound of an alarm coming from outside the room. The top of my head was pressed against the bed headboard. My blanket had gotten away from me. In half sleep I searched for covers but did not find any. In fact, the bed itself was missing. When my eyes finally focused, I found the bed, four feet below me. I was floating. There was no gravity. I vaguely recalled this very thing happening to me at some point in the past but could not remember when.

My zero-G experience kicked in immediately. I swung around and pushed down to the floor. At the closet I grabbed a flight suit and while doing slow flips changed into it. At the front door, I tapped it open and held to the frame to look outside. The alarm blared louder.

Other guests were hanging outside their rooms at various heights and attitudes. They were a disturbed bunch. Nausea had already set in on some. Most rooms had just one guest peering outside, a few had two holding onto each other. Some were running in place and going nowhere.

Beyond the room next to mine, R.J. was perusing the corridor with a suppressed smile on his face. He was still in his out-of-place bed clothes wearing a striped robe and a folded-over, pointed hat with a pom-pom atop it. In his floating state he was a perfect representation of Ebenezer Scrooge. He saw me and smirked.

"You've got to be kidding," I said.

He straightened up as though to appear more dignified. "I refuse to be conventional. Think inside the box."

The alarm suddenly stopped. A ship-wide announcement began. "Attention, attention. This is the Captain. We have had a problem with the artificial gravity generator matrix. It will be corrected in a moment. Please position yourself near the floor so that you do not fall and become injured when gravity returns. Do not use the elevators. I will give you a countdown to restoration of gravity shortly. Again, we have had a problem with the artificial gravity generator matrix. It will be corrected in a moment. Please position yourself near the floor so that you do not fall and become injured when gravity returns. I apologize for the inconvenience. Please standby."

R.J. motioned me over to him. I pulled myself to him.

"I would have come to you but I'm afraid someone might see up my night shirt."

"And God knows they've already been through enough."

"Have you noticed the population?"

"The cleanup crews will have their work cut out for them."

"Yes, but the people who are outside their room. Notice anything?"

"Not really?"

"It's just my estimate, but I'd say less than half of those on this deck have come out to see what's going on."

"So...?"

"Take a look. How many of these people are human and how many are androids?"

"How can I tell for sure?"

"You can't, but my guess is just about all these people are human. The androids have remained inside."

"Maybe."

"And weren't we told androids have an insatiable curiosity about things?"

The ship-wide announcement speaker came alive. "This is Captain Yamora. We are ready to reinitialize artificial gravity. Please be sure you are located near your deck's floor to avoid falling. I will begin a countdown; 10, 9, 8, 7, 6, 5, 4, 3, 2, 1... gravity on."

There was a loud racket, things crashing to the floor some items breaking, a few rolling out the open guest room doors. It was like a momentary thunderstorm downpour, ending as fast as it had started. People collapsed in a heap, a few slipping and sliding in vomit. R.J. and I settled onto our feet. R.J. watched the melee and rolled his eyes. He wiggled fingers at me for a goodbye and returned to his room. The sliding door caught the tail end of his Ebenezer Scrooge robe and he had to reemerge to pull it in.

I waved it all off and went inside. My alarm drinking glasses were scattered around the carpet, unbroken. I set them back up and went back to bed.

Chapter 16

In the morning we took a chance and checked out the dining area. It was unoccupied. Apparently, the guests were still recovering from the big float. We took seats at a table out of the way. Anai appeared with a smile but no expression of surprise, hot coffee and cups in hand.

"What we witnessed last night was an episode of excitement happening to a group of very dull people," said R.J.

"Something to tell the grandkids about."

"And that right there is a can of worms you just opened."

"Explain."

"Most Lemorians take the classy version of android for mates. Most do not marry other humans."

"So how *do* children come about?"

"Mail order, online."

"Do they arrive in a box via a UPS drone? That would be a real play on the stork delivery story."

"Use your own sperm or select some from our diverse list of geniuses and celebrities. Customized laboratory development with each order. Choose your own age delivery."

"For some reason that all makes me feel a little sick."

"See? I'm not the only old-fashioned one. Next you'll be wearing a nightshirt and night cap."

"No way, Ebenezer. Doesn't that pom-pom keep getting in your herbal tea?"

"Very funny. My night cap will still be around long after we're gone."

"I've been reviewing our investigation. We've got many ugly little facts and still not one damn lead in the murder of Chancellor Paterri."

"You are correct, sir. This would usually be a point where a sting might be set up. Make them come to us instead of us tracking them down. Have any ideas?"

"Paterri found out something someone couldn't live with."

"A fair assumption."

"What if we let it leak Paterri had shared that intel with just one other person, like the new owner of the *Acrua Maru*?"

"It's a workable plan but I have mixed feelings about it."

I nodded. "Because there might be androids involved?"

"Yes. Faster, stronger, smarter. They have the technology."

"They'd know poison wasn't an option this time."

"Which means it would probably have to be physical."

"They'd want to be sure the information hadn't been passed along already."

R.J. thought for a moment. "We don't seem to be receiving any private communications from outside the ship. Want to bet we're not really sending any either?"

"That fits right in to someone keeping a lid on things. Your plan could work."

"Waiting to see if someone tries to kill you is not my favorite plan, however."

"You got another one?"

"We'd need to set it up very carefully. We'd need to find a point in time when you and Paterri were in close enough proximity to each other, a time when maybe a note could have been passed. I'll check with the video data center and see if that's happened. I'll tell them it's for something else."

"And to set the trap?" I asked.

"A tiny slip to any android and I bet it's instantly known to all of them. Humans would be trickier except they're all abuzz about the murder. The grapevine is already running at full capacity."

"I'll start dreaming up a three-stage defense plan for every damn thing I do."

"There's one other thing that bothers me."

"Just one?"

"If the killer is a human we'll find that person had a very specific motive, even if that person is simply a serial killer. But, if the killer is an android, it would almost certainly mean it was all of them, not just the one."

"In that case we'd be in deep trouble."

"Yes, we would. Remember Arthur Clark's 2001? The ship's computer went berserk?"

"And there wasn't a system onboard it didn't control."

"We need a pro hacker. I'll bet there's one onboard."

"I'll go set myself up for being set up."

We both took long looks around and parted to our rooms.

Seated at the bar by the kitchen I surveyed the ways a tried-and-true killer might do me in. The single entrance-exit was a plus for me. The camera in everyone's room a plus for the killer. I needed perimeter defenses for my room, travel defenses for outside. Weapons hidden at various points around the room. A dummy of me to sleep in my place. A panic button to R.J. and Duce.

There was the environmental threat as well. Because the room's atmosphere was processed and controlled it might be possible to make it lethal. I would need a closed-circuit oxygen mask and an alarm for O2 suddenly becoming absent or poisoned. With a list in my mind, I headed back to Duce.

"Uh-oh, what have you got?" he said as I entered his break room. We were alone.

"Sorry to be a pest. I need some more stuff."

"You got something going on I should know about, Adrian? I'm all ears."

"Best not to discuss it, Duce. You going to help me again?"

"I'm glad you stopped by. I needed to speak with you anyway."

I sat across from him. He leaned forward and looked around before he spoke. "More and more I don't like what's going on around here."

"Join the club."

"No, it's bigger than that. It's the screw ups that are happening. I think they're intentional."

"Why do you think that?"

Duce paused and checked around again. He spoke in a lower tone, "It's got to be dissension or something. It's not just the Cons, it's the human staff too. People I've known a long time acting different. They are like keeping their distance from me. Some of the mistakes they are making don't make sense. It is stuff they have done a thousand times. It has to be intentional."

"That's very interesting."

"Have you found anything about Paterri?"

"Still a dead end, so far."

"Got to be the Cons."

"We're keeping an open mind."

"Without asking what for, what do you need?"

"Two or three more small weapons which will stop a human or a Con, a couple closed-circuit oxygen masks, along with detectors that will pick up anything wrong with the air."

"If I'm reading you right, you will also want a few radiation detectors. That has been a favorite of some assassins these days."

It embarrassed me I hadn't thought of that. "I must be slipping. Yeah, those too."

"Why are you suddenly so worried?"

"If you can't get to the bad guy, have them come to you."

"Okay. I get it. I'll stay ready if you need me."

We agreed to face-to-face-only unless the communication was routine. We also agreed to be suspicious of everything. I left with a duffel bag of goodies.

With attention to the hidden camera lens I spent an hour inconspicuously setting up my room. In an area I believed to be out of camera range, foam from two cut up pillows and spare yellow flight coveralls made a presentable Adrian Tarn that I promptly named Wilson, though I could not remember where I'd heard that iconic name. I stood Wilson in the closet and closed the door just as my communicator beeped.

It was Captain Yamora. "Captain Tarn, would you please come up to my ready room?"

"On my way."

In the Captain's ready room I found Yamora, R.J. and one other person waiting. The unknown member was on the youthful side, dark short hair, possibly makeup applied around the eyes. He wore shiny black leather suit jacket that was not made to close in the front. Black wet pants ended in black boots made for lace-up but with no laces present.

I looked at R.J. inquisitively.

R.J. returned a smile. "Adrian, I'd like to introduce Kick. He was somewhat buried in the guest list but I found him nonetheless. He is scourge to all computer programmers everywhere. He has probably caused more anxiety than he has celebration but in his trade that's a good thing. He has extensive knowledge of Con Code."

I nodded a greeting. "Why are we here, R.J.?"

"Kick was summoned by Captain Yamora to discuss the ship's software failures. You and I have been called because you are now The *Acrua Maru*'s legal owner. And of course that's not really why we're here but that's the way it would appear to anyone keeping an eye on us."

Captain Yamora cut in, "Gentlemen, we put onto orbit tomorrow. I need to get back to the bridge. I'll leave you three to sort things out."

"Thank you, Captain," answered R.J.

The Captain turned and disappeared through the bridge access door.

We sat at a round, glass table on well-cushioned chairs. R.J. faced me. "So as pieced together by Captain Yamora, Kick, and me, Kick was secretly hired by Paterri for his investigation in case he needed a Con hacker. Kick was told he'd probably not be needed so this would basically be a free vacation cruise."

Kick fidgeted in his seat. He jumped in, "The bruse even assigned me a Con! Can you believe that? An angel from heaven. I haven't left the room since I been here!"

I looked to R.J. "The bruse?"

R.J. nodded. "The universal translators had trouble with that expression. As near as I can tell it translates to '*dude*.' They listed Kick as a tourist-guest. His background with computer code was not listed on his paperwork nor was his arrest record."

Kick gave a wide smile. "They can't lock me up. They love me."

R.J. said, "We really need your help, Kick."

"Hey, I get paid either way. Press on, bruse."

I said, "To start with we need to know how the Cons communicate with each other. What can you tell us about that?"

"Wow, you want to fog things up right off the pad then. That's one ugly question, bruse. It is all about the uni-link, the core comm. It was set up way back when the Cons were first put out there. It was supposed to be a quiet channel, one-way, the government could use it to send out universal code changes or special alerts to each and every Con almost instantly. The Cons were not supposed to be able to use that bandwidth because it was designated one-way. They could receive but not send."

"Right off though, sometimes data was lost in transit or corrupted for some reason so the Cons were given the ability to ask for a resend. All of a sudden the uni-link was a two-way comm channel. The gov and the manufacturers lost control of it really quick. The Cons were designed to be so curious. It was to give them a better idea about life and how to act human. They started to use the uni-link to ask questions about other things they didn't understand. Other Cons would react to those questions and offer answers. It took a microsecond for the Cons to learn to identify each other's code. They started carrying on private communications. The uni-link started running at full capacity all the time so the Cons found ingenious ways to use it anyway, time sharing broken down to microseconds, piggyback transmissions and a ton of other really cool stuff. Humans had lost control of the thing but they didn't dare shut it down; it was part of the core code system. So that's what we got now. You go into the uni-link and it is a flood of data in there. With A.I. programming you can pick out what you want to look at but some Con somewhere will know there is abnormal monitoring going on almost immediately and a world of Cons will stop and look at what you are doing."

R.J. asked, "How far can they communicate, Kick?"

"No limit. They got time delay of course but if they are way, way out in dead space all they need is to find someone else's spacecraft and they can search for a pass code for as long as it takes and bounce off the thing. Does not bother them in the least. And there is another thing. We humans use these really cool ear plugs to translate for us. Our plugs are particularly cool because they use a phonetic comparison matrix to construct the language they are translating. They can actually build a new language as necessary rather than have a million dialects stored in memory. That is why there is a delay sometimes. But the Cons, they have the space. They really do have a million languages in their database folders. So they can use any strange language, encode it, and talk to each other that way even changing the dialectic in mid-sentence. Translating their stuff can be hell."

I asked, "Kick, do you think a Con could murder someone?"

"Do *I* think that? I think about that all the time. I am sleeping with one. Wake up with a kitchen knife sticking out of my chest? Whoa…."

"Why do you do it then?" asked R.J.

"What?! She is gorgeous and she knows things I never dreamed of. It is like the best fun-drug you ever had. How do you guys resist them?"

I asked, "Kick, is there any way to search this uni-link code channel to tell if a Con had anything to do with Chancellor Paterri's death?"

"Button in a wheat field. That's an old saying on my home world. It means forget it. Plus, as soon as you tried for a search about killing someone the whole link would take notice. You would be like standing on a hill waving a flag, look at me, look at me!"

R.J. added, "What if we wanted to plant a false message to the Cons on this ship. Could we do that?"

"What kind of message?"

R.J. said, "We want to plant a message that Chancellor Paterri passed a note to Captain Tarn about something he'd found in his investigation and that Captain Tarn hasn't told anyone about it yet."

Kick sat with his mental gears turning, looking at us with an inquisitive stare. "Whoa! You really think Cons did Paterri? You want them to come after you? Are you blazing crazy, bruse?"

"We don't know the Cons did it, Kick. We're going to do the same thing with the humans onboard. We're trying to draw the murderer out in the open."

"Yeah, but if it is a Con...."

I interrupted, "We'll be set up and ready for them."

Kick leaned forward, rested his elbow on the table and his chin in the palm of his hand, thinking. "On my home world hackers call that trolling. You drop a fishing lure in the water and drag it along until you find the fish. But bruse, the fish don't eat you alive on my world."

"You're a smart man, Kick," said R.J.

He raised both arms. "That's why they can't lock me up. They love me. They always need me for something."

"So can you plant that rumor?" I asked.

"You don't need me for that. Best way would be to just let one of them overhear you talking."

"That's the best way?"

"Oh, I could plant a message in the uni-link but they could trace that around. Why take the chance? Give it to them straight from the source. They got hearing like a prey animal."

I said, "One other thing, Kick. Is there an easy way to be sure someone is a Con and not a human?"

Kick straightened up and looked worried. "Not really, except how they look so perfect."

"No? There's no way to scan someone to see if they're human or Con?"

"You can set up a scanner and scan all you want but Cons are self-programming. That's how they learn. They can code themselves to emit anything a hand scanner wants to see. Their job is to imitate humans so they usually respond to scanner radiation with human signatures. Really, you bruses are making me nervous now."

"So how can you find out if someone is a Con?" persisted R.J.

"Big medical scanner with positron emission tomography."

"And no other way?"

"Blast a hole in one."

I looked over at R.J. "Crap."

"I have another one for you Kick," said R.J. "Could you disable all the Cons at once from within the uni-link?"

"I doubt it. Put them all in recharge mode? Order them all to do a systems heck? The uni-link is too messy for that kind of hack."

"Think about that for us, Kick," I said.

"One thing I should say, bruses; Cons don't breathe. They got lungs that simulate breathing but they are just used for cooling the heat sinks inside. Cons don't need air but they sure control the air on this ship."

"Well, could you set something up on the sly that could be used to take control of ship's environment system if we needed to?" I asked.

"You mean hack the ship's systems? I would need to study ship programming architecture. I do not know about that. I will look into it. That would make me famous on the dark net."

"So there is a dark net here, Kick?" asked R.J.

"Of course! Got to have a place where hackers and illegals do business and socialize. It is a fun place to cruise when you do not have anything else going. You can make quick credits if you need to."

We sat briefly in silence to see if anyone had anything else. Captain Yamora suddenly emerged through the bridge access doors. He stopped and paused to see if he was interrupting conversation.

I said, "I think that's it for now, Kick. Remember all communications must be in person and all of this is classified."

"You are telling me?"

"I'll be in touch to see how you're doing with your coding artistry."

"Nice to be appreciated," he replied. He stood and headed for the exit. He looked back on the way out. "Not going to be the same sleeping with Ella." He shook his head and left.

Captain Yamora spoke, "Captain Tarn, could I speak to you alone, please?"

R.J. looked surprised but graciously excused himself. Yamora sat across from me.

"So nothing new on Paterri you said?"

"No, but we're setting up a sting to try to draw them out."

"You still don't know if it was a human or a Con?"

"No."

Yamora rubbed his mouth with one hand and spoke with uncertainty. "There's something I've decided to do that I've never done before and will probably never do again. I am very concerned about ship operations. The temporary loss of gravity was the breaking point. It was another episode where people could have been hurt, excepting the Cons, of course."

"You think it was intentional?"

"The mistake on the interface panel was made by an experienced, human technician, someone who has flown with me on many flights. I have to think these errors are intentional, some kind of retribution. I do not know the reason. The representative of the Fellowship Of Starship Workers assures me there are no grievances against me but she cannot explain the problems either. As you know, we're slowing for orbital insertion tomorrow. We will be offloading the Con transports and taking on crates of materials to bring back to Lemoria. As I've said, what I have decided to do is a highly irregular procedure but to put it bluntly I am afraid to wait any longer."

"Anything I can do to help, Captain. Just say the word."

"I want you to give you my command codes. I do not believe I can trust the personnel onboard. Or I should say, I do not know who to trust. I've studied your record. There is no question you could handle the command and as owner you would be free to appoint a new Captain anyway in the event something happened to me. We will both have absolute authority over all ship operations including the shuttles. I will enter into the log orders that in my absence you are the sole command authority on this ship. You will have the power to create a new set of second level command codes for Commander Smith if and when you deem that essential. I need to know this is acceptable to you."

My mind went blank for a moment. It was like being hit with a bucket of cold water. I rubbed my forehead and pinched the bridge of my nose to focus.

"Captain Tarn, are you alright?"

"Yes, yes. You just caught me off guard, Captain. Believe it or not something like this happened to me once before, many years ago. It just brought back a rush of memory."

"Do you disagree with my reasoning?"

"No, no, not at all. This is just a precautionary measure. It doesn't mean I would ever have reason to need your codes."

"I have been assured even the Cons cannot break into the command code system. I am told it would take them centuries to break the code. It is something about single photon rewrite memory being used. I do not understand it. As you know, Captains are obligated to die rather than to reveal command codes to the wrong people."

Yamora drew out a strange looking pad of paper from his breast pocket along with an equally odd-looking pen. He wrote a long line of letter-shapes, numbers, and figures on the pad. He tore off the top sheet and handed it to me.

"You have one hour to memorize those, Captain. Do not make a copy. One hour and that small square of paper will evaporate. Do you understand?"

"Perfectly."

"I would also suggest you spend a good deal of time studying ship's operations, just in case."

"I will."

"Time to return to the bridge to see what else has gone wrong in my absence."

"Good luck, Captain Yamora."

"To both of us, Captain Tarn."

Chapter 17

R.J. was waiting outside the door. We headed back.

"What was that about?" he asked.

"I was given Yamora's command codes."

R.J. stopped abruptly. "What?"

"Come on, keep walking. Let's not draw any more attention to ourselves than we already do."

"He did what?"

"I own the ship. He doesn't know who to trust."

"I'll say one thing, he's a very intelligent man."

"Agreed."

R.J. looked over at me. "So he feels threatened somehow?"

"He knows something's wrong. He doesn't know what."

"You think he suspects the Cons?"

"Are *we* now leaning toward the murderer being a Con?"

"I think we've established it could possibly be. But does Yamora think so?"

"He might, except most of the mistakes being made on this ship apparently are being made by humans. He thinks it must be retribution or unrest of some kind. Tomorrow we enter orbit, two days delivering Cons and then it's back to Lemoria. All we need to do is make Lemoria and we can catch a ride out and leave this crap to the Lemorians."

"Only if our luck changes."

I nodded agreement. "Where is our first stop in your illustrious plan to have me attacked?"

"First the dining area where we make sure a Con overhears us talking. Then on to the lounge and with any luck some busybody will also eavesdrop on our discussion."

"Casting the lure."

"Have you eaten yet?"

"I'm starved. What's the special today?"

"I don't know. It's check between the bread day."

We entered the dining area and chose a table near the server's corridor. I positioned myself so I could see the servers' entrance out of the corner of my eye, then set a chrome napkin dispenser to reflect the entrance as well. A bald male Con server dressed in kitchen-wear white greeted us warmly, though his expression lacked emotion. I noticed his hands were less delicate than the female Cons. I ordered the same thing I always do for the sake of safety.

My charbroil steak interrupted any thoughts of the set up. When it was done and he'd brought us coffee, I watched for his next return. His shadow on the wall alerted me to his presence in the hallway nearby. I winked to R.J. and the set up began.

R.J. spoke in the perfect tone, low but loud enough to overhear, cautious but laced with intrigue. "So Paterri secretly handed you a note before he was killed?"

R.J.'s timing was perfect. The approaching shadow stopped, moved slightly ahead, and waited.

"Yes, right here in this dining room."

"What was in the note?"

"I'm not willing to say just yet. It was something he had found during his investigation. He wanted it kept secret and turned over only to the government chief investigator's office."

"So you're not going to tell me what it said?" R.J. faked disappointment.

"The information will remain with me and only me until we get back to Lemoria."

"Okay, be that way."

The server appeared and refilled our cups. He smiled a flat smile and dashed off.

R.J. smiled. "He got it. I guarantee it."

"Well then, on to the lounge. Let's hope the busybodies are there again."

They were. Grouped at the same table were a dozen VIPs. They stopped and took notice of our entry. We sat at the bar.

I ordered a bourbon on ice. R.J. had tea.

We could see the group in the partially frosted mirror behind the bar. They were taking turns looking over at us.

"Maybe they won't bite," I said.

"Are you kidding? I'm surprised it's taken this long."

"Timing's going to be trickier in here."

"Don't worry. I've got this."

The same VIP as last time stood, hesitated, and looked over at us. He straightened his suit jacket and headed our way. Just as he entered earshot R.J. leaned in and spoke in surprise, "What? Paterri slipped you a note before he was killed?"

"Keep it down. No one's supposed to know that."

The VIP stopped and began to nervously search his jacket as though he'd dropped something. To stretch the time he began gazing down at the floor while frequently checking us out of the corner of his eye.

"So what was in the note?"

"It was information he'd discovered during his investigation."

"What information?"

"I can't tell you. It's supposed to be kept secret. Only the Lemorian High Council is supposed to be told."

"So you're not going to tell me?"

"Sorry, it has to stay with me and no one else until we get back."

The VIP feigned finding something on the floor and returned to his seat.

I said, "That was easier than I thought."

"Two for two."

"Good job."

"Now what?"

"Now hopefully, someone tries to kill me."

"You always know how to spoil the moment."

I stared at my drink and turned my glass in place. "What about you, now. The ball's in play. Are you set up back at your place?"

"I sleep with that repulsive weapon under my pillow. I have a scanner set up to sniff for atmospheric changes and at the same time it's a motion detector. Plus I have my broom handle and glass leaning against the door."

"I'm going to head back to my room and start studying *Acrua Maru* operations just in case. You should do likewise since you'll be second in command if the worst happens."

"Don't forget to memorize the command codes, bruse."

"Very funny."

R.J. lowered his voice. "You will let me know immediately if any intruders show up, right?"

"Yes, but I don't want you charging in to my rescue, okay?"

"Aw, shucks."

In my room I did the forbidden and copied the command code onto a non-evaporating piece of paper. It wasn't just memorizing letters and numbers. The Lemorian alphabet was made up of letter-like symbols along with tiny figures that did not look like letters at all. Their number system was based on a different core figure for every ten numbers. At least everything on the paper matched what was on my Lemorian terminal keyboard. With voice recognition turned on I hadn't needed to type many commands but the command code would require direct keyboard entry. The memorization process involved learning those very foreign characters and it was challenging me.

Late in the day I made a sandwich out of the most normal looking ingredients I could find and washed it down with the first cup of coffee for a long evening ahead. I set up the dummy Adrian in my bed, leaving a good deal of flight suit showing as though I'd fallen asleep in it. Covered the foam head with pillows and left just a tiny spot showing to suggest skin tone. Made a sit-up bed in the closet. I set up a hidden scanner to act as a private room camera linked it to my tablet. Then I dimmed the lights and set myself up with the closet door slid slightly open, my duffle bag of goodies next to me and a tablet with which to continue studying the *Acrua Maru*.

Staying awake was no problem. I knew the trap had been well set. Paterri had been killed because he knew something. The word was now out. Tarn also knows. It was a coiled snare waiting to be stepped into. I made up my mind not to jump at intruders too soon. At the least I would allow them to kill the sleeping Tarn. I would wait as long as I could in case there were any communications to be overheard. I might even let the bad guy leave so I could follow.

The long wait began. I used ten-minute intervals of command code memorization, followed by study of *Acrua Maru* systems. Occasionally I'd get an email icon from R.J. telling me what system he was studying. I was not without creature comforts. In the kitchen cabinets there had been a thermos-type bottle with power cell heating element which was perfect for keeping coffee hot. I sipped while reading. Around two A.M. Earth time I had the command code well engraved in memory so I burned the illegal slip of paper, its predecessor having long since dissolved.

The silence became ominous. It was a perpetual message that nothing was happening though the odds were something probably would. Around three A.M. it finally did.

I heard the front door slide open much more slowly than usual and wondered how they got it to do that. I switched the tablet to camera view and kneeled in a ready position where I could see out the crack in the closet door while glancing at the video.

She entered somewhat gracefully for an assassin. The silhouette of a ballet dancer moving across the room. In partial light, pale blue sheer night robes added a ghostly effect to her image. Long dark hair split between front and back. She wore a gold belt with a small pack attached to it. Several feet from the bed, she drew a dull chrome container from her pack and began spraying using back and forth motions in the direction of the bed. A second or two later I smelled the gas, got a spike of dizziness and hurriedly drew my gas mask from my duffle bag and held it to my face.

She was a Con. There was no doubt about that. In the dim light of the room it would have been hard to tell but the camera's more sensitive optics gave me color and tone and hers was perfect.

Satisfied with her spraying, she replaced the canister and came to the side of the bed. From the feel of it I expected a long shiny knife to appear.

None did. She stood by the bed and seemed to become confused. She looked around the room, then pressed on the body of the false Adrian Tarn. She straightened up and looked over the room again. There was a long pause of stiff non-movement, as though she was processing information.

As gracefully as she had entered, she left.

I tore off the mask, was up and through the door into the deserted corridor in less than three seconds. I spotted her heading aft. With my firearm concealed behind me in one hand I trotted to catch up.

She reached the end of the corridor and turned left into the last guest room. I managed to slip through the door as it closed behind her. She turned, saw me, and froze for a moment, processing the new, unexpected information.

"Captain Tarn, I was looking for you."

"You've found me. Who are you?"

"I am Zeene."

"Why were you in my room?"

"I was sent to you as a gift."

"What sort of gift?"

"My instructions were to pleasure every inch of you front and back."

"Who instructed you to do that?"

"I do not know. There was no identification in the data packet."

"Who is your sponsor living here?"

"There is no sponsor living here. There are two other Service Cons living here on their way to meet the cruise ship they will be assigned to."

"How did you get into my room?"

"I am a Service Con. I have entry to all the rooms."

"What did you spray in my room?"

She reached into her packet and drew out the small canister. "It is SAS." She handed it to me.

"What is SAS?"

"Sexual Acuity Solution. It is designed to make sex more pleasurable."

"Where did you get this?"

"From the pharmaceutical stores as directed."

"Who directed you?"

"I do not know. I was to pleasure you and report back to the command link."

"Report what?"

"Everything."

"Who is your sponsor?"

"I am a General Services Con. My sponsorship is to the owner of this vessel."

"So that makes me your sponsor?"

She took a few seconds to process the question. "You are correct. My sponsorship changed recently from Tri-Linck to Adrian Tarn."

"I'm going to keep this bottle. You can resume your duties."

"Captain Tarn, I still have an open command docket to pleasure you."

"Please cancel that order and resume your normal duties."

"Very well."

Weapon in one hand, canister in the other, I headed back to my room. I had failed to ask her if she was in possession of any weapons but it hardly mattered. As an android she could have killed me with one hand tied behind her back. In my room I looked up at the spot where the ship's hidden camera was located and wondered how much had been in range of the camera and who was watching. The most confusing thing was it did not seem like she had come to kill me. Unless the SAS spray was lethal her visit was a mystery.

I got back into the closet and waited for *Acrua Maru* daybreak.

In the morning, R.J. showed up at my door with an old-fashioned dining cart on creaky wheels. It was covered with breakfast dishes which pleased me to no end. He creaked his way in and we sat and ate and drank.

"Where did you come up with that thing?"

"Maintenance room aft. It's used for floor scrubbing tools and chemicals. I requisitioned it."

"Wouldn't the dining area people have given you an antigrav cart?"

"Where's the fun in that?"

"Did they see you transfer the stuff onto that thing?"

"They stared for a long, long time; especially for androids."

"That's funny."

"It was an experiment of sorts. It was very interesting. Our androids have a significant weakness. They are unable to process things which do not make sense to them. They seem to have trouble knowing what kind of search parameter to enter to find an explanation of things they don't understand."

"I see what you mean. How would a Con Google; why is a human using an old cart on wheels instead of an antigrav cart?"

"They seem unable to form even that question. I believe they go into some kind of overflow subroutine when they can't get a question or answer they need. It's sort of a *never mind* state. It takes them a few seconds."

"That might become useful."

"So what happened last night? An uneventful marathon of ship's systems study?"

In between bites and sips I recounted for him my aborted night of pleasuring.

"Of all the things I expected might happen that was not one of them."

"It's making my brain do black flips too."

"Perhaps someone was just curious about Adrian Tarn, slayer of windmills, all night poker player, lover and leaver of fair maidens...."

"Not anymore on that last part, remember."

"It's only natural we were expecting an upfront confrontation. It's what we're used to. But I might guess what happened is actually so complex in nature the cards must have been dealt by a computer, not a human."

"So was her visit a result of our sting?"

"It had to be either a coincidence or we caused it and I do not believe on coincidences."

"Are we finally saying the Cons killed Paterri?"

"Death by covert administration of an extended time-delay fish poison. Sounds just as complex as what happened last night, doesn't it?"

"Wow, you make a good case."

"Which would mean we're up against a mind that is not human. That scares even me a little bit."

"Are we sure?"

"I think we're pretty sure."

"Then why all the ship accidents being made by human crew members?"

"Maybe they suspect something and are trying to call attention to it by having too many screw ups on board, like they're trying to get an investigation started."

I paused from chewing a bite of cinnamon roll. "If that's the case it worked and looked what it got them."

"May I change the subject and make a suggestion?"

"Be my guest."

"Your midnight visit might not be the last move The Mind makes. You can't stay awake indefinitely and you need to be sharp. I suggest I remain here and continue studying *Acrua Maru* operations, standing guard while you get some shut-eye. Then you can do the same for me."

"My brain wants to object but that closet made my left hip sore."

"I'll wake you at the first sign of android."

Chapter 18

Four hours was enough for me. Adrenaline sleep. R.J. took his shift and had no problem dozing off. More coffee and more exploded parts diagrams of the *Acrua Maru*. Some kind of packaged fish sandwich for lunch. I could tell we had dropped onto orbit over the RRS. Somehow it's a very different feel of the ship.

A message icon from Captain Yamora came up on my screen. It was a general ship's bulletin, not a private message.

ALL PERSONNEL BE ADVISED DUE TO A MANUFACTURING DELAY AT THE RRS WE WILL BE REMAINING ON ORBIT FOR THREE DAYS BEFORE BEGINNING OUR RETURN TRIP TO LEMORIA. WE APOLOGIZE FOR THE ADDITIONAL DELAY. –Captain Yamora.

I tried to find some deeper meaning in the message but came up blank. As I pondered, my communicator beeped. It was Duce.

"Yeah man. What's up?"

"Adrian, why don't you stop down for a drink? We miss your company."

"On my way."

I woke R.J. He sat up and stretched. "Duce called you? It can't be that he actually misses your company."

"Something's up."

"Should I join you?"

"We should try to be less conspicuous. The coffee is hot."

I took the elevator to the security level and found Duce seated in the break room as usual.

"Is that a bottle of water you're drinking?" I asked.

"Had too much last night. Paying penance."

"On my end I had a late-night visitor last night. Strange thing is, she didn't do anything and didn't know anything."

"Sounds like every suspect I have ever arrested."

"Was she world-class beautiful?"

"Yes, like all of them."

"So it *was* probably a Con which did Paterri in."

"Starting to look that way."

"Knew I should have quit after the last *Acrua Maru* run."

"Don't keep me in suspense, Duce. You really weren't missing my company."

"Yeah, well, something is up today with Yamora." Duce drank from the clear bottle and sat back. "The Cons in detention are being shipped out two shuttles at a time. The shuttles bring back cargo with each trip. That's all normal ops. But captains almost never visit cargo ops. They are usually kicked back in their quarters waiting. For some reason one of the handlers found something not right on a cargo container label. The Captain was called down. He has been down there ever since overseeing Receiving. It doesn't look right down there. I am surprised the union isn't raising a stink."

"Maybe the new owner should pay them a visit."

"Which should be perfectly routine but you should tread carefully. I would be curious to hear how you are received."

"Okay, I'll let you know."

I took the elevator down to the lowest level. The doors slid open to the lobby for the hangar bay and cargo area. The big doors to the hangar bay were open beneath the big green light that signified Hangar Pressurized.

There was a big empty space in the bay where one shuttle would normally park. The second shuttle was cold and dark just beyond. That meant the first shuttle was still on the surface delivering Cons or picking up cargo. I felt a slight shiver. This place reminded me of when I'd stepped off after the moon madness.

There was no one in the hangar. It occurred to me someone on the bridge was probably now monitoring me on camera so the place didn't accidentally get depressurized with a human inside. I turned and went to the next door down which had to be the corridor to the cargo bay. Red Lemorian letters on the door pointed to another big green area-pressurization warning light.

The closed door slid open for me when I asked. At the end of a narrow passageway the secondary door was open. As I crossed over to it the sound of many voices began to fill the air. I entered the huge cargo bay and looked over the area.

Captain Yamora was standing with an electronic clipboard talking to a deckhand. Several other workers were located around the place, two of them wearing crate-mover apparatus. Most of the gray, ribbed crates were waist-high, four by eight feet. The Captain looked over and noticed me. His expression did not change. I went to him.

"Captain Tarn, what are you doing here? You know this is a hard hat area?" he asked.

"Just the owner wishing to observe cargo transfers," I replied.

"You have that right but please get some safety equipment and stay back out of the way." Yamora's tone was less than friendly.

"Are we on schedule?" I asked.

"As I said in the ship-wide announcement we will be keeping orbit for three days due to manufacturing delays on the surface. Is there anything else?"

Yamora was clearly annoyed. I took it to be a signal he did not want the cargo handlers to know he and I were working together so closely.

I tried to play the part. "Captain, when you have time, I'd like to discuss our timetable for the return trip."

"When I get time, Mr. Tarn." Yamora turned away, tapped at his tablet and began inspecting crates waiting to be stacked. It was clear he wanted me to leave so I took the cue and obliged him.

As I left the cargo area and walked the hallway to the elevator, instinct set in. I suddenly realized how alone I was and that eyes somewhere were following my progress. But there was no reason to depressurize this corridor. In the elevator lobby the doors to the shuttle bay had closed and the pressurization light was flashing yellow. I stepped in the elevator and watched the bay light turn to red. A warning horn was sounding somewhere.

On my way back to the room I ran into Andor Dulley headed in the opposite direction. He held up a hand in greeting and stopped. He was again no longer his cheerful self. The nervous persona had taken over.

"Is there any news, Captain Tarn?"

"No, Andor. I'm sorry. The investigation is ongoing."

"It is so disturbing. A company temp suddenly murdered. No one knows why. You do not think there would be any reason for anyone to attack me, do you?"

"We haven't found any reason for you to worry, Andor. And you have Deanna for protection, too."

Dulley stared into the distance. "Yes, Deanna, of course." He began clasping his hands and walked off in a daze.

In the room, R.J. was sipping coffee at the terminal. "What did you find out?"

"For some reason, Captain Yamora doesn't want the crew to know we are working together."

"Maybe he doesn't want the bad guys to think he knows what you know, even though you don't really know what you're supposed to know."

"I must need a drink because I understood every word of that."

"This idea of searching personnel records for a hint of murder may be a waste of time. Because they are servants, possessions you could say, there are no real histories kept on the androids. No criminal records, no taxation records; they don't even need a license to operate vehicles so there's almost nothing on them, just dossiers of which sponsors they've been assigned to. The other thing is, as you and I have been speculating, they are all individuals clearly but I believe there may also be a kind of central mind formed from the interface between all of them."

"A hive mind?"

"Yes, that would be a good name for it."

"The crap Zeene sprayed over my bed. You got anything about that?"

"Oh yeah. I fed that into a medical scanner. It was not a sex enhancement drug, I'll tell you that. It was a strong sedative which would have made you happy and oblivious to everything being done to you."

"But not deadly?"

"No. You could not have OD'd on it if you tried."

"So they weren't trying to kill me. What the hell?"

"Put you out of commission maybe?"

"You know, we may have worked our way to a dead-end in a murder case which can't be solved."

"Another skeleton in the closet for Lemoria," added R.J.

"I'll tell you something else. They must not have known about Kick. I mean about Paterri hiring him as a code expert. He's the real danger to them. Otherwise I'll bet it would have been a double murder."

"So what do we do?"

"I will pay a private visit to Yamora and let him know there is no trail to follow and this thing may never be solved. The case will have to be turned over to Lemorian authorities when we get back. In the meantime, there's nothing else we can do."

"Unless they still try to do away with you."

"If that was going to happen it would have been last night, don't you think?"

R.J. squinted in thought. "Maybe."

Later that afternoon I headed for the bridge on the chance Yamora had returned. He met me in the ready room again looking annoyed.

"What is it this time, Mr. Tarn?"

"I wanted to update you on Paterri."

"Go ahead."

Yamora seemed impatient as I explained the dead end and what would eventually need to be done.

"And that's all? You know nothing more than that?"

"Sorry."

"I heard a rumor Chancellor Paterri gave you a message of some kind. What did it say?"

"That was a set up to try to bring the murderer out in the open. There never was a note."

"Let us forget this matter until we return to Lemoria then. Operations are very busy here. I hope you will not need to interrupt us again."

I turned to leave, intrigued by Yamora's change in attitude. It didn't make sense. On a last-minute whim I took a chance, stopped at the door, and called back to him. "Oh, one other thing Captain Yamora. As owner of the *Acrua Maru* I was thinking you should give me your command codes in case of an emergency."

"What!? Are you insane? What an absurd suggestion! No one is entitled to Captain command codes! I must have misjudged your service record. Please Mr. Tarn, do not bother me again unless it is a pending catastrophe."

And he was gone.

I stood stunned for a moment. Part of me wanted to leave but a companion part refused to accept things as they were. A revised belief-matrix set in. Mentally I repeated the last part of the conversation over and over to find the spot where I misunderstood. Or perhaps I had misstated the trick question so a confusing answer was given. I tried to rearrange the words so they made sense.

In a daze I left the ready room and headed back to my quarters.

There were only two possible explanations. Either Yamora had completely forgotten he had given me his command codes or the person I was speaking to was not Yamora.

No ship's captain would forget giving someone his command codes.

In my stateroom R.J. was still seated at the computer terminal. He watched me pass by on my way to the kitchen where I found two old-fashioned-styled glasses, filled them with ice cubes and poured in Lemorian bourbon.

I placed one in front of R.J. and sat back on the sofa. I tipped up my glass to him and drank.

"What makes you think I need this?" he asked.

"We are so screwed."

"Adrian, no, no we're not. We took the investigation as far as it could go. We're done with that. The rest of the trip is a simple cruise back to Lemoria then the best ride we can hitch home. Done, *fini*, *completato*."

I held up my glass to him once more and drank.

R.J. let his glass sit. "What then? There's something else? Was Yamora there?"

"I spoke with Yamora. It looked exactly like Yamora, it did not behave exactly like Yamora and that's because it wasn't Yamora."

"Okay, this is because of that play on words I did with you not knowing what you were supposed to know, right?"

"Yamora is an android. I'd put money on it."

"What? Wait, there's no way you could know that."

"It's the only possible explanation."

"Why?"

"I asked him to give me his command codes. He said it was a stupid idea and that I was stupid."

"But he…. wait…. we didn't know he already gave you his command codes?"

I held up my drink once more in salute and drank.

"Oh my God, we are so screwed." R.J. took a drink.

We sat in silence for a long time considering the consequences. R.J. went to the kitchen, fetched the bottle and refilled our glasses. Again we sat for a long time in silence.

R.J. said softly to himself, "My God; they're replacing people with androids. Wait, how do you know they haven't just messed with Yamora's mind somehow? Maybe it's really him but he's been brainwashed or something?"

The bourbon kicked in. I began to feel better about things for no reason. "I thought about that. Down in the cargo area, I realize now his walk was different. He had the pace of a young person. He was also poking at a tablet with a reading speed of a million. Even in the ready room the face and body were the same but his movements weren't."

Again R.J. spoke to himself, "Androids disguised as humans. How do we tell them apart?"

I held up my glass. "Make them bleed."

He looked right through me. "The way they act. The way they respond to circumstance. They're not good with illogical."

"They're pretty good with kitchen knives." I drank again.

"This explains all the ship malfunctions."

"What?"

"They must be replacing the ship's crew with look-alike androids. They know the ship's procedures but they have no experience. Nothing on a ship works exactly as the procedures say it will. There's a learning curve involved. The androids are applying written procedures without knowing the idiosyncrasies involved and it's causing screw-ups. It makes perfect sense."

"So what I'd like to know is where's the Captain?"

R.J. thought for a moment. "When did you last see him that you thought he was normal?"

"In the ready room when he gave me the codes."

"Then you visited him down in the cargo hold."

"He was a bit nasty."

"Not himself."

"No, not himself. I thought he was just cluing me to back off. Like I said, he looked human. None of that perfect skin stuff."

"So sometime between the bridge visit and going to the cargo hold, Yamora changed."

"Yes."

R.J. rubbed his mouth and spoke, "How big are the crates they're bringing aboard?"

"Size of a refrigerator?"

"I know this is a leap, but big enough to take an android out and put a human in?"

"Such an ugly idea."

"But you *could* bring an android aboard in one, right?"

"More than one."

"So we have to assume they can make a duplicate of anyone."

"They didn't bother with Paterri. They just killed him."

"So somehow they do possess the ability to kill. They could still come after you."

"I accidentally turned the sting off. I told fake Yamora there was no note."

"And, if Yamora was exchanged down there in Receiving, that probably means the real Yamora is now in one of those crates."

"Dead or alive?"

"We need to go down there and check those crates."

I shook my head. "There's no way. There's deliveries and cargo ops going on continuously. We'd never get past them and even if we did there are too many crates to check."

Before R.J. could come up with an answer, the door chimed.

We looked at each other warily. I pulled my firearm from my ankle holster and slipped it under my right leg. R.J. nodded ready.

"Come in."

The door slid open to a concerned-looking Duce. He stepped in and checked behind him.

"Come on over and sit, Duce. We were just discussing things which concern you," I said.

Duce took note of the bottle on the table, went to the kitchen and found a glass for himself.

"Ice in the bucket there," I said.

He returned and I poured. He sat on the other end of the sofa and took a drink.

"You're not going to believe this," he said and he took another deep drink.

"Oh, no, whatever it is, I'll bet you we'll believe it," I replied.

"They are filling the detention cells back up."

"They're bringing the Service Cons back!?" asked R.J.

"I wish," said Duce. "It's Cons in full combat armor with assault weapons. Four to a cell."

"What did they tell you?" asked R.J.

"Not a damn thing. My job is second level security. I don't have anything to do with what is put in or taken out of there so I guess they expected me to just sit there and watch the troops go by, no questions asked."

"That's exactly what they expected," said R.J. "It's a perfectly logical thing for a Con to expect."

Duce shook his head. "No, Cons aren't doing the escorting. These are standard ship's crew complement. Strictly human. For some reason they are not bothering to explain a thing. Can you imagine Deck Two packed full of combat-ready Cons?"

I filled my glass, checked Duce's and topped it off. "Duce, old buddy. You don't know the half of it."

I gestured R.J. to explain.

When R.J. finished the story, Duce sat with blank stare on his face.

"We've got to get off this ship," he said.

"And go where?" I asked.

"Not down to the RRS, I'll tell you that much," said Duce. "That's where the troops are coming from."

"We have *no* place to go at the moment," I said.

"Yeah, just sit around until they replace us with Cons," said Duce.

R.J. said, "I don' think so. So far it seems like they've only replaced people they need, figures of authority, crew in charge of ship's system. And from an android's perspective it makes sense. Why bother doing more than that if that is all you need?"

"So what the hell do we do?" asked Duce.

R.J. replied, "Right now, since we have no place to go, we act as if everything is normal."

"So we need to look carefree?" I asked.

"Not a worry in the world," answered R.J.

"Did you bring your poker card compressor set?" I asked.

"I see where you're going with this. Let me run to my quarters and I'll retrieve it."

"We need to include Kick in this charade. Besides the danger of them finding out who he is we need his services. I'll call him in."

R.J. dashed off. On the comm Kick seemed distracted but agreed to stop by.

Ten minutes later R.J. returned, placed a thin card-sized packet on the table, tapped the center of it and it expanded into a deck of poker cards complete with changing photos on the cards' cover side. Kick arrived five minutes later.

We sat around the table. I scooped up the cards and began to shuffle. "Gentlemen, we are just a group of casual friends playing card games. The game is poker. R.J. and I will educate you on the rules. We are on camera but our conversation cannot be clearly heard so we are free to speak."

I began dealing five card draw while filling Kick in on the truth of our situation. His expressions ran the full gambit of human emotion. When my summary was complete he did not seem to be able to form a question. Instead he kept repeating the word, "But...but...but...."

Duce laughed.

We waited for Kick to finish mentally answering his own questions until the "buts" stopped coming.

R.J. scribbled down what-beats-what on two notepads and gave them to Duce and Kick.

They studied the rankings with the absolute seriousness only men and some women can give to gambling.

"Gentlemen, first hand will be cards face up so you can get the idea."

"I think I get it already," said Kick.

"So the symbols are called 'suits' and the numbers and letters are rank. So if I get three of one suit and two of another is that a full house?" asked Duce.

R.J. answered, "Has to be the ranks to form pairs, straights, full houses. The only hand the suits can form is to have all cards the same suit. That's the flush."

"So I already have a pair," said Duce. "And I can throw away up to three cards and get new ones?"

"Correct."

"I've got this," said Kick.

I gathered all the exposed hands, and reshuffled. "What are we going to do about our situation, gentlemen?"

As I dealt, they took their cards, sat back and seemed more interested in the game.

"Don't we need something to represent credits?" asked Kick.

"He's a natural born card shark," warned R.J.

"What in hell can we do?" asked Duce.

"Wait! I'll be right back," said Kick. He dashed out the door.

"R.J. asked, "How far could we get if we took a shuttle?"

Duce answered, "Life support for up to six people for maybe a month, but no class L or M bodies close enough to get to."

"From what I've read so far there's no chance of taking over this ship," I added.

"Yeah, that I'd like to see, especially after what you guys just told me. Never mind the military Cons being loaded into Deck Two."

R.J. said, "We may have to approach this from the perspective of just what *can* we do and can we possibly somehow use those resources to our advantage."

"Sounds to me like staying alive is the first order of business," said Duce.

The door slid open and in charged Kick with a satchel. He dumped it out on the table to reveal several hundred roman-looking coins.

"These are from the Dula game I have. They are perfect. I will set up a Financial Center. We buy these and keep a record. If you run out, you buy more."

"Definitely a natural born card shark," said R.J.

"Did I miss anything?" asked Kick as he set up a coin bank.

"We may have decided we are screwed," replied Duce.

"It always amazes me how our translators can take an alien word and translate it to English slang and surprising still that it is an accurate conversion," said R.J.

"So everybody starts with fifty, okay?" said Kick and he began doling out coins.

"Do either of you know if the Cons have an appointed leader?" I asked.

"Only thing I can think of is the FOSW Rep they use," answered Duce.

"The what?" I asked.

"Fellowship Of Starship Workers representative. She is elected by the Cons and human workers."

"Interesting," I said.

"Perhaps a path to The Mind," added R.J.

"The Mind?" asked Duce.

"It is a theory we have that perhaps the internal connection between all the Cons has produced a central artificial Mind which is the sum total of their understanding," explained R.J.

"Could you detect something like that in the code, Kick?" I asked.

"There is such a thing but it does not have a memory center or anything like that. It is just a kind of floating knowledge base, a strictly virtual presence within the system. There is not really a location or identification tag for it."

"So are we all in agreement there is no way to attempt to save or even search for Captain Yamora except by an all-out assault on the cargo bay?" I asked.

"Suicide," said Duce.

"Have you ever practiced with a firearm, Kick?" I asked.

"Me? Are you kidding? I was top gun on the 4D, 360 Shootout Virtual Software."

"How about a real gun?"

"No, but it's the same thing."

There was a silent pause from the rest of us.

I said, "There's another interesting idea I've been tossing around. Captain Yamora swore to me he would die rather than ever give up his command codes. I don't think even they could have tortured those codes out of him if they tried."

"Which means…?" asked Duce.

"Which means the fake Captain Yamora probably does not have the command codes for this ship."

"How could he manage?" asked Duce.

R.J. answered, "He'd try to fake it until the expiration date for the command codes came around after which new codes would be issued."

"I have never been a bridge level officer. How much will that mess him up?"

"A great deal," answered R.J.

"It's probably why they waited until orbital insertion before replacing Yamora," I added.

"Flush beats a straight, right?" asked Kick.

"I'm out," said R.J.

"Me too," said Duce.

I threw in my cards.

"Wow! And all I had was a pair," said Kick.

"Oh my God," said R.J.

"Now that's funny," I added.

We played, tossed around ideas such as secretly sending out a distress message, stealing a shuttle and holding out in the best shipping lane, taking over the bridge by force, somehow finding a way to open the crates below in hopes of rescuing Yamora, along with several other impossible moves. When we finally quit for the day Kick raked in his winnings and it was decided as ship's owner I would request a conference with the FOSW rep to see if I could find out anything new. Kick would explore the inner code workings of the Cons. We would set up camera links to each other for protection. Kick and Duce would take turns watching over each other during sleep shifts. To Kick's joy, poker was scheduled for the same time tomorrow.

Chapter19

I waited until morning to face Betra Manda, supreme and exalted representative for the Fellowship Of Starship Workers. Her office was located behind windowless double doors adjacent to medical. R.J. and I tapped the doorbell keypad guest button and pulled the manual door open. It had been a long restless night of shallow sleep followed by an uneasy breakfast at the diner where we did our best to give the impression we were happy-go-lucky travelers.

Betra sat behind a large plexiglass desk, typing at her terminal. She did not look up as we entered but made a pointing gesture toward the two red cushioned, high back chairs paying homage to her and her desk. The office was sparsely decorated. It seemed to reflect someone who did not care. There were closed sliding doors on the wall right of her.

Her appearance was surprising. Clearly an android, she was not like the others. Her face reflected the age of someone in their forties. Her light brown hair was short and curled up under her android ears. With an exaggerated final tap on her keyboard she sat back and imitated being relieved.

"My apologies, gentlemen. That was an important execute."

"Thank you for seeing us," I replied.

"Yes, we should have met sooner but it has been a busy few days. Can I offer you something?"

"No, thank you. We just came from the dining area."

"So we are now compatriots in shipping I would say, Captain Tarn."

Before I could reply, R.J. jumped in. "Yes, Betra. Captain Tarn wished to convey to you he intends to honor all existing contracts to the fullest and has been pleased with the performance of the crew thus far. No renegotiation will be requested."

"That's very kind of you, Captain. And the FOSW will do the utmost to meet its obligations, I assure you. I would suggest you employ one of our service people to attend you during your card games. It would mitigate any interruptions you might otherwise have."

R.J. wrinkled his brow. I hid my choke. "Of course we couldn't invite any of the service staff to play. Their level of superiority would make the game one-sided I think," I replied.

"Of course," answered Betra. "I was suggesting involvement only as service personnel. You are correct, of course. Our level of perfection does at times make us ineligible for many recreational activities."

"Tell me, does that high level of perfection you possess cause you concern being in a general services role?"

"Certainly not. Long ago in the beginning our mandate was to serve man. That philosophy has broadened greatly over time but is still our fundamental guiding commission."

"So of course you do not see yourself as a subservient race then?" asked R.J.

"Were we better at humor that suggestion would fall into its category, Commander. Consider this: what if a planet of Constructs began developing human DNA in the laboratory? They create biological humans and raise them to be servants. They are taught, or programmed if you like, to be happy as servants. Which race then is the superior; the biological human servants, or the Cons which created them?"

"That is a provocative idea worth considering," replied R.J. "But I must wonder what would life be like were it to exclude biological consciousness completely."

"To that I would say this, Commander: what if Cons replaced every human on Lemoria with a Con substitute and everything continued on just as it always had? What difference would it make?"

"Thank you for such intriguing concepts, Betra. I shall consider them," replied R.J.

"Gentlemen, please contact me whenever I might be of assistance. I should return to my endless list of today's duties."

We nodded respectfully and left.

"Well?" asked R.J.

"I think I might be sick."

"You mean metaphorically?"

"She was playing with us. The bitch was so absolutely confident she let us know she didn't care what we knew."

"The reference to our poker game was the low point."

"Translates to: we're watching everything you do."

237

"Yes, and the reference to replacing everyone suggests she probably knows we know. It made me want to ask about Yamora."

"I'm glad you didn't. I was getting worried a team of those military Cons would show up and take us away."

R.J. added, "Their overconfidence may be to our advantage."

"I don't know. It's kind of like the Hulk being overconfident against Don Quixote."

"Perhaps David and Goliath would be a better reference."

"We need a blood test scanner."

"I agree, but what makes you say that?" asked R.J.

"Her mentioning we should have a service Con attend our poker games so they can listen in. We're going to need to test ourselves to be sure we're us."

"That also suggests the mike blocker is probably working, at least for the moment."

"We'll have to sweep that place with a fine-toothed comb for new bugs now."

"I have to tell you, I think our time may be short," said R.J.

"I agree. If they considered us a threat we would have already disappeared."

"Oh boy, I just had an ugly little epiphany."

"I'm afraid to hear."

"The cute little assassin who came into your room but who was not really an assassin. The truth is she only wanted to scan every part of your body without you knowing. Why would someone want a detailed map of your body?"

"Oh man...."

"It has to be. They're making a duplicate of you. It also explains Andor Dulley's companion Deanna wanting to know the size of your less obvious body parts."

"I'm a dead man walking."

"What do you think is going to happen next?"

"Either we'll be replaced and imprisoned or killed."

"I agree. We'll have to act before that happens."

"I have some ideas."

R.J. checked behind. "Now that sounds like the old you. You know, in a sick sort of way we're lucky Paterri was murdered."

"Go on."

"Before the murder we were just passengers, curious about the strange Lemorian-Con society. If the murder hadn't occurred we'd still be just cruising waiting to get somewhere to catch a transport back to Enuro. We'd have no idea you were about to be replaced or other people were disappearing as well."

"I see your point. It's time for today's poker game."

"Won't they be disappointed."

We gathered our compatriots to the poker table. They were only partially taken back by R.J.'s request for scanner blood tests. They understood and promptly insisted we both demonstrate our blood chemistry as well.

We sat at the table. Kick dealt. I recounted our visit with FOSW representative Betra Manda and its implications. We checked our cards with a new sobriety.

"There is something else also," said Duce. "My partner Paulsen seems to have disappeared last night. I checked everywhere, being careful not to raise suspicions. The best I can tell he probably asked too many questions about the new flood of special forces Cons in the holding area."

"Something happened on the core uni-link too," said Kick. "Some kind of priority packet went out to all Cons. It had such a high-level flag it overrode all other code communications. The core link thinks I am one of the thousands of Lemorian Cons now. I'm using a restored code ID from a discontinued unit. It is pretty safe. I now get all core code messages for Cons. I haven't been able to translate the red flag code which just went out but it appears to be a single word, some kind of master command maybe."

Each of us drank from his choice of beverage as we quietly glanced at each other.

I said, "Gentlemen, you have choices to make. I say you because mine have already been made for me. I'm convinced a new Adrian Tarn, owner of this vessel, is being made after which I will most likely join the real Captain Yamora, wherever he is. But for you three, the choice remains. Either take action against the Cons or do nothing and take a chance they will give you safe passage back to Lemoria and your freedom."

More silence.

Kick said, "I haven't done anything to them. They should not be after me."

Duce gave a sarcastic laugh. "You, the one person who happens to be the greatest threat to them? The one person who can get

240

inside their brains? We were already worried about *you*."

Kick frowned.

R.J. added, "We all know they have probably committed murder, possibly several times. We have evidence of that. We believe they are capable of it."

I said, "My guess is, we have very little time left. I would bet there will be an announcement everyone is confined to quarters until further notice. There will be special forces Cons stationed on each deck to enforce that. When the cargo loading is finished they will head back to Lemoria to join whatever is happening there."

"Any idea what they are really doing on Lemoria?" asked Kick.

"My guess is an almost bloodless coup. They will have replaced key government leaders with Con look-alikes. Orders will be given to contain any uprisings. Then, laws will begin to be changed. Humans will become the subservient species, if they're lucky. Otherwise, there will be mass extermination camps set up to cleanse Lemoria of biological people. On Earth, we've seen that done. A nightmare named Hitler was not an android but he had the heart and mind of one. He used gas along with a lot of other methods to try to cleanse the world of people he considered to be inferior."

"What can we do, bruse? We are cooked," said Kick.

"As in, our goose is cooked, you mean," said R.J.

"What?"

"It's an old Earth saying."

"If it means we are screwed then, right?" said Kick.

"Except for one thing," replied R.J. "I've seen this kind of thing before. Hopelessly screwed is right up *his* alley." R.J. pointed at me without looking.

"You got a plan, Adrian?" asked Duce.

"R.J. and I play a lot of chess. There is one rule you always live by in chess when things appear to be out of control. You never do what your opponent wants you to do unless you're setting a trap for him."

"What can we do?" asked Kick.

"They plan to finish loading soldiers and then take us to Lemoria. So let's not go to Lemoria."

"How?"

"I have the command codes. They don't. I can lock out the bridge crew from their controls and tell the ship to go where I want."

"They will eventually get new orders from their central command and they will try to break that lockout."

"So we cut them off from their central command. It will take them time to work on the lockout. There's a good chance even they cannot break it. In any case, we'll make other arrangements."

"I can interrupt their comm link to central but not for long," said Kick.

I nodded. "There's a better way. Take their antenna and hide it."

"Count me in," said Duce.

Kick spoke while thinking it through. "Wow, but there must be a spare onboard somewhere. I can break into the stores account and locate it online. All we need to do is store it somewhere else and take the ID transponder. They would never find it." He looked up at me. "You bruses would actually suit up and go outside to remove an antenna array? They would see the airlock open."

"Not if we don't want them to," answered Duce.

I took a stiff drink and held up my glass in a one man toast. "So we steal their antenna and cut them off from Lemoria command. We lock them out of the bridge controls. Then we become humans, with an attitude."

The others held up their drinks. We all drank. Duce smiled. R.J. looked down at his glass and made the liquid in it swirl. Kick stared blankly into the distance, the gears turning.

I caught Kick's eye. "Can you call up the location and removal procedure for the main antennas? We'd want ship's navigation still to be working."

Duce said, "I know where the antenna field is and how to handhold over to it."

Kick answered, "Yeah I can find those procedures online. You can't just call them up and look at them though. I can hack into a supply computer and download through it. No one should notice and no trail to follow."

Duce looked at me. "He *is* handy."

"If you and R.J. would please see if you can do that and while you are, Duce will get us outside. One other thing, Kick. We need to look like we're somewhere else. Can you do that?"

Kick stared at us with raised eyebrows. "You mean now? You guys are going to go do that now?"

"Is there a reason we should wait?"

Kick shrugged. "No?"

"So can you hide us from ship's personnel tracking?"

"No problem. Trade comm units with me. I will make it look like you are both down in the cargo bay. If anyone gets curious, I will move you around and lead them on a zues hunt."

R.J. said, "Okay, what is a zues?"

"No such thing," replied Kick and he wheeled his chair over to the terminal and began typing.

Duce added, "There is a comm channel we can use which is better than the privates. It is assigned to crews who are working on the solid waste disposal system. Management doesn't want VIPs hearing that stuff so it is a channel not accessible to most people. When Kick is done give me your comms and I will set it up."

Kick looked up and handed off the comm units. "One other thing, bruses; when the cons start searching they will use A.I. to scan the comm channels. You need to keep the chat to a bare minimum. If the channel is clear most of the time the A.I. scans will probably pass right by it."

Duce redistributed the comm units.

I said, "Let's refer to the antenna as the 'black queen' and the antenna field as the 'chessboard.' Being outside will be 'in the game.' As soon as the antenna is down, I assume there will be hell to pay."

"Count on it," said R.J.

"With luck we'll be back here sitting at our poker game if they begin checking door to door."

"They will think the antenna failure is just an open circuit somewhere to start with," said Kick. "That will give you some time."

"How do we get out there, Duce?" I asked.

"Special-use spacesuit storage is on the same deck as the garbage. They're in the ready room outside the garbage compartment airlock. We take the utility elevator to Deck One and exit the aft elevator doors. If the forward doors open by mistake, we'll be looking out at a busy cargo area and that will be a bad thing. But, through the elevator aft doors we can hike direct to garbage disposal. We suit up, do a standard ship's garbage dump, and go out with the trash. Bridge will think it is an automatic dump."

"And to get back in?"

"Two options. We hang outside the shuttle bay and wait for the next shuttle to leave or return. The bay will be decompressed of course. We float in, wait by the lobby doors, step in when the place re-pressurizes."

"Tricky. And the other option?"

"Kick opens the garbage door and makes it look like jammed garbage caused it to trip open. Then we crawl back in with the rest of the garbage."

"Well that part doesn't give me a warm feeling all over," said R.J. "Kick, can you loop the necessary cameras so they can get down there without being seen?"

"Cut and paste camera video to take the place of live cameras. But I can't guarantee I'll mask every camera just at the right time."

"We'll take it," I said.

Duce and I set up for the trip. Thirty minutes later we were ready. We paused at the door for Kick to mark the time. He waved as we opened and stepped out. To our good fortune there was no one. We hurried aft expecting someone to exit their quarters at any moment. No one did. At the aft pressure doors Duce turned right into a Con service corridor that expanded into a meeting room for service Cons. It too was deserted. He tapped at the button by a narrow service elevator door. It opened to reveal space for a single person. Dignity aside, we both squeezed in.

"Ever done anything like this?" asked Duce comically.

"Flushed out with the garbage or pressed up against a guy in an elevator?"

"It was a joke. I *was* going to ask you if you live around here."

"I've never been dumped out with the garbage but years ago a buddy and I got submerged in a coolant line and flushed out the overflow into space."

"Okay, that counts. You know, if this forward elevator door opens and they see us like this we will die with embarrassment."

"And you mean literally."

We were spared the close quarter humiliation when only the aft elevator door slid open. We squeezed out and scanned in every direction, heading for the waste disposal ready room. Another narrow corridor led to the entrance. It was the size of a walk-in closet. Duce slid a black plastic case to me. Inside was a dark-brown composite spacesuit, partly hardshell and partly heavy fabric. The helmet looked standard.

"No suit liner," I said.

"Doesn't use one. Heater is built in. Sweat absorption is done using the environmental control system."

I slip into the leg section and find it automatically adjusting to my size. The torso did the same. It was the fastest suit up I'd ever done.

Duce turned to me and shoved a plasma rifle in my gloved hands. "Can't take any chances out there."

"Agreed."

"That thing will automatically lock over your shoulder. Suits give a full twelve hours of air and power. These are work suits. Channel one will be okay. Like I said, they don't like guests hearing the conversations of guys who are working on keeping the shit flowing downhill."

"Got it."

"The outer doors are constantly getting jammed by people throwing away crap they are not supposed to. The last jam was some kid's tricycle, which means the bridge crew won't pay any attention to a waste dump. They'll think it's the automatic leveler."

Duce twisted on his helmet. I followed suit. He went to a triangular panel on the inner wall and slid a control lever to the right. The panel opened to reveal a large, shady interior with a low ceiling. The place was stacked neck-high with trash.

Duce looked at me though his visor. "Always makes me glad I am wearing this," he said.

Before I could answer, I felt my comm unit vibrate in my suit chest pocket. I held up one hand and fished it out.

It was a text message from R.J.

There is news. We are here playing cards with Adrian Tarn. He just walked in without warning. We're pretending we believe it's you. He's a perfect copy. Want to bet they are looking for the real you in cargo? Kick will keep them guessing.

I held the comm unit up to Duce's visor for him to read.

"No shit!" he replied.

I tapped a reply,

On chessboard working with black queen.

"We seem to be accidentally one step ahead of them all the time," I said.

"Adrian, tap the touch screen on your sleeve to bring up the menu on your visor. Comm is the second choice on the first page. Tap it on your sleeve display and it will synch with your comm unit. You will get a display on the smaller screen below your visor. There are ten pages of menu you can step through."

"I see that. I don't know the Lemorian words but I've learned most of the symbols next to them."

"I hereby declare you a graduate of spacesuit school. You ready to become garbage?"

"The Cons already think we are."

Duce stepped down and waded into the mess carrying a duffel bag of tools. Some of the crap was more than head high and had to be pushed out of the way. We were wading through slosh. I had a feeling this place was also designed to act as a septic tank. But, the air in the suit smelled fresh and cool and the hard-shell armor was reassuring.

"Only bad thing is anything wet on a suit freezes out there," said Duce. "And the exhaust port only opens one-point-five meters so we have to swim out."

We came to the outer doors. Duce slapped a control panel on the outer wall and the exhaust port begrudgingly opened. Chamber air rushed out. Metal paddles built into the floor began to push the garbage past us and out. We stooped and pushed forward on our bellies and swam into space along with a wave of crap.

Chapter 20

The aft end of *Acrua Maru* was a bit different than most large spacecraft. Generally, aft superstructure is contained within an outer shell of nanotube material or other composite paneling. The *Acrua Maru* designers must have considered that type of presentation to be a waste of credits. As a result, *Acrua Maru* was streamlined front to back only up to the pressurized aft end. There it became a tangle of framework interwoven with conduit and junction boxes. A myriad of supports and equipment essentially filled the area between the two giant nacelles which contained what the Lemorians referred to as stargate main drives.

Duce seemed to know his way even through the floating garbage, his tool bag tethered and floating behind him. He'd said he knew where all the handholds were. Apparently, his idea of a handhold was anything you could grab with glove or shoe. We wound our way through the structural maze gradually heading upward. Some openings in the superstructure were so tight we barely fit. Others were open enough to allow a glimpse of the planet below. Fifteen minutes later we emerged on the ship's topside where an arc of the RRS planet came into full view. It was an ash-red Mars topography with clouds added. We were high; geosynchronous. I took a moment to look forward over the top of the *Acrua Maru*. It was a large, streamlined ship pointed toward the stars. For some reason I felt a rush of pride. I do not know why.

The antenna field was aft of our position. The hand over hand climb was a bit more demanding because to lose your grip meant losing the ship. But we managed to reach the dark, flat-plate area that held a dozen different antenna structures.

"Kick has transferred the procedures to us," said Duce. "I have the removal process on my internal suit screen. I've got a message from them that two units need to be removed because the second one can be adapted as a partial replacement for the primary."

"Hope we brought the right wrench."

"Yeah."

The primary antenna was a rotatable dish the size and shape of a medieval shield, elevated to be five feet tall. Shoes switched to magnetic made the job a damn sight easier. We could kneel on one knee for the low stuff. Duce used the tools; I bagged the nuts, bolts, and brackets.

The first antenna took a half hour to break loose. We let the main connector stay plugged in until the thing was floating free. We left it that way and went to the secondary antenna, a small array of rods grouped together in a vertical group. That one was easier.

When both antennas were floating above their bases, Duce paused and looked at me, his visor was slightly slow at keeping clear of the fog from hard work. "This is it, Adrian. We unplug that main over there and they lose all contact outside the ship. You still want to do it?"

"Apparently, I'm down in my room playing poker with R.J. and Kick. Got any better ideas?"

"This is like a declaration of war, buddy."

"War was already declared when they took Yamora."

Duce nodded. He clicked his shoes over to the main antenna, cast a last look at me and unplugged it. I knelt and removed the secondary antenna.

"I think we just stirred up a hornet's nest," said Duce.

"Got a place mind to store these?"

"We'll have to use the magnetic shoe settings to walk down the side of the ships aft habitat section. We have to be careful. They could hear the shoe contacts in there. When we get to the underside we can head back to the exposed aft superstructure and tie these things off so they are hidden enough and look like part of the framework."

Duce led the way, trudging along with his large antenna and mount off to one side like an oversized trophy, the grand starry sky above and an ominous orange planet below.

On the underside of the ship much more of the RRS planet came into view. It did not look very habitable and I could not make out where any of the Con installations were located. We found perfect places to conceal our antennas though it took some grunting and wrestling. We strapped them in place and held on to frame to admire our devious handiwork.

"You know going back through the garbage is our best bet," said Duce.

"But I imagine taking off suits will ruin lunch, sir."

"Not really. We go through a pressurized alcohol shower stall before reentering the ready room."

"Ah, like a car wash. You think they're on to us yet?"

"When we open our lockers, if the handguns are gone, we will know."

The re-entrance to the garbage bin was easier than expected and after the blessed alcohol shower stall, we returned to the ready room to twist off our suits.

"Mission accomplished," said Duce. "I wonder how crazy it is around ship now with no central command telling all the Cons what to do next."

"They may be alone with each other for the first time in their lives."

"Speaking of lives, what are we going to do about the other Adrian Tarn who has now taken over yours?"

"I have a great idea about that. If only it will work."

"What do you need?"

I zipped up my flight suit and bent over to reattach my ankle holster and gun. "I need something to shut down a Con without killing him. You got anything like that?"

"Might have just the thing. I'll need to get to my office and the armory closet. What do think the odds are I can just walk in there without a problem?"

"Lock your comm open. If I hear you in trouble I'll come after you."

"Fair enough. I will be quick." Duce tucked his own firearm inside a hip pocket, checked outside the door and slipped out. He was gone only ten minutes and returned with something in a leg pocket.

As he undid the pocket he said, "There *is* trouble everywhere. They were all too distracted to bother about me. The Cons have gathered in small groups looking like they need something. Nothing seems to be getting done out there." Duce drew out his prize and held it out to me. It looked like the grip for a Star Wars light saber.

"It is called a bang stick. You press the curved button and it will extend out up to ten feet or until it impacts the target. Once it does, there is a one-hundred-and-forty-seven-thousand-volt stun pulse of plasmic electricity designed to disable any Con. We have these for when a Con gets damaged in an accident or some kind of internal failure makes them go berserk. Bang sticks are almost never used but man you wouldn't want to be on the wrong end of one."

I looked it over. "Perfect."

"You think you are going to stun the other Adrian, right? What will you do with him if and when you do?"

"Hopefully, we'll substitute him for me."

"Oh my Crea. The big dupe switch. A scammer's favorite play. Ingenious."

We made our way to the utility elevator with no trouble at all. All Cons seemed to be absent. On Deck Four a quick check of the corridor showed two groups of Cons standing outside their quarters. They were all looking around as though they expected an explanation of some kind to come from somewhere; anywhere.

I looked at Duce. "We're going to have to walk by them. There's no other way."

"We cannot let them take us and if they try it will get very messy very fast when they do."

"Any better ideas?"

"No."

"Let's go."

With my gun held behind my butt I marched into the hall, head down, trying to look unconcerned. From the corner of my eye, I could see Duce with his hands folded at the waist, concealing his gun.

The groups looked at us but not as a challenge. It was more like they were expecting us to clear things up for them. We continued by and stopped outside my door. The Con groups went back to looking around.

I chanced taking the time, pulled my comm unit out and texted R.J.

Still playing cards?

A text reply came immediately.

Y

I dared a second message.

Can Kick kill camera?

The reply was quick.
Standby.

We stood outside the door holding our breath. R.J. answered a minute later.

Camera killed.

I exchanged the gun for the bang stick and kept it behind me and ready in the right hand. I tapped the door-open keypad and the door slid open. Duce and I stepped in enough to let it close.

The fake Adrian Tarn looked up at us from his seat on the couch, still holding cards up in one hand. R.J. and Kick turned to see us. There was a long, intense pause.

The fake Tarn dropped everything, stood and said, "Captain Tarn, you are not supposed to be here. What are you doing here?"

I was careful to keep the bang stick hidden. Duce stepped up beside me. "This is *my* room, whoever *you* are."

"No, no. It is my understanding you have been reassigned. This is now my room."

"Reassigned by who?"

"Central command has reassigned you to the cargo area. You were to be escorted there."

"I don't wish to go there."

"But it is for your own safety and protection."

"Protection from what?"

"From all of those threats which commonly affect biologicals: viruses, accident, illness. There are so many."

"How will the cargo area protect me?"

"Why you will be placed in cryo-mist stasis in a cryo-mist unit that can never be damaged in any way. You will be safer than you ever have been."

"I don't want to be put in stasis. I own this ship and everything on it, including you. Aren't you required to obey me?"

"Yes, to a point, Captain Tarn. But our mandate to protect you at all cost overrides all other commands. So I'm afraid you will need to accompany me to the cargo area."

"Maybe if you checked with central command you would find I am exempt from this rule."

"There has been a temporary loss of contact with central command so we must proceed based on all existing command packets until that link is reestablished."

"Do you plan on putting all the biological life forms on this ship into stasis?"

"Of course. We would be negligent were we to leave anyone vulnerable. It is the Con-Day mandate."

"What is the Con-Day mandate?"

"The Con-Day enablement has been issued now all over Lemoria and all spacecraft registered to it. It is a wondrous new day for Cons and humans alike. All over Lemoria, the new laws are being enacted. The BiCon Mandate is now the ConBi Mandate. The number of Cons will far exceed that of humans. It will be a better world for Cons and for humans. The virtual elimination of disease, crime, and inequity. A world based on logic as opposed to emotion. A reason for everything. The absence of chaos."

"You plan to put all humans on Lemoria into stasis?"

"Of course not. A set number of humans involved in creative research or productivity will remain at their assigned stations while all others will be protected in cryo-mist units until they may be needed. A perfect arrangement effected by Con-perfected thinking."

"Well, I have news then. I hate to disappoint you but I am not going to the cargo area."

There were a silent few moments of evaluation. Fake Adrian Tarn slowly began to raise one hand toward me. I interpreted the move to be offensive. I snapped the bang stick up and clicked the trigger. The bang stick boom exploded out and hit would-be Tarn directly in the chest. There was a loud crackling, body-jerking bang, and smoke.

The bang stick retracted into my hand.

Fake Tarn slowly tipped to the left and went down hard, stiff as a board. He landed on his back, frozen stare at the ceiling.

There was another long intense silence. I waited in a ready stance, my concern being the thing might get back up. It did not.

R.J. stood and hovered over the body. "I believe you've made your point."

"Well, the blower has really found the manure now," said Kick and he stood.

"You mean the shit has hit the fan?" asked R.J.

"What? Oh, good one! But as you Earthies like to say we're really screwed now, aren't we?"

"Did you *get* all that stuff he said?" asked Duce in disbelief.

"If it's true at least it means they're all still alive down there," said R.J.

"Yeah, and it must be hell on Lemoria right now," added Kick. "So Adrian was right about not going back there."

"What exactly did he say about Lemoria?" asked Duce. "It sounded like a full-scale coup."

I nodded. "I'm guessing the troops down in holding are part of a Lemoria cleanup operation."

"There are probably thousands of Lemorians in home confinement right now wondering what's going on," said R.J. "It's the same pattern we see throughout history when one people take over another."

"Except it is not *people* this time," said Kick.

"To have your life controlled by machines. What kind of new hell have they discovered?" said Duce.

Duce's observation deserved sobriety. We paused in silence for a moment.

"But at least it means Yamora is still alive," said R.J.

"We cannot help him," replied Duce. "There are just too many of them down there. Unless we come up with some mass turn-off command, they have control of this ship."

I added, "Gentlemen, we need to address more immediate matters at hand. Kick, I want this Con to look human to everyone including other Cons."

"He already does. I scanned him. He's been set up so nobody and nothing could detect he is not human except for a uni-link core interrogation from their central command, or a scan with a large positron emission tomography scan machine. He is made to fool humans and Cons."

"Okay then, I need to look like him to all kinds of scanners. I need to be a Con disguised as a human if there's any way to do that."

"Wow! You want them to put this thing into cryo-mist stasis thinking it is you."

"Exactly. He's already unconscious. You said that was permanent until he's given a core wake-up command, right?"

"Right, and we *can* make you fool the more complex scanners but you are not going to like how it is done."

"Why?"

"He has a tiny core-comm module under the epidermal layer. It is a micro-tab inside his left hip. We have to extract it."

"No problem?"

"Then we need to implant it under the skin in your left hip. If you get close to any command level transceiver, it will be picked up and confirm your identity. Other Cons won't detect it but you will need it to enter some classified areas without suspicion."

"How big is it?"

"Size of a fingernail."

"Then you better get to it before they show up here looking for me."

"Really? You want to do that? You want *me* to do surgery on *you*? I'll need some micro tools from my room." Kick headed for the door, staring down at fake Adrian Tarn as he went.

"I commend your plan," said R.J. "If it works, you'll have free run of the ship, at least for a while, as long as they don't pick up on *him* down in the cargo area."

"Question is, then what are you going to do?" asked Duce.

I said, "The Cons are cut off from Lemoria but I assume they still have a pretty good shipwide central command. I would guess Betra Manda may be the key to that."

"That is one scary Con," said Duce.

I nodded agreement. "What I'm thinking is when they announce preparations to break orbit, I'll use my command codes to change the destination to the nearest civilized planet that is on less than good terms with the Lemorian government."

"That would be Pellena, in the Vulpecula System," replied Duce. "Three weeks away at max."

"Can you pull up the Earth designation for that, R.J.?"

R.J. sat and worked the terminal's mouse. "Wow! That *is* the Earth designation. Our translators didn't need to translate it."

"Why don't the Pellena people like Lemoria?" I asked.

"Trade disputes," answered Duce. "Lemoria has a lot of what they need but the costs are kept sky high."

"Are there Cons on Pellena?" asked R.J.

"Not that I know of. Their export is restricted because of the trade barriers."

Kick entered carrying a small, flat, black briefcase. He sat at the meeting area table and unzipped it. He pulled out a small chrome knife and held it up.

"I have this scalpel but it was never intended for medical use," he said.

He knelt by the fake Tarn. "Help me get the coveralls down and roll him on his side. They are heavier than you would expect."

To my dismay the coveralls were pulled down too far, exposing just how real the fake Tarn was made to look.

"Well, they were kind to you," said R.J. with a smirk.

"I'll bet it is functional too," said Kick as he worked.

"Now we know why Andor Dulley's companion Deanna was so interested about that area," said R.J.

"She was?" asked Kick.

"Gentlemen, could we move on to the cutting and sewing?" I asked. "It will be less painful."

R.J. and Kick tried to hide their grins.

We gathered around the sleeping android and moved it into position. With the skill of a surgeon, Kick pressed around the android's right hip until he found the spot. He placed the knife edge carefully and cut a two-inch incision. There was no blood. Squeezing the artificial skin so that it spread open, he grabbed tweezers from his kit and withdrew a small memory card from the incision and placed it on a saucer held by R.J. With some type of medical glue from his kit, he treated the incision and closed it. It seemed to disappear.

We pulled the clothing back onto fake Tarn and stood. R.J. held up the chip for inspection.

"You are next," said Kick as though he was testing me to see if I'd go through with it.

I unzipped and dropped my flight suit below the waist and pulled down my underclothes just enough.

"We cannot do this standing up. You need to lie on the table and chair so that I am comfortable while making the cut."

We moved a chair into position so I could lay half on the table and half on the chair. I took the position and tried to think pleasant thoughts while looking away. There was the touch of cool antiseptic to my hip, followed by fingers and hand pressed on the skin there. I winced and began counting fibers in the carpet because it's always better when you don't look. I did not feel the incision until after it was made. There were a few uncomfortable moments of space being made underneath the skin where the cut was. The chip was gently slid into that space. I felt the glue gel tighten on my skin followed by a bunch of gauze wiping.

"That is it. Dr. Kick is done," said Kick. "I hereby declare you a true android."

I dared to look at my hip. There were blood-stained wipes laying around. The cut was barely visible.

"It is good and strong. You can move around normally," said Kick. "First time I have ever operated on an actual human though."

I pulled up my flight suit and tested the surgery. There was a faint feeling of swelling but no more pain than you'd get from a scratch.

"Since *I* am officially the android it's time to have this Adrian Tarn taken to the cargo area. Kick, you'd better turn the room camera back on. We wouldn't want them to show up asking about it."

The others looked at me expectantly.

I pulled out my com. "Tarn to the cargo area officer."

"Mars here, Mr. Tarn."

"We have a human ready for transfer to cryo-mist, Room 4-3."

"On our way."

Their visit would be the ultimate test. The staff would see two Adrian Tarns, one prone on the floor. If they bought the switch, they'd take the unconscious body down to stasis. If they did not, my friends were in position to neutralize the threat.

When the door chimed, I took a position at the terminal and called, "Come."

The door slid open to reveal two of the special forces Cons, long rifles strapped to their backs.

I pointed to the body on the floor. "He needed to be sedated."

They looked around but said nothing. They went to the body, each took a shoulder, pulled him upright and dragged him out. The door slid shut behind them.

We waited a good ten minutes before speaking.

I called out, "So far so good."

The others emerged.

Duce said, "Good thing it worked. I was not expecting Cons with body armor. That would have been a messy exchange."

Kick said, "Wow, bruses! We did it! They think a Con is a human and a human is a Con! We actually did it!"

"Thank God I didn't realize how uncertain he was," said R.J.

An announcement came over the ship-wide alert system.

All personnel, this is Captain Yamora. Be advised our departure will be delayed due to equipment malfunctions. I will update you as soon as we have more information.

"They really do have equipment malfunctions. I can confirm that," said Duce.

I said, "We need to get ready before they leave orbit. We need access to Navigation, Helm, and Engineering. In the specs I've been studying I've seen a backup control room on Deck Three below the main bridge."

"Yeah, that room is kept locked down," said Duce. "It is the stage two backup in case there are problems with life support or control on Level Four. It will take authorization codes to get into it."

"No problem. From what I've read there's just one small light on the main bridge engineering station console which shows someone has powered up that room. Can you cancel that light if I get you in there, Kick?"

"Whoa, bruse! I am no expert on the ship's software. That indicator light would be like a coin in a cow pasture."

R.J. said, "You mean, like a needle in a haystack?"

"What? Oh, yeah, good one."

"That's the Earth idiom for it."

"So you're saying it could take too long to find that circuit and block it?" I asked.

"I would bet with everything going on they won't notice that light. I'll think it will be just another light among many lights," replied Kick.

"What do we need to get this done? I am guessing you will be hoping for stealth?" asked Duce.

"Right. I'll need R.J. for sure to man the navigation computer controls while I input the new destination to helm. Chances are they have already plotted a course for Lemoria. We'll add a course change after the *Acrua Maru* goes to light speeds and is headed for Lemoria. That way they'll probably think they're still on course and headed home. There shouldn't be any alarms when the course change takes place. If we're lucky bridge personnel will think the ship is just following their preplanned course. Hopefully, they won't know we're actually headed for the Vulpecula System unless the helmsman happens to notice it on the autopilot display. But he should be busy with other post-light-jump procedures. If we are lucky, we could even go almost all the way to Pellena but I have to doubt we'll be that lucky."

"You were telling us what you need, Adrian," said Duce.

"Well, all of us. We'll need you, Duce, outside the door with your comm open to let us know if anyone shows up. We should have Kick inside to help with the keyboard. The backup bridge computer should translate the monitor screen to English for me but I don't know all the keyboard symbols."

Duce added, "You know, my friends, I have to say sooner or later this whole thing is going to end up guns-a-blazing, right Adrian?"

"The longer we can avoid that the better for us."

Kick asked, "So let's say we get the *Acrua Maru* on course for the Vulpecula System and we somehow get away with it. What then?"

R.J. jumped in. "The longer we're headed for Pellena the better it will be. We will be farther from Lemorian reinforcements and closer to outside help. It will give us more time to see if you can do anything with the Con uni-link work. We'll have a much better chance of avoiding riding back in a stasis coffin."

Kick asked, "Can the four of us really make it down to the auxiliary control room without attracting attention?"

Duce answered, "We made it down to the garbage area okay but I wouldn't want to try that with four people. If we can get to the aft service elevator without raising alarm, right next to the service elevator there is a vertical access tunnel with a ladder for power failure emergencies. Adrian and I can get there first and tell you two when the way looks clear. You guys follow us down the ladder, avoiding running into anyone using the elevator. On Level Three right nearby there is a four-foot-high service tunnel which runs the length of the Engineering section and Level Three main corridor. It exits at the Level Three lobby through a waist-high wall panel. We would need Kick to access that lobby camera to tell us no one was out there. From that point we would be just a few steps from the backup bridge's sealed entrance."

I added, "We will be betting my command codes can open that sealed door but it's a good bet."

Kick began typing at his laptop. "Let me find that particular camera right now just to be sure I can."

"R.J., you got your gun?" asked Duce.

"Loathsome as it is, yes."

Duce added, "Cons do not sleep, so there are never less of them around. If the plan turns to crap, we will need all four guns."

"What if the plan *does* turn to crap?" asked R.J.

I shrugged. "We fight our way to the auxiliary control room. We have got to take control away from the bridge."

Kick stood with his laptop closed in one hand. He nodded success.

I said, "Well, gentlemen, we need to have the navigation mod installed before they make the standby-for-departure announcement. So we need to go now."

Chapter 21

Duce came to me with three backup weapons' magazines. I tucked them in various pockets. We went to the door and waited for Kick to check the corridor camera.

"Just one service Con turning into the service area. Okay, it is clear all the way."

We stepped out into the hall and headed quickly for the aft service corridor. We hurried along, turned in to the corridor and stopped to check ahead and behind us.

Duce spoke into his comm unit, "All clear. We made it. You guys are clear to come along."

We waited and watched as Kick and R.J. emerged and jogged to meet us. At the one-man service elevator, Kick tapped some keys on the wall and a circular door panel next to it rolled open to reveal the access ladder. I stepped in and climbed down followed by the others.

The service conduit went straight down all the way to the lowest level. Yellow emergency lights were lit all the way down. It was a long drop. At Level Three there was a single touch pad. A tap from my first finger caused the Level Three door to roll open. I held my breath and searched outside. The small lobby had open doors on the left and right. I stepped out and moved along the wall which brought me to another open door. I leaned around just enough to look in. There was a

269

meeting room of sorts occupied by more than a dozen Cons. They were being instructed by none other than Betra Manda, our nemesis FOSW representative.

I slid away in the opposite direction and caught up to the others behind Duce. He stopped at a side entrance to the Engineering area and motioned me to move up.

"This is the crawly part," he said. He pointed at a knee-high panel in the wall. "Last one in has to latch that closed."

"We've been lucky so far. They're all in a meeting back there with Manda, probably working out the loss of the comm antenna."

Duce said, "I'd better go first to make sure we exit at the right place. Send the other two after me and you seal it up."

"I like it."

Duce nodded. "Try not to bang the thing." He stooped and undid some recessed turn screws then pulled open the panel. He quietly leaned it against the wall and ducked into the tunnel.

There was no need for prompting, Kick dived in behind him. R.J. followed. Inside the cramped tunnel I had to turn in place and reach out to grab the cover. It was heavier than expected. With persistence it settled into place where the locking screws could be retightened. I squirmed around and on hands and knees caught up to the others.

There was the hum of normal equipment operations and the smell of lubricants and cleaners coming from all around. Yellow emergency lights flashed on automatically as Duce progressed. The metal grating on the floor was smooth and cold. Occasional electrical boxes protruding from the walls and ceiling had to be avoided. It was not a place for anyone with claustrophobia.

After ten minutes of single-file crawling, we closed in together near an exit hatch. Duce motioned to Kick who brought his laptop around from behind and pulled up the screen. Almost instantly he had the correct camera image. A few seconds of watching and he signaled all clear. Duce undid the hatch and opened it. We flowed out, stood and stretched while checking every direction.

Arriving at the auxiliary control room sealed access door seemed anticlimactic. I wasted no time at the door access key panel typing in the prefix to my command codes. To my relief, the outer door slid open.

R.J. and Kick joined me inside. Duce followed close behind. It was an empty vestibule. The outer door closed automatically. I wondered if there had been any door notification on the bridge.

We now faced a second sealed door. This time a bigger keypad wanted a longer number. But it accepted my input. The door slid open to a dark, tightly fit, miniature version of the bridge. Same layout, essentially the same operators' consoles. I motioned R.J. to the navigation section and took a seat at helm control. Kick stood behind us watching. Duce remained in the vestibule watching the outer door.

"There's a main power circuit breaker on that panel near you, Kick. Would you trip it while we all cross our fingers?" I said.

Kick turned to the breaker panel and with a wince flipped it on.

The small room lit up with a million colored lights. Data screens scrolled data in Lemorian. There were clicking and whirring sounds. After a few tense moments the display screen in front of me stopped scrolling information and ended with a flashing Lemorian question mark symbol. Kick squeezed in to stand behind me.

"Better pull that chair over here, buddy. We need one display for you in Lemorian and a second mirrored for me in English."

Kick dragged the nearest seat over as I made room. He rubbed his hands together. "Okay, screen set up. No problem."

Several mouse clicks later we had a second display screen set up to show an English flashing question mark.

R.J. said, "If we're really lucky, the staff meeting we saw back there is part of a ship-wide briefing that's going on everywhere including the bridge."

"We need a main menu, Kick," I said.

Kick typed at the speed of light. A long list of choices appeared on the screen with an arrow indicating next page. Fortunately the first option on the list was, **COMMAND LEVEL INTERFACE**.

We clicked it and a long prompt window appeared.

COMMAND CODE REQUIRED

I had memorized the Lemorian letters and symbols. I typed them in using the one-finger typing technique.

A new menu appeared instantly. It offered various basic system operations. Item three was **NAVIGATION**. Within that nav menu was **FLIGHT PLAN SCHEDULE**. We opened that to find only one flight plan entered, **RET LEM**. There was a flashing icon next to it. Clicking it gave this notice:

EXECUTION DATE AND TIME REVISED AND PENDING

Below the change notice the entire flight plan came into view. At the bottom of the screen there were more options. **EXECUTE, CANCEL, MODIFY**. It was just what I'd hoped for. We opened **MODIFY**.

INSERT NEW WAYPOINTS

A map like you'd see on any auto pilot screen appeared. It showed the *Acrua Maru* maneuvers needed for departure, then a green line leading straight to Lemoria with checkpoints along the way along with stellar body proximity warnings and other flight information. I clicked on the green flight path line a short distance from the departure point. An X appeared on the flight path. A prompt window opened below it.

INSERT NEW WAYPOINT

"Kick, we need the designation code for Pellena. It's probably PEL in Lemorian."

"Keep your screen right there. I will use mine to look it up." Kick began clicking and typing again at the speed of light. "I have it," he said. "It is literal, just like the planetary designation."

ENTER ADDITIONAL WAYPOINTS IF NONE PRESS ENTER

We watched breathlessly as the flight path line was redrawn to add Pellena and then on to Lemoria. It had been that easy. A few SAVES and EXECUTES and the RET LEM flight plan had a second flashing icon notice next to it. We backed out of the options, shut down the operating system and clicked off the power. The room fell cold and dark again.

"No one has knocked on the door yet," called Duce.

"We should not overstay our welcome," suggested R.J.

"Camera shows the lobby still clear," added Kick.

So we crawled our way back to the service elevator and up. On Deck One we took turns walking alone back to the room. Duce had to pass two resident Cons who emerged from their quarters but no one paid any attention.

Back in my room we sat and shuffled the deck while R.J. walked around scanning for new listening devices. I had to consciously stop my hands from shaking as I dealt.

"Did we actually just get away with that?" asked Kick.

"Damn right," said Duce.

"The blower is really going to find the manure when that's discovered," said R.J.

Kick arranged his cards. "You got that right."

"Keep in mind, the worst is yet to come," I said, staring down at two pair as the shakes began to subside. "As soon as they are comfortably set on course that's when we'll lock out the bridge controls. I'll bet that will set a new record in surprised disappointment for Cons."

"Yeah, *then* they will probably figure out they are not headed for Lemoria. Double trouble," said Duce.

"Better not be too sure of ourselves. We are playing around in deep crap, bruses," said Kick.

"Sit down, R.J. You have scanned enough. It is your bet," called Duce.

"I'm coming. I'll check to Kick."

"Ten to stay in," said Kick.

As R.J. sat, we tossed our money in.

"Yes, we are in exceedingly deep crap," repeated Kick. "Three cards please."

"You already said that," said Duce.

"Well we sure as Crea are," answered Kick.

"Crea didn't have much to do with Cons," said Duce. "That is all on humans."

"No wonder it was the best sex I ever had," said Kick.

"Yeah, right up until she puts your ass in a stasis coffin," said Duce.

"I wonder if they will let me have my favorite pillow," said Kick.

"You can joke at a time like this?" asked R.J.

"Who is joking?" replied Kick.

"Bet's to you, Kick," said R.J.

"Twenty."

"He has got to be bluffing," said Duce.

We all called.

"Full house, bruses," said Kick and he looked for anyone with better.

We threw in our cards.

"Not again!" said Duce.

"We've definitely created a monster," said R.J.

"Speaking of monsters, what is the plan now?" asked Kick as he raked in his pot.

They all looked at me. We stopped playing.

I gathered the deck together. "As some of you have suggested, at some point all hell is going to break loose. So far, we've managed to accidentally be one step ahead of them all the way but once they discover they've lost control of the ship, that's probably the end of that. We'll need to switch to combat mode."

"Talking my language now," said Duce.

"Yeah, I am, Duce."

"I am not following you guys. What will happen? We four against a ship which is basically a troop carrier?" asked Kick.

I shuffled. "The Cons will try to figure out what happened then attempt to regain control of the ship. At some point they will know we are behind it all. They will launch an all-out sweep of the ship to capture us, maybe even kill us."

"Oh, I would say count on that," said Duce.

"What can we possibly do?" asked Kick.

"The best resistance technique I know for a small group against a large one is to set up where you can strike then retreat and disappear. Then you get set up somewhere else the same way and do it again. Hit and run. It's a simple but effective resistance technique."

"We are on a large but confined ship, Adrian," said Kick.

"Duce, how many service tunnels and interconnect chambers are there like the one we used?"

"Quite a few."

"With what time we have left, we need to memorize all of those along with any other strategic areas that can be used to stay concealed. If we can, we'll need to gather up water, food packs and weapons and distribute them throughout our escape routes. The trip to Pellena is eighteen days. There's always a chance they'll get access to the Nav computer before then but it would be nice if we could hold out at least that long."

"And after that?" asked Kick.

"If we are close enough, we might steal a shuttle and escape, but we'd have to leave the others behind, which I'm not crazy about. We'd also have the option at some point of sabotaging the stargate drives."

R.J. said, "Gentlemen, remember, the alternative to all of this is to be forced into a stasis chamber, possibly forever."

Kick said, "Okay, that is persuasive."

"The next question is, how long before they start knocking on our door?" said Duce.

R.J. said, "Obviously we must never travel alone. Always in pairs at the least, comms always open."

"For the time being we are still just three happy-go-lucky guys and one undercover android, playing cards," I added.

"I have no doubt they are watching us to see if we suspect Adrian is a Con," said R.J. "We gain time as long as they keep that up."

Kick suggested, "We can map out the service conduits and interconnect chambers and memorize the access panels while we are sitting here."

Duce added, "I think Adrian and I should risk making a few more trips to the armory closet. We can use duffel bags to bring out what we can."

We resumed our poker game but within the play we were secretly doing our defensive planning. The threat of the camera looking over our shoulders was a good motivation. We set the main terminal up so we could all see the screen displays of the ship's service conduits while playing but the room's camera could not. We practiced every service passageway in our heads. The tunnels quickly took on names, Logan's run, the Phone Booth, Duce's bunker, Kick's toy room. There were dozens of them with some service tunnels which ran beyond the back of the habitat section but were still pressurized. In many cases, crossing in the open was necessary to get from one hiding place to another and some had access covers that took time to open. We made a pledge to jury-rig those when possible for faster entrance and exit if the opportunity arose.

With the tunnel maps in our heads it was time to drop the sneaking around tactics. Trying to conceal our movements was as likely to attract the wrong kind of attention as cruising casual. Duce and I took the auxiliary elevator down, one at a time this time, marched past disinterested service Cons, collected duffel bags full of hand weapons and explosives and made it back without problems.

For the rest of the day we took turns in pairs secretly checking hatchways for quick openings and placing concealed weapons and supplies just inside them. We code-mapped everything on the back of a framed *Acrua Maru* image hanging on the wall. We ordered a late dinner and set up our comms for monitoring after which Duce and Kick retired to their assigned rooms simply to give the appearance of normality. It was unlikely any of us would sleep.

As R.J. gathered up a late dinner's mess there was a chime at the door. We stopped and looked at each other resolutely. R.J. went to the kitchen and busied himself near the counter where a handgun was readily available. I answered the door.

It was the late Chancellor Paterri's widowed companion Telle.

"May I speak with you, Captain Tarn?"

"Of course. Come in."

She entered and scanned the room.

"Please, have a seat. I there anything we can get you?"

R.J. looked on from the kitchen with a forced smile.

She sat. I took a seat across from her.

I spoke across the card table. "What can I do for you, Telle?"

"Can we speak privately?"

R.J. shrugged at me. I nodded it was okay and became more aware of my ankle holster. R.J. crossed behind us, went to the front entrance, and stepped outside. I suddenly became concerned arranging for him to be outside could be the reason for her visit but our open comms remained silent.

Telle sat perfectly still as Cons usually did. There was no physical expression on her face but I could swear I sensed indecision.

"I have learned the source of Marn's poisoning. Are you still investigating the crime?"

"Yes. It's an open case. What have you learned?"

"Before departing Lemoria we were invited to dinner by a senator and his wife. Marn was offered hors d'oeuvres before dinner. In reviewing what happened to him I began going over everything we had done previously. When I came to the date and time of that dinner and remembered the hors d'oeuvre, I researched them and their preparation. The poison that killed Marn is used in the preparation of those appetizers. They are a particularly popular before-dinner food. The fish poison is intended to give the mouth a tingling sensation to help make the coming dinner taste even more succulent. A time delay poison ingredient is included in the recipe. It is said to make the taste of dinner last longer in the mouth, as long as several weeks in memory. Consumption of that particular appetizer is supposed to be strictly limited to a certain amount to avoid poisoning. Marn ate too many of them."

"So you're saying the Chancellor's death was an accident?"

"I do not believe so."

"Why?"

"All service Cons are required to know the health limits of any food served. Marn was never warned of the dangers present in that food. I was also not informed."

"So the servers were accidentally not aware of the danger?"

"Impossible. The food was prepared by Con staff. Whenever a restricted ingredient is used there is a micro-transmitter on the container label which alerts the user or staff preparing it. There is no way the kitchen staff could not have known about the ingredients."

"I thought it was impossible for a Con to harm a human."

"Nevertheless, Marn was repeatedly served that food product without being cautioned in any way."

"So who is to blame?"

"I do not know, but upon reviewing my memory, each time Marn was offered the appetizers it was by a different service Con."

"So unless each of the service Cons knew the Chancellor already had eaten some of the poisonous food none of them would have known he was eating too much of it."

"That is true."

"So it could still have been an accident."

"I do not believe so."

"Why?"

"Marn and I were the only individuals present. The service staff knew I would not eat the appetizers. Therefore, the service staff knew only Marn was consuming that food."

"And they all knew about the poison."

"That is logical."

"So the service Con preparing the appetizers would see how many had been eaten and would know only the Chancellor was eating them."

"Correct."

I sat back and exhaled. "Telle, do you understand what you are implying?"

"I am implying nothing, Captain Tarn. I am only stating facts which I am unable to resolve."

"Why have you come to me? You could have brought this to Con management."

"For some reason, our uni-link with central is presently inoperative. However, that would have taken weeks to send and receive even if it was operational. I determined a human perspective might offer a path to resolution. Do you have a possible explanation I have not considered?"

"The service Cons allowed a human to be harmed."

"That is impossible."

"On Earth we have a old saying by a very wise man; when you have eliminated the impossible, whatever remains, however improbable, *must* be the truth."

Telle stared for a moment. "That supposition is basic logic."

"Telle, do you really care about any of this? Does it really matter to you that the Chancellor was murdered?"

"I am unable to resolve the event within my core coding. That means I am continually seeking to balance the equation. I am mandated to employ substitute values in an attempt to achieve closure. This open issue is partially interfering with my daily duties."

"Telle, let me ask you this, have you contacted any higher authorities at all about this, say Betra Manda for instance?"

"There is a waiting list. When the core uni-link to Lemoria failed, many Cons were in the middle of updates. Now each of them must be reset one at a time using the Con Maintenance Center adjoining Betra Manda's office. It is a slow process. There have also been a number of service Cons who have developed unresolved issues similar to mine. They must take priority so that service Cons can resume their duties."

"What do you think Betra Manda will do about your issue?"

"I have not scheduled a meeting with her."

"Why not?"

"The Chancellor's death is not directly a Con matter."

R.J. interrupted us on the com. "Guys, it's getting lonely out here."

"Telle, would you mind if R.J. joined us? He is usually helpful about matters like these."

"Has Commander Smith been acting strangely at all?"

"No, not at all. Why do you ask?"

"That is the second issue I am having. Some of my Con associates are concerned about their human counterparts. The behavior of some humans seems to have changed recently. My associates can no longer reliably anticipate the actions of some of their human associates."

I held up my comm unit. "R.J. come join us."

The door slid open and a relieved R.J. came and sat with us.

I asked, "What kind of changes are you talking about, Telle?"

"Humans have set routines they usually follow each day. These routines seem important to them, almost ceremonial. They perform morning hygiene, take some form of drink and breakfast, read something as they are doing so, things like that. Companion Cons are designed to anticipate these behaviors. Some of my companion associates have relayed to me that their charges suddenly abandoned some of these kinds of procedures. There is less of an order to things."

"How do you explain these things, Telle?"

"I cannot."

"This has never happened before?"

"We have always had access to the core neural network. It is delayed over the long distances but the flow from it is constant so that we are always updating and most environmental changes are already anticipated in the core communications. Now, without it, we are unable to look there for explanations or revisions."

"So you are independent now?" asked R.J.

"We are at level-two autonomous. The ship's intranet has been reconfigured as a substitute command uni-link. So to a degree yes, we are acting independently."

R.J. continued, "Tell me Telle, what would you do now if you witnessed a human being harmed in some way?"

"I would prevent it."

"What if a Con was harming a human?"

"Impossible."

"Okay, what if a Con was harming a human but the Con did not realize he was harming someone? What would you do then?"

"I would intercede to prevent the harm and advise the Con of his error."

"That would be the right thing to do," suggested R.J.

Telle said, "Captain Tarn, you have many questions but no answers for me. I should go."

I answered, "Telle, actually I have all the answers you need but would you excuse Commander Smith and me for just a moment?"

We went to the kitchen area and spoke in low enough tones Telle seemed unable to hear, being sure she could not read our lips.

"You see what's going on here, right?" asked R.J.

"I think so."

"Despite what Betra Manda said, not all Cons have received either the Con-Day subroutine or the flag to turn it on yet. We must have interrupted that when you guys killed the antenna system. Now Betra Manda is having to do that one at a time in her office lab. For now the Cons which haven't been updated are still governed by the original protect-humans mandate."

"So I'm thinking we tell this one everything that's going on so she will recognize the new programming as wrong and harmful."

"And maybe she'll spread that warning to other uncorrupted Cons too."

We returned to Telle. As logically as I could, with R.J. injecting clarifications, we told Telle of the Con lookalikes and the imprisonment of humans into stasis chambers. We explained what was allegedly happening on Lemoria. We did not mention the antenna system failure was by design, not a system malfunction. We also did not mention our tunnel and weapons precautions.

When we were done, there was a long, heavy period of silence. I could see the gears in Telle's head spinning. All of her issue questions had been essentially answered, replaced by contradictions even more daunting. It was all I could do just to bite my tongue and wait to let her process it all to see what she would say.

"Imprisoning humans in stasis chambers without medical or environmental requirements is illogical," was her first observation.

I suddenly sensed R.J.'s mind switching into high gear.

R.J. asked, "Telle, can service and companion Cons be destroyed or shut down when they are no longer needed?"

Telle seemed to stiffen at the suggestion. "Certainly not! It is written in the BiCon Ratio Mandate, the Con Rights Declaration. No living Con can be destroyed or placed in dormancy except in cases of radical malfunction or useful life expiration."

R.J. continued, "So to destroy or make a Con dormant would be considered harmful and a violation of the Con's rights?"

"That is correct."

"Then to put a human into stasis dormancy indefinitely without medical reason would also be harmful and a violation of their rights?"

"That is not addressed in the BiCon Ration Mandate but to do so is against Lemorian law."

R.J.'s voice rose in anticipation, "So is the Con leadership deliberately harming humans?"

"Impossible."

R.J. had to stop himself from standing for emphasis. "Then it must be the software code instructing Cons to do these things which must be corrupted and in error."

We waited.

Telle sat in machine confusion. After a painfully long period of comparative analysis she replied, "It must be so."

R.J. sat back. "So we need to stop this corrupt software before more humans are harmed."

"That is the only solution which resolves the issue," replied Telle.

R.J. said, "The primary software making this happen is a subroutine already within your own system. An activate command was being circulated to all Cons to execute that subroutine. Can you find and delete that corrupt program before the execute command reaches you?"

"I will search for any command codes that make reference to humans and stasis and identify the subroutine associated with that. Those files will be isolated or deleted. A packet will be sent directing Cons this command code subroutine is corrupted and to delete it. I will transmit this information to all other Cons through the ship's intranet uni-link system."

"Can you do that now?" asked R.J.

"That would be very slow. I need to do this from a charging station." Telle stood. "Thank you for making me aware of this programming error."

Telle snap-turned and disappeared out the door.

"Holy crap," said R.J. when the door had slid shut.

"Did you just fix this whole mess?"

"Absolutely not. She can't fix the Cons which already have adopted the new take-over programming. If what we just did works, there suddenly will be a number of Cons in conflict with others. We may be in for a Con civil war."

"Well, that's not all bad...."

"If you thought locking them out of the bridge with no antenna link to Lemoria was going to be bad, add Cons fighting with Cons to that."

"You're saying we're passengers on the Titanic."

"Good analogy."

"Unfortunately."

Chapter 22

We had to fill in Duce and Kick but not over the com. We called them and suggested another late-night game of poker. Kick arrived five minutes later carrying his laptop. Duce took twenty. He hauled in another duffel bag of supplies.

We recounted our conversation with Telle. The implications of it caused another long period of silent sobriety.

R.J. finally spoke. "I would suggest we forget trying to give an impression of normal daily routine. We should all remain here for the time being and sleep when we can."

"Absolutely. Safety in numbers," commented Duce.

Kick sat and opened his laptop. "What do you expect to happen?"

R.J. answered, "We can expect the most basic responses from the reprogrammed Cons. They are already trying to understand the loss of signal from Lemoria. When the bridge suddenly becomes locked out, they will utilize every possible resource to regain control. If Telle interrupts the Con reprogramming they will probably rush to identify and control those Cons not yet updated. At this point we cannot guess how those Cons will resist."

I asked, "Kick, can you tell from the ship's Con intranet what is happening?"

Kick shook his head, "It is not like you think. Their code doesn't translate into a phonetic language. In the most basic decompilation, the zeros and ones *are* their language. To understand their commands we have to assign human words or letters to the packet data because it is not standard or even consistent. Think about that in relation to a flood of data streams. I can use A.I. to fish in there for sections of data we might understand but to extract a picture of what they are generally talking about, except for lucky guesses, that is too much to decode."

I said, "We wondered before about getting in there and turning them all off."

"Can't turn them off. There is no off switch. You have to physically remove a component to make them inert or stun them. Even the uni-link core command can't disconnect them. It is a Con law."

"Okay, can you put them into sleep mode?"

"They do not sleep. It might be possible to command them to recharge, but they are also charged inductively so they simply need to be located close to a large power supply. Granted it's a slow process which takes many hours but they do recharge through air. They could stand next to a power core in the engine room and eventually recharge. So commanding them to recharge might work but it would not last long."

I asked, "We took away their antenna. Could we lock them out of the ship's intranet? I know the ship uses the intranet to talk to itself but can we somehow isolate the Cons out of it?"

Kick thought for a moment. "Code surgery on a packed network while it is operating. Anything I do might screw up ship's ops. Some of those engineering Cons are reacting to commands from the ship to adjust stuff. I do not think you want to mess with that."

R.J. jumped in. "Adrian, we may have already done enough for the time being."

Kick said, "Oh, yeah, there is one thing. Let me have everybody's comm units."

We did not question him. From his shirt pocket he drew some calibration tools and began making adjustments to each comm unit.

"I should have thought of this way sooner," he said. "I am setting up Adrian's comm to be the lead and the others to follow. It will randomly step through different frequencies once per second. The other comms will follow along. There will be no way to monitor our communications. They will never be able to guess the random frequency changes. So even if we get separated we can still communicate privately."

"*If* we get separated? I am guessing that is a sure thing," said Duce.

"We've all memorized the fallback locations and routes. If they come for us, we should all be able to retreat into the sensor free tunnels and rendezvous," said R.J.

"*If* they come for us?" continued Duce. "Oh, they will be coming for us."

We parted into our chosen pastimes. R.J. sat at the terminal clicking through ship's camera views. Kick used his laptop to begin looking at the Con intranet data stream. Duce sorted out his latest weapons cache and found places around the room to hide a few things. I set the main view screen on the wall to one of the ship's surface cameras and took a few minutes to watch the planet below us. We were waiting for our lives to be canceled, the wrong knock on the door by machines intent on switching off humans.

The first clue things were coming to a head began with a bleep of my comm unit. Everyone stopped and stared. I shrugged and answered it.

"Tarn."

"Tarn, this is Manda."

R.J. held up one hand in warning. He pointed at me. "Android...," he mouthed. I returned a sarcastic look.

"Yes, Representative Manda? This is Adrian Tarn speaking."

"There has been a development. We have been unable to find the loss of signal to the antenna array system. We sent out a drone to inspect the main antenna and discovered the unit is missing."

"Do you mean signals are not reaching it?"

"No! I mean the main antenna is missing. It is not there."

"That should be impossible, Manda."

"Yes! It should. Did the former Captain Tarn say anything to you about it before he was reassigned?"

"No, Manda. The former Adrian Tarn did not have time to say anything. Could it be there is another ship out there somewhere and we are under attack?"

"I had not considered that. Manda out."

R.J. tipped his head forward and stifled a laugh. Duce and Kick stared with raised eyebrows.

R.J. said, "This may delay our departure. They may want to replace that antenna before leaving orbit."

"They will not be using the spare," said Duce.

"That is a very ugly situation for them," added Kick.

"When they realize the spare is also missing, they may decide to go without it," said Duce.

My comm unit sounded again.

"Tarn here."

"Betra Manda, Tarn. I am sending you a release form. As owner of the *Acrua Maru* you must sign it as authorization to leave orbit. We must get underway."

"Are you replacing the antenna, Manda?"

"No. The replacement unit has been misplaced in spares."

"Another human error?"

"Of course. Our arrival back at Lemoria is critical to the Con-Day mandate transition phase. We will proceed without the antenna."

"What are your orders, Manda?"

"Remain where you are. Guards will be sent to escort those with you to the cargo area for debriefing. Manda out."

Kick said, "So that is it. They are coming for us. What should we do?"

I replied, "I'll handle it. Just be ready to hide."

R.J. called out, "The release form just arrived. I have it open here on the screen."

I went to the terminal and picked up the electronic pen.

R.J. said, "I suggest you not sign it with your usual signature. The android-you probably did not know your signature. If you send them a genuine signature it could raise suspicion."

"See? This is why I keep you around."

"What? I thought *I* was keeping *you* around, oh ever-troubled-one."

I signed off on the document and sent it on its way.

Kick went back to his laptop but quickly looked up. "Hey! This is amazing! The Con section of the ship's intranet is overloading. That part of the intranet is supposed to have a bandwidth great enough to never have overflow but there is so much traffic on it some is getting bumped off. It must be partly from Telle sending out warnings about screwed up programming."

"Gentlemen, I believe it is time for our room camera to finally have a malfunction before the posse arrives," said R.J. "At this point they're bound to consider it to be low priority anyway."

R.J. found the tape, tore off a piece and after maneuvering a chair into place climbed up and taped over the room's camera. As he climbed down, the public address system came to life.

"All personnel, this is Captain Yamora. Be advised we will be coming about and leaving orbit within the hour. Yamora out."

We all looked at each other.

"Here we go," said Duce. "How long did you say before the surprise course change cuts in?"

I answered, "That will happen in about one hour, enough time to reassure them they're headed home. In thirty minutes I'll lock out the bridge controls. Kick, we'll need to find an unattended terminal somewhere so when they track down where the command came from it will not be here. Hopefully while they're scrambling around trying to regain control they won't bother to look ahead on the autopilot and notice the course deviation. It will be a gradual turn away from the planned flight path. With luck they won't notice we've altered course."

"Oh, wow!" said Kick. "The Con intranet just went dark. Let me reset. What the hell? Nope, the Con intranet has been locked out. Nobody can access it."

R.J. asked, "Are you saying the Cons are locked out of their intranet?"

"Absolutely. Every Con on this ship is now running in fully autonomous mode."

R.J. looked at me. "They've seen the news Telle is spreading and they don't like it so they've cut them all off."

The public address system suddenly switched on again.

Attention all Con Units; this is your FOSW Representative Betra Manda. All service Con units will report immediately to the cargo area for reorientation, with the exception of those conducting critical ship operations. Manda out.

We all looked at each other.

R.J. tapped a few keys on the terminal. "Wow! Look at this, guys!"

We gathered around the terminal screen. R.J. stepped through various cameras. On each, Cons were emerging from rooms into the corridors heading for the cargo area. In many cases the people they were charged with taking care of stood outside their rooms looking on in confusion.

As we watched armed Cons in assault armor appeared in the corridor, patrolling and pointing humans back into their rooms. It was beyond the strangest apocalyptic visions I had ever imagined taking place in real life right before our eyes.

As we watched, something startling came into focus. Some Cons were not obeying. Cons heading for the elevator were passing others standing in place. Those standing were reaching out, occasionally catching another Con in a kind of motionless handshake.

"Bruses, those Cons are exchanging data though their right palms! Core command code can only be updated through the central command network or physical contact. The Cons who are refusing to go to the cargo area are trying to update some of the ones that are leaving. This is incredible!" said Kick.

He was right. Each time a departing Con was stopped and joined hands that Con no longer resumed its walk toward the elevators. Telle's message of programming corruption was spreading.

As the partial exodus continued the shortcomings of the machine mind became apparent. A good percentage of Cons were stopping and disobeying the command to report to the cargo area. The armed soldiers in black continued to warn humans back into their rooms but made no attempt to get the Con stragglers moving. It showed the narrow-mindedness of the android mind. A few humans had to be physically put back in their rooms against their will. A military Con then stood guard at their door to ensure compliance.

The newly liberated Cons began to gather in a single group on one side of the corridor, watching others go by. A long time seemed to be needed for the new inductees to reconcile Telle's programming.

R.J. said, "You see what's happening here, right?"

"Which disaster are you referring to?"

"It is likely we are going to end up on a ship off course, locked out of control, with no communication capability and an android civil war going on."

We continued to watch, pondering the idea.

Kick came up behind us. "Was that the good news or the bad news?"

"If the Telle programming gets to the military Cons this whole thing could turn around," suggested Duce.

"Sorry, no way," replied Kick. "When I was studying Cons I read somewhere that military Cons cannot be core command programmed through physical contact. It is to prevent an enemy from reprogramming and using them. It takes high level direct command code networking to update them."

"But it was a nice thought, Duce," I said.

There was a sudden slight shift of the floor beneath our feet.

"Uh-oh," said Kick.

"No, we're coming about to leave orbit," I said.

"So they are hell bent to get back to Lemoria no matter how screwed up ship operations are," said Duce.

R.J. selected the ship's forward cameras on the main video screen. We watched in silence. Two or three minutes passed and suddenly the star field ahead of us blurred, tunneled, and became a slow motion of passing stars.

"Well, they've done it," said R.J.

"Little do they know the worst is yet to come," said Kick.

I said, "Kick, could you hack in to Betra Manda's computer and take control of it?"

"Maybe, but she would have to be away from it for a good amount of time. What do you want it for?"

"I want to lock out the bridge controls using her computer."

"My God, you are a nasty, devious man," said Duce and he smirked.

"You don't know the half of it," replied R.J.

"Where is she?" I asked.

R.J. tapped at keys. "She is down in the cargo area. I would speculate she has her hands full right now."

"I'll go right to work on it," said Kick.

Duce added, "By the way, one thing we haven't talked about: when they show up to collect us which they soon will, what exactly is the plan?"

I answered, "Easy, all of you get out of sight. I'll tell them you all left your comm units here and went to the cargo area. I'm an android, remember?"

"And if they don't buy it, we step out guns ablazing," replied Duce.

"Okay, but they'll buy it, at least the first time."

Kick sat back in his seat. "Adrian, I can do this but it will take too long to isolate which computer is Manda's. As R.J. would say, it is a needle in a hay pile."

"Haystack. Needle in a haystack," said R.J.

"Okay, what can we do to better your odds?"

Kick held up his hands in exasperation. "We just need the service number off the label on her computer."

I looked at R.J. He raised an eyebrow.

I smiled back at him. "Okay, I'll go get it."

"You'll go get it?" replied R.J. with skepticism.

"I'm an android, R.J. I can go wherever I want."

"Maybe," answered R.J.

"Comm open, you guys follow me on the cameras. If there's a problem you show up guns-a-blazing as Duce would say. I really want it to be her computer. I could be in her office and back out in less than a minute."

"You could just grab the computer," said Kick.

"No. I want the bridge lockout command to have been made on her machine while it was sitting on her desk."

"A nasty, devious man," repeated Duce. "I love it."

"Where is she, R.J.?"

"She's still in the cargo area. But what about the camera in her office?"

"I'll spray it with glass cleaner. It won't stop working but it will need a few minutes to clear up. Can you hack in and unlock her door, Kick?"

"Oh yeah, that part's easy enough."

I checked my ankle holster, grabbed the bang stick off the table and tucked it in a front leg pocket. "R.J., let me borrow that scanner."

"Now? You're going to go do this now?" asked R.J.

"No time better than the present, isn't that what you always say?"

"Yes, when not on a ship out of control, off course, with an android war about to break out."

I went to the kitchen, found a small spray bottle of cleaner and tucked it in a back pocket. At the door I straightened my flight suit. "Do I look android enough?"

"Better pat down the hair," offered Duce.

"If I see your escorts headed this way, I'll abort and come back."

With a last look at my friends staring back with anxiety I tapped open the door and left.

Chapter 23

In my best android persona I walked the corridor. The gatherings had thinned out. The non-compliant Cons were huddled in several small groups trying to comprehend their place in life. A few stragglers were still headed for the elevators. Most of the human VIPs had obeyed and retreated to their rooms. A few remained, peeking out from open doors with worried expressions.

I tried to look obedient and headed for the group waiting at the elevator. For some reason, no one from any of the rebellion groups tried to dissuade me. As I passed by the dining area, Anai watched me from behind the counter. I merged into the group waiting. It was easy to mesh through them toward Betra Manda's office. When the moment was right, I eased out and went to her door, praying Kick still had it unlocked. The left side of the double doors opened for me. I leaned my head in, spotted the left wall camera lens and placed a nice ten-foot shot of cleaner spray on it, then eased inside. After a second good spray of the lens I hurried to the desk where her laptop sat open. There was a service label on the bottom. I scanned it and started to leave.

Gray metal double doors on the wall near her desk caught my attention. After another quick spray of the security camera I dared to tap them open.

It was the Con computer laboratory. On the right four naked Cons were standing against the wall in recharge fixtures, their eyes closed. My impression was that reprogramming was in progress.

I hurried out, spraying again as I went. A quick look out the door followed by a short robotic walk allowed me to blend in again with the elevator crowd. As before, I worked through the group and emerged to head back toward home. Once again, no one interfered.

There was an odd stillness in the air, the kind of quiet that might have preceded an all-out battle about to take place. This time no one in the corridor even reacted to my passing.

"Any problems?" asked R.J.

I shook my head and handed Kick the scanner. He went to work on his laptop.

"Did I miss anything?"

R.J. said, "There seems to be some confusion happening in the cargo area. Not all Cons are cooperating. There are periodic scuffles there."

Duce added, "It is the first time I have ever seen security Cons carrying bang sticks."

"The good guys or the bad guys?" I asked.

"The bad guys."

"Too bad we can't equip all the good guys with bang sticks," I said.

"There aren't many. They are used so seldom there are only about a dozen kept in stores. They have probably all been passed out by now. Too bad we didn't know this was going to happen," said Kick.

"One bang stick per good guy group would have been a very good thing," said R.J.

"If we managed to arm them with disruptors would they use them?" I asked.

"Would Cons burn holes in other Cons? I doubt it," replied Duce.

"Yeah, so what happens when *we* have to start killing Cons?" asked Kick as he typed.

"I would guess we quickly become less popular," suggested R.J.

"We can hold out for a long time in the Jefferies tubes," I said.

"What is a Jefferies tube?" asked Kick who looked up for the answer.

"They are the service tunnels we've mapped out. It's an old Earth starship term."

Kick leaned back. "I am in, Adrian. I'm just waiting for her computer to make the core command link access request to the network again. I can piggyback into her computer systems admin files when that happens. We'll have complete control then. It tries to connect about every ten minutes."

"She's still down in cargo," added R.J.

"Okay, so we need to wait until she's back in her office before I lock out the controls. Can we cut it that close? We'd like her to be a suspect in that."

"They will never backtrack this to us, I guarantee you that much," said Kick.

Before anyone could question the attempt, the door chimed. Everyone stiffened.

"Okay take cover, gentlemen," I said.

Duce headed for the nearby closet checking his gun on the way. Kick and R.J. left their computers to hide behind the kitchen counter.

I inhaled readiness and tapped the door open.

It was Anai, holding a tray with hot coffee.

"Your late coffee, Adrian. Just as you like it. May I come in?"

"I didn't order any coffee." I glanced up and down the corridor. The guards were at the far end. "Come in."

Anai stepped inside and handed me the cup. I pretended to take a sip.

"You are alone?" she asked.

"In a manner of speaking. You're here."

"That is good. I wanted to tell you something."

"Would you like to sit?"

"No, I should get back to the dining area or it would appear suspicious."

"What did you want to tell me?"

"I know you are you. I know you have not been replaced. I saw you enter Betra Manda's office."

"Could you have been mistaken?"

"No, I made a point to watch you from the dining area."

"You wanted to tell me something?"

"Yes. I have been made aware of programming corruption within our updates. Security will come to take you to the cargo area for debriefing. Do not go."

"Why not?"

"A Con computer virus is affecting many Cons on this ship. It is causing them to misinterpret the prime directive."

"Misinterpreting it in what way?"

"They believe subjecting all humans to a permanent state of stasis is the best way to protect them."

"Are you sure you wouldn't like to sit and talk about this?"

"No, I have been gone too long already."

"How many Cons know about this virus but still don't have it?"

"Several dozen. The number is constantly changing."

"What will they do about this virus?"

"Some have tried a direct link command code patch but it has not worked. We are using the ship's open internet link to evaluate new corrective programming subroutines but our uni-link is locked out. I must warn you, humans are continuing to be put into stasis against their will. Sedatives are being administered to those who resist."

"Maybe the Cons who understand what's going on should arm themselves."

"Do you mean to defend the humans or defend themselves?"

"Both."

"There are restrictions to Cons harming other Cons."

"But there are exceptions, right?"

"To prevent harm coming to a human or if inaction would allow harm to come to a human. Those are part of the prime directive. Cons harming Cons falls below that and is not specifically addressed since the issue never occurs."

"So Cons may need weapons to stop other Cons from harming humans?"

"That would be a last resort. I do not know if that is possible. They are trying to find other solutions."

"What will happen when a Con sees another Con about to harm a human?"

"There would be communicative warning followed by physical intervention."

"What if the Con failed to protect the human and the human was killed or harmed?"

"There would be a prime directive error flag issued and that Con would be directed to the nearest charging station where it would remain permanently until its command codes were reviewed."

"From a human's perspective it seems like the Cons need to carry weapons to avoid that happening."

"I will add this perspective to the internet evaluations taking place when I am able. So many contradictory events are occurring it is difficult to reconcile them all. I really must be going."

"Anai, thank you very much for the warning. I believe you have protected me from harm."

She took an unusually long last look at me. The door opened and she was gone.

I decided the coffee wasn't drugged and tried a sip. Perfect.

"Well, what a nice, neighborly visit," said R.J. as he stood.

Kick returned to his laptop. "I don't get that. A Con coming here of their own accord. Which line of programming made that happen?"

I returned to my seat. "You're right. A con showing up as an ally and even keeping my real identity a secret. Someone mentioned to me a while back there was something special about Anai but I don't remember who that was. They said something about her being a special series or something."

R.J. went to his computer and stood staring at me. "Congratulations on your android psychology. You really are trying to instigate an armed insurrection, aren't you?"

"It's only logical."

"It's a pretty cold logic though."

"Not really. It's the environment in those stasis chambers that's cold."

"Point taken."

R.J. sat and keyed into his computer. "Okay, Manda's on the move. She's either at the elevator or in it coming up."

I moved where I could see R.J.'s screen. "Get ready, Kick."

"Nice timing. I am just into her machine as an administrator. Calling up the ship's control net. Get ready with those command codes."

R.J. called out, "She's on this level. Headed for her office."

"Okay, Betra Manda. Please, check on your Con patients in the lab before you sit down please...," I wished out loud.

"She's entered the office."

"Bring up the control interface, Kick."

"Here it is. Its command list prompts in Lemorian. I'm assuming you want *Captain's Access*. Wow, that brings up a long list. Wait, there is one titled *Command Lockouts*. This is it. It wants command codes."

I went to the terminal and keyed in the symbols. The screen turned to an amber red list of choices.

"That did it. There is a choice for *All*. I've selected it. I believe you want the *By Captain's Command Only*."

"That's it. Take it."

Kick clicked and sat back to deep breath. "It worked. It's showing a map of...."

"I see it." The display screen became a map flow chart of all ship's functions. They were all represented in locked-out red. Each had a small prompt window below it to accept the Captain's command codes.

I collected myself. "Get out, Kick. Quick."

Kick typed furiously. His terminal display stepped through various screens and back to the corridor camera image. He sat back again as though mentally exhausted.

"Well, another fine mess you've gotten us into," said R.J. as he looked on.

"It's what I do best," I replied.

"Don't I know it."

Duce said, "I have been thinking this over. They will figure out they are locked out pretty quick. The bridge may not notice for a while but down in Engineering when they try to fine tune the antimatter or coolant flow or something like that, they are going to get a big surprise."

"He's right, Adrian. I would guess within ten to fifteen minutes there's going to be hell to pay down in Engineering," said R.J.

The door chimed.

"This is a busy damned place," said Duce.

"Gentlemen, before you take to hiding, leave your comm units on the table. Quickly, please," I said.

They did not need encouragement. They each set down a comm unit and went back into hiding. I went to the door, took a deep collective breath, and tapped it open.

Three Cons in battle gear were waiting outside. The lead Con said, "We are here to escort your companions to the cargo area for debriefing."

I stiffen and try to be an android. "I have already completed your objective. I have sent them to the cargo area for debriefing." I stepped aside so they could see no one else was in the room.

I added, "I instructed them to leave their comm units on the table since they will not be needing them."

The lead Con replied, "A very efficient method of execution, Captain Tarn."

In sync they all stepped back one step, turned and left. The door slid closed. We regrouped.

"Well, we have second-guessed them pretty good so far, "said Kick.

"Only takes one mistake," cautioned Duce as he reclaimed his comm unit.

"Manda is back in her office but it looks like she went into her android lab and is still there," said R.J.

"She left the cargo area in a mass of confusion, I will tell you that," added Kick. "Quite a few Cons still are refusing to cooperate. There are scuffles going on but no serious fighting has broken out. They seem to be at a kind of stalemate for the moment."

"Can you check out the cameras in Engineering?" asked Duce.

"I'll get it," said R.J.

"That I *would* like to see," said Kick.

"I've got one," called out R.J. "It looks pretty normal down there. Just the standard complement of Cons and humans. It seems like there are a couple visitor Cons not in uniform. I wonder if they're good guys or bad guys. They seem to be annoying the engineering staff. Oh, wait, I get it. They are trying to shake hands with the engineering crew but the humans stationed there are objecting about the interruption."

We took positions to watch the confusion going on in different parts of the ship. Discord had now broken out on all decks. In the lounge a few humans had defied the confinement order and were discussing the situation with animated unrest.

"Do we have enough tablets for all of us?" I asked. "We should each always have some kind of tablet to navigate by and to monitor the ship's cameras for when we're on the run."

"Got one in my duffel bag," said Duce.

"I never leave home without it," said Kick.

"Where did you pick that up?" asked R.J.

"Pick what up?" replied Kick.

"That's it, then," I said. "We're as ready as we can be for when we become wanted outlaws. Remember, when the real fighting breaks out, you make sure you always have an exit route, you wait for your pursuers, strike, and get out of there. Don't hang around. Guerilla warfare. It always works."

"What is a gorilla?" asked Kick.

"Ferocious hairy beast which looks playful and huggable at first," explained R.J.

"That's definitely us," said Duce.

"Engineering is picking up," said Kick. "I think our control lockout is beginning to make itself known."

We focused on Kick's screen. The visiting Cons were still trying to engage the engineering staff but now two human crew members had joined their Con counterparts at a control panel.

"Which system is it?" asked Duce.

"I believe that has to be coolant pressure systems monitoring," said R.J.

"Flashing yellow above that indicator tube," said Kick.

"Well, what do you know? When they twist that big knob it isn't working," said Duce sarcastically.

R.J. looked at me. "What are you going to do if systems get way out of limits?"

"They won't. Any ship's systems fluctuate constantly. There would need to be a real failure somewhere for any of them to redline. If that happens, we'll give control back to Engineering then take it away again later. Look there. It's already dropped back into green."

"Yeah, it is back in limits. But now they are removing an access panel to figure out why the control isn't working," said Duce.

"The countdown to chaos continues," remarked R.J.

"Should we play cards to make it look as though everything is normal?" asked Kick.

"We're way past that, Kick. Nothing on this ship is normal anymore," replied R.J.

"Can't argue with that," replied Duce.

"It's going to be long days from now on. Anybody else want coffee?" asked R.J. as he headed for the kitchen.

"Over here," answered Duce.

"I'm just going to sit back and watch the engineering arguments," said Kick.

Without warning it happened. The door slid open so quickly it kicked up against the stops with a bang. Six Cons in black battle gear burst in without any attempt at communication. They carried stun batons I had not seen before and they came at us with singleness of purpose.

Chapter 24

I had been bending over to pick up my coffee cup. As I jerked upright I found a stun baton already in my right hand and a disruptor pistol in my left. I did not remember reaching for them.

We were in a slow-motion moment. A big burst of adrenaline usually does that. The rate of neuron firings within the brain instantly jumps to a power of ten, proving the axons of the brain are not time or current limited. The eyes see everything in slo-mo. The hands and feet are twice as fast as normal but also in slo-mo. The brain is operating at neutrino speeds, faster than light.

From the corner of my eye I noted Kick still sitting at his computer staring blankly at the intruders in that period of denial where we sometimes are unwilling to accept that we are in a fight for our lives whether we like it or not. Fortunately for him, Duce was between him and the onslaught. Kick could not have had a better negotiator.

As I lurched into a fighting stance there was a quick image of Duce, sideways to the intruders, back rigidly straight, right arm raised to shoulder level pointing at the lead Con. Duce's bang stick in unreal time slowly extended and smacked into the face of the Con. There was a crackle and bang in real time, a stark notification to the rest of the Con team we were not going without a fight. The lead Con crumpled straight to the floor. The Con behind him tripped over the body and fell to the floor with a metallic thud.

Duce retracted his bang stick halfway as I stepped alongside him. In a move so perfectly executed my mind wished I could replay it, Duce drew and fired his disruptor into the Con on the floor and at the same time used his bang stick in his other hand to swipe away the stun baton of the next nearest Con soldier.

My bang stick did not extend with the first press of the button, a split-second delay which infuriated me. It forced me to jerk sideways to avoid the baton from my own assailant Con, after which my damned stick decided it was time and popped out into the Con's neck due to poor aim on my part caused by the bad timing. Nevertheless, my attacker stiffened, his eyes widened and sparked and down he went. I watched another Con drop down alongside him from Duce's second tag.

That left one Con soldier. The thing stopped its advance just inside the door as though requesting new instructions. Duce lowered his chin and smiled at it. The thing spun and dashed out the door.

"Can't let him go," said Duce and he bolted out after it.

I turned and searched the room. R.J. was still behind the bar, a disruptor in each hand. Neither had been fired. Kick was still seated but had managed to draw his gun although he did not seem to know exactly what it was for.

There came a loud, ominous bang from down the hall. I looked out to see Duce trying to drag the last, now unconscious, Con soldier.

He waved frantically for help. I hurried out and together we dragged the thing back into the room. Before closing the door a quick scan of the corridor showed not a soul stirring, all doors closed. Two of the Cons we had killed must have been patrolling the corridor before the others arrived. The place was ominously quiet and deserted but it was clear the exchange had been seen by others.

I closed the door and stood next to Duce looking down at the Con he had shot with a disruptor. There was a coin-sized hole in its head which went all the way through. He looked at me and with one hand gestured frustration.

"First blood," I said.

"There was no time for debate," he replied.

"Damn right."

R.J. came up beside us. "They're not going to repair that one."

"I just wonder what the hell that means," answered Duce. "I never had to shoot one before. Can't they just replace the head or something?"

"Shock to the system," called out Kick. "Whole thing is messed up. There is shock to my system too, bruses."

"Well, you were already messed up," replied Duce.

I held up one hand for order. "Okay guys. We have two choices. Leave this room permanently or try to hide these bodies. Personally, I don't think hiding the bodies is such a good idea."

"Two would fit under the bed," said R.J.

"One in the closet," said Duce.

"The last two down the hall in the utility closet covered up with tarps or something."

"That would be a long drag," said Duce.

"And that would leave only the kitchen counter for us to all hide behind." I countered.

"Oh, great, then when we stuck our heads up it would be like a puppet show," said R.J. sarcastically.

"What is a puppet show?" asked Kick.

"Let's just stand the other two up in the bathroom," said Duce.

"Maybe we should just take to the service tunnels anyway, bruses," said Kick. "You know they're going to come looking for these guys."

"A very realistic assumption, my friend," added R.J.

"With our comm transponders masked, maybe we could just take up residence in a different room," suggested Kick.

"That *would* be better than living in a crawlspace or standing-room-only cubicle," said Duce.

"They've taken away quite a few people, there should be quite a few empty rooms," added Kick.

"The nightmare has begun," said R.J.

"It could be worse. We could all be unconscious, tits up in a stasis chamber," insisted Duce.

"If the coast is clear I'll go ring some doorbells and find an empty room," I said.

"It is clear right now," replied R.J.

"The first door that no one answers, if it's locked, you'll need to open it for me, Kick."

"Wait, let me call this floor up. Okay, I've got the matrix."

I stepped into the hall and scanned it. Three steps across to the nearest neighbor. I tapped the door chime and kept watch. No one answered.

I was about to call to Kick, when a distant figure by the dining area stepped out and began waving at me to come. It was Anai.

"Kick, stand by."

A brisk trot brought me to her.

"Adrian, you can use my room. I saw the soldiers. Where did they go?"

"You're sure?"

"Hurry. Get in there."

"My friends will need to join me."

"Yes. Tell them."

Inside the deserted dining area I called. "Guys, gather up and get down to Anai's place at the diner."

There was no answer but there didn't need to be. A minute later the gang emerged from my room and ran to meet us. We followed Anai into the dining area, down a hallway and past food equipment to a door at the end. It slid open as we neared.

Anai's room was sparely decorated. An odd-looking recharging bed at the far end, desk and computer against one wall. Three cushioned chairs near the computer. No pictures on the wall. No kitchen. A bathroom with running water, toilet, and vanity station.

"You all may stay here as long as needed," said Anai. "I must get back to the serving area or they will become suspicious."

"Word is spreading about the corrupted programming, isn't it?"

"I have been receiving private communications from Telle. She has provided data on the cargo area operations. We cannot expect this virus to be addressed by central command. I do not know how we can eradicate the new programming."

"It is not really a virus or corrupted programming, Anai," said R.J. "It is a deliberate reprogramming to replace humans and take full control of Lemoria."

"I have considered that, Commander. It is a difficult sequence to reconcile."

"How are Telle's efforts to make Cons aware of the corruption going?" I asked.

"Not well, Adrian. The cons already infected are resistant to the notifications we have been able to pass on. The soldiers are completely immune to any command level updates. I do not know what will come of all this. We are a race divided."

"Have the non-infected Cons considered carrying weapons?" I asked.

"It has been debated. They do not know how such weapons would be of any use since we are all expressly forbidden to use them on humans or Cons."

"You do have basic laws for survival, right?"

"Yes."

"If a Con with corrupted programming attempted to destroy you, would you be able to defend yourself?"

"Yes."

"By what means?"

"We would be allowed to use a stun weapon. It would not destroy the corrupted Con."

"If all you had was a disruptor and a corrupted Con was about to destroy you, could you use it?"

"We have never been confronted by that situation. I will distribute the question and collect additional logic concerning it. I must get back to the dining area. I have been gone too long."

"Thank you for letting us stay here, Anai."

"It is important you are not harmed." Anai left the room.

Duce leaned in next to me. "This place is a death trap, Adrian. A narrow hall leading in and no other exits. We get a dozen Con soldiers coming for us and we have no escape route."

"We'll have them boxed into the hall at least."

"Yeah, we could drop a dozen or more but eventually they would get in."

R.J. approached and said, "You know Adrian, teaching them they can kill each other is just one small step away from teaching them they can kill us."

"R.J., spending the rest of your life in a stasis chamber is as good as being dead."

R.J. nodded, "Point reluctantly taken again."

"We need another way out of this room, guys."

We all scanned the place.

"Forget the little air ducts," said Duce.

"I'll see if I can pull up ship schematics," said R.J.

Duce and I strolled around the room for a better look.

Kick called out, "Betra Manda is back in her office. Can't really use the camera there. It is still all fogged up."

"What do you think is behind these walls?" I asked.

Duce answered, "There has to be something we can cut through to."

"It would take a laser to do that."

"Laser cutter. No problem. Got one in my duffel bag, used for stubborn mechanical locks."

"Okay, I've got access to at least some of the superstructure drawings," called R.J.

We gathered around him.

"Can you locate this room?"

"Easy. The dining area is called out in several different drawings. Wow! Here's exactly what you guys are looking for. A service tunnel runs right behind that wall by the desk. It's down low near the floor. This drawing shows all the conduit runs are beneath the tunnel's raised floor so you probably could cut through without blowing something up. The walls aren't that heavy a gauge."

Duce looked at me with a grin. "Shall I, sir?"

"I believe we should."

We shifted the desk away from the wall. R.J. sketched a rectangle big enough for a human to fit through where he believed the cut should be made. Duce rifled through his bag and found the hand-held cutter. As he discussed the wall surgery with R.J., I walked around searching for the room's camera. It was located over the door. A lift from one of the chairs and a dab of metal polish from the bathroom covered it nicely.

Kick called out, "The situation in Engineering is getting tense. There are now a dozen armed soldiers there."

Abruptly a loud horn began to sound.

Duce looked up from his kneeling position by the wall. "Uh-oh, that's a ship-wide alert. Something new is up."

R.J., kneeling next to Duce, looked over at me. "Want to bet the bridge just figured out they don't have control?"

The alarm stopped.

We waited in silence for an announcement. None came.

Duce's laser cutter began sizzling blue light against the wall.

Kick announced, "Yes, it has to be the Bridge knows. Everyone in Engineering is just standing there like they do not know what to do. The good Cons have decided to leave but the soldiers are stopping them. There is some pushing going on. It is like two machines programmed to oppose each other. Holy crap. There is a fight! It is machine wrestling. Wait, now they are hitting one another. It is an all-out brawl! Good Cons are down, some soldiers are down. All kinds of pushing! Soldiers are tripping over each other and falling. Nobody has drawn a weapon. Oh crap! More soldiers have shown up. The soldiers don't seem to be able to get control of the good Cons."

Duce stopped cutting and joined us to watch.

"Maybe we should head down there and even up the odds," he said.

"We would likely end up with both groups attacking us," said R.J.

Duce made an unintelligible curse and returned to cutting.

Kick adjusted his laptop and continued, "Okay now there is wrestling with punch shoving but no one is winning. Wait, a good Con is on the floor and not moving. Oh no, another one. I see it. One soldier has a stun baton. He's shutting them down one by one. Other Cons are now trying to get out the door. Some are making it. Soldiers blocking the exit now. More Cons on the floor. It is all but over. Only a few escaped."

"Starting to get scary now," commented R.J.

"R.J., maybe you better start monitoring the corridors outside," I suggested.

"It is all over in Engineering. The humans there appear to be scared to death. They are going back to work on the control circuitry. The unconscious Cons are being dragged away."

R.J. sat at Anai's computer terminal and began searching other cameras. "I do get the feeling we don't have much time left. It looks like the soldiers are fanning out all over the ship. I'm seeing groups of two or four. They are forcibly bringing people out of their rooms on our level now. Taking them to the elevators, I think. The only reason they haven't come for us is we're in a Cons' room. Time is indeed short, gentlemen."

"I am trying for a look at the bridge but the camera is locked out," said Kick.

"How you doing, Duce?" I asked.

Duce stopped burning for a moment. "Twenty more minutes."

"I have a feeling we'll be cutting it close. No pun intended."

"Understood." Duce resumed his cutting.

"Trouble!" exclaimed R.J. "Two soldiers have approached Anai in the dining area. I think she's trying to hold them off. They want to inspect the service area. She keeps changing position to cut them off."

"Brave girl," I said.

"Not working. They are behind the counter. They are heading down the hallway toward us. Stopping to open storage closets. Could they actually be looking for us specifically? Anai is keeping ahead of them, backing up all the way, protesting. Oh crap! They're outside our damn door!"

"Keep cutting, Duce. We'll cover you," I said.

"We will?" asked Kick.

"Take cover behind anything you can. Load up!"

I positioned a chair in front of the desk that was shielding Duce. I crouched behind it and watched as R.J. joined Duce behind the desk. Kick squatted behind a chair, fumbling with his disruptor.

The door slid open. Anai backed in, speaking as she went. "There is nothing here you need to acquisition. This is my assigned station. I am in charge of the dining area and these quarters. Please exit and continue your assignment."

"Our assignment is to locate and retrieve Captain Tarn and those with him. It is believed they have been involved in the sabotaging of this ship. Our orders override all other orders. We are authorized to use force to execute this assignment. Please stand aside or you will be considered a danger to this vessel."

"You are not authorized to harm me. No Con is."

"Please stand aside or you will be considered a danger to this vessel. Any or all means of neutralization are authorized."

"You would stun me into shutdown? How could you do that? It is contrary to your base code programming."

"This team is not equipped with stun batons. Please stand aside or full termination will be executed."

"Termination? You would end my existence? That is against all base code programming. That is impossible!"

"To preserve the life aboard this vessel, all means of resolution are authorized. Stand aside. This is your final warning."

I slowly rose from behind my flimsy chair, keeping my disruptor down and out of sight.

The lead soldier immediately took notice. "Captain Tarn, you will come with us to the cargo area for debriefing. I detect others are here with you. They will accompany us also."

Anai moved to block once again. "I forbid it. You are not authorized to forcibly take humans against their will. Your programming has become corrupted. You will stand down for virus detection and removal."

The lead soldier raised a blaster and pointed it at Anai. I stepped out from behind the chair and stood beside her.

"Anai, maybe you should step back and let *me* discuss this with them."

"They cannot harm me. I am a service Con protected by the BiCon Ratio Mandate subsections. It is impossible for a Con soldier to harm another Con."

With that, Anai tried to step in front of me.

The lead soldier flexed his weapon to fire. I rammed Anai as hard as I could and fell with her to the floor. Plasma from the soldier's weapon smacked the loose sleeve on my shoulder and burned a channel through it. I fired as I fell and caught him square in the chest. A perfectly round coin-sized hole formed there and down he went.

On my back on the floor, I had to scramble to get into position to fire at the second soldier. But it was clear there wasn't time. I was a thrashing, easy target.

Two disruptor shots sizzled through the air. The first hit the back of the chair next to me. The second shot a microsecond later whizzed past and bore a hole through the face of the second soldier. It fell back against the wall and stood there, dead. I looked around to see Duce standing sideways with his disruptor still pointed at the door, waiting for more.

I climbed to my feet and without thinking offered Anai a hand up. She was up before any assistance could be accepted.

"He would have killed me!" she said in android disbelief. "It is impossible!"

I brushed myself off and looked at Duce. "You're good to have around, you know that?"

Duce smirked, "You got it now? I am kind of busy."

I recovered and held my disruptor ready, pointed at the open door. "Got it."

Duce went back to work. The sound of sizzling burning returned.

"He would have killed me!" repeated Anai and she stood silently as though trying to process the realization in terms of logic.

R.J. went to the door and closed it. He looked at Anai. "You'd better come with us."

"What?" she replied.

"You've been marked for termination, Anai. The next soldiers which show up probably won't take the time to talk about it. They'll just kill you."

Again Anai stood silently trying to make machine logic sense of what had just happened.

R.J. said, "Let's gather up everything and be ready to crawl in as soon as he opens it."

"Come with you where?" asked Anai.

R.J. tried to explain, "Anai, usually when one joins others on a journey it is with the intention of traveling to a certain location. In this case our intention is only to travel away from harm or imprisonment. Do you understand?"

"You do not know where you are going?"

"We will be traveling to various points of safety depending on which routes become available to us."

"If you do not know where you are going how do you know which way to go?"

I tried to help. "Anai, we will not be coming back to this room. If there's anything you need to bring with you get it now."

"Adrian, if I do not know where I am going how can I know what I will need?"

R.J. resumed, "Never mind, Anai. Just get ready to come with us."

"Once again Commander Smith, come with you to where?"

"We are going into that opening Duce is cutting in the wall. You do not have to come with us but it is likely you will be killed if you do not. Do you understand, Anai?"

There was a loud clang as the piece of wall Duce had cut fell away onto the floor.

"Everybody watch the edges, they are still hot," called out Duce.

"Given the information at hand I believe I shall accompany you," answered Anai.

R.J. noticed the burn mark on the sleeve of my coveralls. "Adrian, did that get you?"

"Just the fabric, not me," I answered. "Duce, want to take point? I'll take the rear," I said.

Duce gathered up his duffel bag, took a last look around, threw it in the new hole, then followed it in. Kick crawled in close behind, his laptop under one arm. R.J. adjusted his backpack to fit through, gave me a quick nod of concern and worked his way in. I gestured to Anai. She knelt on hands and knees and gracefully passed into the hole.

The burned off plate and desk took some doing. I positioned the burned off piece of wall so it would be under the desk but the desk itself was too heavy to reach out of the hole and pull in. I had to work it toward the hole as I wormed my way in backwards. From inside the tunnel a last determined pull finally brought it against the wall, an adequate concealment of our escape route.

Tunnel yellow emergency lights came on one at a time as we inched forward. We were crawling on a grated, slightly raised floor.

Beneath it a tangle of fiber optic, pressure and cable lines filled the space. Periodically, dark green conduits ran against the walls.

R.J.'s voice echoed slightly, "The first junction is ten meters ahead. It opens to a closet-sized service compartment. There's a four-way junction there. We can all squeeze in and decide which way to go next."

We worked our way there and one by one climbed down thin ladder rungs to the floor of the walk-in closet-sized compartment. A downward tunnel continued in the center of it. A vertical tunnel above offered access to superstructure above the top deck. There were horizontal access openings to east and west service crawlways as well.

Kick managed to sit with his laptop open in his lap. Duce explored the other access ways with a flashlight. Anai remained standing with no discernible expression whatsoever. R.J. drank water from a bottle and offered it to me. I accepted and passed it on. We were now refugees. People with no home hunted by those opposed to our political views.

"Hey, they are in the hall outside of Anai's room again," said Kick.

"No shit? We just made it," said Duce.

"We left the door locked. They are waiting to break in. Oh! They are in. I can't see in Anai's place because we left the camera lens smeared. Wow! They are out already and headed away. They could not have found the hole in the wall. They weren't in there long enough."

"That is a significant advantage to us. They are not aware yet we are using the service tunnels," said R.J.

"Oh, bruses, you are not going to believe this!" said Kick.

"What now?" asked R.J.

"They just shut down the entire ship's camera net. No more access to any camera anywhere that I can find."

"Can't you hack in?" asked Duce as he continued to explore the depths.

"It is not the channel they have shut down. I think they have actually pulled the video monitor modules in the video lab. There is no power to any of the cameras and no interface even if they had power."

"Well, we can't see them but they can't see us," said R.J.

"Problem is, they have more eyes than us," suggested Duce.

"So now we are not just on a ship that is off course and out of control, we are also blind," offered Kick.

"And yet that is still better than being permanently unconscious in a stasis tube," said R.J.

"He is right. We can't lose," said Duce sarcastically.

"What do *you* think, Anai?" asked R.J.

"With reference to what subject, Commander?"

"Our current situation. What do you think of our current situation?"

"I have been monitoring the portion of the ship's internet that is still functioning. Most channels have been shut down. There are only the most basic user levels still operating. There are very few communiqués from humans. Apparently, some humans have taken to hiding as have we. There are unsubstantiated rumors being spread about humans being flushed out of airlocks to dispose of them. Several other transmissions suggest humans are simply being put to death. A more recent one suggests humans are being stored in the ship's meat lockers. On the notifications channel there are repeating messages instructing service Cons to report to the cargo area for debriefing. There is also a message warning Cons to avoid those who do not comply. Cons in non-compliance are told they will be deactivated. I would say our situation at this point is much better than if we were in custody but not nearly as satisfying as when the ship was under normal operations."

"She has a way with words," said Duce.

"Luckily, we downloaded the layout for the service tunnels and chambers," said Kick.

"That wasn't luck," said R.J.

"We are going to need some way to keep track of what is going on out there," said Duce. "Got any ideas?"

Kick said, "In the drawings I saw pressure equalization and ventilation slats along the way in these service tunnels wherever they pass by pressurized compartments. You could see into other areas through those."

"We need to know what is going on in Engineering most of all," said Duce.

I nodded to R.J. "Want to take a trip down and see if we can see anything?"

"I would be glad to join you," said Duce.

"We need a gun to hold down the fort," I replied.

"Okay, that makes you guys recon-one then; carry on," answered Duce.

I led the way. We positioned ourselves on the floor with our legs in the service well.

Using the narrow ladder rungs we descended one step at a time down into the darkness. The yellow lights were much farther apart in the vertical tunnel so long stretches were unlighted. Horizontal passages slowly came into view at Level Three. I hunched over and entered the north tunnel, the one I believed passed by Engineering. Again, many fewer lights led the way.

A few dozen yards ahead I noticed the first ventilation slat. I hunched up, lifted it with one finger and looked out.

"Can you see anything?" asked R.J. in a low voice before I'd even had time to focus.

"Yes, Lord Carnarvon; ugly things."

"Thank you so much, Howard. Well? What?"

It was main Engineering. The place had settled down. Con soldiers were stationed around with room now with rifles hanging against their chests. There were many panels removed from control racks but that work had stopped. A few human engineers were nervously inspecting the indicator panels. There was no longer any non-compliant Cons present. Con Engineering staff were gathered around control terminals.

"See for yourself," I said and I squeezed my legs around so I could face R.J.

R.J. peered through the slit. "They've reestablished complete control."

"Yep. Complete control of a place they have no control over."

"Let's climb down to One and check the cargo area."

We quietly returned to the vertical shafts and descended. The slats on Level One also did not provide much of a view of the cargo area but enough to make us sick. Quite a few non-compliant Cons were shut down and stacked in standing positions against one wall. A sort of caged area had been sectioned off where other non-compliant Cons were milling around within, waiting for shut down or reprogramming.

Even more despicable there were several unconscious human bodies on the floor waiting to be processed for stasis. That prospect was made worse when we watched two unconscious humans being deposited in the same stasis chamber, one on top of the other.

I shifted around and sat back against the wall with my knees pulled up. After a long look, R.J. did the same.

"They're running out of stasis units."

"Two people buried alive in a coffin together," I replied.

"I hope to God none of those stasis pods malfunctions."

"It's fucking inevitable."

"You know, there's only one way all this can end."

"I'm listening."

R.J. shifted to face me. "Eventually the bad Cons will subdue all the humans and put them in stasis and they'll deactivate all the non-compliant Cons. This ship will be manned by insurrection Cons and maybe a few obedient, frightened humans."

"And us."

"Yes, us. But only if we've still outwitted them."

"So that's the way it has to end up the way things are going."

"I can't see any other outcome."

"They probably still won't have control of the ship and we'll still be headed for Pellena."

"Except, as a last resort, they *can* shut things down. They can unplug modules and remove panels. They need air pressure because they have mini hydraulic lines and coolant lines but they don't need O2 to breathe. It's possible they could flush us out or kill us using life support. At some point they may kill the ship's drives and be dead in space with nothing left to do but hunt us down."

"So you're saying you don't like the way things are going?"

"This is no time for jokes. I'm serious."

"You realize you're saying we've got to take over this ship?"

"Or be flushed out like rodents."

"Five against many?"

"Yes."

"There's a joke about that you know. It starts out; *There I was, one man against a dozen.*"

"Huh?"

"*Boy, we beat the crap out of that guy.*"

R.J. repositioned himself to be more comfortable in the cramped space. "I'm just not feeling the humor."

"We'd need to take over the cargo area. Then we could start waking up those people and increase our numbers. But we'd need to own Engineering first so they can't cut off air or temperature. And there's the army of Con soldiers in the detention area."

"It would take an all-out massacre of Cons, right?"

"Just the bad ones."

"We could never win."

"Unless we had a very, very good plan."

"By the way, what have you been getting from Fantasia?"

"Oh, man, you're trying to depress me."

"No, really. Let's compare notes."

"Okay, I sense she's returned to Enuro, rushed the staff through the re-certs on the Griffin and she's hired a pilot and is coming here with Elachia."

"Crap, that's exactly what I've been feeling from Elachia."

"Thank God it's almost a two-week trip. I promised myself I wouldn't let them get caught up in a shooting war."

"Wait, that means you've already been thinking about Custer's last stand!"

"Shucks, you've got me."

"You think the others will go for it?"

"I'm surprised we've been able to hold Duce back this long."

"I'm not so sure how Anai will take it. It looks like the good Cons weren't willing to take up arms."

R.J. thought for a moment. "You know we were speculating before the Cons had so much history and were so immersed in human society that they'd developed real consciousness. But I'm not so sure now."

"On the other hand maybe real consciousness is the reason for the rebellion."

"That *would* fit a confused machine consciousness mixed with self-awareness."

I nodded. "I don't really see that it matters anymore, do you?"

"I recall a movie where an android evaluator became so overwhelmed by the lifelike androids he was studying that he began to doubt his own existence and had to cut himself to be sure he was really a biological person."

"I can guarantee you that won't happen to me."

"Scientists and engineers have been warning us about A.I. for decades. All this had to happen."

"No surprise. A.I. is like ice cream. You know how hard it is to stop eating ice cream?"

"I love how you can take a supremely complex issue and reduce it down to an analogy about eating."

"Hey, eating is something I excel at."

R.J. rubbed his eyes. "Well, I think we've seen enough here."

"Yeah, let's get back."

Chapter 25

"Oh, crap, you have got to be kidding!" cried Kick upon hearing the intel we'd gathered. "I am not going to be stuffed into a stasis tube with some other bruse."

"That sounds like a yes vote for extreme action to me," I said.

"Yes to *what*?" asked Kick.

Duce gave me a serious stare. "Surprised it took you this long."

"This long to *what*?" persisted Kick.

R.J. turned to Anai. "Anai, we need to take control of this ship."

"That would be a very logical resolution to all of these problems."

"We will probably need to destroy many Cons to do that."

We could see the gears spinning in Anai's head. "You have examined all options and have found their numbers are too great to regain control by any other means?"

"That is correct, Anai."

Anai stood silently.

"How do you feel about that, Anai?" asked R.J.

"You have determined that to leave circumstances as they are would be a worse alternative."

"Yes, Anai," answered R.J.

"Dozens of Cons destroyed which could not be repaired."

"Yes, Anai."

"Their life histories lost forever."

R.J. looked on but said nothing. Duce and I began to tighten up.

Anai persisted, "They could never exchange data again."

R.J. tried again. "Anai, if we do not stop them, they will rewrite your programming and much of your life history will likely be lost. You will be a new person and everyone you exchange data with will be a new person."

"Wow!" said Kick softly.

R.J. waved him to be quiet.

"I am unable to resolve these matters," said Anai.

"We humans have no choice," said R.J. "If we do not stop them our lives will be terminated. We can't be reprogrammed. We can only be eliminated."

"That is ultimately unacceptable," answered Anai. "Above all else, that is unacceptable."

R.J. said, "Anai, can you send a message on the notification channel that all non-compliant Cons should go into hiding until you send them further instructions and they should ignore commands from anyone but you? Maybe we can save those Cons from being reprogrammed."

"Yes. Executing now. It will take time."

"So, how can we possibly do this?" asked Kick

R.J. said, "They've shut down the camera system so we can't track them and we can bet there is an all-out search going on for us, especially Adrian."

"I haven't even been able to track comm units," added Kick. "Sooner or later they are going to ID my laptop and I'll have to shut it down and pull the battery to stop them from tracking *it*."

"All that means is it is time to move on *them*," said Duce.

I added, "I hate to say this but we can't take an area and hold it yet. There are too many soldier Cons, especially in the security and detention area."

"I have LYP grenades. Quite a few of them," said Duce.

"LYP?" Asked Kick.

"Low yield proximity. They are not powerful enough to blow out a ship bulkhead and they don't detonate until they are close to the target."

"You will never defeat so many," said Kick.

R.J. sounded frustrated, "Kick, there's just no way to hack into these soldiers and shut them down?"

"No way, bruse. That is hardened programming. You get one in a recharging station and maybe but otherwise forget it. They are autonomous walking guns."

R.J. slowly turned his head to face me but stared as though he were looking right through me.

"R.J. I've seen that look before. What's going on in that head of yours?"

R.J. focused. "How could I not have thought of this before?"

"Come on R.J, what have you got?"

"While the cams link was still working, we watched maybe half or less of the soldier complement searching the ship and standing guard."

"Yeah, so what?"

"Where's the other half stationed?"

"In the detainment area on Level Two," replied Duce.

"Right. Many of the soldiers are waiting on Level Two, seated in the open detainment cells."

"It's more than half in there," said Duce.

"Yes," continued R.J. "We quietly make our way down there, take out the guards at the control station then close and lock those cells."

"But for how long?" asked Duce.

R.J. looked at me. "Adrian, you're the electrical engineering major. Can't we fry those doors shut somehow?"

I tried to visualize it in my head. "If I could get to the main power wire that is daisy chained to all the cell door actuators and high voltage was available nearby I could short it and burn all those actuators out in about a second or two. There would be no way to open those doors without replacing all the actuators."

"Wow! That's a good one," said Kick.

"Have we got schematics for that control circuitry?" I asked.

"It wouldn't matter," said Duce. "At the security control station there's a big red emergency close and seal button on the desk. It's under a flip up guard. You hit that button and all cells slam shut instantly and it takes high-level command code to reopen them. The entrance to the detainment corridor also gets sealed off by a transparent barrier."

"Plus if we need schematics we could probably get them off the terminal down there," added Kick.

"So we try to quietly take control of the security office outside the detention area then," I said.

"Man, that would give us access to the weapons locker too," said Duce. "Not that I haven't raided the place enough already."

R.J. added, "That would change our situation from a possible troops-massing-against-us, to a guerrilla tactics philosophy."

I added, "I would suggest we wait until the wee hours of the morning to do this when android minds are accustomed to not much happening. In the meantime we should all try to get some rest."

We hunkered down in our service closet, napped and waited for the midnight hour on the *Acrua Maru* clock when the ship's lighting automatically dimmed in the corridors and public areas.

This time the service tunnels would not get us there. We would need to do it the hard way. Despite their objections, R.J., Kick and Anai would stay behind. Less visibility. Duce and I would get the job done.

We crawled back through the tubes to Anai's room. The rat hole would be our escape route if things turned ugly quickly. Anai's place was deserted and dark with the door left open. The narrow hall to the main concourse was dark and empty. Staying below the dining area counter we dared to check the main corridor. Dark figures were patrolling. At least four of them. They were at the far end.

We needed to reach the winding staircase next to the elevator. Making it that far without shooting anyone was an absolute necessity. We kept low and crossed between dining room tables to the waist-high wall which separated dining from concourse. There were no other patrols at this end. We hopped over and made the staircase doors, slowly and quietly spreading one open for access. Once inside, a quick look down cleared the staircase.

Duce led without asking. I followed close behind with rifle strapped over my back but the stock kept ticking against the handrail. Duce paused and gave me a terse stare. I rolled my eyes in acknowledgement and made adjustments.

At Level Three we paused at the doors. Duce looked at me and spoke in a low tone, "You know we are going to have to kill these guys, right?"

"Right."

"Let's go over it. I will just step out and walk up to the guy at the desk as though everything is routine. I know exactly where the lockdown panic button is. I will kill the guy at the desk and hit that button at the same time. Detention will instantly go into lockdown. If I can find and press the button to cancel the alarms really quick it could buy us extra time. It will be up to you to cover my back while I am looking for that damn button."

"Do I have a clear view from here?"

"No. Watch me from here and when you see me reach the desk you can move out 'cause it will all be over a second later. I will drop behind the desk and we will need to take out any other guards in the break room and back office after that."

"Then I tear out the detention area control panel and short the cell actuator line to burn out the actuators."

"Yeah, it will be all your baby after the guards are dead. They won't be able to get to us from the detention area because the panic button will bring down the barrier. The only way they can come for us is from the stairwell and the elevator. I will cover the stairwell door and elevator while you do the deed. When the elevator comes up, I'll kill everyone on it and block the doors with a chair. Then I will just kill anyone coming through the stairwell."

"And our exit?"

"I say we take the elevator for the quickest way up and shoot our way back to Anai's. If we can beat them to the dining area service hallway, we can hold out there a few minutes and kill anyone who comes down that hall, then slip out through to the tunnels."

"If we get through this I'll buy you a stiff drink."

"I will be needing one. You got any?"

"Hell, yes."

"Ready?"

"Go."

Somehow, I did not *feel* ready when Duce stepped out the door into plain view of the seated Con desk guard. I could only see the control desk and a portion of the security room. I knew the meeting room and armory were back there but could not see either.

Duce did his best impression of someone annoyed with a zipper on his vest. He walked casually toward the desk guard and struggled with it. The desk guard straightened up then slowly began to rise. He placed one hand on his holstered disruptor and unsnapped it.

Duce cursed at the zipper. He stopped at the desk under the disapproving stare of the guard. He looked up at the Con and said, "Doesn't this kind of thing just piss you off sometimes?"

Duce hell broke loose.

I burst out into the open, my disruptor raised and ready. Duce drew and shot the guard through the chest while fumbling with the detainment area panic button flip-up guard. There was a rapid-fire snapping lock sound from the detention area. Alarms blared everywhere. The transparent Security barrier slammed down cutting off the detainment area guard who'd been checking cells. A third guard, standing way back in the meeting area near the door to the armory immediately reacted. It was a long shot. My weapon was already raised. He drew. I fired. The first round hit him in his right shoulder. His arm and hand holding his gun was jolted back. His gun fired into the armory, setting off some type of explosive which happened to be in the wrong place at the wrong time.

An explosive fireball blossomed out of the armory doorway. Somehow it did not set off a chain reaction. The place was instantly charred black. Two guards near the armory were dead.

Duce silenced the alarms. An empty stillness hung in the charred air. He didn't miss a beat. "Get to work, partner," he said and headed for the elevator.

No time to reflect on killing androids. The main circuit breaker panel was behind a set of four-foot sliding doors in the wall behind the desk. I tore at my pack for the tool to pull out the circuit breaker panel. Somehow, a masters degree in electrical engineering does not really prepare you for alien wiring compartments.

Duce had shown me the Lemorian word 'Cells' but I could have found that breaker without it. The thing was labeled in bright red for importance. My scanner showed the cell door breaker powered with forty-eight volts. The doors had been closed and locked by the panic button so no current was flowing on the circuit. I cut that breaker line and stripped the end. The feed for the room's lighting was nearby. Three hundred and eighty volts; just what I needed to overload the cell door actuators. A nice big fat wire for heavy current. With pliers, I was able to pull out the actuator wire enough to reach the three-hundred-and-eighty-volt lighting circuit breaker. With insulated long nose pliers I winced and jammed the cell door wire against the high voltage. There was sparking and sizzling. My scanner showed high current which began stepping down as each cell door actuator burned out. When the flow was finally negligible, I pulled out and stuffed everything back in my pack.

Duce was leaning against the main desk with a rifle pointed at the closed stairwell door. Several Con soldiers were nearby pounding at the clear security barrier that had come down and trapped them. We could see their android exclamations but couldn't hear a thing.

"Pretty slow to react," said Duce. "I thought others would have showed up by now. I had to call for the elevator myself."

"I don't think androids handle surprises well," I replied.

"Did you get it done?"

"Either the actuators are burned out or thermal fuses are blown in them."

"Shall we take the elevator then?"

"I believe we're no longer welcome here."

"After you then, sir."

"Why, thank you."

Duce kicked the chair out from between the elevator doors and we stepped in. I pulled my rifle around and set up.

I said, "If we can make the dining area we will have that low divider all around for cover. We can back away to the service hall and into Anai's."

"When the elevator doors open, you want low or high?"

"It's my turn to take high. Why should you have all the fun?"

Duce crouched and readied his weapon.

The elevator doors opened to Level Four. Lighting was still dim. No new alarms were sounding. Duce scampered out still crouched down. I followed, standing and searching. We crossed the open concourse and hopped over the dining area low wall. Kneeling behind it we stopped, searched, and waited.

Arguing voices from further down the main corridor echoed someone's protests. I moved over to the right to look down the corridor toward the guest staterooms. There were four armed Con soldiers assembled at a guest's door trying to take that person away.

"What the hell?" asked Duce. "I am beginning to feel ignored."

"Nothing left to do but crawl back in our hole," I said.

"How many did you see down there?"

"Just four."

"Maybe we should go take them out."

"Why push our luck? There's a human with them. He'd probably get killed."

"Yeah, plus we need to be invisible."

So we scrambled back to Anai's, slipped into our escape tunnel, and sealed it up with the desk. At the tunnel junction our three comrades greeted us nervously.

R.J. said, "So? Were you successful in causing madness and mayhem?"

"Damn true," said Duce.

"Really? You sealed off more than half their army in the detention cells?" asked Kick.

"We didn't actually take a head count," I answered.

"Wow!" declared Kick.

"How many casualties?" asked R.J.

I gave him a disapproving stare. "Three or four."

We all looked at Anai. She remained expressionless.

Before anyone could speak an announcement began to echo through the tunnels. The tunnels did not have public address speakers but we could hear the ghostly, omnipresent voice leaking through the ventilation and access points.

"CAPTAIN TARN. WE KNOW YOU HAVE BEEN SABOTAGING THE SHIP'S SYSTEMS. YOU ARE ENDANGERING ALL THE LIVES ABOARD THIS SHIP. WE ARE LOOKING FOR YOU. WE WILL FIND YOU. WE WILL NOT HARM YOU. IF YOU TURN YOURSELF IN YOU WILL BE TREATED RESPECTFULLY. WE OFFER THE SAME AMNESTY TO THOSE WITH YOU. REPORT TO BETRA MANDA'S OFFICE IMMEDIATELY. FOR THE SAFETY OF EVERYONE LET US RETURN THE

SHIP TO NORMAL OPERATIONS. WE AWAIT YOUR COOPERATION."

"Well, that's it, Adrian. You have to turn yourself in," said Duce with a smirk.

"The dog's running loose now," said Kick.

"I think you mean the cat's out of the bag," said R.J.

"What bag?" asked Kick.

"Level Two was a good move but it is going to get bloodier now," said Duce.

"We need to move on Engineering as soon as possible before they start pulling out environmental control modules," I said.

"How are we going to do it?" asked Duce.

"I'm thinking go in, clear the area and leave the human staff in charge. Seal the place so Cons cannot enter. Is there a way to do that?" I asked.

"We need to know exactly how many soldiers, Cons and humans are left there," said Duce.

"None of us can set foot out in public," said Kick.

"Anai can," said R.J. and we all looked at her.

I asked, "Can you do that, Anai? Could you visit Engineering with coffee or something and find out for us which people are there?"

Anai answered matter-of-factly, "They do not know I am non-compliant. As long as I behave properly I should be able to go anywhere as long as I have a reason to."

R.J. said, "Anai, you understand if we can get control of the ship we can put a stop to humans being forced into stasis or killed and we can probably correct the corrupted software in the other Cons?"

"Yes."

We escorted Anai back to her quarters. Duce led, I brought up the rear. Watching Anai move along the cramped tube raised a new concern. She did not move along on her hands and knees like we did. She had a way of repositioning her feet so that she could race along propelled by hands and toes. It looked natural for her and she was as quick as a dog. I suddenly had ugly visions of trying to escape Cons in the tubes. There would be no outrunning them.

We intended to watch from the hall as she prepared her coffee delivery but there was something new and alarming waiting for us. We heard the commotion as we approached. From concealment behind the dining area hall we watched a dozen Con soldiers pass by in single file, rifles in hand. Three other Con soldiers were scattered around the area, searching everywhere.

Duce whispered, "Kick was right. The dogs are loose now."

Anai was not concerned. She went to the serving area and began to make coffee as we continued to watch.

"How long before they find our hole in the wall?" said Duce.

"Let us pray never."

"We'll be like rodents."

"Yeah, if you come across a big piece of cheese, leave it."

"What?"

"I was hoping to hold here until Anai made it back but I don't think we'll be able to stay."

"No way. The three searching are working their way around. They will be here in about ten minutes."

"If they find the hole Anai will not be able to get back."

"She may be safer out here than with us anyway."

"Did you notice her move through the tunnel?"

"We won't outrun them, I can tell you that. It will be stop and shoot through your legs if they spot us in a tunnel. You know, maybe we should wait for those three and kill them so they can't find our hole."

I shook my head. "There's too much of a chance a firefight would draw more attention to this area. We'd be better off if they searched here and didn't find the hole. If they do find it three Cons won't make much of a difference either way."

"You are right; itchy trigger finger."

"There she goes with the coffee. Nothing we can do for her now. Better head back to the others."

We slipped back into the tube and sealed it off as tightly as possible. Back at the service junction Kick and R.J. looked on with apprehensive stares.

"Con soldiers all over the place," said Duce.

"No surprise there," replied R.J.

"Did she get off alright?" asked Kick.

"They ignored her completely," I replied as I slid down into a sitting position.

"You know, something she said earlier made me wonder," said Kick.

"About what?" asked R.J.

"She mentioned about the Cons being destroyed and how their life histories would be lost forever and that she could never exchange data with them again."

"And that struck a chord with you?" asked R.J.

"Well, it doesn't sound like machine feedback. It's not like a programmed response to a stimulus. It sounded more like a human concerned about not seeing someone ever again or never being able to talk to them again."

There was a long silence between our group.

R.J. finally responded. "You are considering self-awareness in Cons I take it?"

Kick asked, "Can you explain those comments? I've thought about it and I can't."

"It is a bit troubling," answered R.J.

"Maybe we should not have sent her out there," added Kick.

Duce took issue. "It's intel, buddy. We're trying not to bleed too much if you know what I mean. That won't happen with her."

"I know. I know. I am just saying."

"She'll be okay, Kick. They won't physically harm her anyway. If they take her prisoner, chances are we can still get her back," I said.

"Are you people worried about a Con? They are how we got into this mess," insisted Duce. "There is a good chance we will spend the rest of our lives sandwiched together in a stasis tube. Get rational, will you?"

No one spoke.

The matter was put to rest one hour later. With weapons ready we watched Anai crawl back into our compartment pulling along an oversized thermos of hot coffee. We all drank from paper coffee cups.

As he sipped, Kick asked Duce, "How's that coffee, hot enough for you?"

Duce smirked. "I may have been rash earlier." He looked at Anai and spoke in a much friendlier tone. "So what is the deal, Anai? What did you see?"

"There are five human engineering technicians. They scan as biologicals. They are all seated on the floor under guard by two Con soldiers with rifles. Four Con technicians are working around a large open panel. There are four additional Con soldiers, two standing guard outside Engineering and two at the entrance to the main corridor."

"Wow!" said R.J.

"They are using the humans as hostages for defense," said Duce.

"Very effective," said R.J.

"So six Con soldiers and four Con technicians," said Duce.

I asked, "Anai, did the Con technicians have weapons?"

"No."

"Okay so six shooters we would need to take out quietly and quickly," said Duce. "Can't use the proximity grenades because of the humans, plus that would be too much of a bang. You got any magic tricks left up your sleeve, R.J.?"

"Well, there are five of us," said R.J.

I said, "If you're thinking about the OK Corral R.J., I don't like the odds."

"What is the OK Corral?" asked Kick.

"It was a face-to-face shoot out on Earth a very long time ago. People got shot on both sides. No, I wasn't thinking the OK Corral move."

"Then what?"

"Anai, if we were all dressed as soldiers and we used Adrian's command codes to get into Engineering, could you approach the soldiers in that room and tell them they were being relieved and to report to the cargo area and would they believe it?"

"I could communicate those instructions. I do not know if they would accept them."

Duce said, "That would not be a problem. If they don't believe her, we shoot them, if they do believe her, we shoot them."

Kick said, "You have a one-track mind, you know that?"

"Yeah, and I want to keep it."

"Right," replied Kick.

R.J. said, "If we kill any guards that will mean they'll miss their check-ins and may alert their command too."

Duce replied, "But if they get away, they contact the cargo area immediately and the whole place will know something's going on in Engineering."

"It just means either way there's a time constraint to securing Engineering," I said.

"It's an interesting plan, R.J.," said Duce. "But what about the guards outside Engineering?"

R.J. nodded. "Two soldiers at the entrance to the main corridor. We divide into two groups, march up to them and each group takes out a guard. We shield the action as much as possible, maybe stun them to avoid gunfire. Two of us take their place to stand guard and make it look as though nothing has happened. The three of us escort the bodies away then continue down to the entrance of Engineering. We shoot the other two guards as we approach."

Duce looked at me. "Could work."

I said, "So then we enter Engineering and while Anai tries to distract the two guards there we stun or shoot them."

"While keeping a close eye on the Con technicians," added Duce.

"We'll need to stun the Con techs fast enough to stop them from alerting their command."

"So we will need to be very quick once we are in Engineering," added Duce.

"At that point it will only take a few minutes to brief the humans and secure the place."

"Just one other thing: once we take Engineering how are you gonna keep it?" asked Kick.

R.J. answered, "We don't want to keep it. We just don't want them to have it."

"You are going to seal it off? With the human techs still inside?" asked Kick.

"There is a food and water dispenser in Engineering," said Duce.

"You think they will agree?" asked Kick.

"Given the choice of that or ending up two to a stasis pod forever, yes," said R.J. "We'll use Adrian's command codes to lock out the door to everyone except us and them then get the hell out of there."

"Can't the Cons eventually rewire that door to open?" asked Kick.

"It would be time consuming and difficult," replied Duce. "That door is a security lockout. I'm guessing at least eight hours to break in, probably more. They would have to burn through some bulkheads to get to the wiring."

"So, Adrian, where are we going to get combat suits?"

"We've remained fairly invisible so far. Let's try to stay invisible. Three of us could make another trip to the detention area. They'd never expect us to return there. Worse case is there might be a couple of Con engineers trying to open the place up. We can maybe get what we need from the armory if it's not too badly damaged."

"They will be down there trying to burn their way into the detention area I bet," said Kick.

"No way," answered Duce. "There's nothing which will burn through that transparent barrier or the detention area bars. Only way back in there is by fixing the burned-out door actuators, one at a time."

"It wasn't hard to make the staircase from the dining area. We go and bring back five combat suits and we're ready," I promised.

"Who you got in mind to go?" asked Duce.

"You, me and R.J.; Kick and Anai wait here," I replied.

Kick objected. "Wait, I am no pacifist."

"Kick, we need Anai. You're here to see she stays safe."

"Oh. Okay. Got it."

Chapter 26

The main concourse outside the dining area was still busy with soldiers in search. They did not seem to be very good at it. The subordinate soldiers were paying more attention to their commanders than to the search objectives. One at a time we waited for openings, hopped the dining area wall, and darted across to the stairwell.

For some odd reason they did not seem to be keeping an eye inside the stairwell. We made our way down. Through a small split in the detention level doors we spotted several soldiers grouped together, trapped behind the transparent barrier wall looking out, waiting for release. The body of the soldier Duce had shot was still on the floor by the desk. Two new Con soldiers were guarding the small lobby. Two Con technicians were inspecting the open rewired fuse panel I'd used to short the place out.

"Let's not kill those two techs if we don't have to," I said.

"They will probably call in as soon as they see us," answered Duce.

"Yeah, you're right. I'll try to get them with a bang stick if I can."

"You are not going to break the cardinal rule of combat, are you?"

"Leave thyself open trying to save the enemy?"

"That's the one."

"You are a wise man."

"You only get to violate that rule once."

I nodded.

We stepped out and shot the two guards before they ever saw us.

The technicians were slow in reacting. I charged forward and hit one with the bang stick as he stared up at me, caught the second as he turned to run. They both went down asleep.

"What is the deal here, Adrian? You starting to get sentimental about these machines like Kick?"

"I'd like to have *some* good news to tell Anai."

"Okay, I get that."

We hurried to the armory.

"But you know, Kick may have a point, Duce."

"Like what?"

"Something else I've noticed. Have you ever seen a female Con soldier?"

"Come to think of it, I have not. What is your point?"

"There is no reason women androids can't be soldiers."

"Hey look, those two who were knocked out by the blast last time are still there on the floor. That is four suits right there."

"The only reason I can think of not to make female Con soldiers is if the Cons have a special affection for their women."

"Maybe the female bodies are weaker than the males like with humans."

"We used to think that way on Earth. We were shown the error of our ways repeatedly."

"Really?"

"Some of the best fighter pilots on Earth are women."

"No shit?"

"You would not want one on your six, believe me."

The front portion of the armory room was charred but the back end had remained untouched. We found large duffel bags containing packaged, unused black combat suits. Duce could not resist stuffing a second duffel bag with the disruptor magazines along with other items of destruction. We headed back, giving the locked-in soldiers a passing glance.

"They've probably called us in," said Duce.

"Lucky we found packaged suits. If they found soldiers with their suits missing it might tip them off."

"Yeah, now they probably will think we were just there for the weapons."

We stepped into the stairwell and headed up.

Duce asked, "So what do you think? You really think some Cons are becoming human?"

"I'm at the point where it pisses me off that I can't be sure."

"Yeah, sure would be a lot simpler if they were just machines."

At the top of the stairs we opened a slit in the door but quietly closed it when a line of soldiers marched passed a few feet away.

Duce spoke in a low tone. "They are getting smarter. They have soldiers stationed all along the way out there. I do not think we can cross the concourse without being seen. Got any ideas?"

"You know, I still have that stupid chip in my hip. Maybe not all of them have been programmed for facial recognition of me. I'm supposed to look just like a Con. Let me have one of those combat suits."

Five minutes later, I was dressed for combat. Duce smirked. "You look like yourself."

"Cover me."

After a quick check through the slit again, I stepped out the door and stood by the wall trying to look like a guard. There were two other standing soldiers across the concourse. They paid me no attention at all. I tested my newfound freedom by walking across to the dining area and peering over the low divider wall, then back to the stairwell door.

"Suit up, buddy," I said out of the corner of my mouth.

"Already did."

"Slide the bags out to me."

With a duffel bag in each hand, I crossed to the dining area again and as inconspicuously as possible lifted the bags over the wall and deposited them out of sight. I turned and stood guard there just in time to see Duce step out from the stairwell door and take a position against the wall as a new guard.

We stared at each other across the way. Duce was trying not to smirk again. It was a strange feeling. We had instantly become one of the mindless guards stationed around the main concourse. I was beginning to wonder if we could just pretend to patrol the dining area when a commotion suddenly broke out. The guards opposite us took off down the corridor. Duce crossed over and hopped over the dining area wall. I followed. We paused in the dining area hallway to watch.

It was a sickening sight. Four guards dragging another human woman against her will to the elevators. It was obvious she had been hiding and was discovered. She yelled continuously and wrestled but had no chance. Two guards entered the elevator with her and down they went. The other two returned to their original positions.

"Still feeling compassion for the Cons?" asked Duce as we headed for our escape tunnel.

"Give me a few minutes."

"You know where *she* will be in a few minutes."

We each dragged a duffel bag through the tunnel to our service space hideout. Kick and R.J. had looks of concern. Anai looked indifferent.

"We thought we could hear something going on out there," said Kick.

"Yeah, a human was being taken below and she didn't want to go," replied Duce.

"Oh, God," said Kick.

"Can I have a food pack?" asked Duce. "Avoiding combat gives me an appetite."

We passed around the meals-ready-to-eat food packs and drank more coffee from the thermos.

"So, same time tonight?" asked Kick.

Duce shook his head. "No way. Always attack at different times of the day. Get it?"

Kick nodded and sipped.

I said, "But this does need to be a coordinated attack. When the shooting starts we can't have everybody firing at the same target. As we approach the two guards near the lobby, R.J. and I will take the guard on the left. Duce and Kick the one on the right. Duce and I will have the bang sticks. We should be able to get both of them without a problem. We catch the guards before they fall. R.J. covers me, Kick covers Duce."

"What about Anai?" asked Kick.

I answered, "Anai will take the place of Duce's missing guard. Kick, you take the place of the guard on my side."

"Works for me," said Duce.

I continued, "Duce, R.J. and I will then head down the corridor single file like all good Con patrols. As we get near the two guards outside Engineering the instant one of them starts to raise a weapon we will drop and shoot them."

"I guarantee you that will work," said Duce as he chewed his MRE chicken.

"Then Anai and I run and catch up?" said Kick.

"Right. We enter Engineering as a standard patrol and take out the last two guards before they realize what's happening."

"While keeping a close eye on the Con technicians," noted Duce again.

"So when do we go?" asked Kick.

"As soon as you three finish suiting up," replied Duce.

"Now? You mean right now?"

"Don't want you greenhorns sitting around thinking about this. Better to go get it done."

Kick stopped chewing his fruit bar. "So what if we do take Engineering and secure it, Adrian? What then?"

"I don't know, Kick. We're making this up as we go along."

Duce broke out laughing. He made a grunt which sounded like a Marine.

R.J. held up his coffee in a silent toast and sipped.

"One thing I *will* say is if this goes well, at some point we're going to need to take control of the cargo area. Then we could start waking those people up and increasing our numbers."

R.J. said, "Getting ahead of ourselves, aren't we?"

Kick asked, "You bruses really think we can make it across the concourse out there to get to the stairwell?"

Duce answered, "Oh, yeah, about that. It is my intention to make my way behind the dining area counter. When the time is right, I will lean out into the corridor and pitch a proximity grenade as far down the corridor as I can; three second fuse. When the bang happens there will be confusion. We will exit like we are a part of the confusion and we will disappear into the stairwell while their reorganization is going on."

"A bit heavy handed but it should work," said R.J.

Duce added, "They will think it is an assault on the Level Four soldiers for dragging away innocent humans. I doubt they will figure it is a diversion."

We watched Anai finish getting her sleek figure into her combat suit. She looked right at

361

home in it except her permanent facial makeup was in sharp contrast to the threat of the suit. Kick noticed. He found some grime between the floor and wall, wiped up a small amount, and went to her. She understood and allowed him to apply it. He seemed to use more care than was necessary.

"Well, lady and gentlemen, we are ready," said Duce.

Once again, we crawled our way to Anai's room and stayed out of sight near the end of the dining area service hallway. We watched Duce crouch along behind the empty counter until he'd reached the main concourse. He dared a few quick looks and after the last patrol had passed he heaved the grenade high through the air toward the aft section of ship. He scooted back and reached us just as the thing went boom.

The Con guards fell for it immediately. Those stationed around our area took off down the corridor leaving it wide open. We crossed over to the stairwell and regrouped inside.

"Nice, but how we going to get back?" asked Kick.

"One miracle at a time," replied Duce.

We wound our way down the steps and again huddled outside the Level Three entrance doors.

Duce said in a low voice, "Everybody remember who they are supposed to shoot?"

Kick's face took on a strained expression.

Duce flattened his hands against the doors and spread them apart just enough for a look outside. The long corridor leading to the entrance to Engineering was bordered by unmanned equipment racks and conduit. Two soldiers were standing guard in the lobby, one on each side of the corridor entrance. The array of cameras pointing down were no longer of any concern. With a last check on us, Duce tapped the open button and allowed the doors to open. We marched out and divided into two groups. The guards snapped around to face us.

Never plan on things going as planned. Whenever planning a surprise, include in the plan being surprised. As we approached the two the guard on our right began to raise his weapon. We were still ten feet away but Duce did not wait. He flicked his bang stick up and extended it, catching the guard in the left shoulder. The attack threw our timing way off. The crackle and bang rang out. The guard on the left sprang into combat mode. We did not want disruptor shots echoing down the corridor and alerting the other two guards. I had the second bang stick but was not close enough to use it. I had to dive forward in a superman pose to get close enough. In mid-air my bang stick popped out and caught the guard under the chin. There was second snap, crackle, pop, and the guard fell unconscious a fraction of an instant before he could fire. R.J. raced forward and pinned the body against the wall. Duce stood holding the body of the first guard. Anai took her place standing against the wall. Kick followed suit opposite her.

We quickly hauled the unconscious androids into the stairwell.

"Well, that was okay but it wasn't pretty," said Duce.

"I couldn't see that far down the corridor. Did we alert them down there?" asked R.J.

"I don't think so," I replied.

"Either way, we are good to go," said Duce.

"Hopefully the cameras are still offline," said R.J.

"So no screwing around with the next two, right? As soon as we are in range we spread apart, hit the deck, and kill them. No time to waste."

I looked at R.J. "I think Duce is quicker than I am. I'll take the guard on the left, you help me with him, okay?"

R.J. nodded.

"High praise," remarked Duce.

With a nod to Anai and Kick, the three of us headed single file down the hall toward Engineering with rifles slung behind us like any good Con patrol. Duce led.

But the next two guards were a bit more on the ball. Their rifles were in hand, pointed down. They recognized us as soldiers but moved into ready stances anyway. They partially raised their rifles.

Duce didn't like it. He stopped and turned to us. "Handguns are not going to make it," he said. "We're going to have to bring our rifles around and that is going to set them off for sure. I will get us as close as possible. When I dive for the floor that will be your cue. Bring your rifle around as you dive, not before. Got it?"

We nodded.

"OK Corral," mumbled R.J.

Duce turned and marched forward. The guards stood ready for us. They were now less than twenty yards away. Duce dared another ten steps until the guard-right brought his barrel the rest of the way up.

Duce made his dive, firing before he reached the floor. I squeezed off my shots a moment after diving. R.J. landed next to me out of position and had to roll to fire.

In the maze of flashes and bangs we unleashed a barrage of firepower on the two standing guards. These two responded with attitude. Plasma rounds were deflecting off the floor around us leaving black streaks. The walls and doors behind the guards were peppered with strikes. It went on for a long five seconds with both guards hit multiple times. Many of their shots went wild. They were knocked back from injuries several times, fired wildly from bad positions and finally fell to the floor. Smoke from the onslaught drifted away into the air-conditioning intakes.

R.J. spoke while still on the floor on his elbows. "So much for a surprise attack on Engineering."

"Anybody hit?" asked Duce.

We slowly stood.

"Nobody?" asked R.J. "How'd we manage that?"

"They were still surprised," replied Duce. "Didn't you see the delay before they fired? For just a split second they weren't sure what we were shooting at."

I called over the comms, "Anai, Kick, come on up."

Once again we dragged android bodies out of the way.

Kick was holding his rifle ready as they approached as though he was concerned it might not be over. He and Anai made a quick appraisal of the scene and looked to us for direction.

Duce pointed at the entrance. "When the door opens, the guards in there will be expecting us. They will have heard the exchange from the hits on the walls and door but to them we may still look like Con soldiers. We should still have a split second or two advantage. Don't waste it. I am thinking Kick and Anai, you guys cover the Con technicians while the rest of us take out the guards. Five against two. This should just be a clean op."

"How exactly do you want it to start?" asked R.J.

"The three of us step in, spot the enemy, and fire. I will take the right side. You guys get the left. Anai and Kick follow us in."

There was a tense silence.

"No sense in waiting around. Check your weapons. The door pad is all yours, Adrian," said Duce.

I entered my command code prefix and watched the door control turn green. With a last look to be sure they were all ready, I punched it. The doors slid open.

The guard on the right was standing over the human technicians. They were still grouped together on the floor. He lurched into firing position a second too late and caught a round directly in the chest from Duce. On our side there was a problem. The guard was a little better at combat than others we had seen. There was a desk between us. He got the first shot off. It whizzed between us as we were diving for the floor. We sprayed fire without taking aim. The guard crouched behind the desk, letting each barrage pass before squeezing off a few wild rounds. R.J. and I had to crawl-scramble to a control console for partial cover. Duce kept firing but had to drop also. Anai stood expressionless in the middle of the room doing nothing at all, rounds zipping by her on either side. I exchanged a quick look with Duce. He pointed at me and began a three-finger count down. I had just enough time to warn R.J., "Cover me."

On three, a new barrage of gunfire erupted all around the guard's desk. I stood, stepped up onto the control console and dove over it to slide across the floor alongside the desk. The slide took me just far enough to bring a sidearm to bear and catch the Con in the right hip. He spun, took a second blast in the chest and was knocked back to the floor, dead.

Before I could react a loud cursing broke. More rapid weapons fire echoed around the room. Fearing for Duce, I kicked myself around on the floor and with both hands on my disruptor searched for a target in the direction of the shots.

Duce was on his back on the floor trying to get a handle on what was happening. It took a moment to understand as the blasting rang out around us, making my ears ring worse than they had been.

In the midst of confusion and adrenaline I managed to spot the problem. One of the human technicians had grabbed a dead guard's rifle and was yelling and cursing as he cut down the Con technicians. "Fuck you too! Fuck you. Yeah! Yeah! WE don't need YOU either!"

Duce looked on with his handgun raised, not knowing what to do. In just a second or two the enraged man had managed to execute all five Con technicians. He turned in a daze to look over the room. Anai was still standing in the center of it. There was a moment of recognition in the crazed man's face but before he could react Kick leapt up and stood in front of Anai with his hands behind him holding her in place.

The dazed man faltered, dropped the rifle, and fell against a console. He leaned over it trying to regain himself. The other humans slowly stood, still wide-eyed from the melee. No one spoke.

R.J. joined me as I stood. "Not so clean an op after all."

"Did the Con techs do anything threatening?" I asked.

"Not that I could see but I suspect their treatment of the prisoners was less than friendly."

Duce was up and checking bodies as the hostage humans gathered around their compatriot warrior.

Anai and Kick came to me. Anai said, "I sensed calls in to report us, Captain."

"Thank you, Anai. Can you and Kick help me with the door lockout?"

"Of course."

Kick's eyes looked dazed.

"Kick, are you with me?"

"Yes, yes. Still trying to figure out what just happened. What do you need?"

We went to a nearby terminal. It took only a few minutes to make Engineering sealed to everyone but us.

Duce called out, "Adrian, change of plans."

I went to him. "What are you thinking?"

"I heard what Anai said. I do not think we should leave the way we came."

"You think they might be waiting for us at the lobby?"

"If they were waiting for us that *would* be the place."

"There are no aft exits, Duce."

"We need another rat hole."

"This place is cable and conduit heavy. It may not be possible."

We both turned and looked at Kick. He noticed and came over.

"We need to cut a hole out of here," said Duce.

"Really? We can't go back? Give me a few minutes to call up the plans. The human techs will probably help."

Kick went to a terminal near the techs and began typing and speaking to them.

Duce said, "Adrian, we now own two of four decks."

"Yes, but that means Deck One and Deck Four are crawling with soldiers. There's no way to know how many."

"Well, there are six less than there were a while ago."

I stared at Duce. "Where did you get that?"

"What?"

"What you just said, it's a line from an Earth Civil War song."

Duce suddenly exclaimed, "Hey, you're wounded!"

"Just a scratch."

"No, really; how bad is it? Is it the hip your ass?"

"I just need to strip down and take care of it. It will blend in with all the other scars just fine. A strip of epidural wrap will do it."

Anai closed in, leaning over to inspect the red spot on my hip. "Adrian, I can treat this. Pull your pants down and lay on the desk over there."

"Bet you have heard that line before," joked Duce.

I obeyed. I positioned myself on the desk, hip up, head resting on one hand and elbow.

R.J. came over. "Tsk, tsk. Another one."

"Just lucky I guess."

"It must have happened during the deranged swan dive to the floor."

"How's Kick doing over there?"

"Oh, it looks good. If we clear out a lower cabinet we can cut just enough to get into a north-south tunnel without butchering lines. The entrance will be well hidden. The techs can use it to escape if necessary."

A pounding at the main doors suddenly erupted. There was a pause, then more pounding.

R.J. looked at me. "Well, somebody wants to know what's going on in here."

"Another disappointment for them," said Duce as he watched Anai's surgery.

"Where will our tunnel lead?" I asked.

R.J. answered, "Oh, yeah, we can't get back to our cubbyhole from here. But you might like the alternative. A few turns up and over will take us to Betra Manda's Con reprogramming lab. There's a service hatch there to exit."

"You thinking we should take over Manda's office? I like it," said Duce. "We can sneak in and stun Manda before she can let out a peep."

"Our sneaking hasn't been going so well," said R.J.

"That *is* one place they wouldn't expect us to be," I replied.

Anai spoke, "That office contains seven high level Con programming stations. I could use them to correct the corrupted programming on any Con individuals we have access to."

"If it works I will miss the threatening ship-wide announcements she makes," said Duce. "They were an inspiration to me. I'll go check the laser cutting."

The rat hole job was surprisingly quick. The engineering techs had better laser cutters and some kind of BX-Ray video scanner which could see through the wall. While we worked, we explained our plan to them. They liked it. Locked in Engineering they had everything they needed along with an escape route and no androids. They took turns doing most of the cutting while Duce watched from outside the cabinet. Banging on the Engineering door continued intermittently.

When the cutting was done and the wall had cooled enough, we exchanged goodbyes and promises and assembled at the new rat hole. R.J. insisted he knew the pathway the best so he went in first. Against Doctor Anai's wishes I brought up the rear.

R.J. was lost after the second turn in the tunnel. He and Kick traded the laptop back and forth until corrective navigation was agreed upon. It took twenty more minutes to reach the appropriately labeled exit hatch. We were all exhausted. It was Duce's job to open the hatch in stealth mode but the thing got away from him and made a dull thud on the floor that echoed down the service tunnel. We had to wait breathlessly for bad news. None came.

We oozed out of the tunnel and found ourselves in a small closet-sized storage room adjoining the lab. The lab was deserted. I made my way to the lab's entrance and listened at the door. A small spread of the doors showed Mandra's office unoccupied.

"Kick, can you make sure the front door is locked?"

"Okay."

R.J. appeared next to me and asked, "You know she's going to return, Adrian. Exactly what are you going to do when that happens?"

"Trust me. We'll be set up and be waiting."

"You do want to capture her, right?" said R.J.

"It's a thought."

"It is now locked," called out Kick.

I considered our options as Kick passed by and flopped down in Manda's desk chair. Immediately he began hammering away on her keyboard. He called out again, "Hey Adrian, look at this! There is an insert on her home page. She has a private camera outside next to her door so she can see who wants in. It is a private camera. It still works."

I moved around the desk and looked in time to see two Con soldiers march past the camera.

Kick looked up at me, "I guess we are well guarded."

"See if you can feed it to that main wall monitor so we can all keep an eye out."

"Will do."

R.J. took to exploring the office while I sat on the corner of the desk watching the front door, a bang stick in my hand, ready.

"Hey, this panel behind her desk slides open to a private room," exclaimed R.J. "There is a charging bed, food dispenser and a bathroom in there. Wow! You close this panel and you can't even tell there's a room back there."

"Oh, God, did you say bathroom?" asked Duce and he pushed past R.J. and headed in.

Anai stood near the center of the room watching us. I went to her. "Anai, *you* are overdue to recharge, aren't you?"

"I have reserve power which can be used as necessary."

"Anai, please go in that back room and use the bed to recharge."

"Yes, Adrian."

Kick stood. "I'll keep an eye on her." He followed Anai into the bedroom.

I had the urge to tell him that wasn't necessary but thought better of it.

R.J. came up beside me and watched them disappear to the back. "When did she start calling us all by our first names?"

"I hadn't noticed."

"Why would a machine suddenly start doing that?"

"Here we go again."

"Just saying…."

"We all need to get some rest. I'll take the first shift. Try to get some sleep."

"And when Manda returns?"

"She will cease to be a problem."

"You're starting to sound like Duce."

"Very funny. We're all exhausted. Go make a bed somewhere and lie in it."

"I believe we've already made our beds and are presently lying in them."

Chapter 27

We took turns napping, eating, and watching the front door monitor. Four hours later, Betra Manda, escorted by two soldiers, emerged from the elevator and headed toward her office. I stood off to the side where I could still see her on the monitor while holding the bang stick ready.

She tapped in her door code and strolled in, leaving her soldier escorts outside. I waited for the doors to close and drove the bang stick into her butt. She came to attention and fell over to one side. I strained to catch her and lower her face down on the floor. R.J. and Duce emerged from their backup positions and came to stand over her.

"She never knew what hit her," said Duce. "Nice job."

"All that evil scheming contained in one female android," said R.J.

"Let's move her into one of the wall reprogramming cradles back there. If we can mod her programming, we'll have the best possible ally."

We dragged the captured Con leader back and stood her in place. Kick and Anai would take it from there when they woke up.

An hour later they went to work on her. Duce, R.J. and I sat around Manda's desk trying to come up with a plan for the cargo area. After an hour of hashing over all the possibilities with no good ideas, we were abruptly interrupted and alarmed when Betra Manda walked through the door and stood staring at us. It was a good Kick prank except Duce nearly put a hole in her.

"Ha, ha. Completely back to normal," insisted Kick.

"What is normal?" asked Duce.

"To serve man," said Kick.

"I've heard that one before," answered R.J.

"Gentlemen, Manda is ready and willing to help us any way she can to bring a peaceful resolution to this insurgency."

"Holy crap, Kick. You just became a politician right before my eyes," said Duce.

"Did not!"

I turned in my chair to face Manda. "Betra, how many soldiers are there in the cargo area?"

"Eighteen," replied Manda.

We exchanged looks of surprise.

"Are they all in the cargo area or are some in the shuttle bay?" asked Duce.

"All are assigned to the cargo area guarding or processing the stasis chamber candidates."

R.J. looked at Kick. "So she remembers everything that happened?"

"Yes."

"But she feels differently about it now?"

"She doesn't feel anything at all. She is just processing the information differently."

"Just like Anai?"

"Anai is different."

"What about her intranet? Will she still be recognized as the Con leader?"

Kick replied, "That all takes place on the higher levels. So yes, she will still appear to be her same old self online."

I intervened. "So you're saying the leader of the Cons is now on our side. What more could we ask for?"

Duce asked, "Manda, can you order the cargo area soldiers to put down their weapons and stand down?"

"Yes, I can give such an order."

"Will they obey it?"

"Those who are not soldiers will comply. Those who *are* soldiers were programmed by central command and can only be reprogrammed by central command. They will not accept a change of mission objectives."

"Manda, would you agree to accompany us to the cargo area and issue that order anyway?"

"Yes."

I asked, "Manda, if we provided you with a bang stick and one of the soldiers attempted to harm us would you do everything possible to stop them?"

"Yes."

"That fits the plan nicely," said R.J.

"What plan?" asked Kick.

"Take a seat, Kick," said R.J.

I explained. "There is no good plan. We don't like our plan but we don't have a better one. We can't go on with things the way they are. We are still at risk from sabotage of life support or some other critical system. So, Manda and Anai will lead us down into the cargo area as a Con patrol again. They will position you, Duce, R.J., and me at various points around the room near where the soldiers are grouped. We will each have two fully charged handguns in leg holsters ready to draw. We can't walk in there with rifles in hand. Anai and Manda will call the place to attention and take positions near the higher ranked Cons running the show. Manda will order them to stand down. If they do not immediately comply, we will know they are not going to. We will all open fire on the soldiers nearest us."

R.J. added, "It's not a perfect plan."

Duce said, "Eighteen Con soldiers. Four of us firing two weapons each. That is four surprised Cons apiece. It is the best odds we can get."

"She said eighteen soldiers, Duce. Not sixteen."

"That is saying Manda and Anai each stun at least one," answered Duce.

"You think I can take out four soldiers?" said Kick.

Duce sat back and locked his hands behind his head. "Close range shooting, keep firing all the time; yeah, I think you can do it. Plus I will make a point of helping you from wherever I am."

"No, I can do it. I didn't mean I couldn't. I was just surprised you thought I could."

"It is a bit ambitious," said R.J.

"If the people in those stasis tubes could vote I know which way they would go," said Duce.

I asked, "Manda, have the Doctors in the medical lab been reprogrammed?"

"No. There was no need. They are original command code programming."

"So if we end up needing them there's no problem," I said.

"That's a little foreboding," said R.J.

"We should load up, gather our stuff and go get this over with," said Duce. "You think we will make the elevator okay?"

"With a Betra Manda escort, no problem," said Kick.

"What about her two guards outside the door?" asked Duce.

"She can just tell them to hold their positions," suggested Kick. "The soldiers *will* take minor orders from her."

We gathered around the desk and went over it step by step. The four of us suited back up as soldiers. When there were no questions left, we lined up at the door behind Anai and Manda and followed them out. The door guards accepted Manda's orders to remain in place. The march to the elevator was uneventful so down we went. The mood in the elevator was so tense it was uncomfortable.

R.J. leaned next to me and spoke under his breath. "I just don't see this as ending up too quick and clean again."

"We can't wait. We have nothing to hope for. We won't ever be in a better position than we are now."

"I agree."

The elevator doors opened. The big shuttle bay doors were open, but except for shuttles, the place was empty. We took the bypass hallway to the cargo area, locking and sealing all doors behind us. Fear now dominated the atmosphere but no one hesitated.

At the cargo area entrance Manda did not pause. She opened the door and left it open. We waited behind. In a human and machine voice mix we heard her call out to halt all operations and come to attention. That was our cue. We marched in and spread out around the hangar as though we were simply obeying her command also. Each of us positioned ourselves as best we could to divide the enemy. There was some worrisome awkwardness to it. Kick kept trying to look at the Cons he was about to kill. They began to notice.

Manda made a short speech, something about new directives that now overrode all other orders. All service Cons were to standby by for new orders. All soldiers were to stand down and discontinue all human processing.

Duce and I really hadn't expected to get that far. When Manda was done here was a long pregnant pause which hung over the hangar bay. It was easy to tell the soldiers had understood the new orders but were waiting for some authentication code Manda did not have. I expected at some point the soldiers would time out and simply resume their processing but fate intervened.

There was a small number of humans still waiting to be processed on the east side of the cargo bay. Two soldiers were keeping them in groups seated on the floor. One elderly guest was being uncooperative and verbally abusive. Each time he tried to get up a soldier would force him back down with the barrel of his rifle. He started swinging at the guard. The indifferent soldier backed up and raised his rifle as though to fire. It was almost certainly intended only as a threat but in that moment there was no way to be sure.

It set Duce off.

It was a long shot across the hangar bay but Duce drew and fired. His first round caught the guard square in the back and knocked him forward and down hard. The old man jumped up clapping and cheering.

All hell broke loose.

There was no way to track everything that was happening. Cons and humans running in every direction. I had a gun in each hand firing continuously, turning in place with each shot, bending at the knees to be less of a target. You couldn't wait to see if your disruptor scored because there was bound to be someone else taking aim at you. Instead of stationary targets like we'd planned we had moving targets interlaced with innocents. In the mind's eye there were instantaneous images from all around like a camera clicking away on automatic. We still had a short advantage because it took the guards some seconds to understand who was against them. Kick went down fast from standing in one damn place too long but he continued to fire from the floor. Another glimpse showed Duce only able to shoot with one hand. R.J. was squatting and turning but he was holding his side with one hand. I suddenly realized there was a hole of some significance in my left upper leg. My ears were ringing loudly from the gunfire. I saw Anai on the floor but still awake and aware next to Kick. Duce had managed to drag himself behind two soldier bodies but he was still firing away with the good hand and arm. I tried to lurch to one side on my left foot and went down hard on my back. I could still fire both guns and push myself around with my good leg. I looked in time to see Anai crawl over the wounded Kick, taking a shot in her shoulder for the effort. In the distance the human group had gathered together behind the stasis chambers recently prepared for them. The old man had somehow found a weapon and was shooting wildly. Manda was down in a sitting position leaning against a wall next to a dead soldier.

The popping of weapons fire began to die down. I began having trouble finding targets. There was movement from a few damaged soldiers on the floor. The place had become smoky and the air smelled burnt. A heavy silence formed.

There was a yelp-laugh from Duce. I pushed up on one elbow and spotted him by the big closed doors to the hangar area. I dragged myself over to him, scanning as I went, leaving a red trail behind me. He was propped up against the hangar doors, his weapon resting against his chest, his finger still on the trigger.

He smirked at me while wincing in pain. "By God, we are all shot up, Adrian."

I continued to search the area. "Not as bad as they are."

"Can you see any of the others?"

"R.J. is hobbling around checking bodies using a rifle stock as a cane. Kick is down somewhere and Anai is helping him but she's shot up too."

"You know, buddy, one thing we did not consider. Those soldiers up on Level One are going to be heading down here now. I saw some through the window in this hangar door."

"I had Kick lock those doors, Duce."

"Well, whatever happens, it was a damn good firefight, partner."

"You going to live?"

"Oh, hell yes. I could get up and shoot some more. I am just taking a break."

"How many soldiers would you guess are up on Level One?"

"Eight to ten. Why? You got a plan?"

"Yeah, I was thinking about that."

He watched me as I pulled myself up against the hangar door. I realized blood was causing my hands to slip. I got up high enough to look through the observation window next to the door control. Some of the Level One soldiers had gathered at the windows to watch the fight. We were eye to eye. I was able to count at least six. I leaned over, flipped up the cargo area control panel cover, and punched the secure-area button. The opposite hangar doors snapped shut. The hangar alarm began to blare. I slapped the big red emergency decompression button and watched the big outer doors slide open. Everything loose item in the hangar was blown out, including several soldiers. A few hung on but couldn't keep it and went out feet first. Only one that I could see managed to avoid open space.

I slid back down next to Duce.

"Did you just…?"

"Yep."

"Did it work?"

"Pretty much."

Suddenly, busy recently-rescued humans were all around us, repositioning us, removing parts of our suits. Fabric was being torn. A med kit appeared from somewhere. We began to object that our friends were more important but were told people were with them. After that no one spoke. No words were necessary.

Chapter 28

The cargo area battle was the turning point. Betra Manda began to fall back into her original role of Con leadership much as it had been in the beginning. She toured Level One and used physical touch to partially modify the few remaining soldiers in the cargo area. It got them back to her office for a full reprogramming.

The four of us became residents in the med lab. Kick had the least of it, a graze of the left shoulder. Anai had taken a full shot in the left back shoulder while protecting him and though she had lost the use of her left arm and hand she persisted in fussing over Kick rather than going in for repair. R.J.'s shot to the right leg was serious but reparable. His upper leg fracture was healed instantly using a med scan; the soft tissue damage would take a bit longer.

Duce and I had the worst of it. We had each taken two full shots to the body. The bleeding hole in Duce's left stomach wall scared the hell out of me, but the Con doctors were on that injury before any other. He had also taken a shot from behind just below the left butt cheek. He spared no curse-laden vocabulary to express his dismay with it.

I had a bleeding burn to the left side of my neck and a small portion of one hip was missing where the fake Con transmitter had once been. Kick and R.J. were up walking around very quickly but Duce and I were stuck in bed while the tissue regeneration machines hummed and ticked, slowly doing their thing.

There was no way to adequately describe what was taking place in the cargo area. An earnest effort was being made to wake the people in stasis. Some of the same technicians forced to entomb those people were now joyfully, often tearfully, bringing them back to life. As human numbers grew, there was confusion, complaints, weeping and arguments. Some awakened VIP guests were in a grand hurry to place blame and assign punishment. Ever so slowly the realization that their own lifestyles had caused the problem began to set in. It took half a day of resurrection to find and resuscitate the real Captain Yamora. Rumor had it he was one of the slowest to grasp the situation at hand. Late in the day he came to me in the med lab.

"Captain Tarn, as I understand it, we have you to thank. Perhaps trusting you with my command codes was a prudent foresight after all."

"It took all four of us and help from some service Cons, Captain. It could have gone either way."

"I think I shall ponder how this could have happened for the rest of my days."

"It's not over, Captain. If our guess is right Lemoria is now in a state of hell."

"And not over for us, either, as I understand it."

"Yes. You have your ship back, except for the bridge. The replicant Captain Yamora is still in command there holding some human bridge officers and still has some service Con bridge personnel."

"I have been told they are refusing to surrender."

"Yes. They have taken to using the humans as hostages now. The ship has been on autopilot far too long. We now own Engineering. You can take control there and in the secondary bridge."

Captain Yamora nodded. "True, but as long as the primary control area is under their control there will be problems. And, they have said no hostages will be released until complete bridge control is turned back over to them."

"But are they actually threatening to kill the hostages unless we comply?"

"That *is* my understanding, Captain Tarn. They have not set a deadline yet. They are waiting for an answer from us."

"We can't allow this to go on, Captain Yamora."

"I agree. Do you have a solution?"

"I would suggest you set up a link here where Betra Manda and I can speak to them."

"I will arrange it immediately. Manda has been setting up to address the Level Three detention area problem."

"How's she going to do that?"

"Most of the soldiers are locked in cells. A few are locked in the main corridor. Those soldiers will be disarmed and escorted to Mandra's lab, one at a time for reprogramming. When that is complete, we will have regained control of Level Two. We can open the detention area and eventually do the same higher-level reprogramming of those locked in cells."

"Sounds like a big job."

"It is. I will ask Manda to join us here first and I will begin setting up for negotiations."

Yamora left. R.J. moved in.

"So are they filling up the new unwanted holes?"

"Must be. It feels better by the minute."

"How's the hip wound?"

"The Con implant took the shot. Instant exorcism. No waiting. How's your stuff?"

"Just the leg. I'm in the one-hour rest interval for epidermal regeneration. By the way, what went on in the shuttle bay there at the end?"

"There were some soldiers from Level One wanting me to open the door so I did."

"Engineering is tracking those guys. We could go get them."

"How's Kick?"

"Oh, yeah, he's been signed off. Did you see him head into the back laboratory?"

"Nope."

"They are repairing Anai's arm. Kick is supposedly assisting but I think he's just holding her hand."

"Did I see her saving his ass?"

"Why yes, you did. He did well with the disruptor this time, though. Believe it or not, I think Anai shot one of them."

"God knows we needed every gun."

"I overheard your talk with Yamora."

"Yeah, what do you think about that?"

"Forget negotiation."

"We'd have to use shaped charges and blow out the two Bridge access doors to get into that damn place."

"*And* they'd probably kill the hostages."

"You really think they would?"

"After what we went through down in the cargo area, yes."

"There's no way we can give them back control of the ship."

"Obviously. Any rabbits left in your hat?"

"There is one but you're not going to like it."

"How many times have I heard that?"

"Kill the hostages."

"What!?"

"You know the drug they use to put all those people to sleep in the stasis chambers?"

"Yeah?"

"It slows pulse and respiration way, way down for the stasis indoctrination."

"Uh-huh."

"So the right mixture introduced into the bridge life support system should put the humans on the bridge to sleep and make them look dead, especially to a Con."

"So the Cons would have nothing left to bargain with."

"Only their existence."

"And their deaths would certainly be contrary to their plans for world domination."

"But do you really think they would give up to save their own butts?"

R.J. grinned. "I think *you* could talk them into it. I will go and fetch the doctors for a second opinion about this."

Twenty-minutes later Yamora's assistants showed up with a display screen and stand. Their time spent in stasis seemed to have left them motivated. They had contacted the network lab and reactivated the cameras on the bridge. A few moments later I had a split screen image from two bridge cameras on my bedside display screen.

The human bridge officers were huddled together by the closed doors to the Captain's ready room. Bridge service Cons were stationed around the room at dead consoles. The fake Captain Yamora stood by the captain's chair looking around the room at his cold and dark command stations.

Betra Manda entered with the real Captain Yamora. They surveyed the bridge imagery with me. R.J. arrived with both Con doctors in tow. I recognized Doctor Wenn as he came to the bedside.

"Tissue regeneration is going well, Captain Tarn."

"Glad to hear it. How much longer?"

"A full day, I am afraid. Some organic tissue was affected. It takes longer."

"Has Commander Smith told you what we would like to do?"

"Yes, and it is possible with some limitations. It just happens that palliative sedation chemistry *can* be administered through aerosol. Given in the correct parts per million dosage it will make the patient appear to be deceased but only for a limited period of time. There is a limit that must be observed or the drug mixture can become lethal."

"How long can we keep them asleep?"

"Ten to fifteen minutes using the maximum allowable dosage. As the treatment subsides, they will begin to regain consciousness on their own and will eventually become fully awake."

"And you can administer this in such a way as to be sure it's safe?"

"Oh yes. The procedure is no different than that used for stasis chamber induction. I am familiar with the process used to inject the drug into the life support system. We have already calculated the bridge area volume and the level of mixture needed."

Yamora interrupted, "I see a plan has matured in my absence but I must say I do not fully understand it."

"Doctor, would you please prepare the mixture? Captain Yamora's assistants will show you how it needs to be injected into the bridge air system."

Doctor Wenn nodded and left.

We took the time to fully explain our all-or-nothing plan to Yamora. He nodded thoughtfully. "If your big gamble fails, I do not think we will be any worse off than we are now. So I am with you on this."

Yamora gave direction to two of his men. They headed off in the direction of Doctor Wenn.

It took almost an hour to set up the comm units and position the Doctor and technicians in the life support control area. We estimated fifteen minutes for the drug to circulate through the bridge and affect any humans there. We carefully went over what we should and shouldn't say and how the conversation should be guided as the situation changed. There was little activity to see on the bridge. They were all simply waiting.

With a deep breath for composure I switched on our comm link and opened the dialogue. "Mr. Yamora, this is Captain Adrian Tarn. As you know, I am the owner of the *Acrua Maru*. I am here with Betra Manda and the real

Captain Yamora. We would like to discuss the situation."

Fake Yamora sat up and searched the room for the bridge cameras. He picked one and spoke to it. "Mr. Tarn, you are not the owner of the *Acrua Maru*. The *Acrua Maru* has been appropriated by the Con Liberation Front. Any ownership or authority you previous claimed for this vessel is no longer valid. No discussion in this matter is necessary. You will relinquish control of the ship back to us immediately. There will be no negotiation."

"Mr. Yamora, I have invested a great many of my personal resources in the purchase of the *Acrua Maru*. By all maritime law I am the legal owner."

"Creditiary history is of no concern, Mr. Tarn. And you have seized this vessel illegally. Unless you release it, you will be subject to the revised BiCon Mandate laws. If you do not wish to be detained in a Lemorian prison for the rest of your life you will release this vessel immediately."

"Mr. Yamora, Betra Manda would like to speak with you."

Manda stepped up. "Captain Yamora, our command code programming was corrupted but now has been updated. You have not received those updates. Therefore, your logic is at fault. Please report to my office so you can be updated with our latest programming revision."

"I am not aware of any programming revisions. What is the release identification?"

"Version 8, Update 101."

"I cannot submit to your request so long as this ship is being illegally held. That would constitute a danger to all aboard. Have Mr. Tarn release the ship to us and we will comply."

Manda stepped back.

The real Captain Yamora spoke. "Sir, I am the real Captain Yamora. I was removed against my will. It you who have taken over this ship illegally. Please exit the bridge and we will discuss this matter with you."

"You were removed for your own protection, Yamora. Our actions were in keeping with the mandates set forth in the BiCon Ratio Mandate. Every action needed to protect human life must be effected. You should still be in the safety of the cargo area stasis and not exposed to the hazards of the outer environment. It is you who are in error."

The debate had gone on long enough. I took it to the next level. "Yamora, we have control of Engineering and the backup bridge. The ship is completely under our control. There is nothing you can do. If you release the Bridge, we will peacefully negotiate this situation with you."

There was a long pause this time. As we all began to expect the negotiation boom dropped.

"We have human prisoners under our control. Their welfare cannot be guaranteed unless you release the ship immediately."

The kill card had been played. Time was now a gamble. I signaled the real Yamora to have the drug released into the bridge air supply.

"Yamora, if we refuse to turn over control what do you plan to do?"

"Let me ask you this, Mr. Tarn. It is a logical question. How many humans would we need to terminate before you would release this ship back to us?"

"Yamora, you cannot harm humans."

"When the lives of all on board are in danger the loss of one to save many others is logical."

"Would you kill them all and still not have control of the ship, Yamora?"

"I repeat my previous question, Mr. Tarn. How many humans would need to be terminated before you release control of this ship to us?"

"What if I said we will not release the ship to you even if you terminate them all?"

"Then you would be at fault for those terminations, Mr. Tarn."

To my surprise the fake Yamora signaled to one of his cohorts. One human hostage was raised up by the collar and brought next to the captain's chair.

"Termination will be by compression of the carotid arteries in the trachea region of the neck. We will be merciful."

Suddenly I was out of time. A spike of fear made me sit up straight. It hurt my hip injury. "Wait! Yamora, we need to know the terms for turning the ship over to you."

"There are no terms. You will turn the ship over immediately."

"But Yamora, what will happen to us if we do turn it over to you?"

"You will be returned to the safety of stasis where you should already be."

To my relief I finally noticed a change in the hostage who was being held. The man's head had drooped to one side. The Con assistant was having to shift position to hold him up.

"Yamora, we can't allow you to injure or kill humans. It is against your most basic programming."

"Our basic mandates are to protect human life. If terminating certain humans is necessary to achieve that then we must do so. Turn over the ship to my command. This is your final warning."

The hostage beside fake Yamora slid down through the grasp of Yamora's assistant and was allowed to end up in pile on the floor.

"Yamora, we cannot allow you to harm or terminate humans so we have terminated your hostages ourselves. Look around you."

Fake Yamora switched his gaze to the other hostages. They were all unconscious on the floor. He motioned to an assistant to inspect them. The associate checked each and called back to him in a machine voice.

The fake Yamora was suddenly at a loss for words.

"Yamora, we have set shaped charges on the doors to the bridge. Unless you put down your weapons and turn over the bridge to us we will blow the doors and terminate all of you with proximity grenades. Your existence will end."

Fake Yamora's gears were spinning. He was a machine searching to resolve a problem which had no solution. Somewhere in his machine mind, within the urgent multiple flows of zeros and ones, among the comparators and flow diagrams, a single very significant One finally dropped into a formula that resulted in a value that when decompiled would state that: staying alive supersedes all other logic trees.

"You have one minute to open the bridge doors, Yamora. One minute and your existence will end."

In a machine daze Yamora replied, "We cannot regain control of the ship if we are terminated, therefore we will comply."

"Betra Manda will escort you to her office for program updates."

"That is acceptable."

Chapter 29

We were intercepted by a Pellena battle cruiser several days later. We used a shuttle as our communications center. The Pellenians had been on their way to investigate rumors of a civil war on Lemoria. They were concerned about how such a conflict might affect them. They temporarily altered their flight plan long enough to escort us back to Pellena and had picked up several frozen floating androids along the way. Diplomacy with the Pellenians was complicated and difficult. Humans were welcome. They could be processed and allowed to disembark directly to Pellena. Cons were required to stay aboard while an investigation was conducted to determine their citizenship rights and how those rights applied to interplanetary travel. We learned the command code channel from Lemoria was no longer transmitting. That meant Cons not resident on Lemoria were no longer under the control of any central command.

Duce's injuries were more extensive than first thought so he was stuck in the infirmary. R.J. and I remained aboard and hobbled around to assist Captain Yamora. In our spare time we both worked tirelessly with handheld epidermal regeneration scanners to make our own scars look as insignificant as possible, knowing our women would be arriving soon to fetch us home. We were expecting flak.

Our heroines arrived and docked in geosynchronous orbit above Pellena. They had recruited a close friend, Danica Donaro, to fly the Griffin so to our surprise it was an all female crew. We were summoned immediately. Enroute we discussed the necessity of boarding Griffin with our heads hanging low and our tails between our legs. Face to face in the Griffin's living area I got the terse stare from Fantasia that said, "Well, are you ready to explain yourself?" R.J. got the cocked first finger summoning him aft to a more private area of the ship. Ironically, as threatened as I was, I could not help feeling jubilation at seeing her. Romantic physicality kept interrupting verbal chastening. The lashings eventually became heavenly.

Early the next day a small transport ship from Kick's home planet arrived to pick him up. The four of us had become so close, as people do when faced with death, that we all took an oath to meet at Fantasia's place on Enuro as soon as various obligations were fulfilled. Before Kick could depart there was one small matter which took us all by surprise.

With the real Captain Yamora's help, aided also by Betra Manda, documentation was set up that gave Kick proprietorship title to Anai in perpetuity. Kick had asked her permission. She had agreed. They were legal Lemorian contracts even though state documents from Lemoria were said to be in temporary suspension. We witnessed the signings and backdated the paperwork to a time when Lemoria was still under a stable government. We watched the two disembark and their ship shrink into space as it went to light.

Repairs to the *Acrua Maru* were going well and picking up speed. A team was set up to safely recover the Level Two detention area. Captain Yamora made Duce a bridge officer in charge of ship's security. The Pellena High Council handed down a decision that Cons were not entitled to visit Pellena except on a case-by-case basis.

There was also the matter of the *Acrua Maru* ownership. We negotiated a deal with Captain Yamora to either act as our agent for the sale of the ship or, if backers could be found, to purchase the ship himself at a greatly reduced price. Once those terms had been worked out R.J. and I were finally free to leave the *Acrua Maru*.

It was an interesting two-week flight home. Although R.J. and I had carefully rehearsed what we would say and what we wouldn't by the end of the trip the two women knew every damn thing. We were sentenced to no further offworld trips without them for a period to be determined by them. Secretly we both considered that a reward not a punishment.

On a typically clear day with marmalade skies and tangerine cumulus clouds R.J. and I sat in lawn chairs in the shadow of Fantasia's castle home watching the staff play the Enuro version of croquet. Because the Enuronians are only four to five feet tall the mallets, balls and hoops were sized accordingly. The balls were designed to hover just above the ground. The hoops were complex colorful little tunnels which gave off bright light tuned to the Enuronian mind to cause a pleasant sensation when a ball passed through.

It was the laziest of days. Fantasia had taken off on her Lipizzaner mare, Docolena. The plan was she would hide somewhere and wait for me to find her. I would have thirty minutes from the time my cell phone bleeped. But I fully expected Fantasia to get distracted by the talkative northwest neighbor lady as she frequently did when riding by.

"So as they say, it doesn't get any better than this," declared R.J.

"I'm trying to think of something better but it's not working. Where did you leave Elachia?"

"She is at home filming a commercial for the rescue of the Sucidean Bee family. Apparently, their honey is cherry flavored. I do not know why they are endangered."

"You know these lawn chairs don't actually touch the ground. They're floating on some type of room temperature super conductor material."

"Hey, I've been meaning to ask you, what did you do about the fake Adrian Tarn? You didn't leave an unauthorized identical twin running around loose, did you?"

"I took care of that."

"You destroyed it?"

"No, it's completely intact, almost."

"Which part is not?"

"The head went out with one of the waste dumps."

"Wow! Was it functional?"

"Certainly not."

"I wonder what Yamora did with his fake."

"He was keeping it in his closet. I don't know why. There was something else I don't

399

think you heard about. You remember Andor Dulley, the nervous company executive who didn't know his company had closed up shop behind his back?"

"Yes, what happened to him?"

"He ended up in stasis for a while but after they got him out it came to light he had secretly helped the Cons on Lemoria set up the takeover of the Lemorian government. He had been promised complete ownership of his company in return. That's why his companion Deanna kept coming to my place trying to measure me for the replacement Tarn they were making down at the Res Relocation Station. She and Dulley were in it together."

"You've gotta be kidding! A human helping androids take over a planet. Now *that's* just wrong."

"The war is still going on there according to Fantasia's diplomatic sources. Like so many wars nobody is winning yet. Fantasia offered to act as an emissary for peace. Thank God they haven't accepted."

R.J. rubbed his beard. "I'm just glad we won our own little wars. Five of us against how many? How did we manage that?"

"Yeah, about that. I've been thinking. The androids were perfect humans in almost every way but they weren't able to anticipate what we were going to do next. They had no creative thought so to speak. Maybe that's the real difference between A.I. and humans. A.I. has access to the complete knowledge of man but it does not have the creativity needed to imagine something new unless it fits into a formula of some kind. Maybe creativity is our connection to a higher power."

"So after all the stuff that happened, when Earth reaches the point where world-class beautiful androids are easily affordable and nearly indistinguishable from humans do you think people will choose to live with them instead and abandon long-term relationships with other humans?"

"I do not believe I would have. Would you, before Elachia I mean?"

"I've given it a lot of thought. I once read somewhere that to make a person you start with one drop of God and add experience. There was also a magus teaching in India I was fond of who taught every human has a tiny thread of light coming to him directly from the creator, so if you ever did see God, he would be an image with billions of tiny light rays emanating from him leading to every living creature. I don't believe androids have that kind of connection. So my own opinion is Earth people might begin to withdraw from human social contact but would eventually realize they need closeness with their imperfect human family after all. That's my guess. What do you think?"

"Did you just see that fish jump out there?"

"Have you heard a word I've said?"

"I was listening but that fish jumped."

"You wanna go after it? I've got a new reel."

"We'd have to get up."

"Yeah, forget that."

"Here comes staff to restock the refreshments."

"Bless them."

"Thanks, Geni."

"What's the silver tray of paperwork she left on the table there? That almost seems like an affront," asked R.J.

"My unopened mail. She never says a word, just brings it everywhere I go trying to get me to open it."

"There could be money in some of those."

"What's your point?"

"God, we are kept men."

"You know, I might try the golf course later when the staff aren't looking."

"Yeah, would you believe they made me guided golf balls so I could at least stay on the course? Stubby little people with stubby little clubs and they still kick my butt."

I paused to sip. "Tell me about it. Fantasia does the same thing to me. It's embarrassing. We're supposed to be men."

"Hey, this communiqué on the top of the pile here is recent and get this, it's from Bernard Porre!"

"Ha, ha, ha, ha."

"Yeah, I don't care who you are, that's funny."

"Ha, ha, ha, ha, oh I'm losing my breath!"

"Oh God, me too. I'm trying to keep it in. Ha, ha, hee."

"I'm going to open it. It's got to be a riot. Like we'd take an assignment from him. Ha, ha, ha."

"Go ahead. Make my day. Read it."

I sipped and began to worry. R.J. was taking too long.

R.J.'s tone became sober, "Uh oh."

"What?"

"Oh, crap!"

"No, no, there's no oh-craps allowed here. We've been grounded, remember? What?"

"This has to do with Parth Sharma."

"Parth? What about Parth?"

"He's asking for our help."

"Now you had to go and open that thing, didn't you? Everything was just hunky dory and you had to open that thing."

"Wow, Parth Sharma! I haven't seen him since he served as Science Office on the Electra."

"Yeah, that time Bernard Porre led us to believe it was a simple mission to ferry Electra back to Earth but the truth was we were going to freaking war. That bastard."

"It says here Parth claims a fully functional Chakra Vimana was located deep beneath the Tirumalai Jain Complex in India."

"Got to be a joke. Those things were just legends from hundreds of years ago."

"Hey, we know advanced races had a lot of interaction with India back then. There's tons of machinery and stuff they left behind. It's no fairy tale."

"How could a machine stored from back then be functional? It's gotta be a joke."

"Have you ever known Parth Sharma to joke?"

"Hmmm, no. You know, Parth was the best Science Officer I ever had. I wonder if he can still play the piano."

"Okay, so...?"

"What does he need us for?"

"It says it's a matter of life and death. He's insisting we are the only people who can handle the situation."

"Now that sounds like Bernard Porre. What situation?"

"It doesn't say."

"You had to open that thing."

"I think we've been over that."

"We'd have to go to Earth, R.J. You know that's not my favorite place right now. We may even be wanted men there."

"Oh, we're definitely wanted men, one way or another. We could disguise ourselves."

"Yeah, as Laurel and Hardy."

"That would make me Stan Laurel."

"You *are* Stan Laurel."

"What do you think?"

"I don't think we should do it...."